k. larsen & mara white

MISSED CONNECTION

MISSED CONNECTION
Copyright © 2015 by K. Larsen & Mara White
Cover by: Cover Me Darling
Editing: Indie Edit Guy
Formatting: Integrity Formatting

This story was inspired by a real Craigslist missed connections post.

Missed Connection
A Novel by K. Larsen & Mara White

PROLOGUE

May 2016

Alarms beeped. Machines chirped. He couldn't quite place why the noises were familiar. His throat was dry and his body ached in the worst way possible. When he tried to open his eyes, he panicked. They seemed to be sealed shut.

"Mike," a voice called out. Something squeezed his hand. "Mike, you can do it. Open your eyes."

He struggled to do it. Mike forced his eyes open. The room swirled with light. Blurry shadows appeared before they sharpened and focused. Doctors, nurses and his sister.

"Oh, thank God!" Kim, his sister, leaned over and rested her head on his hand, which she was also still holding.

"Mr. Blackard, I'm Dr. Hemphill, do you know why you're here?"

He shook his head, he thought, *no*. There was a great weight resting on his chest and he wanted to bring it up to the doctor but the man just kept speaking. "You were hit by a drunk driver, and Life Flighted here to St. Mary's Hospital in critical condition. During surgery, you suffered a massive heart attack but you're a very lucky man, Mike. A heart became available and we were able to transplant it in you." Mike blinked three times. He was sure he'd misheard the man. The steady rhythm in his chest was his. It couldn't be someone else's. "You'll remain in the hospital for a week or two, and then you'll be closely monitored at an outpatient transplant center for about three months. We can talk about all of this a little later. Right now, just rest while we check your vitals."

"Kim?" He croaked out. His sister lifted her head. Tears streamed down her face.

"I thought I'd lost you." Sadness filled him. He didn't want her to worry. She had kids and a husband at home who needed her. She should know that he'd never abandon her. His throat felt too dry to speak. He patted her hand and looked at the ceiling. Someone else's heart. Inside him. He wasn't sure he liked the idea of it. Mike believed that the human heart was where the soul lived and not all souls were good. He closed his eyes. He had, apparently, plenty of time to feel out this new heart during his months of recovery. As his sister stroked his hand and softly spoke encouraging words, Mike drifted to sleep. Tiny anchors and azure eyes filled Mike's dreams.

CHAPTER 1

Titan

While she's in the bathroom, I chug one last bottle of water before we head out, per Bridget's request. I'm happy and feeling good. Bridget and I had a great time tonight at our engagement party. She's laughing up a storm as we get into the car. As we pull out to make the hour drive home, she cranks the radio. "Regulate" is playing. We both sing along and laugh. Bridget holds my hand between good songs. Her new engagement ring sparkles every so often and makes me feel proud. Snow has started to drop down from the sky. The back roads are dark and twisty and unlit but it's the fastest way home, which is still another ten minutes out. The moment I hit the brakes, I know something is wrong. It's like my brain isn't talking to my leg fast enough or maybe the road is too icy. I stomp down harder on the brake. I stomp down. Bridget screams next to me.

⚓⚓⚓⚓

I gently hold the matchbook between my thumb and index finger in my pocket. It's worn and frail now, but it still anchors me. I'm standing next to the truck in the driveway. I blink twice.

Doctor's appointment.

Groceries.

Unloading.

Right.

I hate it when I zone out like that. I've been fatigued lately.

"Hey, Dad," my son says, as he brushes past me with bags of groceries. I grab an armload and follow him in.

"Luke—" I say, as he sets them on the counter. He turns and pushes his too long hair from his eyes. I need to remember to get him to the barber.

"You ready for a night of fun, old man?"

I laugh and shake my head no. "It's just a birthday. No need to get crazy."

"Yeah. Well, a birthday means cake, at the very least. Oh, can I have twenty bucks? Dillon and Max and I want to go to a movie later."

"Who's driving and what movie?" I ask, while putting dry goods away.

"Dillon's mom is going to drive us and I don't know yet."

I raise an eyebrow at him. "You don't know yet?" I wait expectantly for his response, even though I know it's not worth it. It's rare that teenagers have answers to anything these days.

"What? We'll just decide when we get there," Luke shrugs. If I try really hard. If I dig down to the recess of my forty-five year old brain, I can almost remember what it was like to be a fifteen year old boy.

"Okay," I tell him.

Luke puts groceries away with minimal complaints, while I start dinner. It's just the two of us now and although he misses his mom and God knows I do, too—she was much better at parenting than I—we do well together. Then again, we've had the last five years to get our routine just right. When he's finished with the groceries, he sets out two place settings at the kitchen island. It is rare for us to use the dining room anymore. It seems too formal for us. It's reserved for Friendsgiving and Christmas Eve. I dish out the chicken cacciatore to each plate, before joining him.

"Did you post it yet?" he asks, between bites. He sounds like a savage beast when he eats. His mother would be horrified. I really need to remember to chastise him more about that. What happens when he takes a girl out for dinner and eats like that?

"No. And chew with your mouth closed." Luke gives me a lopsided grin. Never mind. If girls run for the hills over his poor table manners, it saves me a world of stress over worrying about him knocking her up by mistake. Chew away, son, chew away.

"Dad, come on. Just post it. Seriously, it's like a one in a gazillion chance that anything will come of it."

I finish chewing my bite; mouth closed. I think dinner needs more pepper. "I know. I know," I answer. He's right, though. I could put it out there into the great interweb and it may never even be seen. The odds . . . well the odds are not in my favor at all. I'm not sure which is more comforting—knowing that nothing may come of it or the fact that it could find its way to *her*.

"I mean, just, you know, time and all that. Plus your birthday is a good time to do something like that. Mom always said . . ."

"Birthdays are good luck," we finish in unison, which makes Luke grin again. The kid has the easiest smile I've encountered.

It looks just like his mother's. Wide and genuine and kind. He's a good kid, with a lot on his plate. Rory's death hit him hard. I don't want to think about his mother. Not right now anyways. And I don't want to think about *time*. "What time is Edie picking you up?"

"Seven thirty," he answers. I nod my head and clear the dishes, while Luke cuts two massive slices of birthday cake for us. He stabs a candle into the center of one slice and licks the stray frosting off his fingers. He pulls something out of his pocket and slides it across the countertop to me.

I unwrap the newspaper wrapping and smile. A matchbook from *Sloane's*. How he managed this one, I have to know.

"Thanks, Luke! This was the missing one." I run my free hand across my salt and pepper hair. Life's funny like that, sneaking up on you, adding lines and colors to your body that didn't used to be there. Forty-five. I've already loved and lost and loved again and lost again, but still feel like I have lifetimes left to live but I don't want to do it alone. Dating scares the pants off me. I haven't done it in so long, I'm not sure I can anymore. There's too much baggage. Too much history to share. Too much hassle.

"I know. I had to mow the guy who hadn't done his lawn for *three* weeks to get that, but it was worth it, to complete the collection." Luke's smile is shy and he won't really look me in the eye. He's going through the I-don't-really-do-touchy-feely-talk-about-my-emotions stage. It's been an adjustment from the mama's boy Rory left me with, but we're making it work.

I've collected matchbooks for the last twenty years. The goal started as one from every diner in the great State of New York. After Luke was walking and talking, we decided to collect them from anywhere we travelled. But the *Sloane's* matchbook was the very last diner in New York that we needed. People don't really make matchbooks to give out anymore. It's a shame. They're like mini postcards. Memories. I put the matchbook aside for the moment. Luke lights the one candle and sings terribly and loudly the *Happy Birthday* song for me. I blow out the candle and this year, I make a wish. But I can't tell because then it might not come true.

Luke finishes his cake just in time for his pick-up. Dillon's mom, Edie, honks the horn and Luke leaps from his chair. He slaps me on the shoulder and yells happy birthday on his way out the door. I sigh and lean back in my chair. The house is still.

Quiet.

Lonely.

I put the radio on the Nineties station. I rinse all the plates from dinner and dessert and load them into the dishwasher. "*Regulate*" comes on. A chill runs through me and I shudder. I touch my hand to my pocket. To the matchbook and then I resolve to make my birthday wish come true.

It's time.

New York >Fairfield >personals >missed connections post
The last day of 1995—m4w

I met you in the snow on the last day of 1995, the same day I decided to kill myself.

One year prior, I'd killed my fiancé, and a mother, a father and a daughter. We were at a party and I was intoxicated when I drove my fiancé and me home. Only I was the only one who ended up making it home. The lives and families I'd destroyed in that accident, haunted me. They still do.

On the morning of that New Year's Eve, I found myself in a desolate house with a fifth of Jim Beam and the pangs of guilt and shame and grief permeating the recesses of my soul. When the bottle was empty, I made for the door and vowed, upon returning, that I would retrieve the Glock from my nightstand and give myself the sentence I deserved.

I walked for hours. I looped around the town before roaming through the riverside park.

By the time I reached the riverfront, the whitewashed sky had begun to drop snowflakes, which soon became a blizzard. While the other people darted for homes and restaurants to keep warm, I trudged into the onslaught of snow. I hoped that it might wash away the sludge of guilt that had congealed around my heart. It didn't, of course, so I started back to the house.

And then I saw you.

You'd taken shelter under the awning of Hope's Diner. You were wearing a green gown, which appeared to me royal and ridiculous. Your blonde hair was matted to your face, and a constellation of freckles dusted your shoulders. I'd never seen anything so beautiful.

When I joined you under the awning, you looked at me with big, sky blue eyes, and it was obvious you'd been crying. I asked if you were alright. You said you'd been better. I asked you if you'd like to grab a cup of coffee. You said, only if I would join you. I still don't know why I bothered to ask you. Before I could answer, you snatched my hand and led me into Hope's Diner. Despite the blizzard and lack of coat, your hand was warm and soft.

We sat at the counter of that diner and spoke like long lost friends. We laughed as easily as we grieved, and you confessed, over cheesecake, that you were engaged to a man you didn't love, a stockbroker from some line of New York nobility. A Van Buren, or maybe a Rockefeller. Either way, his parents were hosting a gala to ring in the New Year, hence your gown.

I shared more of myself than I could have imagined possible, at the time. When I mentioned the drunk driving, I got the sense that you could see there was a war waging inside me. Still, your eyes offered solace, not accusation, and I loved you for it.

After a little over an hour, I excused myself to use the bathroom. I remember watching my reflection in the mirror. Wondering if I should kiss you, if that was completely ridiculous, if I should return to the Glock that waited for me at home. I decided that I was unworthy of the solace this gorgeous stranger in the green ball gown had given me, but to turn my back on such sweet happenstance would be the real disgrace. My mind was made.

On the way back to the counter, my heart pumped in my chest like a jackhammer, and a future—our future—ran through my mind. But when I reached the stools, you were gone.

A matchbook next to my mug caught my eye. I turned it over, nothing but the diner's name and number on it. When I flipped it open, the inside top flap had a drawing of an anchor.

That's it.

No number.

No note.

I can't even be sure you drew the anchor.

As strangely as our time had begun, so, too, did it end. I was distraught. I went back to Hope's every day for a year, but I never saw you again. Ironically, the torture of your desertion seemed to swallow my self-repugnance, and the prospect of killing myself was suddenly less appealing than the prospect of discovering what had happened in that diner. The truth is, I never really stopped speculating.

Obviously, I'm an older man now, and only recently did I recount this story to my son for the first time. He told me to post this on Craigslist, I told him I didn't know anything about Craigslist, and all I knew about you was your first name and that you had lived in New York once. And even if, by some phenomenon, I happened upon you, I'm not sure I would recognize you. Time is unkind that way.

But as I cast this proverbial coin into the wishing well of the universe, it occurs to me, after a thousand what-ifs and years of lost sleep, that our connection wasn't missed at all.

You see, in these intervening twenty years, I've lived a decent life. I eventually fell in love and married a wonderful woman. I'm raising a great son. And I've forgiven myself—mostly. And you were the cause of all of it.

You breathed your essence into my lungs one snowy New Year's Eve night, and you can't possibly imagine my gratitude.

I have difficult days, too. Sometimes I can still smell the smoke from the burning car in the accident with my fiancé. My wife passed five years ago. And then, a few dozen times a year, I'll receive a gift. I remember you. Your words, your kindness, your eyes and that dress. I remember the way you got my heart beating again.

So whatever you've been through in life, wherever you are now in life, and wherever you're going in this life, know this: you're with me still.

This is the worst idea. I read the post a thousand times. Maybe more than that. I've written and rewritten it. This is the best idea. I want it to be just right. Or maybe it doesn't have to be right at all. This is ridiculous. I am a grown man. What am I thinking? The clock reads eleven fifty one. Luke is home and asleep already from his movie and I'm losing steam. I have nine minutes before my birthday good luck runs out. Deep within my soul, I have a need to do this, no matter how ridiculous it is. I hover the mouse over the submit button and close my eyes.

Click.

Jesenia

I hang up the phone gently and let out a deep breath. The wedding planner quit on my daughter, looks like I'm the only one left standing. Am I a terrible mother, if I say I'm not all that surprised? She can't keep her opinions to herself; she is forthright—to a fault. Angie is the definition of a bridezilla and I'm the one to blame because I created her.

"*The Yacht Club,*" she said. "*I want to make the Times.*" "*At least two hundred guests, if we want to invite Andrew's client list.*" I should have stopped her. I should have reeled her in and demanded a package deal on some little island. A remote spot where only one in five guests invited would be able to swing it. I am too passive when it comes to my daughter. I chose nurture over discipline, indulgence over rules. Angelina is what I turned her into and I'll just have to deal with the demands of the bride monster who is my one and only daughter.

I pull up the spreadsheet she's emailed, while drinking jasmine tea at the marble island countertop. Ten thousand yellow roses shipped in from Ecuador costs more than ten thousand dollars. Of course, it does. I know all too well and so does Angie. My daughter and I are both designers, that's why she wants the wedding to be "*better than perfect.*"

Interiors Made Easy with Jess and Angie is the top design podcast on iTunes most weeks. It often sneaks up the charts and settles in right beside NPR, if we happen to have a strong topic project underway. *Room Partitions and Folding Screens* was a huge one for us. But if I remember correctly, it was *Vegetable Garden in the City*, which really put us on the map. My parents, however, did not send me to an Ivy League school to learn how to do interiors. They sent me to meet my husband and I did; John was more than they could have even asked for. But being a New York State senator's wife can get boring. There are only so many luncheons and yoga classes and charity galas one can take. So when Angie was just in tenth grade, we started getting crafty. It turned into an obsession for us both and out of a hobby, we built an empire. We have our own line of paint and fabrics and crafters tools, and whatever gets refurbished on the show, goes into an online auction for charity, the minute we close the episode.

For the last five years, we've been offered network deals—full creative control, an entire crew, ridiculous dollar amounts for every single episode. But I turned them all down, to Angie's dismay. I like the anonymity of the podcast and it's worked out so well for us this way.

I believe, on a fundamental level, that our success comes from the soothing tone of our voices when we talk about easy ways to make everyday life more beautiful. Visuals would destroy the therapeutic experience, we'd become like every other glossy television host with a spray tan and a complicated wardrobe fit for the wife and daughter of a politician. And, of course, it helps that John likes us to be less visible; in his eyes a televised DIY design show is only steps away from a "Real Housewives" episode.

So for now, we work out of the studio on Madison Avenue, we give verbal instructions and listeners can simply go to the website to upload simultaneously aired photos and short videos. This way, I can work in overalls or a pair of comfy jeans, my hair thrown back in a ponytail, Birkenstocks on my feet. Angie and I are spending quality time together while we work and that's part of the appeal. Listeners tune in just to hear our banter, we're funny together and smart and spontaneous. We love what we do and our enthusiasm shows through. Both of our voices are low tenors, without a smidge of a New York accent. That's the pedigree of private school and hundreds of thousands in tuition. We could be from anywhere in New England, the Eastern Seaboard, the Rocky Mountains, even California, if that's how they want to envision us. We could be anyone's neighbor or aunt or mother-daughter team at the local flower shop. That's why so many Americans welcome Angie and me into their living rooms, kitchens, garages and craft sheds.

The podcast takes up all of my time. It makes me happy, it fills a void that I've been unsure of how to fill, ever since Angelina grew up. John is busy, he's important, work has *always* come before family. I'm not complaining. I'm grateful. I'm used to being an extraneous ornament. I say it without malice. Why would I complain? My life, relative to most lives, is gorgeous. I'm a woman who owns far too many formal dresses for the average walk-in closet. Yet, I am still compelled, from someplace deep inside, to obsessively beautify.

I set up a date for tasting canapés and cakes. A meeting with a sommelier who also advises on champagnes. In one afternoon, I have imported fabrics from India for fifty table runners; candles from a small family manufacturer in Vermont, hand poured, scented with lavender from their own thirty acres; truffles from a tiny, vegan bakery in Northern California. I peruse images of centerpieces from yacht club weddings from across the globe, searching for something that will grab my attention. I don't want seashells or starfish, no fishing nets on Angie's tables.

We, the Van Burens, don't even own a boat. It's Andrew's family that is big into yachts. His parents live in Cape Town and Andrew came to New York for law school. He met my Angie on a runner's pub-crawl and they immediately took a liking to each other. John had ideas about the kind of man he wanted her to marry.

"Cape Town is not an area I want her traveling to for the holidays."

"John, she'll marry who she loves."

I put my foot down, I wouldn't budge. This is one area of life where I will not make accommodations. Angie deserves true love and not a recipe prescribed by her father, not a political liaison, not a merger, not an investment, or a pardon. My daughter will marry for love, if it's the only hard stand I make on this earth. I don't ever want her to be like me, a profoundly lonely woman, who didn't even want a passionate marriage, who just longed for a real partnership. An equal, with someone to share my life, my fears, my dreams, even my missteps. What I got, instead, was a lifelong commitment to the façade. A charade. And sure, I love John. I do. But we're not a real couple, who carry a burning flame for one another. We are a presentation to the public, that's constantly undergoing editing and shuffling. Our relationship accords to the public's demand, it doesn't run on a heart clock; John gets paid by the feds.

Love, to me, seems like the most delicate pastry; divine, indescribable, and so very fleeting. I want love for my daughter.

I will guard her chance at happiness like a rabid dog, if that's what it takes, from the media, from my husband, from the whole goddamned state.

I decide, on a whim, to drive out to the Yacht Club. Get a better lay of the land, start the enchanted, nautical theme brewing. I make phone calls from the backseat of the town car, as I sit in traffic. Angie never should have hired a designer, it was doomed from the get-go. What idiots we both were. We're a *do it yourself* design team that hired a designer.

The ballroom is huge and really quite beautiful. The hardwood floors shine with the late afternoon sun. Giant bay windows line the wall that leads out to the floating deck on the water. It will be stunning. I can see it already. This is a magical room and Angie will be so radiant in it. There's an ornate fireplace that takes up a large portion of the back wall. It's hard to tell if it's usable, or just for show. The mantle houses various nautical minutia, scrimshaw, ships in bottles and a rusted, old-fashioned anchor.

That's it. Right here in front of me. My table centerpiece, well, Angie and Andrew's. How charming and how perfect. A rusted anchor.

I pull a yellow legal pad from my messenger bag. Sketching it out quickly, I add antique blue hydrangea in yellow-hued Mason jars. But an odd sensation moves through me when my pencil tip hits the paper, like a wave of nostalgia that overtakes me so fast, I feel dizzy. It's drawing the anchor that makes me remember him.

CHAPTER 2

Titan

"We're going to be *really* late, Dad," Luke yells from the entryway.

I know this. I can't quite figure out why I'm dragging my feet but I've been staring at myself, lost in time for the last—I check my watch—ten minutes. My salt and pepper speckled hair appears lackluster. My light brown skin looks sallow now. My hazel eyes, dull. I haven't been able to sleep for the last two weeks—and I'm exhausted. I haven't been able to sleep since my birthday. Since I posted that damn missed connection. If I hear nothing by tomorrow, I'm taking it down. I mean, what did I actually think was going to happen? My mysterious girl would magically appear after two decades? Maybe I'm really that desperate to see her face again. To touch her warm, soft skin— so different from my rough hands. Maybe I hoped for the chance to see those sky blue eyes and her genuinely kind smile. Those lips. That voice. Maybe I just miss having someone to care for. Someone to hold at night. Someone to come home to. Maybe I just wanted to rekindle hope.

"DAD!"

"Coming!" I tear myself away from the mirror and trot down the stairs. Today I'm being awarded some plaque or award or something like that for best general contractor in the area. I started my own business fourteen years ago. It was a rough start. My wife was pregnant with Luke and we were living off her salary until I got up and running. You'd have thought that people would be well past their biases by then, but even now, the fact that I'm biracial, affects some people poorly. As if the black in me will affect my ability to build their houses. Or perhaps that pesky black percentage of my DNA precludes me from knowing what rich people want when building their homes or maybe it's that I'll steal something. It's impossible to know. At this point, my business has boomed enough that I don't take on jobs where I don't like the vibe the customer gives off. It's a nice place to be.

The town does a 'best of' award for all sorts of local businesses. The ceremony will even be in the local paper. It's prestigious for our small town. Rory and I moved here just before she got pregnant. It's quiet and lush with open greenscapes and forest. The big entertainment is hitting the lake on a sunny day.

"Lookin' good, Dad," Luke says eyeing me. I smile at him and ruffle his hair, as I reach the door. He squirms away and tries to fix the unruly nest he calls hair.

"It's sharp," I say.

"What is?"

"The saying. It's 'lookin' sharp."

"Whatever, old man. Can we just go and get this over with, already? You know Tara will be there, right?" Luke looks at me expectantly.

I sigh and pinch the bridge of my nose. Tara. A year after Rory died, I had tried dating. It was a disaster; a disaster with the local news anchor. She really didn't want it to end; and when I ended it, she took it poorly.

"Yup. Thanks for the reminder."

Luke chuckles. "She was bat—"

"Do not cuss, Luke," I cut in.

"Shit crazy!" he yells and starts running. I can't help but laugh. She was. And he was on to her from day one. I chase him out the door and to the truck. Giving him a stern look as I cross around to my side, he mock shrinks before cackling. I can't keep a straight face when the kid laughs. I start the engine as we both laugh at ourselves, together.

⚓⚓⚓⚓

The event was fairly painless. The local paper is doing a write up of it and Luke saved me from Tara. With the ceremony over and it being a near perfect Sunday, I drop Luke at a friend's house and head to the local bar to meet up with some of my friends. The parking lot is full; when I check the clock on the dash, I realize it's because the football game has already started. The gravel crunches under my boots and the crisp air fills my nose.

I pull open the door and am met with the smell of beer and dirt. It's an odd combination.

"Hey, Titan!" Cherise calls out. Her palm is flat on the bottom of a large tray full of steins of beer. Her breasts bounce with each step she takes. Every man in here has wondered, at one time or another, whether those breasts are real or not. Even me.

"Hi, Cherise."

"Usual, Ty?" she asks.

"Please and thank you," I say, as always.

"Your boys are over there," she says with a smile, pointing with her free hand to the corner. Rusty, Dan and Matt are huddled together across from the largest flat screen television, already hooting and hollering at it.

As I approach the table, Rusty reaches his hand up to slap mine, followed by a head nod from Matt and a shoulder slap from Dan. Good ol' all American boys. Cherise shows up with a fresh round of beers for them and a tall water for me.

"So how was Tara today?" Rusty asks during a commercial.

"She cornered me in true Tara fashion and Luke had to rescue me because none of you numb nuts seemed to notice."

Dan laughs and when he does, his large nose moves in the strangest way. "I noticed but I'm not getting anywhere near Tara. I have a scar from the scratch on my back from your breakup." I roll my eyes at Dan and take a sip of water.

Matt hushes us all when the game's back on. I watch my three closest friends stare intently at the screen before them. I'm not drawn to the game today. My state of mind has been all over the place. I keep dreaming of warm hands in the snow. Green gowns, blue eyes and long forgotten conversations. The ghost of this woman kept alive only by a matchbook, a tattoo and now, a post, just hanging out somewhere online.

"Want anything else?" Cherise's voice snaps me from my strange longing. I look up at her and she smiles and winks at me, before leaning over and tracing my anchor tattoo on the inside of my wrist. "I'm happy to get you *anything*, Titan."

Cherise seems like a really sweet lady but she's not my type at all. I suppose, I could use a good lay though. It's been a long time and I'm tired of my hand. I shake the thought. No. I can't do that to her. But I would solve the mystery of the fake or real breasts. The cons outweigh the pros in my mental list and I pull my arm away from her.

"I'm all set, Hun." Her smile falls just a little, before she straightens up and shakes my dismissal off.

"I swear, Titan, one of these days, she's going to figure out a way to get you to drink, so she can take advantage of you. Male rape is no joke." Rusty quips. Matt spits beer with his laugh and Dan just shakes his head at Rusty. "What? It's true. And it's a serious thing," Rusty says. Leave it to Rusty to be the weary female of a very masculine group.

"Speaking of women, did anyone respond to your ad on Craigslist?" Dan asks.

"What?" I ask. I heard him but I'm confused as hell. How does he know about the post?

"Come on man, you think Luke didn't tell us?"

At this particular moment I want to ground Luke for the next fifty years or so. "I'm gonna kill that kid," I grumble.

"Well?" Matt pushes.

"Nope. Well, yes. I've had lots of strange responses, but not from *her*," I tell them.

"Yeah, but come on, that post—damn, man, you made my wife tear up. The ladies must be overloading your inbox," Dan says. I want to crawl in a deep dark hole.

"Titan Breaks the Internet," Rusty laughs, using his hands to mimic a news ticker.

"I didn't post it to meet women," I say, a tad too defensive. "I am seriously going to kill Luke when he gets home."

Embarrassment washes over me. Strike that, it's not embarrassment, it's shame and fear. There are very few people who know about my life before Rory. I met her at a job site I was working. She had an infectious laugh, a kind, warm, broad smile and eyes that danced and sparkled. I'd been instantly smitten with her. I'd told her everything after a few months of dating. I told her about Bridget, about the accident, about the fact that I got away with it, simply because I was *just* under the legal alcohol limit by the time the cops and paramedics arrived at the scene. I told her of my overwhelming grief that followed. My suicidal thoughts and the woman who smelled like strawberries, who'd taken away that desire simply by sharing a coffee with me on that snowy night. I only shared my story with Luke last year, during a bout of depression he experienced surrounding the anniversary of the death of his mother, Rory. Of course, Rusty, Dan and Matt know, too, but that's it. Five people know all of me. The idea of my history suddenly becoming public knowledge in this small town terrifies me. What would people think? How would it affect my business? My thoughts run wild. Spinning and swirling in my head. Scenario after scenario playing out like a movie reel.

I am barely entertained by the game, so I decide to take off. Half way home, I pull through the coffee shack drive thru for a black coffee. The weather's still warm enough to have the windows down. So that's what I do. I roll down all the windows in my F350 and crank the radio, all the way to the lake. A quick boat ride alone, on a dark glassy canvas, is just what I think I need to clear my mind. When I see my boat, *The Anchor*, a calm washes over me. I grab my coffee and head down to the dock.

Jesenia

I press the buzzer long and hard on Angie and Andrew's apartment. I know she's asleep. I should have just gone home. It's rash and it's rude. I'll probably scare her half to death. I once promised myself that I would never be the kind of mother who intrudes on their child, who doesn't believe in their privacy because she gave birth to them.

"Hello?" Andrew's voice sounds gravely in the middle of the night.

"Andrew? It's Jesenia. Is Angie around?" My voice sounds strained and high-pitched, too cheery for almost—I glance at my watch,—two o'clock in the morning.

"Of course, I'll buzz you in. Is everything alright?"

"Oh, yes. Sorry to bother you two. I just had the most splendid idea that couldn't wait until morning."

Silence.

"Andrew?"

"Alright, then."

The door buzzes. Somehow I'm coming off older than my

forty-five years. Like a batty old mom who's losing all of her tact with old age. Andrew's accent is regal, even at two o'clock in the morning. No wonder Angie fell so hard, he can say "taxes," or "proctology" and make it sound magical. They may think I'm crazy and I'll admit, I am acting a bit manic. But I'm her boss and I know, for a fact, she doesn't have to be at work in the morning. Our next episode isn't until Friday. We're making tables out of industrial wire spools for outdoor entertaining.

I nod at the doorman, who looks up from the game. He recognizes me, tips his hat and goes back to his deli-wrapped salami sandwich and two-liter of Diet Coke.

I take the elevator up to the tenth floor, they have beautiful views of the park. The carpeted hallway is absolutely silent, like a library after hours. I glance in the mirror and rub the mascara from under my eyes. I second-guess my decision to come wake up my daughter. She is my best friend in this world and I'm not repeating a cliché. God gave me Angelina to save me from a life of boredom, built on fabricated friendships and endless dinner parties.

"Mom! My God, what are you doing? Where's Dad? What's going on? Is everything okay?"

She popped open the door before I even had a chance to compose myself and rehearse what I was going to say. I smooth my hair back where it's fallen out of the low chignon. My Burberry raincoat is wet from standing outside of her building, staring and debating.

"Angie. Nothing is wrong, nothing at all, my love. I was just excited and I couldn't sleep, so I went for a long jog. But the jog woke me up and now I've been pacing and sketching and I've got some amazing ideas and I just couldn't wait any longer to share them with you!" I say it enthusiastically and hold up a now dampened bag of yesterday's croissants I picked up at the deli. Andrew runs his hands through his handsome long hair, shakes his head and marches back to the bedroom.

"Okay, Mom, what is this? Midlife crisis? Perimenopause?

Dad is involved in a political scandal? You caught him cheating? Because I know you didn't come over here at—two in the morning—to talk about wedding decorations."

"You are the only person I can call at two in the morning. The only person, Angelina, so I'm using that card," I say. I make a pleading face. Angelina shuts the door, just like that, practically in my face.

This is what it's going to be like, I guess. She's getting married, she'll have Andrew. She won't need me anymore. I turn on the rich carpet, back toward the elevator. I can't help but hang my head. I really should have called her first. What was I thinking?

Then the door swings open and there is Angie in her anorak. She's pulling on her L.L. Bean duck shoes and passing me an umbrella, one we bought together at The Met. An umbrella with Monet's *Water Lilies* on it and when I take it from her, my face breaks out into a full, genuine smile.

"This better be good, Mom. I'm expecting really juicy stuff. There's a twenty-four hour diner on Amsterdam—the potato pancakes are good. Did you bring a car or are we walking?" She asks and then throws her arm around me.

"You are everything I'd always dreamed you'd be and so much more."

"And this better not be about the fated night when you almost left Dad for some mysterious guy who appeared out of nowhere."

Shit. She knows me far too well, this daughter of mine. There goes the dramatic retelling and anchor story I had planned for our night.

"Only exciting wedding stuff, Angie. How about the best wedding ever, for my very best girl?"

"Save it, Mom. You are coming to the hospital to hold my hand through contractions and even spending the first few nights to get up and do feedings," she huffs, feigning anger.

"Lovey, are we having a shotgun wedding? You failed to

mention that to me."

"No, Mom, not yet. Like I could keep that kind of news from you for a second."

"Angelina, if that were the case, your father would show up to the wedding with a shotgun."

"You don't need to tell me twice. Mom, what do you think of blue lights?"

"Honestly, depressing. Almost tacky."

The wind whips our blond hair up as we step into the street. I squeeze Angelina's hand in mine and she smiles at me. She is an exact replica of myself, when I was her age. Thick, naturally blonde hair and big, sparkling blue eyes. A spattering of freckles that travel down her neck and chest and generously dot her shoulders. Somehow, seeing her in the rain, tromping along to an all-night diner, becomes one more piece of evidence in tonight's overwhelming puzzle. My memory is waking up and somehow coming back to life. I remember everything about that night, down to the smallest detail. How he drank his coffee black and used one finger to guide his thimble of creamer over to my side of the table when he saw I liked mine light and sweet, an intuitive gesture. I remember thinking, as I poured the second creamer into my steaming mug, *this is not a man who would ever do me wrong.* There was tragedy in his eyes and it was clear that he was hurting, but he was inherently good, it was simply written all over him.

Then I see his kind eyes, almost as if they were right there in front of me; I remember the snow, the awkward weight of the ridiculously soaked dress. I can almost taste the bad coffee, hear the soothing sound of his voice. I swear I can feel his hand, how it clasped mine across the divide of the cheap, laminate table. It was only a few hours we spoke but they left such a deep impression. God, I remember the grounding effect he had on me, how he seemed to pull me down to earth and put me back in my body. That's what made me draw it before I ran out, on the matchbook that sat in front of me on our table. He was a stranger but somehow he drew me in, like a ship that drops anchor to steady against stormy weather.

I make a decision not to let Angelina get away without hearing the real reason I came. The memory is growing and expanding and suddenly becoming a real thing. It's breathing life into me and everything around me. Something is happening and I've never felt so simultaneously scared and excited.

CHAP TER 3

Titan

I'm supposed to take the post down today. I told myself I would. I *want* to, yet every time I sit down at the computer, I find a reason to stand back up and do something else. It's as if my desk is repelling me. I can't live like this, though. Distracted. Checking my inbox is my new religion. Crushing disappointment when it's full of messages from everyone but *her*—the norm. I can't focus on much. I'm a slave to my phone, tethered to it on the off chance that one of the notification dings is going to be an email response from *her*. I might as well be nineteen again, at the level of ridiculousness happening. I don't have the stamina for this much longer.

⚓⚓⚓⚓

A loud frustrated cry fills the house. Luke must be under the gun for homework. He only yelps like that when he's stressed about schoolwork.

"Luke?" I call upstairs. There's no answer. Needing to avoid my desk anyhow, I make my way to his room, picking up stray laundry and shoes as I go. This place needs a good scrubbing. It's obvious that two men live here with no woman to keep them in line.

"Luke? Bud, everything okay?" I yell through the door. It flies open and Luke rushes out like a hurricane.

"My laptop crashed *again* and I have a report due tomorrow, Dad!"

"Use my computer."

"All my notes and stuff are up here and it's not quiet downstairs. You know I need to be alone to focus."

I want to laugh and tell him to settle down but when he's this worked up, that never works. "Your Mom's laptop is under my bed. I'm sure it works perfectly still, just plug it in, since the battery is probably long dead by now."

Luke stares at me for an extended moment. "Are you sure?"

I nod. "Yup," I answer. "Just don't delete anything, please," I add as an afterthought. All the family photos are on Rory's laptop. Videos. Memories. It's a comfort knowing they're there, if I ever wanted to crack it open. I don't, though. Or haven't yet. I just like knowing I can access them, if I want to.

"Um, yeah. Okay."

I watch as Luke goes into my room and drops to his knees before gingerly pulling out the laptop. He carries it back to his room tenderly, as if it's fragile. I squat, arms full of dirty clothes and swipe up another sock from his doorway before walking to the washer and dropping all the clothes in. I don't separate colors or fabrics or any of that crap. If you own it, you risk it going in with anything else in the house. My system's only failed me twice. One load ruined when Luke left a package of gum in his pants pocket. I pulled the sticky mess from the dryer and put everything right in the trash. And one load half ruined because I left a Chapstick in my pants pocket. I isolated all the Chapstick stained clothing and tossed those, too.

⚓⚓⚓⚓

My phone buzzes and I'm instantly on it. "Larry! Can you tell the crew lunch is in ten?" I yell across the frame of a new house. I swipe my screen and turn away before he answers. An email from Jessica someone at something-or-other. My heart picks up its pace.

There is no way.

It can't be.

I open the email and step into the shade so I can see the screen better.

Dear Mr. 1995,

Damn. Right there I know it's not her. She didn't use my name, but then again, maybe she doesn't remember my name. Maybe the effect I had on her wasn't what she had on me. It's entirely possible.

I am not your green dress beauty. Sorry. I simply wanted to tell you that your post touched me deeply. I thought it brave and bold and sweet. It's evident from your writing that you are a kind and thoughtful person. I posted the post on Facebook to help spread the word because I found myself unable to leave it. I felt compelled to help out somehow.

Anyways,

Best of luck

Jessica

Facebook. Damn. I'm not on it and don't care to be. I'm plenty connected to everyone I want to be, at this point in life. A chill runs through me. This Jen person could have endless contacts, friends. If my post goes viral, then surely it will make its way back to *her*. Right? I can't determine if I'm jacked up from the idea of that or terrified.

"Hey! Ty. Come here. There's someone I want you to meet," Larry shouts to me. I look up and see a pretty redhead standing next to him. I let a sigh escape before plastering a smile on my face and making my way over to them. I holster my hammer.

"Hi. Ty," I say extending my hand to the redhead.

"Emily," she answers and shakes my hand firmly. She has the lightest brown eyes, almost like they're clear with just a tint of golden brown to them. She's a good foot and a half shorter than I am, but most people are, when you're over six feet tall.

"Larry, care to fill me in on why this pretty lady is standing in the midst of a job site with no hard hat on?" I say.

He laughs and his gut bounces with the sound. Like Santa. "Emily is here from Custom Builder Magazine. Remember? The article you're being interviewed for?"

My eyes go wide. How could I have forgotten the Titan Homes feature in Custom Builder Magazine? "Emily! Right. God, I'm so sorry. It slipped my mind," I offer. She smiles and bats her lashes at me. Larry backs away slowly. He knows that look, as do I.

"I think all can be forgiven, if you can help a girl out with where to have dinner in this town." Her front tooth is chipped but it sort of makes her cute instead of homely. It's been too long since I've had dinner with a woman.

"This a date or an interview?"

"Does that matter?"

"Well, sure, how am I supposed to know which kinda restaurant to pick?"

"Date," she interjects quickly. "With a little shop talk, of course."

"Of course. What hotel are you staying at?"

"The Staples Inn."

"Nice place. I'll pick you up at six. Nice to meet you, Emily,"

I say and give her a wink. She blushes and backs away a step or two before turning her back to me. It's little moments like these where I am reminded how much fun flirting can be. I love making a woman blush.

Jesenia

A day later, I've got my phone cradled to my chin as I organize dried flowers into color-coded bins in the basement. Angie is worried about me and has called twice already this morning.

"I don't like how your eyes look, too animated or something," she told me as she dragged a large bite of waffle through syrup last night at the diner. She's as overprotective as her father is when it comes to my mental health. And sometimes it drives me crazy and I want to rebel like a kid, kick my feet, pound on the floor, scream until my face turns beet red. Why is it that every time I'm even a little bit off, "Did you take your meds, Jessy? When's your next scheduled appointment?" It's what he says every time, it's what he's always said.

That's what I'm referring to as "maintaining the façade," Mrs. John Van Buren, Jesenia, designer extraordinaire, married to a state senator, also suffers from bipolar disorder. But no one can ever know it because it's too scandalous for politics. I'm "susceptible to migraines" is the reason we use for meds and all the doctors' appointments. I was misdiagnosed for decades, all through my teen years and I've had my fair share of experimental therapies and trials. In my first year of college, my psychologist tried to tell me I had borderline personality disorder, which felt like a personal insult. When I was finally diagnosed, it was like coming home for the first time. I'm bipolar II, the supposedly more depressed kind. I regulate my moods with a small dose of lithium and sometimes a strong cup of coffee or a simple glass of wine.

But with the way John acts, you'd think I was stark-raving mad. Yet, I've never had any inpatient stays, never suffered an episode that's put me in danger or ended me up in the hospital. I'm not the kind of manic depressive who has unstable behavior, I don't get reckless during mood swings or violent or do things that I regret later. Sure, mania delivers me some sleepless nights. But I'm not out roaming the streets or engaging in questionable behavior. Mania makes me craft—and craft I do, like a motherfucker. I once spent forty-eight hours without any sleep. I refurbished two armchairs in the garage that I'd bought at an estate sale. I figured out how to reupholster the velvet myself, read a whole book on upholstery in one single sitting, without even a trip to the refrigerator or bathroom. During those same two days, I alphabetically organized every bookcase in our English Tudor style home in Albany, the state capitol. I planted tulip bulbs through the permafrost and made collapsible scrapbooks of every sport Angie ever played from kindergarten through the eighth grade. I vacuumed all of the drapes, after laying them out in early spring, on top of the pool cover, in order to get every edge. John woke up to the sound of the vacuum in the back yard and he thought I'd totally lost my head. He dragged me back to bed by pulling me by the arm. I cried for three hours after he fell back asleep, then I tiptoed down the stairs and righted myself by baking four different rum cakes.

I didn't hear John complain as he slid his fork through the dense, buttery, golden slice. He didn't once reprimand me as he washed it all down with a fresh brewed cappuccino I'd foamed and frothed with the espresso machine.

"This is incredible! They'll think I'm drunk at the press conference."

"The alcohol evaporates during baking. There are three more of those beauties on the counter in the pantry."

"Come here, Jessy," he said as he pulled me, standing in my apron, over to his seat at the eat-in kitchen breakfast table. He rubbed my hip and my thigh through my robe. "No vacuuming after ten. The neighbors will talk. Okay?"

"The Dyson is amazingly quiet," I whispered in my defense, as I slipped another perfect slice onto his empty plate.

"I'll call Dr. Fitzpatrick today. You might need a slight adjustment."

I've never adjusted my low dose of lithium ever since they started me. Only one occasion ever called for that and the result was my life's greatest accomplishment. See, I stopped my meds when I found out I was pregnant with my daughter. The situation forced me to open up to John—to tell him there was something wrong with me. And to tell him I was pregnant. He didn't know because I was too afraid to tell him. John *would* be furious if Angelina were pregnant. The only shotgun wedding in our family was the one *we* had right before I'd finished my last year of college. It was our one and only scandal and we kept it as quiet as it possibly could be.

The pressure to stay together after the wedding was extreme. We had to save face and at the same time, prove any naysayers wrong: my parents, John's political allies, our peers who had respectfully waited until graduation and beyond. We had to get married, survive the pregnancy, have Angie and never look back. We had to pull it all off, so that no one would ever even question that it hadn't been our plan in the first place. The Van Buren's don't make mistakes, they are a perfect family and they set the bar high.

Except for one fateful night, when an impressionable Jesenia escaped like Cinderella from a dreadful New Year's Eve party; she was just twenty-two, six weeks pregnant and wearing an emerald ball gown. Her fiancé was impeccable in a tux as he announced their engagement. Jess, on the other hand, was far from okay, her emotions swirled around her like a tempest threatening to steal her plastered-on smile away. She was off her meds, drowning in pregnancy hormones. She wasn't sure if she was in love, if she was doing the right thing. As John spoke and lifted his champagne flute high to the whole room, Jess cowered and felt fear run through her instead of the cheer everyone else seemed to relish in. She had a sudden vision of the rest of her life, a fancy, shining exterior with nothing substantial inside, a giant, luxurious balloon, filled up with nothing but lies.

It was then that she took off running in the slush of the oncoming Nor'easter, her hand pressed to the almost imperceptible rounding of her belly. *Come fly away with me, my child and we will find honesty and beauty someplace in this world.* But she only made it a measly mile away, where she crept into a doorway to find shelter from the wet snow that just wouldn't give up. She splayed her hands across her belly and tried to peer into the future. *Just give me a sign that it will be okay and I will stay anchored in the place where you put me—forever.*

Then out of nowhere, there was a gentle hand lifting her up. She was lost in the doubt of tomorrow and whether or not she could force herself to go on or to even stand up.

"Mom, are you there? Are you listening to me?"

"I'm here, Angie, I am. I just got lost in some memories."

"Well, tomorrow, after the podcast, I thought if you're up for it, we could hit the flea markets. Do Chelsea first and then head over to that newer one in Brooklyn."

"Oh, honey, I'd love that so much."

"Are you sure you're okay, Mom? You sound kind of distracted?"

"I'm good, Angie. I'm excited for tomorrow, they just dropped off the spools at the studio this morning."

"I love you, Mom."

"Me, too, Honey. So much."

So we come to find out that the princess wasn't perfect, that the clock struck midnight and she still had a whole slew of real life problems to deal with. And those problems would remain and she'd dedicate so much energy to covering them up—to pretending to be what she wasn't—so that no one got offended or thought less of her and her family. But Jesenia never wanted a fairy tale, she was okay with reality.

I am a politician's wife who suffers from mental illness. But

I can't be candid about it or ever let it rear its ugly head in public. I must constantly be aware of the impression I'm making. I'm not allowed to do things on a whim or ever speak without thinking.

My disease is like a dark pit that sits deep inside of me. I'm not allowed to explore it, so I overcompensate on the outside. I don't have episodes that look like anyone else's, I rectify my ugly inside by obsessively, compulsively, creating beauty around me.

CHAPTER 4

Titan

It's been a long time since I've gone on a date. Even longer since I've been laid. The prospect of both has me nervous, as I walk through the door at four p.m.

"Luke, Bud, you here?" My voice sounds weak, even to me. I draw in a great breath and try to bolster myself.

"Hey, Dad," Luke says from behind the fridge door. I walk to the island and set down my folders from the Vanderbilt project. Luke pops his head up and nods at me before continuing to rummage through the barren fridge.

"This old fart has a hot date tonight," I say. Saying it out loud seems to take some of the pressure off. The family therapist was right. Rory made me promise to take Luke to family therapy for a year after she passed. She was always thinking ahead like that and knowing what we would need. Of course, it was a necessity, as we were both devastated and a mess. No matter how much preparation you have for losing a loved one, you still hurt the same when it happens. It was actually that advice, 'speak it out loud,' that led me to tell Luke about Bridget, my suicidal thoughts and *her*.

⚓⚓⚓⚓

A few months after Luke's depression started to subside, I'd sat him down and told him that I understood feeling hurt and lost and hopeless. From there, he asked what my experience was and I finally said it out loud. To him. It was a very pure moment for us. We cried together over Rory, he cried for his feelings and I cried for mine. Together. United. And it felt damn good. Of course, for the last year, at least once a month, he's pushed for me to reach out and try and find this *her* until I finally caved and put that damned post up. I never would have done that, if not for Luke. I'm still undecided if having it out on the internet is a blessing or a curse.

"Shut up." Luke removes himself from the refrigerator and bumps the door shut with his hip. His arms are loaded with various snacking items.

"Okay?"

"No, Dad, I mean really? With who?"

"Yes, really. With a woman named Emily. She's the reporter doing the story for Custom Builder on THB."

Luke's eyes start to bulge out of his head. "That is . . . awesome! Where are you going? What are you going to wear? You aren't going to take her out in that, are you?" His questions come in quick succession. They make my brain hurt.

"Slow down there. Take a breath, Bud." Luke smiles and brushes some hair from his eyes. "I'm taking her to Poutine's and I'm going to shower and change before I pick her up at six."

"Poutine's—yeah. That's a good place," he says.

"Since when do you have so much dating knowledge?" I ask.

"I don't." Luke shrugs and unwraps a string cheese. "Leave me a twenty for dinner, will ya?"

I can't help but laugh at my son. He's a good kid, with a good heart. "Yup. Order whatever you want."

Luke rounds the island and throws his arms around my waist. "Try and have fun tonight, Dad. It's just a date. It doesn't have to lead to anything more." I wrap my arms around him and squeeze tight. When his fingers start tapping on my back, I know he's attempting to tap out, so I release him.

"No girls over while I'm out."

"As if."

"If you need me, call my cell."

"Dad. Go get ready, you're so old, it will take you a while to look good enough for this Emily." Luke draws out her name. Emmaaaleee. He's taunting me. I toss a twenty on the counter and check my email before getting in the shower.

Nothing from *her*.

⚓⚓⚓⚓

Emily is standing at the entrance to the Inn in a black skirt and gold translucent blouse. I can just make out the shape of her breasts through it. I pull up and hop out of the truck. As I approach her, I start wondering about *her*. How she's aged. What she would wear, if I was picking her up for a date. Did she marry that guy? Have children? Is she happy? I mentally slap myself. There is a pretty woman standing right in front of me. A real live warm blooded female and I'm off in lalaland.

I grin at Emily. "Hey there." *Hey there? God, I'm a jackass.*

"Hey there, yourself, handsome," she says and tucks some hair behind her ear. It's slightly comical, considering she passed bashful earlier today.

I adjust my stance. "You look nice."

"Thank you."

"Ready to head out?" I ask. She nods. I escort her around the truck and open the door for her. It's quite a step up to get in, even with the foot runner. With one foot up, her purse under one arm and the other hand holding the "oh-shit-handle," she looks over her shoulder at me. Crap. I place my hands low on each hip and help push her up into the cab. When she's seated and straightened herself out a bit, she says thanks and I close her door for her. She fills the drive to the restaurant with small talk about the Vanderbilts' house and about the magazine and how she sees the article portraying Titan Home Builders. I don't speak much, but then again, I don't need to, as she's doing all the talking.

"So tell me how you came to be the building world's most eligible bachelor?" she asks before sipping her wine. I stare at her a beat before laughing boisterously. This chick is funny.

"Excuse me?"

"You are, you know," she says. She's serious. This is news to me, though. I live a quiet life and keep to myself. I rarely ever date, so it's hard to imagine me as a playboy or eligible bachelor.

"I don't know anything about that. I wasn't aware the building community had a list going."

She leans forward and rests her elbows on the table. Her chin is perfectly perched on her fists. "Oh, there's a list and you are at the top of it, Titan." Her smile is cunning.

"I wasn't trying," I chuckle. The dim lighting in the restaurant makes her red hair glow ever so slightly and her skin looks milky and smooth. I grab my glass and take a long slow drink of water. Our conversation isn't riveting, but the longer I sit here and the longer she gives me that come hither stare—well, I'm only human.

"Maybe that's why," she says, "When you're trying, it shows. Naturally, those who don't give a damn are just that much more appealing."

Our dinner is wrought with shameless come-ons from her and she's pretty and willing and I know the facts right in front of me, but my brain is with a blond, blue-eyed stranger who only knows me as Ty. She couldn't even happen upon me in a Google search because Ty wouldn't ever come up with me.

When we've finished eating and I pay the bill, she takes my elbow as we exit. She's flushed, warm and I think, ready to pounce. Our drive back to the Inn she's staying at is tense with sexual vibrations. She adjusts the stereo volume and lets her hand linger in the middle between us. I reach down and cover her hand with mine. She flips hers over, palm up, I twine my fingers through hers. By the time we park, I've resolved to have slow and sweet, then hot and fast sex over and over until I can erase my need for *her*. That's what all this restlessness has been. My own need to come. For a release. To have a warm body for a night. It's not about *her*, it's about me. And right now, I am determined to be all about Emily.

Emily stops me on the farmer's porch of the Inn and pushes up onto her toes as her arms wrap around my waist. I lean down to her mouth. "Ready for dessert?" I whisper before our lips meet.

Jesenia

"Oh, my God, Mom, look at that yellow glass chandelier!"

Angie is smitten with anything girly. She'd paint every piece a pastel color, if I'd let her.

"What are you thinking? Bathroom or kitchen? Kind of small for an entryway."

"Hanging really low over a dark wood, oval dining table. Almost looks like candlewax how those glass beads lay on top of one another."

Angelina has a great eye. I didn't just hire her because she's my kid. She's got a natural talent and her enthusiasm is contagious. Like the one time upstate when we went to visit a dump. We had to lie to John about a charity lunch, because the man would fall into an early grave if he knew we were dump diving.

"I'll buy you brand new things!" he exclaimed when I told him right after marriage that it was one of my favorite pastimes.

"That's missing the whole point, John. Creativity can

transform nothing into something, what's discarded by one gains a new life through another." He shook his head in disbelief and made me promise to stop doing it.

"It's unsanitary. You could get hurt, even worse, arrested."

The first time I took Angie to a dump, she was thirteen. She'd insisted on green rubber gloves and we buttoned her father's discarded old flannels backwards over our clothes. It never occurred to me that it was dirty, I just thought of it as plentiful. Her find that day was shoebox full of black and white photos from the 1920's. She lugged them home and together we pored over them and sorted them into piles that made sense to us. It was entirely her vision to build the book. She made up stories behind each photo and glued them down in a scrapbook. Some of the photos she traced and colored the images in with colored pencils. The end product was stunning—pretty high-art for a seventh grader.

We've made multiple trips back, always on the sly from John. He doesn't get what we do and instead of trying to understand, he's always busy trying to cover for us.

"Just try to stay out of garbage in the City or in Albany. Last thing I need is a front page photo of the two of you in dirty smocks, dumpster diving for broken furniture or whatever it is you do."

We purchase the yellow glass chandelier for twenty-five dollars.

"I'll throw in these wrought iron hooks, if you make it thirty. I think there's six more of them there in the box." The vendor is wearing a winter hat and what looks like two or three jackets. He's got a space heater by his feet, running on a long orange extension cord.

"Deal," Angie and I pipe up in unison and then giggle.

"Mom, are you still thinking about him?" Angie asks me, as we make our way back to the car.

"Honestly, yes, I have been. I don't know what it is. I'd

pushed it to the back of my mind so many years ago, but now, here it sits, right at the forefront. Almost like the memory is trying to tell me something."

"Why don't you try to find him? Maybe you need to know he's okay, to get some kind of closure?"

"Well, Honey, it's not like I'm hiding away. I've got a widely released show, I—"

"Yeah, but it doesn't show your face!"

"Angie, what would your father think, he'd surely not approve."

"Mom, if Dad ever listened to our show once in his lifetime, I'd go into shock. The man wishes we'd call it quits tomorrow, regardless of how much money it brings in. Dad prefers us quiet and hiding in the background."

"But, your father and I are married," I say unlocking the doors to the sedan.

"You don't have to sleep with him. He's probably married, too. Just find him and see what he's up to," she says casually and shrugs.

I feel like telling her she doesn't understand, that the meeting was anything but casual. But maybe my daughter is right and I should listen to her advice. It doesn't have to be the big deal that I'm making it out to be, a cup of coffee at a diner that transpired over twenty years ago.

"What would you have me do, Lovey? Write up the story and put it on our Facebook page?"

"No, Mom," Angie says as she scrolls through her phone.

"What then?"

"Mom, we have a national broadcast, we'll add it into the show."

"But your father!"

"We could have a show about aliens landing on Earth and stealing all of our glue guns and running off with the button collection and Dad still wouldn't notice. Believe me, Dad won't find out. And if he does, who cares? Tell him somebody advised us to come up with something juicy for ratings."

"You are far too talented with deceit and it scares me," I tell my daughter, affectionately, as we pull into traffic on the BQE heading back to Manhattan. She is a smart little monkey and sometimes, still, I can't believe she came out of me.

"Well, I had a good teacher." Angie reaches into the bag of local apples we bought at the flea market and polishes one on the knee of her denims.

"I hope by that, you're referring to your father," I say, giving her a slight smile.

"Yeah, Mom, whatever," she says and takes a bite of her apple.

⚓⚓⚓⚓

We do show prep on Thursdays. Sometimes Angie shows up, some weeks I do it alone. Either way, I'm happy. I make a supply checklist, a bulleted outline for a loose script is all we ever use. Angie and I fill the rest in with our chatter and it seems to get more talked about than our actual show. Some people say Angie is bold and brash and I'm sort of conservative and old-fashioned; maybe it's the contrast between us that makes people tune-in to the station. Or maybe it's not that at all, it could be because Angie and I are so much alike, listeners like to gauge just how far the apple did fall. Today she is here and we are sipping Matcha Lattes and munching on water crackers with brie. Angie is in socks and sweats and a tunic and I'm in my usual jeans and Birkenstocks, wearing a painter's smock. I'm painting the iron hooks we picked up a beautiful teal, we've got a planned episode titled, "Hooking Up," that I'm sure will capture the attention of a wide audience.

"So, tomorrow are we going to bring it up on the show? I don't see a bullet point on here that says: "missed connections, hot black guy who drinks black coffee or wet, emerald ball-gowns from when we were twenty."

"Haha. Miss Comedienne. You are qualifying for nagging at this point. Besides, I don't actually know if he was black. His skin was darker, could have been Indian or Middle Eastern or South American, for all I know." I stick my teal hook in a clamp to dry and peel off the electrical tape where my fingers were holding it.

"He was black. Quit changing your story. Next you're going to tell me that he's actually my real dad."

"Angie!" I say and my eyes shoot up to meet hers. She's sitting in a swivel chair and lets my notes drop haphazardly to the wide crafting table. I take a sip of my latte and cradle the mug in my hands.

Dipping my brush in the paint, I dab at where the iron still shows through.

"I'm not nagging, I just know you won't do it on your own."

"It doesn't seem proper. A woman in my position. It would get back to your father."

"Screw him!"

"Angie!" I say, but I can't help but feel lighthearted. My daughter defends me before I even get in trouble.

"Dad never should have hid your disease like it was something to be ashamed of. You are so high functioning, Mom. You could have been a great advocate, an amazing spokesperson for other people who are out there suffering."

"My work with the Children's Aid Society has been really important, in both my life and your father's."

"I'm not saying it hasn't, Mom!" Angie grabs a furry, white throw pillow and hugs it to her chest. "All I'm saying is that what he did wasn't fair. You deserve to be who you really are and I don't know if Dad *ever* gave you a chance. We only get one life, Mom, I want you to be happy."

"I am happy." Tears are coming fast and silent and I wipe them away, probably marking up my face with streaks of teal paint.

"I'll say it, if you don't. I don't care what anyone thinks."

Our show is unscripted and live and suddenly my daughter has me petrified of what she might say.

"Let me do this one thing for you, Mom, and if nothing happens, we'll put it to rest. You can't walk through your life with a heart full of unsolved mysteries. Don't you think it's important to thank the people who shape your life? Who made you into who you are? What if mystery man is walking around just as curious as you are?"

CHAPTER 5

Titan

Lips. Gorgeous, pouty, cashmere lips. *Her* lips. Soft kisses pull me from blue eyes and blond hair. Kisses. They flutter across my abs and up, up, upward until lips meet lips. This is heaven. This is . . . this is real life.

"I fell asleep." It's a statement. "What time is it?" I ask.

"It's only eleven," Emily says.

"Wow, okay, I should probably get going. Luke will wonder where I am, if I show up any later than midnight."

"Who's Luke again?" she asks as she lays her full weight on top of me. I roll left and wrap the sheet around her as I go.

"My son." Emily's hair has that sensual, just fucked looked. It's that look that can't be replicated, no matter how hard women try and how many products they smear in their hair. Her skin glows and her eyes are hooded still. I give myself an inward pat on the back for a job well done. When both parties are sated, you're allowed to congratulate yourself. I stand and stretch.

"No need to rush out, Ty," Emily says looking a little deflated.

"I'm not rushing. I'm just being a decent parent," I say, while pulling my boxers on. I lean over her and give her a quick kiss on the mouth. Plus, I'm out of condoms.

"Do I still get that trip on *The Anchor* tomorrow?"

"Of course. I don't break promises." I button my shirt up. "Why don't you pack a lunch and we can do the interview on the boat. The leaves are gorgeous this time of year." I pull my pants up, zip and button them.

"Okay," she says.

"Emily," I say pulling the comforter from the floor up and over her. "Thank you. I needed tonight."

"Just tonight?" she pushes. I nod my head and she frowns but reaches up and hooks her arms around my neck. Just before her lips touch mine, I hope like hell that I will feel something; a connection; a spark, something. We kiss and it's anti-climatic, for me, anyway. I smile and tuck her in, turn off the lights as I go and whisper goodnight as I shut the door.

The second I walk in the door, Luke is all over me. Questions are flying and all I want to do is pull on some pajama pants, a wife beater and slump on the couch to relax and enjoy the feeling of my happy balls.

"Yes, I had a good time. No, we aren't 'together.' Yes, she's pretty. No, I'm not seriously interested in her. Yes, LUKE, it's time for bed," I ramble off.

His brow furrows and he huffs at me mumbling 'whatever' before stomping off to his room. It's these moments where I'm unsure how to be a good parent. He's my son but he's my best friend, too, and the line has to be drawn somewhere. He doesn't get to hear all the nitty gritty details. He isn't old enough to understand yet.

Now that Luke is in bed, I can relax, and relax, I do. I throw my feet up on the coffee table after changing into pajama bottoms and decide that it's time to catch up on some recorded shows. Wouldn't you know it, hours later, when I'm drifting off to sleep, I realize I haven't thought of *her* since I got home. I end up falling asleep with a slight smile on my face.

Morning comes too fast. I feel well rested and more like my normal self. A good lay *was* really all I needed. I stretch and crack my neck. It's stiff from my position on the couch. Sunshine fills the windows. It's going to be a great day for a ride on the lake with Emily. I get up and pad to the kitchen barefoot and topless. Once the coffee is started, I pull out all the ingredients to make apple pancakes, Luke's favorite. I've got the bacon frying and pancakes flipping, when Luke stumbles into the kitchen. He moans. "The smell motivated me to get up."

I chuckle and toss him a strip of cooked bacon. He shoves the length of it in his mouth before grabbing a mug and making himself some coffee. It's these moments that I live for. These easy, lazy Saturday mornings. The smell of a hearty breakfast, the moans of bacon love from my son and the way the sunlight filters through the house, as if to say the day is too gorgeous to waste away indoors. It gives the illusion that there isn't a damn thing wrong in the world.

I fill a plate with bacon and apple pancakes and slide it across the island to him.

"Any big plans for today?" I ask. Luke douses his pancakes in butter and syrup, while crunching on another bacon strip.

"Nope." His reply is mumbled from food in his mouth. It makes me laugh. "You?"

"Taking Emily on the boat for lunch and to do the interview. Two birds, one stone and all that nonsense."

Luke whips his head backward, sending his hair flying out of his face. "Cool."

I pile my plate with breakfast and refill my coffee before sitting next to him and digging in.

"Yeah, cool," I say.

Jesenia

I'm sitting at the dining room table surrounded by folders. I ordered blue lights for Angie after all, I can visualize where she's going with it. The wedding will be pricey but I think that's what John expects. I've made a spreadsheet to show him where I cut corners anyway, even if he won't be impressed. My phone buzzes and I glance down to see it's Angie. I take my reading glasses off and lift the cell to my ear.

"Morning, Honey. You're up early."

"Barely up. I'm chugging coffee. Dad home?"

"No, Angie, he left almost an hour ago. Did you need him?"

I notice my coffee cup is empty and stand to fill it in the kitchen.

"I don't want him to be there. Are you sitting down?"

"No, I just got up. What's going on?" I hear the pop and hiss of a soda can opening. "Angie, are you drinking soda for breakfast?"

"I don't live at home anymore, Mom. This is Redbull. You're going to need one, too, turn on channel four, or six even. It's on all of them."

"Terrorist attack? What's happening? Darling, you're scaring me." I fumble with the remote control for the television in the kitchen. God knows I've never turned it on before and I don't know how to use the damn thing.

"Not quite. More like friendly fire. Seems Mr. Black Coffee is looking for his woman, too. His letter moved from Craigslist to Facebook, and all the way to the morning news."

"Shut up!" I yelp and finally get the damn thing on. There's a group of women sitting around a circular table and leaning in toward one host who is reading. I push every button trying to find the mute and when I hit it, of course, the volume is blaring.

"Listen to this, it gets better: *But as I cast this virtual coin into the wishing well of the universe, it occurs to me, after a million what-ifs and a lifetime of lost sleep, that our connection wasn't missed at all."*

"Oh my, he's so poetic," another woman at the table says, her hand clutching her heart.

One of the ladies, who appears younger than the rest, is trying to salvage her mascara by running a perfectly pink fingernail along the rim of her eye.

"He has to find her!" she warbles dramatically. "I've never read anything so touching."

The camera pans out to the audience and there are some women actually in tears. *Histrionics*, I think. They encourage the audience to react and promise them time on camera. Seems like a lot of hoopla, but of course, I didn't hear the whole letter.

"Kind of like my thing, you're thinking?" I ask Angie while I pour creamer in my coffee.

"It is your freaking *thing*, it's your story, genius! Turn the channel!"

And just like that I drop my mug on the floor, hot coffee splashes onto my beige colored capri pants and I can feel the heat of it on my ankles. Because when I turn the channel, it puts me in front of his face. I'm staring at a screen containing a photo of the same man who sat across from me that night. Of course, he's aged a bit, has some greys and a few lines, but if anything, the years have made him even more gorgeous than he was when I met him. He has the most kind and simultaneously vulnerable gaze I've ever seen in my life. I could never forget it, even when I tried. That gaze somehow penetrated me and left its signature on my being. I'm breathless and paralyzed and speechless at seeing him again.

"He's hot," Angie says dreamily.

"That's him," I whisper, fighting the urge to burst into tears.

"Yeah, it is him and his name is Titan."

"Ty," I whisper and his name buzzes on my lips.

"He wrote you a letter and everyone in the world read it.

Some people put it up on Facebook and then the entire universe shared it. One of his buddies uploaded the picture to help it along."

"He is beautiful," I say and frown and quickly change the channel when they move the shot away from his face.

"You're not the only one who thinks so. Apparently, *Titan* has gotten everything from marriage proposals to offers of no-strings-attached sex. He's a single dad with a kid. He's got his own construction company."

"Floozies," I say and finally find a channel that has a picture. It's a different shot on this one, he's on a boat and looks to be fishing with his young son. Then they pan into an interview with some random couple who met and married via a lost connection.

"Mom, he wants *you*. You've got to contact him!"

"I'm a married woman, Angie. I made my choice that night in the diner."

"Mom, you and Dad have had separate rooms since I started high school!" She's screeching into the phone and I feel dizzy with the onslaught of information.

"Honey!"

"What? I'm not blind, for crying out loud! What, are you no longer a person, you're not a human being anymore? Since when is forty-five old, Mom? Look at Demi, look at Elle. You're gorgeous, people ask us if we're sisters all the freaking time! Go live a little!"

"Angie, what's gotten into you? Don't you want your parents together?"

"Fine, don't take it! This one chance that the universe is offering you!"

"I will write him. I will. But this is crazy talk, Lovey, it is. We might not even feel anything at all after all these years. A lot has come to pass in that time."

I'm on my hands and knees with a sponge, a tea towel and a spray bottle of homemade cleaner. My knee catches on a broken chip of ceramic and pinpoints of blood begin to appear through my pants.

"Just read the damn letter," she huffs and then hangs up the phone. I shake the broken pieces of the coffee mug out of the towel and into the garbage. Skimming through the channels, I see the daily news shows have moved on to new fodder. A storm that caused tornadoes in the Midwest, left hundreds of thousands without power. The election. Commercials for adult diapers. No more of *his* face. Creeping hesitantly toward my laptop, I pull up our Angie and Jess' podcast page to see what all the fuss is about.

An hour later, I've read and reread the letter a thousand times. My eyes are red-rimmed, my heart is pounding and nervous energy is running through my limbs like an ungrounded electrical current. His words are *more than* poetic. They were meant for me. Ty is looking for me. I feel like I somehow heard him through space and through time. It was his outcry and his need that reached me and woke all of those hidden memories up. I feel so connected to him, that I'm at once, terrified and ecstatic. I never thought I'd see him again in this lifetime or the next. What was a once a distant dream has suddenly burst through the void and blazed smack into my reality.

It looks like I have a letter to write.

Ty, I am the girl from Hope's Diner that New Year's Eve in the snow. You have been with me, too. For whatever reason, I was somehow unable to let you go. I always wondered what my life would have been, had I left with you that night instead of returning to my dorm. I was later reprimanded by my future husband, for leaving without telling anyone, for not wearing a jacket. He accused me of being rash and irresponsible and foolhardy. None of those things sounded so bad to me and I wondered if you would have thought so. I don't even know if it was an option, to take your hand, to go with you, to see where the wind would take us.

I have to tell you that I never would have left you alone, never, had I known the path you'd walked down before ours crossed. I never would have let you question your worth. I would have told you that you deserved to thrive and to live a full life, like you have. You deserved that and more.

Ty, I don't know what to say to you, except thank you. That night meant so much to me. I wish, in some ways, that I had been braver than I was—that I could have offered you more solace, even if it were just my two arms and the warmth of my body. I wish, too, that I had spoken aloud what I was feeling, a connection so strong it was all consuming and overwhelming. I didn't know what to say or do or even how to broach the topic. So I did the only thing I knew how to do in my naïve, twenty-two years. I ran. I ran away from things I didn't understand.

And now, twenty years later, I can only apologize for my behavior. I can say now, that I wish I had stayed and we had explored what it meant. I wish I had given reign to the thing that was happening between us. What would have happened had I trusted my instinct, or your instinct? I wish my fear could have been replaced with spontaneity, with a healthy sense of adventure. But I was scared, Ty. I was young. I'd just found out I was pregnant, carrying my daughter, who is the love of my life.

I didn't tell you my whole name. I'm Jesenia Van Buren. I'm married. I have one daughter, Angelina. I'm very preoccupied with crafts and home design. My Angie and I have a podcast where we broadcast do-it-yourself design projects, step by step to our listeners every week. I still live in New York, back and forth between the Capitol and the City. I've led a good life this far and I find myself mostly happy these days. I hope you are happy, too. I hope, with the exceptions that you mentioned in the letter, that life has been good to you.

If you are ever in the City, please drop me a line. I'd love to meet for coffee again, maybe share a slice of cheesecake. I will wear a green dress and you just be sure to bring that same look in your eyes.

Better twenty years too late than never.

Jesenia

CHAPTER 6

Titan

It's Sunday and the weekend's almost over. The interview with Emily went really well, I think. And our picnic boat ride wasn't too shabby either.

"Any response?" Rusty asks while searching my house for his son. "You know it was Dan who sent those pictures in." I'm mortified that my picture has made television. I'm mortified that anyone outside of *her* has been reading my post. It's not something I took into consideration when I posted it.

"Figures! You know what? I haven't checked my email since Friday. Probably not though." At this point, I've committed to the idea that getting an answer from Jess is a lost cause.

Rusty grabs his son, Dillon, by the collar as he walks by. "Do not go out of earshot boy, we're leaving in five or your mother will castrate me." Dillon nods and walks off toward the backyard with Luke. "Well there's always this Emily chick."

"Nope, *that Emily chick*, has already checked out and is on her way back to Albany to write the story." How Rusty ever landed a wife is beyond me. And Edie is about the sweetest thing you've ever met.

"You better hope you were a good lay or the story might turn out hostile." Rusty laughs at his joke but I don't join in. I had two rounds with Emily to confirm that we were both satisfied. I'm confident the article will be a good one.

"Dillon!" Rusty bellows.

"You could walk to the back door and call him," I say, laying the sarcasm on as thick as possible.

Rusty just looks at me. Dillon comes barreling through the house and heels at his father's side.

"Thanks for having me over, Ty," Dillon says.

"Anytime," I tell him.

⚓⚓⚓⚓

At eight, I sit down at my desk to finish up some paperwork before tomorrow morning. Luke is locked away in his room doing homework. I finish up logging receipts, I enter everyone's payroll and balance the books. Mindless stuff. Boring stuff.

"Eight forty-five!" I holler from my seat. Luke knows that he has ten minutes to wrap up whatever he's doing because it's our TV time. We pick a show and watch it together, Sunday through Thursday nights before bed.

I pull up my email and log in.

Two hundred new messages.

Two hundred. Jesus. I start scanning through, quickly marking the obvious ones for spam and leaving the ones I'm unsure of. I'm down to seventy-five when Luke appears.

"Whatcha doin'?"

"I had two hundred new emails."

"Dang, Dad." Luke bumps my shoulder.

"Yeah, I've weeded out all but seventy-five." I lean back in my chair and wrap my palms behind my neck for a good stretch. Luke pulls up the spare chair and sits next to me.

"Let's go through these and see if she's here."

So we start opening emails and scanning. Twenty minutes later, I'm ready to leave the rest until tomorrow.

"Last one, Bud." I close my eyes and rub the heels of my hands over them.

"Dad." I look to the screen, knowing something's up from the tone of his voice.

Ty, I am the girl from Hope's Diner that New Year's Eve in the snow. You have been with me, too, for whatever reason. I, too, was somehow unable to let you go. I always wondered what my life would have been, had I left with you that night instead of returning to my dorm.

"It's her," I breathe. Suddenly, I'm frozen. I hear Luke's excited voice yammering on about *her* name, Googling something, pictures and other nonsense, but he sounds miles away. My stomach feels like it's on a rollercoaster. My mouth is stuck open. I don't know what to do except read and re-read her email and blink.

Jesenia

I crawl into John's king size bed in the middle of the night. The mattress is soft and the down comforter is billowy, there's a mountain of pillows he's tossed to the bottom of the bed and onto the floor around the bedroom.

"John!" I whisper, shaking him gently. This was once my room, too, and I haven't stepped foot in here for ages.

"John! Can you hear me?" I try to rouse him again. He's always slept soundly, like he hasn't got a care in the world. John always said I burned all of my calories by worrying too much.

"Christ, Jesenia? What time is it?" He barrels as he sits straight up in bed.

"Not quite three thirty. I wanted to talk to you."

"And you couldn't wait a few hours? What's going on? Are you having an episode, do we need to call the doctor?"

"No," I say slowly shaking my head. I grab a cylindrical pillow with a lace appliqué pillowcase. I slowly untie the ribbon where it's gathered at the end. I tie the bow back up again and try not to be angry with him.

"You know, John, when was the last time I had a really bad episode? Ten years ago, maybe? Maybe even more? It was during the time when you lost the mayoral election. We were all under a lot of stress and I came down with the flu that same weekend."

"How could I forget? They wanted you to do an inpatient stint and we had to pull out all stops necessary to avoid a scandal."

I remind myself to breathe in and out to help keep me from yelling at him. I don't want to blame him. I just wish he could understand me better.

"I'm not so sure myself that the 'episode' needed hospitalization. I stayed up for three days. I knitted and crocheted."

"Maybe fifty pieces, Jess. You painted the den green."

"I paint lots of things a lot of different colors, John. I like to paint, color is important to me."

"You hire someone to do that. You don't spend three sleepless nights doing it yourself!" he barks. John throws back the covers and grabs his robe.

"You almost sound like you're mad at me. That happened ten years ago, John."

I don't get an answer, as he shoves his feet aggressively into his slippers.

"You don't have to get up. I just wanted to talk. "

"Might as well since you've woken me."

"I'm sorry that you feel like my mental health has been such a burden and a disappointment. Sometimes I just wish you would accept it as part of me. I might still do all of those 'crazy' things, even if I weren't sick."

John goes into the en suite bathroom and shuts the door on me. Not a word of forgiveness or reassurance or even common courtesy. I don't think John loves me. I don't know if he ever has.

⚓⚓⚓⚓

Angie and I have been looking forward to the "Hooking Up" episode. We've collected just about every type of hook in every possible material, stainless steel, iron, ceramic and glass. We even found some wooden peg hooks that would go well with more country-style interiors. We're planning on going over simple mounting and stud finding, then decorating ideas and creating patterns out of hanging towels and jackets. At the end of the segment, we take phone calls from listeners. It's our favorite part of the broadcast because Angie and I have to think on our feet and come up with some spontaneous and off the cuff answers.

I remember when I first brainstormed the show. It was born organically out of people always asking me how I got something to look like this or like that in my own house. I found I always enjoyed explaining the process to others, almost as much as I enjoyed creating the object. Whenever we'd have company, the wives would always wander around the house. "How did you make these whimsical bookcases?" "Did you frame all of these quilt squares yourself?" I'd find myself popping a frame off and deconstructing the piece to show the admirer how they could do it themselves in their own home.

John was lukewarm about my idea from the very first mention.

"John, what if I did a podcast about some of the decorating projects? I can have Angie join me because she's got such a great eye and a magnetic personality."

John looked up from his paper, his glasses sliding down his nose.

"Who would *listen* to a design show? Isn't that something that people would rather view on the television?" He looked down at his paper without giving it much thought.

"Have you ever heard of "Car Talk?" I asked him, ever so casually.

"Of course. Loved it! I was a loyal listener to that show for years," he said and took a bite of his Danish.

"You *listened* to it?" I asked him.

He huffed, shook his paper and lifted it up in front of his face.

"Where are we with groupings, Mom? Do you want to do bathroom hooks first and then move onto hallway coat racks? Let's just start with stud finding because no one ever gets that stuff right." Angie says, waving some notes in my face.

"Sorry, I was daydreaming, Honey. What were you saying?"

"So did you really respond to the letter Black Coffee sent or that's just what you told me to get me off your case?"

"I responded. I swear! Already two days ago!" I say, pinning my microphone to my lapel and handing the other to my daughter.

"Why do you think he hasn't written back yet if he was so eager to find you?"

"I don't know the answer to that question. I suppose it could be too emotional for him, or maybe he's shy. Who really knows? Maybe after all of this hoopla, he's just changed his mind?" I shrug it off, as if it were any old email, but really my heart squeezes in my chest with a burn that feels almost like rejection.

We really do look just alike, my daughter and me. Today, my hair is twisted up into a hasty French twist, secured by a number two pencil. Angie's topknot is being held together with a Bic pen. We're both wearing white button up, cotton shirts, and the V on the chest is a gateway to thousands of freckles. We've got the coloring for redheads but without that final detail.

"Let me go see if Catherine has screened the callers."

"Already did it, Mom," Angie says, then sort of steps in my way.

"Well, aren't you industrious! You *never* deal with Catherine, if you don't have to."

Angie just shrugs and then bites on her fingernail.

"Ladies, you're live in two," Catherine says stepping into the studio. "Do you need any water or coffee?"

"Thank you, Darling. I think we're set." I wink at my daughter as the theme music starts to play.

"And on in ten, nine . . ." I hear Catherine's smooth voice over the intercom.

CHAPTER 7

Titan

"Titan?" the woman's voice is nasal and does nothing to calm me.

"Here," I answer.

"You're up next. Do you have your question prepared?" she asks.

"I do. Yeah."

I couldn't respond to the email. I didn't know how. I suddenly had no words to write. Nothing made sense. Nothing was good enough. Jess. My Jess wrote to me. After the initial shock of actually getting a response from the intended person, Luke had slapped the side of my head and told me to look at the monitor. He had pictures of Jess right before my eyes. Luke had Googled her in mere seconds, once he had a first and last name. And there she was. There they were. Blue eyes. The eyes that I had only imagined for the last twenty years were the clearest azure I'd ever seen and before I could stop it, a sigh escaped my lips. I never wanted to look away from those eyes again. I wanted to right every wrong in the world, just to see her smile. I wanted to hear her laugh and know that I made it happen. I wanted to be there when she cried, so I could kiss the tears away. I wanted it all. I want it all with her. And I realized I had officially lost my marbles. She's married and happy. Of course, then I really couldn't form a response that made any sense.

⚓⚓⚓⚓

It's been two days and I haven't contacted her. I feel off-kilter but I'm going to go through with this. Luke said to just do it because she must be cool if she does podcasts. Apparently, they're hip. So here I am, on hold, about to *speak* to her.

"You're on the air, caller."

I let go of the breath I've been holding. "Jess?" I ask. "This is Ty." That's all I can muster. There's nothing.

No sound.

"Hello?" I say.

Jesenia

And I know it's him. It should be impossible to remember his voice. I met with him for a few hours over coffee, more than twenty years ago. Everyone knows that acoustics are strange in restaurants. "Ty" might be short for Tyson or Tyrone or any number of T names on the planet. But, it's him. I can feel it, I know it, and suddenly I have no words left in my brain. Why is he calling the show? Wouldn't a letter have been easier? What the hell do I say now? I've never in my life been left speechless on my radio show. The vision of him hovers before me in my mind's eye, a combination of memory and input from the photo on the television just the other day.

"Hello, Ty. Thanks for calling Interiors Made Easy with Jess and Angie! What can we help you with today?" my daughter pipes in. Thank God for Angelina! I had no words in my mouth, or thoughts in my head. Just the standard answer we give to every caller, it flowed out of her naturally. Except, Lord knows this isn't any old caller to *me*. Angie yelps ever so quietly and we make silent eye contact, eyes wide, wondering if it's even possible. My heart pounds with anticipation. I don't want to make it hard for him, yet at the same time, I loathe to air our laundry so publically. I'll let Angie take over, I can't deal with this situation.

"It's H-I-M," Angie mouths at me.

"I know!" I mouth back.

"What the hell do I say?" Angie mouths. Then immediately follows with her perfect on-air voice: "So Ty, did you need us to help you hook up today?"

CHAPTER 8

Titan

The construction trailer is packed with every crew member. Ear buds are plugged into smartphones streaming the live podcast. I swear I only told Luke and now, all of a sudden, my closest friends know and my crew apparently knows. This is getting out of control. I'm already nervous enough, I really don't want or need the strain of having fifteen burly men watching and listening in on this very personal moment.

"So, Ty, did you need us to help you hook up today?" Right. I was supposed to ask a question. About hookers. No, hooks. Yes. Hooks.

"Uh yeah, I did." Coughs covering up laughs, begin to fill the trailer. Oh, crap. "No! No, I don't need help hooking up," I stammer flustered. This whole idea has already spun viciously out of control into a pathetic scene and I'm the star.

"You had a question though, yes?" She asks. I did dammit, but now I've forgotten my fake question. Hooks. Okay, bathroom hooks. The Vanderbilt's house. Jacuzzi! Yes.

"Oh, yes, I did. I was calling for Jess, this is Jess right?"

"This is Angie, her daughter. What's your question, Ty?" Jess's daughter says. Her daughter, right. I wonder what she looks like, if they are close, and if she knows about me.

I fumble for the right words. "I um, never mind, I won't keep you."

"Hello," it comes out timid. "This is Jess," an incredibly sexy voice croaks out at me. The boys in the trailer all whoop with excitement for me. "Tell us your question, Ty."

My question, what is my question? I have so many. I want to say a thousand things to her but I don't know if now is the appropriate time. So, I relay the only question that seems appropriate. "Oh, ok. Um, let's say you are building a Jacuzzi room in a master suite, one that will have a flat screen TV mounted across from the tub so one can really relax. What kind of robe hooks would you put up?" Robe hooks? Shoot me now. *SHOOT ME NOW.*

That might be the lamest question ever asked. I can't take the embarrassment. The guys are all staring at me like the dunce I am. Wide eyes. Hands slapped over mouths. I wave them all out with a hand gesture and one by one, they file out of the trailer, leaving me alone before I end up firing them all.

"A Jacuzzi room. Hmm, well . . ." That's all I can take. Her voice. The hesitation in it. I hang up the phone. I can't believe I thought calling in would be the right move. I throw my phone on the desk, uncaring if it cracks or breaks. The thud it makes on the desk is strangely gratifying. From the small trailer window, I see the crew start to scatter and I can feel myself turning red as a Fuji apple. I throw open my laptop while simultaneously slamming my rear in the chair. Before I know it, I'm logged into my personal email and typing away. Well, typing is a stretch, I'm more a hunt and peck typist. So I'm hunting and pecking furiously, which frustrates me even more.

Jess,

I am incredibly sorry for calling into your show. I don't know what I was thinking. It was unprofessional and I'm sure caught you off guard.

I delete the message.

I re-type another message.

I delete that one, too.

My desk phone rings.

"What?" I snap.

"Dad."

"Luke?" I say. Shouldn't he be in class?

"You really goofed that one," he says.

"You were listening?!" I crow.

"Of course, I was. Listen, I know you, you're probably attempting to apologize. Don't. Back away from the computer and just do your work today. We can figure out what to do tonight—together." I imagine Luke posed like a police negotiator, trying to talk someone down from jumping off a ledge. His words are clear and soft. He probably has an active stance, arms planted apart, arms up, ready to lunge out and grab the back of my shirt as I start to go down.

"How in the fu—hell did you get so damned smart?" I ask.

"Mom," he says. And I smile.

"Love you, kid."

"Love you, too, Dad."

I hang up and drag a palm down my face and squeeze my eyes shut. Work normally would be fine, but right now, I have to exit this trailer and deal with a bunch of men who will never let me live down the gaff I've just made. This is going to be brutal.

Jesenia

"Caller, are you there?" Angie asks, in full control. My breath has all but whooshed out of me and my heart is pounding full-force.

"I guess we got disconnected—what a shame, Ty. But, we'd be happy to answer that question via email. Ceramic hooks are our go-to for bathrooms, but since it's in the bedroom, which sounds delish, by the way, we'd need to know what kind of décor we're working with there. Also let us know if you're willing to remove tiles. We've got an easy trick for that with barely any clean up time. Right, Mom?"

"Yes," I chirp out.

"We can help one more caller *hook up* and then it's time to wind up this episode."

Angie is unfazed and so good at her job. Tears squeeze out of my eyes in gratitude and I feel so incredibly proud of how good she's become at this. She could run Design Made Easy perfectly well without me.

I'm in a daze through the last question, thinking about Ty and his voice and the image he left with me. I'm imagining him hanging up his robe and stepping into the Jacuzzi. God, he was built back then, the outline of his physique visible through the button up shirt he was wearing, strong arms, broad shoulders. I see myself dropping my robe and clasping his hand to step into the warm, bubbling water with him. How divine it would feel to pull him into my arms, feel his chest against my chest, like I've ached to do for so long.

"Thanks for tuning in! And until next week, remember, the only thing standing between you and a gorgeous home, is the misconception that you can't do it yourself. You can, we did!"

"Phew! That was an averted disaster!" Angie says unclipping her microphone.

"That's a wrap, ladies. Episode Two-sixty going into the

archives. The Jacuzzi caller hung up, we didn't drop it."

"Thanks, Catherine. That's what we figured."

"Did you put him up to that?" I ask, suddenly glaring at my daughter. "You are a scoundrel, Ang! How could you do that to the poor man?"

"I didn't, Mom. I swear to God! Maybe I kind of, sort of, recognized his name when I screened the log but I swear to you that I did NOT ask him to call! He did that on his own. He wanted to hear your voice and then he flipped out at how sexy you were." Angie says, a huge smile overtaking her face. She wags her eyebrows at me and I can't help but burst out laughing.

"Holy Mother of God was that sexy!" Angie yells.

"Pipe down, Angie!" I beg.

"Oh, like Catherine, AKA Lady Elaine Fairchild or Bob the sound guy, care! Mom, he wants to do it in the hot tub with you! I swear, if only *my life* was that sexy!"

"He wants to hang a hook!" I proclaim.

"Pfffft. Yeah. That guy is so crazy about you—he hung up the phone like a kid!"

"I thought it was kind of adorable that he came up with a question," I say. I pull a plastic storage bin off of one of the stainless steel shelf units and start to put all of our hooks away.

"Oh, my God, Mom. Your face, it was priceless! Can you believe that Black Coffee Guy actually called the show? Did you ever think you'd hear his voice again in your life? What are the odds?" Angie stands up from her swivel chair and shoves our notes from the episode in her briefcase. She's in charge of uploading all of the content to the website for our archives.

"I honestly never thought I would, but now that I have—I'm not quite sure what to do with myself."

"You have to meet with him. You've got to see each other. You owe it to yourselves to see where this goes."

"Darling, did you forget that I'm married to your father?"

"Grrrrr, that again? Barely! You're barely married to him."

"Angie, could you elaborate? Your father and I are together as we've always been."

"Oh, you mean living in the same house? Look, Mom, sure, I love Dad. He's been a great dad and a great senator, but let's face it, he hasn't been a good partner. I know you've sucked it up and put your energy elsewhere, but you deserve to be happy. You could use a little love in your life."

I just nod my head because there's nothing I can say. Angelina is right.

Ty's next email says:

> Dearest Jess,
>
> I feel like a fool for my call into the show today. Fool is actually a tame description for how I feel right now. My call was a surprise that was too much for live pod casting (is that what it's called?).
>
> I couldn't find the right words to respond to your email and after two days of thinking it over, I thought calling was the right way to go. If I'm honest, I wanted to hear your voice.
>
> Is that strange? Is this entire situation strange?
>
> I wanted to apologize and let you know that I promise not to call into your show again and disrupt your podcast.
>
> Now, on to the next topic. Would you please tell Angie that I am sorry for catching her off guard, as well? I can't even imagine the consequences of explaining my call to your daughter. I hope it didn't cause a problem.
>
> I'm sitting here having a black coffee and thinking about the way your freckles formed constellations across your shoulders. It's a ridiculous detail to remember twenty years later but there it is—in the forefront of my mind.

Tell me something about yourself now. About what gives you joy. What are your passions, Jess?

I have to ask . . .

Why did you leave without saying goodbye that night?

Very Truly Yours,

Ty

CHAP TER 9

Titan

Gravel flies when I pull into the driveway. The Vanderbilt house is nearing completion and quite frankly, not holding my interest at all these days. Luke is at football practice and won't be home for another hour.

I blow through the front door and drop my work folder on the entryway table, while simultaneously toeing off my boots. In an effort to show a modicum of self-control when I saw her email come in on my phone today, I willed myself to wait and read it when I was home for the day. I practically skid into my desk chair. Using my hands under the desk to pull me back to center, I open up my email and read.

> *Dearest Ty,*
>
> *Never feel a fool for speaking your truth. It was an absolute delight that you called in. I was rendered speechless, too. After twenty years of reliving a memory, it's difficult to come up with any real thing to*

say. Know that I've spoken to you a thousand times in my head. I hope that doesn't sound too crazy.

No need to apologize to Angie, she is your biggest fan in the world, calls you "Black Coffee Guy," and never stops talking about you.

I haven't shown those freckles off in years. I don't even know if they're still there myself. Thank you for remembering so much about me. It touches me deeply to know that a moment that was so pivotal in my life— was important to someone else—that it also lives on through you.

My greatest passion and joy in my life, is being a good mom to my daughter and making sure that she turns out alright. Other than that, I find myself constantly working with my hands. I sew, knit, sand and caulk, I paint, I glue, I refinish—anything that makes the world pretty, makes me happy. I'm not bad in the garden or at baking a cake. I like to dance and swim and hike out by the lake. I'm longing for grandchildren eventually someday. I always wanted more than one but it never worked out that way.

What about you, Ty? What makes you tick?

I'll probably never be able to give you an answer for why I ran like I did. I was responding to fear; I was afraid of my own inadequacies. If I could take it back now, I would. I would stay, and when you came back to the table, I would wrap you in the warmest hug possible. I would take your hand and walk out with you and when we reached the street, I would turn to you and ask you, "Ty, what do you want to do?"

Always,

Jess

I read her email twice through. It takes my brain that long to process each word. Have I missed out on twenty years with her?

Should I have looked for her after that night? I push all the what if thoughts aside and focus. I feel bold and brash. I want to tell her the way I really feel. To tell her all the secrets that reside deep inside my heart, that I'm unable to share with anyone else.

She found my post.

She responded.

She seems open and responsive to my contact and seems to regard our meeting as deeply as I do.

I don't want to waste any more time.

I start typing my response, consequences be damned.

Jesenia

Sweet Jess,

I think, perhaps, you'd be better than some of my construction crew, if those are your hobbies. Want to come help me finish a house?

I live for my son, Luke, work and the comfort of some close friends. I love making breakfast but not dinner. I love music, live or not. I have a boat at the lake here and taking it out on a clear day is just about the best thing ever—something about the way the water laps the boat as I go, the gentle rocking sensation when anchored, it's a kind of peace that reminds me of you. What you gave me, a calm and peace—it has remained for twenty years. It is beyond understanding because it happened on the inside, where my heart is. Not on the outside where life can be so difficult. It is because of you. It feels as though a hundred lifetimes have passed and in each one, you're there somehow. My wife knew about you. She marveled over you and thanked you because if not for you—I would have never been her husband. For twenty years, everything has always come back to you. Please forgive me if my sentiment is too forward but it's been on my mind for a long time and I want you to know.

I think I like your alternative ending to our meeting the best. So, Jesenia, what do you want to do?

Very truly yours,

Ty

That night I dream about Ty. I am stepping into the hot and steamy, bubbling water of his Jacuzzi. He is already in, waiting for me, submerged up to the chest. I drop my robe which is made of slippery, whisper-soft satin—the same color of my New Year's Eve's dress so many years ago. As it falls from my body, Ty's eyes wander from holding my own, to my shoulders, then to my breasts and below. His gaze goes at once soft but hazed over with a shade of lust. I haven't been looked at with desire for so long, that my blood turns warm in my veins and rushes from my head to my heart, then lower. He doesn't speak to me but he reaches out his hand. My hand clasps his rough one, calloused with years of hard and honest work. *A real man's hands.*

I submerge my body in the soft, velvety water. He caresses my shoulder and leans in to gently kiss my freckles. He interweaves his fingers with mine and stares into my eyes. I knew his gaze for such a short amount of time, yet the recognition I feel when looking at him is overwhelming. The connection is still there, blazing as strongly as it did on the night I first saw him. It's a soul-deep, penetrating connection that I can feel all the way down to the tips of my toes. His lips find mine and his kiss sears me with heat. His calloused hand cups my breast and I can do nothing but surrender to this man and lean into his body. I open my mouth to his and he thrusts his tongue deep inside, while his hand possessively searches out my hip. I can't help but moan into his mouth, a sound of deep yearning that races forth from the depths of me. Ty kisses me with an unbridled passion that is unlike anything I've ever known.

This is what it could have been—this could have been us. Twenty years of Ty is what I missed out on. I sit up in bed, awakened by my own arousal. Flipping on my stomach, I groan, frustrated into my pillow. What if I could *have* this? What if real life could be like a never-ending romance?

I want to tell him. I long to jump out of bed and search for his number—let him know just how much the sound of his voice and his email have undone me. How I'm wet and dreaming of him and his hands—that I'm rotating my hips and grinding desperately into my pillow. His eyes, his lips, all of them on me. I want him to know how much I desire his touch, how devastatingly handsome he is to me.

I pull myself to sitting, my back to a pile of pillows. My phone is on the nightstand and I grab it to frantically search for his email. Conjuring the sound of his voice, I read and reread his last email. Then, with a burst of spontaneity, I hit "reply."

CHAPTER 10

Titan

When I finally made it to bed, my hand had found its way into my pajama pants and slowly wrapped around my cock. My other hand had my phone in front of my face with internet pictures of her. As my hand slid up and down my cock, I swore I could taste her red lips, feel the smoothness of her skin and count each freckle that was spattered across her chest and shoulders. I came in mere minutes. I fell asleep, happily, in seconds.

A buzzing sound on the nightstand pulls me from a deep sleep. My hand stretches out next to me and slaps around on the table for the offending vibrations of death. I roll, cell in hand and pull the covers up around me before swiping the screen. It's three in the morning. *Jess.* Opening the email, a grin overtakes my face, despite being grumpy from being awakened.

Ty,

*From so much thinking of you and remembering, I am
unable to sleep.*

Yours,

Jess

I am smitten. I type out a reply and hit send. I know I
shouldn't. I don't know the state of her marriage or really
anything about her life but it appears she's choosing me, as much
as I am her. Thing is, I don't want to be a home wrecker. I don't
want to cause her harm or make her life difficult. And there's
that pesky fact that she doesn't know or need all my baggage. I
roll over and kick my feet against the bed. Life is cruel sometimes
like that. And really, what can I offer her besides a curse? Every
woman I've married or been engaged to has died. That's not
something to overlook. Before I'm able to fall back asleep,
insecurities plague me. Memories of Rory suffering for so long,
slowly dying. Memories of Bridget's bright smile and blood-
curdling scream. Doctor's appointments, Luke's tears, my tears
and trials.

Jesenia

Jess,

*You sure know how to make a man feel rather
immortal. Not sleeping is no good at all. If I were there,
I would hold you in my arms and pull you tight against
me. I'd kiss the back of your neck and whisper how
gorgeous you are until you fell into a deep sleep.*

Your Anchor,

Ty

*p.s. here is my cell # 518–555–7427 you don't have to
use it—but you're welcome to, any time.*

I wake up smiling from a deep sleep, rested and at the same time, bubbling with excitement. I have not felt excited about my personal life in as long as I can remember. Reaching for my phone, I spot it fallen on the floor by the bed. I guess I took the phone to bed with me. I open my email and see he's replied. The excited feeling grows, a carbonation in my belly that runs all through my body. I'm buzzing and grinning at 6:00 in the morning. I hope I'm not manic, yet I hardly care, if I am. It feels so damn *good* to feel good again that I imagine myself strong enough to crush anything that dares to stand between me and this man.

His email is forward, intimate and inviting. He's thinking of me, too. He would *kiss me, he would hold me in his arms*. This has suddenly become almost too real. Too real for a married woman, for a responsible adult—both things feeling like two heavy coats that I would rather shrug off, than let them alter my happy state. He's given me his phone number; the last time a man gave me his phone number was in college, I was twenty. I'm smiling so hard, my face is threatening to break. I want to reply to his note, call him, text him, do all of the naughty things I've been dreaming about with him. But I have to be an adult. I have to talk to John. I won't be a cheating spouse, and this already feels too close for comfort.

Picking up the phone, I dial my daughter's house. She may be my child, but as opinionated as she is, she'll certainly know what to tell me to do.

"Andrew? Hi, dear, it's Jess. Sorry for calling so early on a Saturday. Is Angelina awake?"

"She's knocked out, we had a bottle of wine with dinner and you know how she gets—oh, wait, she's stirring. Looks like she heard the phone. Hold on here a minute."

"Mom?"

Angelina sounds groggy and confused. She's not much of a drinker and even champagne at a friend's baby shower will sometimes send her into a terrible hangover. She gets if from me. John can drink cognac and bourbon, smoke cigars with his friends and wake up at 5:00 the next morning to jog and swim before a press conference.

"Hi, Darling! Are you alright? Too much to drink?"

"God, why are you so chipper? If we talk about last night, I will puke on the duvet. Talk about you. What's the status with Ty?"

"Who's Ty?" Andrew says in the background. His accent is gorgeous, even hung over in the morning. Angelina must be covering the mouthpiece. I can tell she's speaking but everything sounds muffled.

"Back. I don't care what they say, men are so nosy. Tell me about Ty."

"You didn't tell Andrew, did you, Angie? I hope not. What will he think of me? I need to speak to your father before this gets back to him from the wrong person."

"Andrew won't tell anyone, Mom. Who would he tell? I told him you've a got a hot reunion date with some guy you went out with twenty years ago—it's not that big of a deal."

"We've been writing, Angie. Exchanging emails and now he's given me his phone number. The feelings are so strong and it seems we're both equally interested in each other."

"That's amazing! Mom, I'm so excited for you!"

"I'm excited, too, but also feeling very conflicted. I'm going to speak to your father about it this morning. I don't want to do anything rash before your wedding and—"

"Mom, don't worry about the wedding. Just follow your heart."

"Darling, you are so kind, but I owe your father my respect. I don't think he's ever fooled around on me and I, at least, have to tell him that I've been speaking with someone else."

"Well, I doubt he's been celibate for the last—what ten years? You two started sleeping in separate beds, when? After the mayoral run disaster, right? I couldn't have been more than fifteen. It's time both of you moved on. If you're staying together for his political career, you're only hurting yourselves."

I hear Andrew's muffled accent in the background.

"Thank you, Baby," Angie says, and I can hear her lay a kiss on him. "He brought me Starbucks in bed. That man is the greatest thing that's ever happened to me. It's my own fault I'm hung over and he treats me like I've got the flu."

"He loves you, Angie."

My heart swells with joy because my daughter is in love. There is nothing more I can ask for in life than the happiness of my child.

"Let me know what Dad says and if you need my help. He might be really unreasonable and if he is, I'll talk to him."

"I'm genuinely surprised at your reaction and how much you're encouraging me. I would think you'd want us together forever, even if only for unruffled feathers and for the sake of old memories."

"Remember when you went to bat for me and Andrew? How Dad didn't like him and refused to give him permission to ask me to marry him? You fought for my happiness, Mom, and I couldn't be more grateful."

"I knew you two were in love, that's all that mattered to me."

"I want you happy, Mom. Don't take this the wrong way. You've always been a good mother, but you've never had your own happiness. I want that for you. I think you've played the game long enough for both Dad and me. It's time you did something for you, and you alone, before it's too late."

"You are so mature, Angie," I say holding back tears.

"I could care less about the bad press and at the wedding, Dad will, of course, give me away, but as for your date—that's totally up to you. Just because you guys break up, doesn't mean you stop being my parents. Go do your thing, Mom, and I'll cheer you on from the sidelines."

I'm surprised by Angie's reaction. It's what she wants to feel, but whether or not she'll still feel that way if we really split up, is another matter entirely. There are so many changes happening in my life, that I'm coming face to face with the unknown. I stretch and crack my back, pulling my pajamas up over my head. My phone comes with me into the bathroom because it's my link to Ty and I'm hesitant to put it down. If I'm being honest, I'm also scared of leaving it unattended and letting someone else read my intimate emails.

Brushing my teeth in the nude, I contemplate using the number he gave me, sending him a text or else calling to say good morning. I resolve to tell John today. But first I scroll through his emails and retrieve his phone number.

CHAPTER 11

Titan

I wake at five, like always. I stretch in my spot and dread getting out of bed. I check my phone and see a text.

> *Good morning, Ty. I hope you slept well. Even upon waking I find myself thinking of nothing but you. Yours, Jess.*

Instead of giddy, I feel unsettled or maybe just uneasy. I stare at the ceiling and take a deep breath. Rory. It's time. I roll to her side of the bed and reach under the frame. There's a box of dvd's. I grab the one labeled 'when I'm gone' and roll back to where I was. It's been sitting there, in a box, under the bed for just over five years now. Pulling my laptop from the floor, I situate it on my lap and prop myself up before popping in the dvd.

It loads automatically and Rory's face, ashen and sickly, appears on the screen. Is this what I'm destined for?

"Ty, my love. I'm guessing if you're watching this, that it's been at least a year since I've been gone." I smile at her words. Rory knew me so well. *"You really do need to get better at this dealing with crap stuff, dear."* Her tone is light. *"I'm also guessing that, if you're watching this, it's because you've started to really move on. And you're probably getting that guilt ridden feeling that you seem to be prone to. Don't. I want nothing more than for someone else to enjoy your love and for you to feel that comfort again, as well."* Tears form in her eyes and it nearly breaks me. Cancer is the worst. This is not how I remember her. She was so vivacious and loving. She glowed. The person on the screen is simply a shell of who she was. *"Let me just say this one thing before you get into a serious relationship. I want you to look for the woman in the green dress."* She raises her eyebrows at me and leans towards the lens. She's making a point. *"Luke can help you but you have to tell him about her. I know you carried her with you deep inside your heart and before you go dating, willy nilly, I think you should, at the very least, attempt to find her. And if you do, you tell that woman thank you for me. Without her, I would have never met you. I would have never experienced your unconditional love. I would have never had Luke. She deserves your thanks and mine for Luke alone."* Tears spill down her cheeks and I can't hold mine back any longer. Wet, fat, drops drip down and off my chin. *"Find her, Ty."* Rory smiles at me through tears. The video cuts out.

I let myself have this moment to just feel. To feel my absolute love for my late wife. I let myself mourn her for just moment longer. I let myself fall in love a little deeper with her—even though she's gone—for knowing me so well and for encouraging me to find love again, and for knowing that it probably lay in a woman that I met long before her.

A soft knock at my bedroom door startles me a bit. I sniffle and wipe at my face.

"Luke?" I look at the clock, it's almost six now.

"Can I come in, Dad?"

"Yeah." Luke enters, sees me, sees the laptop and cocks an eyebrow at me. "Come watch this, Buddy," I say and pat the bed next to me. He shuffles across the floor, wiping sleep crusties from his eyes and sits next to me. As I replay the video for Luke, I have this hope that anchors in my soul; all my restlessness and unease is swept away. Luke leans into my side. He swipes at his eyes as Rory talks. I wrap an arm around him and squeeze him tight to me.

Jesenia

> Morning, beautiful. Have a great day. Thinking of you.

I stare at the text like it's a revelation. It shouldn't be so entirely foreign for someone to say 'good morning' to me, for someone to call me beautiful. But tears bite at my eyes when I struggle to remember the last time John called me beautiful. It was a very long time ago. Throwing on jeans and a sweater, I rush down the stairs to catch John at the tail end of his breakfast. I won't allow myself to flirt with Ty anymore without telling him something. It has to come from me instead of him finding out from Angie or Andrew or one of those horrid tabloids.

"Morning, John! I'm so glad you're still here. I wanted to speak to you before you left. How are you feeling?"

John clears his throat and looks up from his paper. Displeasure washes over his face and as it does, I have the realization that during every single interaction we have, John looks upset with me.

"I've got a seven a.m. with the comptroller, can't we save it for later?"

"We can speak later, certainly. But I'd like to tell you now, before someone says something to you. I don't want you to think I'm sneaking around."

John folds his paper, seemingly annoyed at me. He takes his reading glasses off and folds them beside the paper.

"Sneaking around, Jess? What in God's name are you talking about?"

"Do you remember the last time you kissed me?"

"I, I—we've been married for more than twenty years. Why would you ask me such a thing?"

I pour myself a cup of coffee and sit down at the breakfast table next to my husband.

"We don't sleep in the same room. You never hug me. Most of our interactions feel hostile and you treat me like I'm a burden or a problem."

"You're going to lay all of this on me right now, right before I have to go to work?"

Taking a huge drink of my coffee, I dig deep for resolve and courage.

"There's no right time to do this, John, today, tomorrow, three months from now—it doesn't make a difference. I loved you once, I did. I love the amazing child we created. But John, I'm not sure what we're doing anymore."

"Are you saying you want a divorce?"

He looks almost annoyed again, like I'm ruining his breakfast, not trying to speak my own truth.

"I don't know," I whisper. I recently reconnected with someone from my past. I don't know if it's romantic, or even what it will be. But the one thing I know for certain, is that it's incredibly meaningful to me."

"Romantic?"

"I haven't cheated on you, John, if that's what you're asking. I haven't even seen him yet, we've just emailed and texted. But to be perfectly honest, it's made me reevaluate everything in my life. Even if absolutely nothing comes of it—I think I owe myself better than this relationship. And I'm not blaming you, it's my fault as much as it is yours. But we aren't a real couple anymore, we haven't been for a long time."

I reach over to his croissant and pull off a corner, I dunk it in my coffee, put it in my mouth and study his face. No emotional reaction. He just looks annoyed. I will chuck my hot coffee at him if he asks me if I'm having an episode.

"If you'd like my opinion, I'd rather wait until I finish my term. I'd hope, out of respect for our daughter, you could put your midlife escapades on the back burner until we walk her down the aisle."

"I understand your requests and I'll consider them, they're not unreasonable. But John, you said ten years in the senate. This term makes ten and I don't see any evidence of you stopping. As for Angie, I've been open with her from the start. She, of course, wants us both at her wedding, but it does not matter to her if we are there together."

He raises an eyebrow at me. So little emotion comes out of him, that I want to cry at the lack of humanity. A crumbling marriage of twenty plus years, a child, a family breaking apart—shouldn't we be devastated? Shouldn't we be lamenting the huge loss? It's a business transaction to John, a political maneuver.

"Do you have a lawyer?"

"No, John. I'm telling you two emails into this. I wouldn't have thought anything of it, if not for the additional contemplation. It made me take a serious look at us and where we're going. I started thinking about what I want out of life for the first time since we had Angie."

"My advice is to wait and see if this blows over. If not, you know how to get ahold of my lawyer."

He pushes his chair back and closes up his briefcase. Not a touch on my shoulder, no hug for old time's sake. I almost long for more tragedy, or even some rage. John walks out of the house without saying another word to me.

CHAPTER 12

Titan

I haven't received a response text from Jess. Maybe I was too forward. Is it possible that I've screwed this up already? My thoughts make me feel crazy. I haven't doubted my actions like this in a long, long time. I chug the last drops of my coffee and chuck the cup in the contractors' garbage bag sitting on the floor to my left. We have another week before we wrap things up for the Vanderbilts. This house is one of my best. From top to bottom, this house is stunning. It's one hell of a legacy to leave my name on, that's for sure. The view of the lake makes this place one hell of a getaway. I'm sure once they get their interior decorator in here, it will be featured in magazines, which is exactly what the Vanderbilts want. I walk through each room of the house, eyeballing all the small details, to make sure everything is as I want it.

My phone buzzes in my pocket. I whip it out of my pocket with the enthusiasm of a teenager.

> Article is live in this month's edition. Congrats, Ty,
> this should really put your name on the map. Care
> to celebrate?

Emily. My stomach drops. It's not the text I wanted to see and not from the person I wanted it to be from.

> Great news. Thanks for letting me know.

My response seems cold even for me but I don't want to lead her on in any way. Across the distance and space between Jess and me, I still feel that inexplicable pull to her. To whatever connection was born that night twenty years ago. Emily has no place in that world or in mine. If someone told me ten years ago that Jess and I would re-connect, I would have laughed at them. It's not that she wasn't there in a corner of my heart, but I was in love with my wife, my family. There wouldn't have been room for Jess in my life, but now, now there is—except for her, there's a husband. She was always an echo inside me because that's all she could be. Now I want a front row seat in her life. The timing isn't exactly perfect. I sigh and rub my temples vigorously. This day has already been a tsunami of emotions. I need to relax. I need a quiet, peaceful boat ride. I need to leave my phone in the truck or something so that I can't compulsively stare at it, willing it to reach through the universe and force Jess to respond to me.

⚓⚓⚓⚓

At lunch, Rusty and Dan pop over to the job site to check out the house and catch up with me. They're stunned that my post reached the actual person it was intended for and that we've been talking.

"Dude, I Googled her. Damn. She's hot, Ty!" Rusty slaps me on the shoulder, grinning.

"I swear, she's barely aged at all since we met," I say. And it's true. Besides looking more mature, she's still as stunning as she was the day I saw her huddled under an awning.

"So, are you going to meet up?" Dan asks.

"We've only emailed a couple times and swapped a few texts

at this point. I don't think we'll be getting together any time soon. She's married, guys."

Dan makes a face at me like he's just bitten into a sour lemon. "Seriously?"

"Uh, yeah, seriously," I say.

"But . . ." Rusty leaves the word hanging between us. I shrug because it is what it is. They can't change that and neither can I. We grab sandwiches from a local deli and eat in a combination of silence and grunting. When we've all finished, I go back to the job site to meet with the Vanderbilts.

"Titan, we just want to say," Mr. Vanderbilt motions to his wife, who is staring at me with a strange look—"that we couldn't be more pleased with the work."

"Thank you, sir."

"Are you the Craigslist guy—you know from TV?" Mrs. Vanderbilt blurts.

"Tandy. I thought we discussed this," her husband scolds and gives her a stern look.

I stare at the ground between us.

"I'm sorry for that, Titan," Mr. Vanderbilt says. It always rubs me the wrong way when a man so clearly controls a woman.

"It's okay. And yes, I am." Mrs. Vanderbilt's eyes look like saucers.

"I knew it. Adelaide was talking about that post that was on that morning show! She said Angie told her something about it because the woman is Jesenia!"

Now my eyes are bugging out. "I'm sorry?" I don't know if I'm asking a question or apologizing.

"Our daughter, Adelaide, is friends with Angie Van Buren."

"Okay," I say. I feel out of place. I'm not sure how to react.

"Tandy, that's none of our business," Mr. Vanderbilt snaps. His voice is commanding and he straightens his back. His wife cowers and tucks into his side like a dog being called to heel. I blink. What the hell just happened?

"Titan, let's connect the end of next week when things are finished to settle up."

"Sounds great, Mr. Vanderbilt." He shakes my hand firmly before taking his wife's elbow and leading her away briskly. I feel guilt. Have I done something terribly wrong? Have I upset her world? The heart is funny like that. It can make you feel like you're bullet proof or cut you down with the smallest truth. How foolish have I been to pursue her after learning she's a married woman. What kind of man am I?

Jesenia

Angie and I are knee deep in silk fabrics and lace at a showroom in the Garment District. Her wedding dress is being handmade and we're taking advantage of the fabric showrooms to do an episode on scraps and all of the amazing things you can do with them. Angie has contracted a fledgling designer from FIT instead of hiring someone well-known. We're both passionate about supporting struggling artists and Angie saw her dresses at a fashion show and knew right away that she wanted to work with her. We've got a list going of possible projects for the next podcast. Table runners, adding lace to pillows, cloth napkins, patches, doilies, framed fabric and anything else we can come up with.

"I can't believe Dad didn't react more. It's just like him to pull away whenever anything gets emotional."

"I did come at him out of the blue, he was not at all prepared for it," I say. I use fabric scissors to cut through a metallic silk that looks both silver and gold, almost a platinum color.

"I guess the little girl inside of me wanted him to fight for you. I think I was hoping that maybe this would shake him up enough to wake him up—so maybe he'd finally let you know that he really does love you."

I fold the yards of platinum fabric into a square and note the item number on our invoice. Angie and I have been coming to this wholesale shop for so long, that they've given us a house account here. Nothing else in this world smells quite like a New York warehouse style building, jam-packed full of imported textiles from every corner of the globe, silks from India and China, raw wool from Italy, bolts of cotton and jersey print from Germany, Duchesse satin from the Arabian Peninsula. I run my fingers up and down an ivory silk on my lap.

"Your father was never very emotive, Angie. Even during the good years, he was more interested in relationships with campaign contributors than he was with his wife."

"He's really good at taking care of other people's needs, just not his own family's. What's the deal with Titan, what are you feeling from those emails?"

"Overwhelmed, if I'm honest. I don't want Ty to feel like he's a rebound, or like he's the reason for a break-up. I don't want him to feel pressure from my actions to do or be something he doesn't want or isn't ready for. Now is not the time, but of course, I have yet to tell him about my disease."

"You don't need to tell him about that yet, Mom. Don't cry over some rejection that hasn't even happened yet! It's not a deal breaker—like Dad always made it out to be. You get depressed, you get a little crazy. Well, so do all the rest of us!"

I reach up to the cutting table and pull myself to standing. Looking down at my daughter, I decide she's an idealist.

"It's unfair not to tell him, but it's a strange thing to mention in a conversation with someone you just met. Who knows if he's interested in dating or even spending any time with me?"

"How could you say that? You're talking about a man who wrote to the heavens, searching the universe for you. He's serious about you and he'll accept all of your flaws. That's what lovers do for one another, Mom—they love the hell out each other, including the tough parts."

I shove a bolt back onto a shelf that runs from floor to

ceiling, so many bold colors and textures, my head is spinning with ideas for creating.

"Let's go get some lunch, Honey. I think we've got enough for ten shows."

"Don't pull a Dad on me! We were talking about Ty!"

"Ty and I are hardly lovers, Angie. Although I'll admit that reconnecting with him has made me evaluate my situation, I don't think jumping into a relationship is very healthy. Nor do I want to burden a man I barely know with the reality of my disease. He'd probably hightail it in the other direction if he could hear us having this conversation."

"What a bunch of crap! I wish you could hear yourself speaking. You're not a disease, Mom, you're an incredible person! You're beautiful and smart, caring and thoughtful. In fact, I can't think of a single reason why that gorgeous man wouldn't want to be with you!"

"I'm going to go settle up with Dominique," I say, tossing the last folded square onto the table.

"Damn, you're frustrating. I should probably talk to Ty myself."

"You will do no such thing, Angelina. Leave the poor man alone!"

"Yeah, well, I read the letter, too, Mom, as did the rest of the world. I don't think anyone who saw it got the impression that Titan is looking to be left alone. I'd say it's more like he's screaming the opposite!" Angie grabs her Starbucks mug and practically flings coffee on our collection. She's blushing hard in her cheeks, just like she has since childhood, whenever she's upset or frustrated.

"I'm scared, Angelina. Just really scared, that's all."

CHAPTER 13

Titan

It's been two days and no response from Jess. I've typed out tens of different text messages but deleted them all. I've typed out a few emails, even just to see if perhaps that route would be more comfortable for her. But I haven't sent any of those either. I'm just going to man up and wait her out. This is all new. She's in a very different place than I am. And the ball is in her court. Time is ticking away and all I can do is wait.

⚓⚓⚓⚓

The air is chilled and the lights at the football stadium illuminate everything. He made varsity this year. I couldn't be more proud of the kid. He's managed to boost his grades, albeit my driving ultimatum probably had a hand in that, made varsity football this year and he's writing for the school newspaper as well. He is a well-rounded kid and I love watching him excel. They just stopped the clock for a timeout. I rub my hands together and blow into them. A young lady three rows down from me shouts, "Good job, Luke!" before waving toward the field.

Who is this creature? I pick up my coffee cup to head down closer to this chick.

"Where the hell are you going?" Rusty asks. I shush him and point out the brunette. He cocks an eyebrow at me. "Little young, even for a 'Most Eligible Bachelor' like you, Ty."

I stifle a laugh and move in behind the girl cheering for my Luke. The advanced copy of the magazine arrived at the house today—complete with my picture on the cover. It was a little embarrassing, to be honest. Emily got me good. The caption under me read; General Contracting's Most Eligible Bachelor Tells All. I stopped there. I didn't have the heart to read the article just yet. Rusty, however, read the entire damn thing before he agreed to get in the truck and go to the football game. It hits newsstands in a week.

The announcer comes over the crackly speaker system as the boys break and the game starts back up. "Here's Pollock back to throw! This offense hasn't had too much success converting on 4th down today, giving our home team a slight advantage." I look up to Rusty, his son, Dillon Pollock, has an arm that any college would be happy to have on their team. Rusty beams.

"Jennings takes the ball. He's running it back!" the announcer shouts. The brunette is wiggling in her set. "GO, LUKE!" she shouts.

The announcer starts speaking but I already know what's about to happen. "Oh! Luke Jennings with the score, folks!" The girl cheering for Luke goes nuts. As does most of the small town crowd. I stand and cheer my son. He spins in a circle and does a curtsy before kissing his fingertips and pointing to his Mom, watching over him with the stars.

Every.

Single.

Touchdown.

My face feels like it always does, as if my smile might break my cheeks. The only thing missing is someone to share these moments with.

Luke runs up to the fence and Brunette Girl scurries down the bleachers to meet him. She blows him a kiss that he catches. I've never seen anything so corny before. And Luke has not mentioned a damn thing about any girl, so we're going to have plenty to talk about later tonight. I know he learned what he needed from sex education in school and I know Rory gave him the basic 'birds and bees' talk when he was younger, but I need to make sure he knows that if he doesn't wrap it up, I will take it off.

"Wow, Luke's got a lady," Rusty chuckles and shoulder bumps me. "Pretty one, too."

"Shut it, Rusty. I still don't know how I feel about this yet. I was just trying to get a better look at her was all."

"Alright, alright. I'd be proud as hell if Dillon brought a girl around," Rusty laughs out.

"I like that there's no girlfriends around yet. More men time. More focusing on the important stuff, less chance of grandbabies," I say sternly.

"Hi, Titan, nice to meet you. I'm Rusty, not your child." Rusty holds out his hand for me to shake and I can't help but let out a laugh. I might be a tad overprotective of Luke but . . . he's all I have.

I stop by the Pizza Shack after running a few errands after the game. Luke is sitting in the corner. The cute brunette is sitting right up against him in a booth, along with Dillon and another teammate. I stop at the counter and grab two slices of loaded potato pizza before heading toward Luke's booth.

"What's up?" I ask as I close in on them. Luke and Dillon's heads snap up in unison. I try like hell to keep my serious face on.

"Uh. Dad, hi," Luke answers.

"Can your old man sit?"

"I have to go anyways," the brunette says in a high pitched voice.

"And who are you?" I ask.

"I'm Bree. Luke's . . . ahh," she shrugs and shimmies out of her seat. Standing next to me, she crane's her head up to my face. The poor girl doesn't even reach my shoulders.

"See you next time, Bree," I say. I slide into the booth and set my paper plate down on the table.

"So uncool, Dad," Luke mumbles and I smile as I chew another bite of the world's tastiest pizza.

When I get home, I know that Luke still has an hour before his curfew. I also know that tonight he will absolutely come home by curfew and not push my buttons any more than he assumes he already has, so I strip off my T-shirt in the hall as I make my way to my room and toss it on the floor. I rub my abs, sore from a day's work. I pull my belt loose from my jeans when I hit the threshold of my bedroom. I let my jeans drop to the floor and kick them aside. I'll pick it all up tomorrow. I crawl into bed in my boxers, plug my phone into its charger and pull the covers up over my head. I dream of a diner, green ball gowns and snowflakes on fire.

CHAPTER 14

Letters

Hey, Luke,

Sorry to mail you a letter like this is 1982. I didn't know how to get your email address and I thought this might freak you out less.

Let me introduce myself, I'm Angelina Van Buren. Please call me Angie and no, never any Brad Pitt jokes or I may have to hurt you. Sorry to stalk you because I know you're just a kid, but my mother is too stubborn for her own good, so I'm resigned to taking matters into my own hands—hopefully that's something you can relate to.

If you're still thinking I'm nuts, let me help remind you: My mom met your dad in a diner in New York, more than twenty years ago on New Year's Eve in a snowstorm. Somehow, in the little time they were together, they left a lifelong impression on each other. I think, if I have the story right, you had some hand in encouraging your father to send the letter. So I'm being proactive, too. My mother has somehow gotten it into her head that she's unworthy of love. I told her that a meeting isn't a lifelong commitment, that getting to know your dad isn't something to be afraid of.

Knowing my mom, I doubt she's written him. She won't tell me shit anymore because I threatened to contact him. You can let your dad know that she has taken action with her life. Earlier this week, she asked my dad for a divorce. Now before you go thinking this has gotten way out of hand—my mom needed a reason to leave and find herself again and the letter was just the kick in the butt to get her moving. They were miserable, I repeat, MISERABLE together. I know she doesn't want Titan to know because she thinks he'll judge her, call her rash and think she's completely lost her mind.

I think they need to meet and I think you and I have to orchestrate it because otherwise, it will take them another twenty years to get up the damn courage.

What do you say to a little conspiracy? You can call or text or email me, Luke. Anytime!

Angie Van Buren

347–877–9532

angelinavb@gmail.com

To: angelinavb@gmail.com

From: L00Jennings@gmail.com

Hi Angie,

I thought emailing would be faster. Plus, I've never sent a letter before and I didn't want to ask my Dad for a stamp. He'd def. think something was up then. You're lucky I got the mail today.

I don't really know how to say this, so I'm going to just be blunt. Even my Mom wants my Dad to find your mom. She left a video for him before she died. We just watched it a little while ago and she actually said she wanted him to find your mom.

I'm 15, so I don't really have funds to make any plan happen, but I'm game to do what I can. Um, my dad and I take a mystery ride a few times a year. Usually he surprises me with a destination but I could turn the tables on him this time and get him somewhere without him knowing in advance. Would that work?

Oh, it can't be during week days because I have school and football but weekends are good.

I'm pumped you wrote to me. And, I don't think you're nuts.

Luke

CHAPTER 15

Titan

Ty, there is so much I would like to tell you. I'm torturing myself because it pains me that I'm not perfect. I'm not the same girl you met in the snowstorm or the girl you shared coffee with in the diner. I'm complicated, I come with instructions and I've spent way too many years now neglecting my love life. Speaking with you ignited something deep inside me. I'm terrified to continue this because I doubt I can live up to the vision you have of me, young, fresh and idealistic—my whole life still in front of me.

I'm afraid of telling you too much or too little. I'm afraid that reality cannot live up to our fantasies or that we remember things the way we want to remember them and not really as they came to pass. How can one cup of coffee give you the feeling that you've known someone forever? How can one letter

*inspire you to radically alter your life as you know it? I
don't know what you do to me, Ty. Never before has
another human had such a profound effect on me.*
Yours, timidly, Jess

It's been a quiet few days. The weekend came and went
without fanfare.

Then yesterday I woke up and had an email from Jess. I've
replayed every word of her email in my head since then. I admit
that when I saw an email from her, a grin as wide and broad as
the Cheshire cat's, overtook my face. I don't have answers for
her questions though. Twenty years is a long time. Neither of us
are the same people we were that night. Life alters you, changes
the fabric of your soul and teaches you things over time. I'm in
the yard raking leaves. I'd wanted to respond immediately but I
didn't. I need time to formulate a response that is just right for
her. I'm contemplating my response, still, when Luke arrives
home from practice.

"Dad," Luke says running up to me.

"Luke," I say while leaning on my rake. He's a ball of energy,
bouncing from one foot to the other.

"You know our mystery rides?" He asks the question as if we
haven't taken a mystery ride once a quarter for the last five years.
Basically, we hop in the car and drive until we reach a
destination—it's a surprise for Luke until we arrive. We spend a
night away together. Sometimes we just rent a room at a local
hotel with a pool, sometimes I take him farther and we look up
fun things to do while we're there.

"Ah, yeah. I'm familiar with them," I laugh.

Luke beams with pride, making me wonder what he's up to.
"I'm taking us on our next one."

"Are we walking?" I tease.

Annoyance crosses his face. "No! Come on. I pick the
destination. I will give you directions as we go but you are going

to be the surprised one," he says animatedly. His smile and enthusiasm are infectious. I can't say no to the kid.

"Deal," I say. Luke grins widely and nods his head. "Do I get a heads up on when this mystery ride will happen?"

"Naw. That'd take all the fun outta it," he says. He tosses his backpack on the grass and picks up a paper leaf bag. "You rake, I'll hold the bag for you."

Jesenia

Jess,

Twenty years has that effect on people. I never expected that you would be the same person. I know I'm not. I don't know how a chance encounter can stay with someone for so long, all I know is that it has for me, too. My only expectation is that, should we ever meet again, the conversation we have be as easy as the one we shared decades ago. Something about you, simply put, set my soul at ease. Maybe just the cadence of your voice or the words you chose to speak. I can't know.

I doubt you come with instructions. Surely you aren't a robot or a dvd player. If I've learned anything in the last twenty years it's this; all women are complicated; all women strive to feel understood and all men strive to give that—while trying to be uncomplicated themselves.

We can always just email, if that's what puts a smile on your face.

Yours, Ty

"You can put them all in the truck that's going to Albany," I say to the movers. I've been bubble wrapping John's pictures from his home office. They consist mostly of framed degrees, various accolades—things of that nature. John has decided to stay permanently at our house in Albany. I'll keep the townhouse in the City until I can downsize to something more reasonable. Things have been moving so fast, that now and again, I've almost lost my footing. But I've managed to stay positive through most of it. I'm living my truth, so I keep telling myself that things can only get better for me.

My hair is tied up in a bandana and I've got paint splatter all over my arms and face and the painter's smock I'm wearing. I painted John's office as soon as I took the frames down, it was a compulsion, probably a subconscious desire to erase him. I don't have any malice toward my husband, I'm more angry with myself for hiding, for not speaking my mind sooner. I wonder if John's voice will stick around, condemning me. When I was putting primer on the window sills, I could almost hear him chiding me, "Jess, people of our standing do not do their own interior painting. Other people need jobs—let me hire some Mexican." Like his voice will always follow me, putting me down, constantly disapproving of everything that's important to me.

"Mom?" I hear Angie shout from the entryway.

"Upstairs, in the office!" I yell back. I'm glad she's here. Angie always helps me get out of that headspace.

"Hey, Mom. What are you doing in here?"

"Changing the color. I never could understand your father's obsession with *bone*, *cream* and *ivory* for every room in the house. I want color. I'm ready for some variety in my life."

"Oh, I know where you can get some color," Angie says, raising a brow at me.

"Did you come over to harass me?" I say, but I can't help but smile. She is a ball of fresh energy and she's unloading take-out cartons from the giant plastic bag she's carrying.

"Don't try to take the high road, Mom. Dad had all of your

interior touches shipped off to the Episcopal Church donation. He bought bachelor furniture, black leather—you'd hate it. Honestly, I bet that's why he got it."

"He's entitled to his vision, Angelina. I've probably been a dominating decorator holding him back from his bachelor dream pad." I wipe sweat off my brow and place my paintbrush in the paint pan as Angie hands me a steaming container of lo-mein noodles.

"Giant, flat screens in both the bedroom and the living room; it's like he's having the time of his life, breaking all of your house rules. Oh, and the herb garden—the one we spent so much time designing? Turning it into a patio. Cement and wood, Mom. Say goodbye to our dreams of aromatic dining."

"It's sensible, I guess. He can't cook a thing unless it's on the grill, so maybe it's smart planning on his part. Hope he doesn't starve to death," I say, as I slurp up noodles with my chopsticks.

"He and Andrew are bonding over it and it's so gross, I could gag. I was like, *he hated you last week and now you're his best friend?* I guess he forgot that he wouldn't give him permission to marry me. Now they're talking about rib-eye steaks and which shitty beers go best with them."

"Well, your father could use a good friend and I'm glad he finally came to his senses about what a good man Andrew is."

"Oh my God, can't you just say something mean about him like a normal person?" Angie yells, gesturing at me with a huge piece of broccoli gripped precariously between two wooden chopsticks.

"He's your father, Angelina. He is a good man, just wasn't a great husband."

"You want to know if he's dating anyone?" Angie passes me her mushrooms, dropping them into my carton. She gives me the raised eyebrow again, like she's enjoying it—like she's up to something.

"No, I don't care. Incorrigible, my dear, that's what you are."

"If you don't run after this, someone else will take him. You know he's a catch. He's Fairfield's *most eligible bachelor.*

I raise my own brow back at my daughter while I'm crunching on water chestnuts.

"Snooze, you lose," she says, then reaches into her plastic bag and waves a magazine in front of my face. I grab the magazine and see Ty on the cover. He's dashing, no, God, he's *sexy.* That might be the problem. He's as sexy as any man who is paid to pose for magazines. "Mom, you're blushing."

"He really is about the most stunning man I've ever seen. I wish everyone else didn't agree with me. It makes it even more intimidating than it already was."

"He's probably seen hot pictures of you on the internet. Don't be such a spoil sport."

"Didn't you bring any wine to go with this take-out?"

"Don't change the subject," Angie says. But she reaches into her oversized purse and pulls out a bottle of Sauvignon Blanc, smiling with glee.

"Look at you, purchasing wine all by yourself. I can't believe you're twenty-one, Angie. Seems like just yesterday you were crawling on these floors."

Rising from my knees, I pull the kerchief off my head. My hair tumbles into my face and I set the Chinese take-out on the desk and look straight at my daughter.

"I would love to—but I'm just not ready, is the answer to your question."

"Will you ever be?" Angie asks as she closes up the containers.

I can't answer. I don't have one. I'm as unsure about this as I ever have been about anything. I don't remember ever feeling so insecure about men, but after twenty years of living with John, I don't feel desirable or even feminine. I'm out of practice and terrified of failing, of making a fool of myself and proving right all of my husband's theories about my inadequacies.

"Maybe we need a getaway. A spa weekend or a hiking weekend in the mountains—just the two of us, some fresh air and some exercise." Angie follows me downstairs with the wine as we go in search of wine glasses.

"That actually sounds divine, but what about the show? We tape on Friday and that would leave only two days for us to hit the road." Angie pours me a huge glass of wine and I've got a feeling she's up to something sly.

"We'll run a pre-recorded episode or re-run a popular show. We could give them Urban Gardening again. People lost their minds over that topic. But don't worry about anything, Mom. You keep painting and packing and I'll get everything in order. You just show up with a suitcase and an open mind. We'll have the time of our lives!"

Angie's smile is too big and she's only had a few sips of wine. But I can't refuse her, I can't refuse my only daughter "the time of her life."

CHAPTER 16

Titan

There is a mountain of invoices and receipts in front of me that I need to reconcile but my attention just isn't there. The air is crisp and people are burning leaves. A smoky petrichor mixes together and makes the distinct smell of autumn. I've settled up with the Vanderbilts and they have now moved on to working with an interior decorator.

The magazine edition with my mug on the cover, came out and the entire town has been buzzing about it. I will never live down this whole *Most Eligible Bachelor* business. This morning, when the sun was barely up and starting to cast shadows through the blinds, Luke and I had coffee together and decided we should do our mystery ride this coming weekend. I need to get away from all the hub-bub here. All the peering eyes. All of a sudden, between the Craigslist post and the magazine, I feel like a slab of meat. Women are so much worse than men and coming from a construction guy, I know what I'm talking about. I've been heckled and cat-called and shamelessly flirted with. The draw of settling down here with Rory and Luke was that it was a *quiet,* small town. A town where nothing ever happens.

Rusty and Dan are the worst. I will be known as MEB for years to come. Luke's mystery ride idea seems like the best idea either one of us have had in a long time. A weekend away at some cabin on a lake would be a God send right about now. I don't even care where he takes me, so long as it is out of our county lines.

I roll my chair away from my desk to stretch. The reconciling can wait. Right now, I need to get out on the water and stare at some clouds in silence for a while. Sunset comes earlier and earlier these days. There won't be too many more boat days, so I might as well enjoy them while I can. Locking the door behind me, I stroll out to the truck and start her up.

⚓⚓⚓⚓

Ty,

Somehow, whatever you say is always what I need to hear. I saw you on the magazine cover. You will not be eligible for much longer now, of that much I'm sure. Your houses are beautiful works of art and you should be proud of how you built that business yourself, from the ground up. I loved reading the article about you. And I can see you haven't changed much. You're still humble and honest, handsome and kind—any woman would be so lucky to have you in her life. I couldn't help but think of how much I'd love to work on a project with you. I guess that sounds silly, but I would love to see you in action, turning those blueprints into something so concrete and meaningful. I'm afraid I'm no good at keeping secrets, Ty. I hope you won't run the other way when I drop this bombshell on you and please know that had we not reconnected—the outcome would have been the very same, eventually. I don't want this decision to put any pressure on you or for you to think that it necessarily signifies something between us. Deep breath. My husband, John, and I have split up.

This is why I've been reluctant to answer. It seems like such a monumental decision requires some down time. So that's what I've been doing. Thinking it through. Trying to decide what my next step will be, now that I'm on my own. I'm repainting the entire house, room by room. It's helping me to recall some of the good memories we shared as a family in this house. As I go, slowly and meticulously, I'm bringing color into my life and meditating on the changes I'd like to make. As much as I try to distance myself from you and the picture you've left in my mind, you keep popping back up, persistent as always in my subconscious. What is it about you, Ty? What happened to us that night? I often dream of falling into your arms. Even though I keep distance from you consciously, in real life, both my mind and my body revel in your presence with me at night.

Always,

Jess

A hundred thoughts snake through my brain as I read her email. A tempest of emotions swell inside me. She's left her husband. I want to fist bump someone. I want to think that it *is* because of me but that's unrealistic. She would have never made such a rash decision based on a meeting twenty years ago and a few measly emails and texts. My ego is out of control at the moment. She liked the article. She likes the houses. She wants to work together. I always say the right thing. If it wasn't weird to stand up, beat on my chest and hoot and holler—I might. It's all very uplifting. It makes me beam with pride. Manly pride.

Yet, I feel let down somehow, too. She tries to distance herself from me. I don't like that. I don't like that at all. The words "*I keep distance from you consciously, in real life,*" send my stomach plummeting like an anchor to the sea floor.

But she dreams of me. When she doesn't push me out of her mind, she wants to be in my arms and God knows, I want her to be there as well. I want to know what her hair smells like; is it lavender or berry? How soft would her skin feel under my fingertips? Are her lips as silky as I've dreamed? How does Luke fit into this if something comes of it? Will she be weird about Rory? About the stories we tell sometimes, the memories and pictures hanging around the house.

Instead of responding, I close my email. She needs a little space and time. She said so and that I can honor. I head into the living room. Luke is sprawled across the couch, one leg over the arm and his neck resting on the opposite arm. I swat his leg and he makes room for me, so I sit.

"So do you have everything you need, like directions, for this trip?" I ask.

Luke rolls his eyes at me. "Relax, Dad, we're all set. You just worry about doing what I tell you to do while driving."

"You sure you finally know your left from right?" I bite my lip to keep from taunting him more.

"You're kinda mean, you know that?" Luke laughs.

"Someone has to keep you on your toes." I tickle under his knee and Luke jumps with a girly little squeal. When he was little, it was much higher, but I always loved the sound of his caught-off-guard laugh.

"Cut it out!" he yells. "Just be ready to go Friday and pack one decent outfit."

"A decent outfit?" I ask. Since when do I need to look nice for a mystery trip? I'm dying to know what he's up to.

"Yeah, like *not* a hoodie. Like, a button up shirt. Just one," Luke says while waving one finger through the air and bugging out his eyes at me.

I wrinkle my face at him in confusion but decide to let it go.

"Right. Okay, will do. Now, what are we watching?" I ask.

He scratches his head and shrugs. "How about the new Terminator movie?"

"Redbox?" I ask.

"And large pizza," he says with a grin.

"Aye, aye, captain." I salute him and stand. I grab my keys from the console table in the entryway and slide on my sneakers, not caring that I'm crushing the heels. Pizza and a movie with Luke sounds like a damn fine night.

When I get back from picking up pizzas, dessert and the movie, Luke has the ten foot bean bag pulled out and two pillows tossed on it for us. Everything is ready to go. Luke grabs the dessert bag and movie from under my arm. I set the pizza boxes on the coffee table and start doling out slices onto paper towels for us. We both plop down into the bean bag. Luke with the remote and me with our dinner. It's these little moments that have kept me going since Rory passed.

Jesenia

"Well, how did you find out about it, if you've never been there before?"

I'm driving the Volvo, Angie is in the passenger's seat, shelling peanuts and drinking a pumpkin spice latte, whose aroma has overwhelmed the whole car.

"For one, I haven't been to every spa and resort in the world yet. You look on the internet, ask friends for recommendations, read reviews—I don't know."

"Did someone you know recommend it?"

"Nope."

"Thanks for doing all the research, Angie. I'm sure it will be fun."

"Are you nervous, or what; you don't trust me? You seem

uptight."

"Not at all, darling, I'm grateful to be spending time with you. I'm not used to traveling without your father is all—and you know those trips were usually scheduled down to the wake-up hour. "

Angie has her blonde hair tossed up in a loose, messy bun. She's wearing jeans and a grey cashmere sweater, her tortoise shell glasses balanced precariously on her head. She's kicked her shoes off and has one leg bent up in front of her, a posture she perfected by the age of four, when riding in the car or eating dinner at the table. Her toenails are painted a shiny, dark purple with little flecks of gold that dance in the sunlight. I can't stop looking at her every time my eyes stray from the road. What would I do without her? She keeps me both sane and totally crazy.

John says she's marrying way too young. I told him we married younger and that pretty much shut him up. But Angie is ready, I can tell by how she carries herself. She's serious about life, serious about starting a family.

"Do you think about him a lot?" Angie asks. She lowers the glass and tosses all of her peanut shells out the window. Any other time I'd scold her, but we're in the middle of nowhere, a winding road in a thick deciduous forest.

"Who, your father? Not at all. Although I feel a little bit guilty admitting it."

"Not Dad, Mom. I was talking about Ty."

I look at her and she's grinning. I don't know what's gotten into my child. Most kids want their parents together forever—no matter what—even if the two parents hate one another. Angie seems more eager than I am for me to move on with my life. She's so enthusiastic about Ty.

We glide around a curve of the mountain, scattering leaves that have fallen onto the road. It's peak season for the fall spectacle and the woods are alive with color—deep red sienna, burnt orange and bright, smiling yellow.

"I find myself thinking about him a lot more than I want to admit. I think about the choices I made and how things could have been different."

"Who knows, Mom? Maybe you'll get your second wind and you two can meet up again. I mean, just to see what would happen."

"Lovey, I don't want to spoil your fantasy, but I'm afraid that ship sailed a long time ago. I had a chance and I blew it. Let's concentrate on your love life and planning your wedding."

Angie reaches past me and fiddles with the radio. Our show is broadcast onto some satellite stations. I sneak a peek at the clock, it should be starting right now.

"Are you going to make us listen to our own show?" I hate to hear myself, but not my daughter. She'll take notes about improvements we could make and ideas for other episodes. She thinks like a producer. She'll become something unstoppable someday. I've watched her execute, with precision, just about everything she's ever put her mind to.

"It's either that or I torture you with pop songs. Mom, did you bring any lingerie?"

I sneak another look at Angie, despite the winding road. She's now kicked off both of her suede booties and is picking at her purple toenail polish. She raises her eyes to meet mine and shrugs—then quickly resumes her task.

"Why would I do that?" I ask her incredulously.

"Because you should seriously think about getting in the habit of wearing nice underwear. You're single now and you never know when or where you might meet someone."

I can't help but laugh at her advice. I thwap her in the arm and she lets out a mischievous giggle.

Then we hear a loud popping sound and the car veers sharply to the left toward the wall of rock on the driver's side. I wrench the steering wheel in the opposite direction and simultaneously remove my foot from the accelerator. I break slowly as the car seems to stagger in the road, weaving shakily before it comes to a stop.

"What the fuck was that?" Angie says, peering into the rearview mirror.

"I think we just blew a tire," I say, both hands on the steering wheel. My heart is thumping and my body coursed with adrenaline. "I should have gone with the rental. I never use this car, it's been ages since it had a check-up."

"When was the last time you had the tires rotated? " Angie asks.

"Had them, what?"

"Oh, dear God. We're in for it. Do you, at least, have Triple A?" she asks me as we unbuckle our seatbelts.

We step out of the car and the air is so clean. It smells of forest and blue sky and leaves changing color. I put my hands in the pockets of my cardigan and survey the landscape. We're at a high elevation and gorgeous scenery pans out before me—lush forest in full fall regalia, an endless bright sky with enough breeze to make the billowy clouds chase one another. A faint smell of wood smoke kisses the air. The only sound is the wind and the distant call of birds. It brings me both peace and joy and without thinking, I spontaneously reach out and hug Angie to me. She marches over to the tire and shakes her head at our predicament.

"It's shredded. Looks like you hit a blender. What the fuck do we do now? I'm calling the resort."

I open the back hatch to see if we have a spare. I don't even know my own car, I'm so used to drivers and cabs or letting John take care of everything. I yank on the trunk covering, trying to get into the wheel-well that holds the spare. It doesn't give at all, making me wonder if it's ever been opened. Angie walks around the side of the car, cell phone pressed to her ear. Her hair has tumbled out of its bun and is skimming her shoulders.

"We're about forty minutes out. I don't think we hit anything. The tire was old, probably needed to be replaced a while ago."

I'm wrestling with the spare, trying to detach it from where it's nestled. I found the jack, pulled it out and almost dropped it on my foot, not expecting the weight of it.

"Are you talking to your father?" I mouth to my daughter. "I'm sure we can change it. Just pull up a Youtube video."

"Yeah, right," Angie says, speaking away from the mouthpiece. "I'm talking to the concierge, maybe they can send someone for us.

I take my cardigan off and roll up the sleeves of my shirt. Grabbing a clip from my pocket, I pull my thick hair back into a ponytail. The tire finally agrees to come free. It's heavier than I thought, so I roll it to the front of the car.

Soon, my knees are aching from kneeling on the road. I ask Angie to pull out something from my suitcase to use for padding. I'm sweating and getting more frustrated by the minute. The illustrations on the directions for changing the spare aren't helping one bit.

"How about you give up?" Angie asks handing me her sweatshirt. I roll it up and shove it under my knees.

"It can't be that hard—people have to do this every day. It seems like the wrench keeps slipping as I go."

When I look up, I see Angie standing by the hood, one hand on her hip and the other outstretched, thumbing for a ride.

"Sweetheart!" I say, dropping the wrench and brushing stray hair out of my eyes. "It's not 1970. It's not safe to hitchhike anymore."

Angie frowns and then rolls her eyes almost imperceptibly, a look she perfected in middle school and hasn't stopped doing since.

"It's the country, Mom, not the city. I'm sure we'll be fine."

"I can get the spare on, I promise. And *the country* is precisely why I'm opposed to it. Didn't you ever watch Deliverance? It would be better to wait for a tow."

I look down the road and see a truck swiftly approaching. It slows as soon as Angie comes in to their line of sight. Through the sunlight, I can just make out two men in the cab.

"Angelina Van Buren, put your thumb away this instant!" I scold her. "We don't need anyone to help us," I say and throw my hands on my hips.

"Speak for yourself. I just got my nails done."

I sigh at my daughter and turn toward the truck. Maybe they could just help us put on the spare and I could give them some cash for it.

The driver's side door opens and a man steps out of the truck. He's tall and built, wearing a green sweater and jeans with aviator sunglasses. His body is graceful and strong, as he makes his way toward us. His body language shows concern and is at the same time reassuring; he doesn't look like he would ever hurt us. When he sees me, he stops dead in his tracks and removes his sunglasses.

I know the face. I know those eyes.

Titan. In the flesh. Mere footsteps in front of me.

CHAPTER 17

Titan

It's been hours since we left the house. I need to stretch my legs and get another bottle of water. My throat is dry. I rub my head and stretch my neck back and forth.

"Left here, Dad, onto two thirty one," Luke says. The roads here in the mountains are winding and mostly deserted. Red and gold and orange leaves create a stunning backdrop for our drive. I still have no idea where we're going but I trust that Luke has everything figured out. I turn on to the road as Luke's directed. He's got his feet propped up on the dashboard and his phone glued to his right hand.

"So how much further?" I ask, while tugging at the neck of my sweater.

"Just under an hour it says."

I flick my thumb up to turn the volume up on the steering wheel. Luke grins and starts bobbing his head to the song. The sun is bright, making the foliage pop just that much more.

We round a bend in the road and I slow as soon as a blond

comes into my line of sight. Through the sunlight, I can just make out two women. The one facing me with her thumb hitched out and another with her back to me.

"They blew a tire, Dad. Should we help out?" Luke's face is all concern. He's a good kid.

"Of course," I say. I put my blinker on and pull over just behind the car. I hop out of the truck and round the hood. When I see who it is, I stop dead in my tracks and remove my sunglasses because there is no way in hell I'm seeing straight. I've finally lost my marbles. But, I know the face. I know those eyes. There they are. Blue eyes. Eyes that I have only imagined for the last twenty years are the clearest azure I've ever seen and before I can stop it, a sigh escapes my lips. I never want to look away from those eyes again.

Her shirt sleeves are pushed up to her elbows and she's holding a tire iron. A lump the size of Everest forms in my throat. I hear Luke exit the truck. I feel him standing at my side but I don't register seeing anything but *her*. I want to take this moment and wrap it up in a box so that I can open it over and over in the coming years and feel this same sense of awe and wonder. My body wants to open my arms and pull her into them. I want to pick up where we left off.

"Jess?" Her name leaves my lips in an inaudible croak. She nods almost imperceptibly. Her lips have formed this perfect, pouty O shape. They did the same thing when I asked her if she wanted to get a coffee. The smattering of freckles still graces her collarbone from what I can see and her shiny blond hair is just as I remember it. I can't form any words. I shuffle my feet to ease some of my body's tension.

"Jess?" Luke repeats with a wide-eyed expression. "Uh, do you want help with that tire?" he asks. Luke looks between me and Jess. Neither of us have really spoken or moved. I'm content just drinking her in. Memorizing every curve of her body available to me. I want to close the distance between us and wrap my arms around her but I can't make my feet move. I feel like

I've just witnessed black and white turn into vibrant color for the first time.

"Mom, I think Luke needs that," the other blond says. Her daughter. That must be Angie. She's standing right next to her mom now. I blink a couple times and focus in on Luke, he's standing just left of Jess, hand outstretched, waiting for the tire iron.

Jess is here.

Jesenia

What do you do when you find yourself face to face with your crush of the last twenty years? You stare him down, drink him in and offer no words to make the encounter less awkward. I'm sitting on a stool in a jewel green gown, he has sad eyes that crinkle at the edges when he smiles. I want to stay here but I have to leave. I have to run. I have to go back to John. I rub my belly.

"Jess?" He says my name again and the sound of it rushes me back to the present. I was lost in his gaze, remembering what it felt like to be under those eyes—to feel the warmth coming off of him.

Angie and Luke are talking about tires and fall and lodges like long-lost best friends, reunited over coffee instead of a flat on the highway.

"Could I have that?" Luke asks me, reaching out for the tire iron.

I stare at him speechless, my mouth hanging wide open. He looks like Ty but he must also look like his mother. Wavy dark hair, a wide mouth, and already as a teenager, the shoulder girth of his father.

"Ty?" I say turning back to his father. I can barely form thoughts. When you've waited so long for something, it's hard to take it in and believe it when it really, finally happens.

He nods his head and his face breaks into a smile. His eyes are full of wonderment and I blush at the way he's looking at me. A sound comes forth from the remnants of the young girl inside me, a squeal or a yelp—something that sounds giddy and excited. I drop the instructions I found under the wheel. It's five steps to Titan. I count them in my head, thinking about the twenty years that have passed and how much I missed out on him.

"Whatever are you doing here?" I manage as I step toward him. Inside I'm cowering at how much I told him. He's probably confused as to why I wrote him that I'd left my husband. I came on too strong; he was only trying to reconnect—not be a lifeboat for my unhappy life or failing marriage.

"I could say the same for you. We're on our way to getaway weekend—some mystery spot up in these mountains."

I'm close enough to touch him, so I reach out my hand. He's just as handsome as he was the night I met him, even better in real life than on the pages of a magazine. Ty takes my hand and pulls me into his chest. Another little sound escapes me, as his big arms find their way around me. His sweater is against my cheek and I can feel his heart beating through his strong chest. My hands timidly move up his sides until I'm hugging him back. It's a bear hug, so huge and warm and honest. I breathe in his scent and smile at how uncomplicated he seems. Ty wears Old Spice, uses Ivory soap and doesn't have a bad bone in his body.

"I have wanted to do this for way, way too long." He says into my hair at the crown of my head. His lips are only touching my head but somehow it's extremely intimate and tender. I love how closely he pulls me in.

CHAPTER 18

Titan

Not a lot else has ever felt so entirely right. She's in my arms. I can't relax them to let her go. This hug has gone from perfect timing to an awkward length of time to hold a near stranger. I don't care. Her hair smells fruity. I could inhale it all day. I doubt she's strong enough to wiggle out of my hold, so maybe I will do just that. Sniff her. Oh, God, I'm a creep now. My heart is pounding in my chest. I'm sure she can feel it. I'm sure it's a dead giveaway to all that I'm feeling. Her scent, the feel of her pressed against me, my heart rate, my jeans slowly growing tighter. Slowly, I force my arms to relax and let go of her. I keep my palms on her shoulders and sort of hold her arm's length away, to really look at her. One hand has a mind of its own and a finger trails over some of those freckles on her collarbone. I want to make constellations out of all of them. She's watching my finger graze her skin. When I realize what I'm doing, I yank my hand away like she bit it. "Sorry!" I say, a little too frantically. *Pull yourself together, man.*

Jess smiles and giggles a little. "It's okay."

"So, ah, what are you doing out here?" I ask. Jess tucks some hair behind her ear, pulls her cardigan from her waist and starts to put it on. *Good*, I think. It's chilly out here. Her face is flushed. The tip of her nose is pink. I want to pull her to my chest again and warm her nose.

"We're having a weekend away," she says then stands ramrod straight and turns to face Luke and Angie. "You two!" she accuses, pointing to our children. Both their heads snap to our direction with mock-innocent expressions plastered on their faces. *The kids?* No way. How on earth would they be able to pull this off?

"Tire's changed!" Luke shouts and starts putting things into the trunk of Jess's Volvo at record speed. His hair is flopping into his eyes as he does and he keeps pushing it out of the way. Angie bites her bottom lip. She looks a lot like her mother at that age.

"Luke," I say sternly. "Was this planned?"

He dusts off his hands before wiping them on his jeans and looks to Angie. "Busted," he says. I have a hand on Jess's shoulder as I stand next to her. Her head reaches my chest. How did I end up next to her, touching her? Why does it seem so natural?

"Mom, you needed a push," Angie explains while approaching her mother slowly. Her face, though, is covered in an enormous grin.

"I most certainly did not," Jess says. She sidles in toward my side a little more. Naturally. It's all natural. I squeeze her shoulder. Again, all so normal—yet not.

"You so did! Luke and I planned a little meet up. We have separate cabins but it will be fun, getting to know each other again and look how beautiful it is out here," Angie gestures to the incredible mountain views surrounding us. "Plus, it's already paid for so—waste not, want not, right?"

Jess's shoulders sag. I remove my hand from her. "Luke, I can't believe you did this," I scold.

"Mom would've . . ." I cut him off. "Stop," I say putting my palm up. "Jess." She turns to me and looks confused or maybe just unsure. "We don't have to do this, if you aren't ready. I think sneaky kids really want it, too, and I'm alright with it, but if you need time—then we don't have to do this. Luke and I can go home." I search her face, her eyes, as I finish—hoping like hell that she agrees to ride out the weekend because I can't lie—I'll be devastated now that I've seen her, held her, if she didn't want to stay.

"You're alright with it?" she asks hesitantly.

Hell yes, I am. "Absolutely," I answer. A weight lifts from my chest.

Jess gives a sideways glance to Angie, then turns her attention back to me. "Okay then. Let's all stay the weekend."

And just like that, I'm pulled in. Hooked, like a junkie. I feel high at just the sight of her. What will I feel spending a weekend with her? There's a brief moment where Jess barks orders at Luke and Angie and people start to head back to their respective vehicles but I'm lost in a sea of what if's.

What if I can't bring myself to leave on Sunday? What if she can't? What if this is the worst idea in the history of bad ideas? What if I just hold her hostage in a cabin until we're old and gray and sickly, so that I never have to stop looking at her? What if she hates me? I'm still thinking about all the what-if's when Jess's arms wrap around my middle. I look down, taken by the contact. She looks up. There's eye contact. It holds me captive. It is intimate. I'm warm all over. I'm on the cusp of leaning down to kiss her, when she says, "I'll see you there, Ty," and lets go of me. I watch her walk to her Volvo. I watch her get in and buckle up and start the engine, only then do I turn for the truck.

"Dad?" Luke says.

"Holy shit," I mutter under my breath.

"You okay?" Luke asks.

I watch Jess pull out from the shoulder and put the truck in drive. "I don't know, Buddy. I think I just had an out of body experience." I pull out behind *her* and try not to freak out while Luke starts laughing.

Loudly.

Jesenia

"Angie, you are a busy body! I can't believe you set us up! What if we weren't ready yet, what if . . . I don't even know where I'm attempting to go with this.

"What if what? If I'd have told you, would you have agreed to it?"

I adjust the rearview mirror and watch Ty and his son get back into their truck.

"Probably not."

"See, it's like therapy, then. I'm helping you move on and reconnect with old friends. You should consider yourself lucky you've got someone outgoing like me in your life."

"Were you just going to let us think it happened by chance?"

"We were going to play it by ear. Hey, he looks even hotter in person."

I glance again in the review and see they're following close behind us. Ty has his sunglasses on and appears to be laughing at something his son said.

"He's a gorgeous man, always was. There is something so, I don't know, wholesome about him."

Angie's shoes are off again and her feet are pulled in close to her butt.

"Right? I know, like he seems like a really sweet person. He works hard and loves his son. Plus—it's like he feels things pretty deeply. If his obsession with you is any indication. He's like a burly, man's man but he's in touch with his feelings."

We take another curve and scatter yellow leaves across the black pavement. My heart is warm in my chest and I can't wipe the smile off my face.

"I wouldn't say it was an *"obsession,"* maybe more like a bucket list thing. We're getting older—it's natural to want to reconnect with those who've made an impression on you in your life."

"Stop with the old thing, would you? Okay, we turn off to the left in about two miles. They've got amazing hot tubs here. Some of them are outside and you can use them at night!"

"I don't know if I brought a swimming suit, Angelina!"

She's working her hair back up into a bun. Even though we work together and talk on the days we're not prepping for the show, it's been a long time since we had quality time like this. I'm not going to admit it out loud, but I'm impressed with my daughter for pulling this off.

"I brought an extra. This is the turn-off, up here at the sign. Oh, now I'm getting excited. We can watch movies, eat in the lodge, sleep in late, do whatever we want. It's going to be awesome, Mom! There are hiking trails all through the woods and a lake at the bottom of the mountain."

"You should have said something about the underwear a little earlier than half-way here."

"Well, then you would have been too suspicious. Why, you already thinking about sleeping with him?"

"Angelina!" I say and reach across the seats to bat at her arm. But right then, we pull up in front of a beautiful old lodge. There are cabins and pathways reaching up to the mountain, all nestled cozily among brilliant fall foliage.

"Oh, man, is it stunning? We couldn't have picked a better time to come! This is going to be so fun!"

I love her enthusiasm and her positive energy. I pull into a parking space in the small lot and Ty pulls in right next to me. I'm nervous about speaking to him, there are so many expectations. But being in his arms felt so easy—much easier than I could have ever imagined.

"Wow, what a view!" Ty says, as he steps out of the cab. Luke hops down on the other side and scans the scenery around us.

"It's amazing, right, Dad? I knew you would love it. When Angie sent the website, it was hard not to show it to you!"

"Apparently, our kids have good taste," Ty says, smiling at me. He moves closer and puts an arm around my shoulders, almost possessively. God, John never touched me like this, so friendly and familiar, Ty is the warmest man I've ever met and we've only ever spent mere hours together. John agreed to link his arm through mine for picture ops at State dinners. I want to roll into Ty's chest and smell his clean and earnest scent. I want to stargaze in the hot tub while sitting on his lap.

He squeezes me in a warm hug, his arm still around my shoulder. Ty kisses me on the side of the head, and I'm almost in shock at how perfectly natural it is.

"Does it look good to you? Are you okay with the place?"

I turn to look into his soft gaze.

"There is no other place I'd rather be than here with the three of you."

"Perfect. I feel the same way," he says, in a low voice just between the two of us. "Luke, are we doing the lodge or the cabins?"

"Dad, I booked us a cabin because it's a little more rustic. Angie got a room at the lodge because it comes with spa amenities and girls like that kind of stuff. Plus, we wanted to be careful, in case you guys didn't hit it off. We could always switch it up a little with the four of us, but I think the rest of the place is booked for the whole weekend."

"I like rustic. The cabins look great!" Ty says as he and Luke automatically help Angie get the luggage out of the Volvo. It touches me just then how wonderful a job Ty is doing raising his teenage son alone. Luke is polite, engaged, and as personable as his father. Not every man can turn a teenager into a gentleman. I can tell the bond between the two of them is ferociously strong.

We walk together up the hill to the main entrance of the lodge. Angie chats with Luke and Ty is back by my side. He gently takes my hand in his hand and heat rushes right through me. Are we moving too fast? Acting like long lost lovers, when we were only ever conversation partners on a night of pure desperation for the both of us. Did we connect back then out of mutual torment and not because we were kindred spirits? Maybe we have nothing in common.

I take a deep inhale of the fresh fall air that surrounds us. The lodge is huge and built to look rustic but anyone could tell that it's a five star resort, if ever there was one. I dare myself to peek over at his eyes again. He smiles at me and looks relaxed, not terrified like I feel I must seem. I squeeze his hand back gently and he pulls me in closer.

At the front desk, Ty and I are left to check in while Angie insists she and Luke go get some of the hot chocolate the lodge is famous for.

"Angelina, can't it wait five minutes?" I ask. Now I'm fearful she's up to something. Why do I feel like this is becoming a trend in our relationship? "What credit card did you use to make the reservation? Is it my Amex or did you use Andrew's? Can I do the check-in without it?"

"Dad's business expense account. Don't worry, I asked him first. Told him it was for me and Andrew to get some quality time away—a little reboot before the big wedding," Angie says, walking backwards and practically shouting. She winks at me like it's all fun and games, and then turns her attention back to Luke. Her words bounce around the giant A-frame of the entrance with low beams crisscrossing every which way above us.

"Oh, dear," I mutter almost under my breath. I'm pretty sure I'm blushing. I'm pretty sure I'm mortified that I told Ty in the letter that John and I had split. He probably thinks I'm desperate, or just looking for a quick hookup. Nothing could be farther from the truth—I'm terrified of both getting close and/or physical with someone.

"Kids. They have good intentions, but sometimes you wish you could sit them in front of Sesame Street and they'd shut up just like they did when they were little."

"Oh, Angie never shut up, even as a toddler. She's all fire, that girl, I think it's why I suffered such heartburn while carrying her."

"Luke's a good kid," Ty laughs jovially. "But we should do this for ourselves and not because our kids are too bossy. Anything you're uncomfortable with, just let me know. I consider myself a gentleman and the last thing I want to do here, is put any pressure on you. I read your letter about the split. I know that can't be easy."

"Thank you, Titan," I say, biting my lower lip. I hand my card to the front desk clerk and my driver's license with it. "It was a really long time coming, so not so emotional, if you know what I mean? Angie is grown, so it was more about logistics than anything. I'm glad it's over, if I'm being honest."

"Me, too," Ty says simply, and it makes the warmth rush through me again, picking up right where it left off. It might sound audacious coming from any other man, but out of Ty's mouth, it's just intense and maybe a tiny bit suggestive. He hands over his card and we check into our rooms and walk toward the great hallway.

"Mom, Holy Crap? You *have* to taste this!" Angie yells. She and Luke are skidding toward us with giant to-go cups.

"Best I ever had, Dad. Better than yours, even!" Luke says.

"How many sugary drinks are you going to consume in one day, Honey?"

"As many as I want, because this chick is on vacation!" Angie says, pointing to herself dramatically. "Speaking of calories, Luke and I took the liberty of signing you two up for an activity.

They've got a wine and cheese thingy by the grand fireplace in the main lodge tonight and it looks really cozy and romantic. It's casual; you can wear jeans or whatever."

"Angie," I say. I'm slightly embarrassed that my daughter is so forward.

"You like cheese, Ty? You look like you could deal with a nice wine and cheese night—right?" Angie asks. Forget forward, she's unstoppable.

"I love cheese. I haven't had a drop to drink since the day I met your mother, though," Ty says good-naturedly. I look up to him. The accident. He told me all about it.

"See, Mom, its fine. He's totally a cheese guy," Angie says. She's so cavalier. She shrugs her shoulders as if this were any random meet up.

"What about you and Luke? Don't you two want to come?"

"Oh, we've got plans alright. Popcorn and The Shining downstairs in the movie room. I'm going to scare myself senseless and enjoy watching Luke freak out. He's never seen it before, can you believe it? What better time than at a remote resort in the woods? Muhahahaha! Come on, dude, can you carry that all the way to my room?" Angie says as Luke follows her, lugging her suitcase in one hand and his hot chocolate in the other.

"Angie can sometimes be a little much," I offer, not knowing quite what to say.

"Don't worry at all, fast-friends, I'd say. Luke thinks she's great, I can tell by his face. Imagine how bored he'd be, if he didn't have Angelina to conspire with."

"We don't have to do the fire-side thing, if you're not up for it. It was a long drive up here and— "

"Are you kidding? There is nothing I'd rather do in this world than sit by the fire with you and catch up. It's been twenty years and I'd love to hear about everything you've been up to."

I smile at him and nod my head in agreement. I can't think of anything I'd rather do than stand under his gaze, drink some wine and get close to him by the fireplace.

"Here, let me get your luggage. What did you say your room number was?"

This is happening. It's real. Ty is standing here beside me. We're in one of the most romantic spots I've ever seen and we've got the whole weekend ahead of us.

CHAP TER 19

Titan

I'm carrying bags.

Jess's bags up to her room.

This place is spectacular. Charming, but rustic. I can't wait to see the cabin Luke and I have. I'm still reeling from seeing Luke and Angie together, like they've known each other all their lives.

"Penny for your thoughts," Jess says and bumps my arm with her shoulder.

"I'm overwhelmed. Luke, Angie. You. It's a lot to take in. And this place is incredible." She stops in the hallway and tries her keycard in the door.

"Mmmhmm, I'm feeling the same." She holds the door open for me, so I enter her room and set the bags on the floor at the end of one of the beds. Her arms are wrapped around her midsection. Like she's trying to hold herself together.

I cross the floor and stop a few inches from her. "I'm going to hug you again, Jess." I can't stop the smile from creeping over my face. "I'm all those things, but mostly, I'm in awe that you are standing right here with me. It's surreal." I pull her into my chest and squeeze. Her delicate arms snake around my waist and squeeze back. "Flabbergasted," her voice is muffled in my sweater.

"Flabber, what?" I ask pulling back a bit to free her mouth.

"Flabbergasted; astonished. I've always liked that word." I laugh at her and pull her back into my chest.

"Flabbergasted is a great word, Jess." I kiss the top of her head. Her hair is like cashmere against my lips. "Should we meet at the grand fireplace at eight?"

She peels herself away from me and nods with the most radiant smile on her face. I let her go and shut the door behind me.

I pass through the lobby and back to the parking lot to get Luke's and my bags from the truck. The walk to the cabin is short, but quiet. The path is wood chips with small lights every ten feet or so to keep it illuminated. The temperature has dropped a bit but it's still comfortable without a jacket on. The canopy of trees offers small glimpses of the stars overhead that have just begun to come out for the night. I arrive at cabin six. It's a true log cabin, complete with a bug zapper hanging from the porch. It looks to be about three hundred square feet. I use the key given to me and push through the door. To the left is a small kitchenette. To the right is a small fold out table with chairs and the bathroom. Straight ahead is a large bedroom with two king sized beds. It's plenty of room for a weekend away. It's perfect for a weekend away when you have a lover and don't intend on leaving the cabin. I wander into the bedroom and set down our bags. The two windows overlook the lake. The water looks smooth and glassy with the moonlight shining down on it.

It's nearly seven. I sit on the chair next to the window and prop my feet up on the windowsill. *Jess.* She's a ten minute walk away from me right now. Luke's a good man for entertaining himself right now. I need quiet to think, to process. Just for a moment. I can't quite wrap my brain around the situation. Jess is here. I've touched her. Smelled her. Heard her voice. It's surreal and it has me twisted up. Are we too old to be doing this? Is it going to scar our kids? Or are we old enough to do what's best for us and trust the kids will be okay? My brain hurts from the constant barrage of thoughts. One thing I don't need to debate is that I want more of her. So much more.

At eight, I make my way up to the main building. I walk through the impressive lobby and into the room to the left. There's a bar at one end. I head over to ask the bartender a question. Jess is standing at the grand fireplace in heels and a comfortable looking tunic and cigarette pants. I sneak up behind her. Place my hand on the small of her back. "There's this song that makes me think of us. Sometimes I listen to it as I fall asleep so I'll dream about you."

Jess whips around with a little jump before she composes herself and grins at me. "What song?" A man hands her a glass of wine.

I can feel myself turning red. "You probably don't know it. I have a thing for old, old songs." I watch the way her lips connect with the glass. The way her throat moves as she takes a sip and swallows.

"Tell me, Ty." She hands me a napkin with a variety of cheeses on it.

"*Trust In Me*,' Etta James," I say quietly.

"Wow, an old soul. Who would've thought?" She's . . . flirting. Her eyes sparkle in the dim light. I suddenly feel like I've had something to drink, which is ridiculous.

"Should we sit?" I ask. Jess nods animatedly. I guide her towards a comfy looking, oversized chair next to the fireplace. She sits, toes off her heels and tucks her legs underneath her. I try to sit on the edge of the chair to give her some room, but she waves me in closer to her. I'm glad. I don't want to lose sight of her, now that she's here. I made sure to use the restroom before I came up here. There is no way in hell I'm taking that chance again and finding her gone.

"So," she says.

"So," I parrot. I pop a cheese sample into my mouth. Jess's eyes go wide. As I chew, my nose starts to tingle and scrunch up. My tongue tastes like, like, pungent, mushy vomit. My instinct is to claw at my tongue and get it all out of my mouth but I can't do that here. Jess starts waving her hand in the air. Tears start welling in my eyes.

"We need some water, please," she says to the waiter. She moves the other cheese samples to one hand while her wine is cradled between her knees. I take the napkin from her and try to purge my mouth of the awfulness that's invaded it. "Epoisses," she says and nods to the napkin at my mouth. "It's actually been banned from public transportation all over France because of the smell."

"Now you tell me?" My words sound funny as I continue to get every last bit out of my mouth. Jess laughs. It's loud and infectious and instantly makes me forget about the taste and smell in my mouth. The waiter brings a glass of water, which I chug before promptly joining in on the laughter. "Okay, great cheese expert, what should I eat that I might actually like?" Jess picks up a sample from her hand and places it in my palm.

"Cheddar is probably safe." And just like that, we're laughing again.

There are a few other couples meandering about when the bartender turns up the music. We've managed to keep the conversation light—for now. I know we both have questions. We're both new at this, unsure of what's appropriate and not. I stand and set my water glass on the hearth of the fireplace before taking her second glass and doing the same. A cover of 'Can't Help Falling in Love' starts and I reach out my hand to her. "Dance?" She looks at me like I've lost my mind. I waggle my outstretched hand at her for emphasis. She hesitates but takes it and I help her up. She's graceful as she slips on her heels and looks up to me. I pinch the matchbook the bartender gave me between my forefinger and thumb, just out of her sight. Reaching forward I slip my fingers into one of the pockets on the front of her pants, deposit the matchbook and pull her hips to mine. She looks dizzy. Her breath comes in uneven gasps, as I take one hand in mine and guide her other to my shoulder before wrapping my arm around her waist. We're flush. Chest to chest. I start to move and she presses into me. A low groan slips from my lips. "You look beautiful tonight. I should have told you sooner."

"Oh, stop."

"I don't want to stop."

"In that case, I suppose you may continue," she says.

"Your eyes are like the sunlight on a clear blue ocean." I twirl her out away from me and back in. "Your hair is like cashmere." I roll her backwards, she kicks up a leg with a little laugh. "The sound of your voice feels like home." And I want to run and hide. I was on a roll there, doing great, but that last one just slipped out. It's the truth, but it's too much too soon. I try my best to cover my gaff. "Your freckles are still there, and perfect." She stops us from dancing and looks directly into my eyes and further, to my soul. It's like I don't need words, she can just see into me and know. It's a strange but comfortable feeling.

"Please don't hold back what you want to say. I don't know what's right or wrong at this point but I know that I like hearing how you see me." She looks bashful but proud that she spoke up. I take her face in my hands. My thumbs stroke over her cheeks slowly. So soft. I should kiss her. It takes all my willpower not to kiss those lips as her tongue darts out and wets them. Her fingers claw at the shirt at my waist. It's almost as if she's willing me to do it. Instead, I lean forward and kiss her forehead. "Just don't leave without saying goodbye this time and we'll be okay," I say.

"I'm sorry, Ty, I'm so,—" I stop her with a finger to her lips. "Shh," I tell her. "I wasn't scolding you. Just letting you know that this time—that won't fly."

Jesenia

This is what second chances feel like, magical and decadent, almost like you've beat the powers that be at their own game and you're dancing on borrowed time and a slowly sinking ballroom—but you won't let it stop you. The fireplace is roaring and the lights in the great room are dimmed all the way down. Ty proves to be a phenomenal dancer and we're not talking about the waltz. His hips pressed against my pelvis, made my insides turn to liquid. Forget everything I ever learned about decorum, if he goes in for the kiss, I'm done for, I'll have no defense against the swell of desire that is quickly overtaking every inch of my body.

My thoughts make me stare at his lips while we dance. His are so full and wide, mine dwarf in comparison. Then my mind blips on the thought that I've never kissed a black man. I haven't kissed many men to begin with, minus some awkward exchanges in high school and then a few frat boys at college before I met John. I wonder how racism has affected his life and if it's been hard for him. It can't be easy coming to a place like this, where people are polite but their eyes linger just a little too long on your face, wondering what your story is. Or where people look back and forth between you and your son, silently questioning if his mother is white and whatever that could possibly mean to them. But Ty is so noble and forthright, if it weighs on him, I'd be hard pressed to tell. Or the simple truth could be that he's dealt with it all his life, so by now he's used to it. He sits me back down in our designated loveseat and does a silly bow in front of me.

"Would my lady like more wine?" he asks and I smile at him and nod. I can't seem to stop staring at his lips. I watch his handsome profile as he goes to the bar. All he said was, "my lady," but I liked the sound of it so much, that I'm holding back everything inside me to not chase after him and throw myself into his arms.

I need to cool down, get my head on straight and try to keep it together. This is more romance than I've had in so long, that I'm getting swept up in the allure of it. We need to talk—we need to be serious about some things. I meant to ask him about not drinking and I haven't even yet broached the subject of his late wife or offered him my condolences. He walks back over toward me and I drink in all of his maleness, from his close cropped greying hair, to the how his button-up shirt molds to him. He's muscular and entirely in shape, a man who works hard with his body and likely hits the gym a few times a week. I'm trying to focus on something meaningful to say when Ty approaches, he hands me the wine and runs his fingers down my cheek.

"You're really flushed. Does the wine do that to you? Maybe we're too close to the fireplace, want to step outside for a minute?"

I take his hand and rise to my feet. I just fell for him a little more from the sweet concern on his face. We step out onto a wide balcony that overlooks the rising hill behind the lodge. The night is crisp and sweet smelling, with just a touch of firewood smoke in the air. The stars are out in droves and the moon is a thin crescent. When I look out over the edge, I can just make out some of the cabins. They look so homey with yellow lights warming up the windows and faint wisps of smoke rising up from their chimneys.

"The cabins have fireplaces, too? That must be so cozy!"

"You should come up to check it out. I'll build you a fire and make you hot cocoa." Ty arms slides around my waist and I lean my weight into him. I can't stop thinking about the kiss and without planning, my lips find their way to his neck.

"Jess," he says. I love the way my name sounds with his voice. I nip at the warm skin on his neck and feel as if I've lost all control of myself.

"I'm sorry, I—"

"Don't be sorry." And in that instant, his lips find mine and we are truly reunited in a tentative, adoring kiss. Our kiss is timid at first and then I open up to him. His hands go to the back of my head and he massages my neck as he deepens his kiss, using his tongue. I haven't kissed like this for so long, maybe ever. It makes my heart race, my loins ache and without even meaning to, I'm slowly grinding into him. When we release for air, we say only each other's names.

"Jess."

"Titan."

Then we're back in the kiss again, reopening all of the doors that slammed shut so many years ago. The two of us under the same unforgiving moon, maybe a little more mature, but still harboring the same craving to connect deeply with the other, someone so mysterious, yet so incredibly familiar, all in the same moment.

In our kiss under the moon, it feels like time folds in on itself. It could be that night. Ty on the verge of destruction and me, running from a man who I knew couldn't understand me. But on this second try, we do it right. We fall into each other's arms and trust the feelings that had overwhelmed us. We give in to the desires that coursed through us back then, this time we don't judge them—we follow their lead.

Ty pulls back and he cups my face in his big palms. He strokes my cheeks with his thumbs and stargazes in my eyes. Then he throws his head up to the sky, almost as if to hold back tears.

"Jesus, is it too weird to say I've missed you?"

I shake my head and now my tears are all falling freely. I wrap my arms around his neck and bury my face into his shirt, breathing in his warm scent.

"I've missed, too, Ty. So much."

"Are you crying, baby? Don't cry," he says and lifts my chin up.

Then I'm kissing him again, more passionately even than the first time. My mind is blurred with lust and I'm losing feeling in my arms from holding him so tight. He responds with enthusiasm and thrusts his tongue deep into my mouth. Calling me "baby," undid me, I'm seconds away from tearing my clothes off right here on the balcony.

"Come back to my room," I say breathlessly, pulling away just the slightest bit.

We rush, hand in hand, to the elevators in the lobby. I'm praying The Shining is still running and Angie hasn't gone back to the room. His hand settles on the small of my back as we wait impatiently for the elevator. It dings and we step inside and Ty pushes me to the back wall. It's not aggressive but it's forceful and it undoes me yet another notch. I can feel my underwear soaked between my legs and this time, I moan out loud into his kiss. My hair has fallen out of its clip and Ty has his hands in it. From my hair to my neck to my shoulders to my ass, I moan again and Ty presses his erection into my belly. I grind shamelessly onto his leg. I have no idea what's come over me. I've never in my life acted so out of control of my own body. What if someone walked in, what if there were press with cameras. I don't care about anything but getting more of Ty and more of this intoxicating feeling he's bringing me.

The elevator stops on our floor and we tumble into the hallway, still kissing, still groping. He's a bit rough and his stubble is bruising my mouth, but I love it so much, I would never tell him to slow down. He takes my hand and leads me to the door, reaches his hand in my back pocket and pulls out the key card.

"Jesenia, I'm going to walk you in and kiss you goodnight and be out in five minutes," he says almost panting. I pout like a child. I can't believe it's already ended.

"Stay, Ty. Please? I'll call and reserve us a separate room. I don't want to spend another moment away from you, it's been too long already."

"I know and don't want to make this any harder than it already is. You've had wine. It's our first night. We *both* need to think about this."

I open the door into my dark room and kick off my kitten heels. I pout more and throw my hands on my hips and then run right back into his arms because I can't stand to be apart from him.

"Believe me, when I tell you how badly I want you. I want to show you what you do to me and I want it to be something we'll never forget."

"Show me then," I whisper into his ear. I nip at his earlobe and suck it all the way into my mouth. I don't even know who I am at this point, I'm so worked up from kissing him. He shoves his thigh between my legs and it provides friction in the right spot. Again I make noises, which is completely foreign to me. I've always been silent in the bedroom and my vocalizations are scaring me. But Ty seems to like them, he kisses me harder every time they escape.

"I would be devastated if you regretted anything we did. I want to make love to you so badly, but I want to do it the right way. Look at me for a minute."

I obey and look into his eyes. Can it really be that we've only ever spent hours together? I've never felt so connected to another person in my life. Ty feels like home to me to and I barely *know* him.

CHAPTER 20

Titan

"I don't want this to be one night or a weekend fling or just sex. You and I are bigger than that, Jess, and I believe wholeheartedly that we were meant to be together. Let's let it breathe for tonight and tomorrow we'll wake up and make sure it's what we both want. I'm not talking about casual or no strings attached or dating or any of that. If I have my way—it means you and me forever, whatever that may look like." They say nights were made for saying things you can't say in the light. I decide to just go for it. This is one of the few moments when I wish I could enjoy a little liquid courage.

"So I've thought a lot on this whole thing and here's what I've come up with—some relationships are anchored by their faith in God, when everything falls apart, both parties come back to their faith and it holds them together. Some relationships are anchored by their deep appreciation and respect for their partner. That's what Rory and I had. When things got tough, our respect and admiration for each other held us together. But you and I?" I take her hand in mine. It feels right. "We have something different, we're anchored by a moment in time. A chance encounter. We're anchored by hope. Hope's Diner. At first, I thought maybe that wouldn't be enough. But, hope is an incredibly powerful thing. The hope you gave me stuck with me for twenty years. It's a solid foundation to build on and I want to at least try." She starts to open her mouth and she looks worked up. Flushed. Beautiful. Brimming with thoughts and words and emotions. "Now, kiss me, woman." Jess smiles at my command. My lips ghost over hers. Warm breath and silky softness. I brush my fingers over her lips and kiss her forehead. Jess closes her eyes and slows her breathing. She nods her head with her eyes still closed. I memorize every curve, line and angle of her face before I slip out the door.

Jesenia

Ty is a gentleman in every sense of the word, but I've never been left in a state of such intense need and desire. I peel my clothes off and hope he'll change his mind, only to come charging back in and find me standing naked in the middle of the room, wanting him.

I've never been so turned on in my life. My skin is on fire from his touch and the memory of his hands tests my sanity, as I feel close to combusting. I drag myself to the shower and turn the water on full-force. I step under the freezing cold stream and just try to breathe, evenly. In and out.

⚓⚓⚓⚓

"Calm down, Mom. It's okay. You are so out of practice. Him saying "no" wasn't rejection, in fact it's the opposite, he said "no" because he's *so* into you that he wants to be careful and do it the right way!"

Angie found me sitting in a dark room on the couch in a towel, crying my eyes out over Ty. I'm trying to think about it rationally but I've never been so overcome with emotion, like my insides were ripped out of me and put back in all tangled and mixed up. Angie hands me my pajamas and I reluctantly pull them on.

"Do you want to dry your hair or are you going to sleep on it like that?" Angie asks. My hair is still dripping down my back. I'm a mess, a ball of pent up sexual energy and confusion and I feel so clingy and needy. I'm doing everything in my power not to run to Ty's cabin and throw myself into his arms like a child in need of a parent.

"You guys will figure it out tomorrow, you both need to sleep on it," Angie says. She's standing behind me gently towel-drying my hair. "In other news, Luke is a great kid. He's smart and mature and really down to earth."

"He's got an amazing dad." I say and then burst into tears again.

"Okay, Mom, that's enough. Let's get you into bed. You and Ty are moving in the right direction and everything is going to be okay."

"I know you're right, Angie. It's just so overwhelming. After all these years, the feelings are so strong. I can't help but mourn for the years that we've lost already."

"Try to stay in the present—those are your own words I'm regurgitating back to you. We're on vacation, we're having fun— you've got to loosen up a bit."

Angie crawls into bed next to me and lays her head on the pillow. I smile at her and wipe my eyes.

"There are two beds, you know?"

"I know, I'm just making sure you're okay. Sorry to secretly spring the love of your life on you without preparing you first."

"I appreciate what you've done, Honey. I don't know if I ever would have been brave enough to do it myself. I'm glad you did it. Ty in my life feels like a whole new beginning. I've never felt so excited about the future, Angie."

"I'm excited for you. I've never seen you like this either. Your face is full of color and your eyes are shining so bright, either you're wasted or you just started living your real life."

"Thank you, Angelina."

"Goodnight, Mom."

⚓⚓⚓⚓

In the middle of the night, I wake up from the urge to pee. I tiptoe to the bathroom so as not to wake Angie. My clothes are strewn on the floor like a teenager who does everything with angst. I sigh and pick my pants up off the floor and give them a hard shake. Something white tumbles to the ground and is illuminated in the ray of light that pours out from the bathroom. I lean down to pick it up and carry it into the bathroom. I can tell it's a matchbook, I just don't remember picking one up. Inspecting it in the full light, a wave of nostalgia washes so strongly over my body, that I reach out to the sink to steady myself against its onslaught. I left him a matchbook that night.

My chest seems to expand unusually large with the breath I take in, then conversely, contracts to the point where I can scarcely breathe. I pull the top up, careful not to tear it. He's sketched an anchor on the inside cover. The night we met. The snowstorm and the tears. Two inconsolable souls who were comforted by the very existence of one another. It didn't matter what we said or what we did. All that mattered was our acknowledgement of the other's pain and fears. A serendipitous encounter, an unforgettable bind, a gift of pure solace, when the universe reached out and connected Titan to me, and me to him for a moment.

CHAPTER 21

Titan

"Did you have a good time, Dad?" Luke asks, not caring that I'm in bed with the lights out. I sit up to look at him across the dark room.

"The best," I tell him and it's the truth. The feeling of Jess in my life, in my arms, on my lips, has thrown me for a loop. I feel like I've been doing flips underwater.

"Why so glum sounding?"

"Just, you know, Luke. The truth has to be told at some point and I'm dreading it." Luke crosses the floor and sits on the end of his bed. I can hear his breathing pick up. "Please, Dad. I don't want to talk about it."

"I know, Buddy."

"No! You don't know," he wails. I climb out from under my blankets and move to him. To me, he still feels like a toddler when I wrap my arms around him. I hold him tight and rock gently. I don't care if he's fifteen. I know he needs it and quite frankly, I do, too. "Please, Dad, I want this one weekend to just be fun. Angie is really fun. I want to have a fun, crazy, *normal* weekend."

I let Luke go and take him in. Really take him in. He's almost as tall as me. He has his mother's eyes and smile. He is growing up so fast but still too young to be saddled with all this. And if he wants a crazy, fun, normal weekend—I will give it to him. "You win, Buddy. A wild, fun-filled weekend it is."

"Promise," Luke says, kicking off his sneakers.

"I promise. We will do nothing but insane things which will make everyone laugh hysterically all weekend. Hey! What about that zip line tour? Nothing says wild like having your junk all scrunched up and on display in a harness," I offer.

Luke gives me a half smile. "Deal. But I want Jess and Angie to come, too."

"Not sure if that's their thing, but we can try," I say. "Now how about some sleep?"

"Yeah, I'm tired."

I get up and crawl back into my bed. "How'd you like the movie?"

"It was freakin' creepy! No wonder you never let me see it before. I'll probably never look at a hotel the same way again," Luke proclaims.

"If you have a nightmare, I'm right here," I chuckle and adjust my pillow.

"I'm not five, Dad," Luke grumbles.

"In my head, you still are. You were much cuter then, too."

"Good night, Dad." His voice sounds irritated but I'm willing to bet he's trying to hide a smile right now.

"Night, Bud."

I tuck my hands under my pillow and stare at the ceiling. Life is cruel. It can light you up or leave you cold, and love, love can tell you every word to say or leave you without any words at all. And right now, all the words that are important seem to have flown the coop. My heart says twenty years from now, I want to look across the dinner table with a handful of grandchildren under our feet and know Jess still makes me feel immortal. My brain says that fantasy is just that—a fantasy.

Luke's got it right. We need a wild, crazy, normal weekend. I push all my conflicting thoughts from my head and instead think of Jess. The hope she fills me with. The peacefulness she radiates. Of the way her body pressed against mine turned my insides to hot and hard. Of her eagerness. Of the way she wanted me and of the way I want her.

⚓⚓⚓⚓

I'm up with the sun, which is normal for me, so instead of waking Luke up, I make a pot of coffee in our kitchenette and take a mug down to the dock at the lake so he can sleep in. My fleece is barely warm enough, but the coffee mug keeps my hands warm and the view is stunning. It's peaceful here. The water is smooth, not a ripple to be seen in the glassy top. Loons cry and ducks bob up and down feeding. The sky is pink with the rise of the sun. It adds to the fire colored leaves of the trees surrounding the lake. Leaves crunch with squirrels and chipmunks running through the woods. I lean back in the Adirondack chair and close my eyes.

"May I join you?" The voice startles me. My coffee sloshes in my mug as I jolt upright.

"Jess?"

She laughs at me. "I didn't mean to scare you."

"It's alright. Sit." I sip my coffee. "Why are you up so early?"

She sits in the chair next to me and wraps her shawl around her. "Couldn't sleep in. You?"

"I'm up at five for work most mornings so . . . habit. I have a pot of coffee in the cabin, should I fix you a mug?" Jess looks beautiful first thing in the morning. She doesn't' have a stitch of makeup on as far as I can tell and it makes her freckles across the bridge of her nose stand out more. It makes me wonder where else I'll find those mesmerizing freckles on her.

"I'm okay for now."

"Alright," I say. "Don't hesitate to change your mind, though."

"This is stunning," she says looking out at the tree line. I move my mug to the arm of my chair and reach across the small gap between us to take her hand in mine. Her skin is so creamy-looking against mine. She squeezes my hand and smiles.

"It really is." *Wild, fun weekend.* I remind myself. I tug at Jess's hand and she looks at me confused. "Come sit here," I say, patting my lap. She bites her bottom lip to keep from grinning. "Come on, I'll keep you warm."

She stands but I don't release her hand. I slide down in my seat a little and pull her down until she's sitting on my lap. She rests her head on my shoulder and I slide my arms under hers and wrap them around her. "Much better," I whisper into her ear, before I lightly kiss her neck.

Jesenia

Curling into Ty, I let myself relax in his arms. I can't remember the last time I watched the sun come up, or the last time I felt this safe, protected and yet vulnerable, all at the same time. He kisses my neck and turning my face into him, I offer him my lips. Kissing Ty is like rolling back into bed, warm, comforting and delicious. A fish jumps in the water right in front of us. I let out a giggle and Ty smiles, then pulls me in closer to him.

"I thought maybe I'd apologize for last night. For being the one who was moving too fast. I wanted to tell you that I'm not usually like that—I mean I haven't been with anyone beside my husband. You know what I mean."

"Don't apologize for anything. I was feeling bad because I didn't want to deny you. I just thought we should slow down so that we're sure of what we want, that we're both on the same page."

I run my fingers through his hair and down the side of his neck. I let them guide me into the V of his shirt and I feel all the way down around his sculpted pec and then up into his armpit. Ty tilts his head back and closes his eyes. Gently, I kiss his lips and then along the edge of his jaw.

"I promised myself I'd be more restrained, but I can already tell it's going to be a problem."

"No problem at all," he coos at me. Then Ty opens one eye and squints up into the sunlight and my face. "Unless restraint is something you're into. Then that can totally be arranged." He's smiling when he says it and I find myself laughing again. He hands me his mug and I take a generous sip of it.

"I like it black, hope that's okay."

"I know how you drink your coffee. I've known for twenty years."

He grabs the nape of my neck and pulls my face quickly to his. He kisses me hard and emotionally, almost robbing me of my equilibrium.

"I was going to say something about you liking it black, too, but then I figured we were too old for those kind of jokes." I smile and take another sip of his coffee and peek out at the blazing sunshine.

"You look like you have a halo. You're beautiful in the early morning light, golden hair, blue eyes, like a Pre-Raphaelite damsel. It makes me want to take advantage of you." He says everything with a mischievous smile, a grin that's contagious.

"I want you to, too," I whisper into his ear and I can feel him go hard right next to my thigh.

"At this rate, we won't make it to lunch."

I remove my hand from the V of his shirt and let it travel down over his chest, his stomach and ever so gently, graze where his erection presses into my leg. I kiss him again and his grip on my hip tightens.

"We just need a room and a "do not disturb sign," I whisper to him.

"I guess as far as getting to know each other before the physical part, we're both failing miserably."

I look into his warm eyes and nod. He's right, before we even finished a cup of shared coffee, we're right back to where we left off last night.

"You're right, Ty, we should slow down. This weekend is about getting reacquainted. The other stuff can wait, it's me who's jumping the gun."

"I didn't say I didn't like it, Jess. Don't get me wrong. You're the sexiest woman I've seen in years and I can't wait to discover that part of us."

I can't help but think about my disease and how I need to acknowledge it. I need to bite the bullet and just get it the hell over with. I tell myself it's not something to be ashamed of, it's part of me–it doesn't define me, it doesn't make me less of who I am. But my blood runs cold when I actually try to form the words and express them.

He thinks I'm beautiful. He thinks I'm refreshing. Tell him the truth and all we'll have is this weekend. I'm sure he would smooth it over, make me feel comfortable, he's a gentleman after all and he would never say or do anything that would hurt me. But I can see it, as if it's already happening, tell him what the whole package includes and we have a fun weekend, a long kiss goodbye and I'm left with the memories and a bunch of unreturned emails. I'll call and he'll be polite and ask how I'm doing, tell me about Luke and then make an excuse as to why he has to get going.

See, no one wants to deal with a complicated mess—sleepless nights, deep depression, random, manic episodes. A woman who keeps it together on the outside, but while you're tossing in bed, she's on the floor in the closet crying. Organizing your ties by style and by color, making a grocery list in the dark and clipping coupons with the zeal of a mad bargain shopper. And not because she likes doing these things, but because sometimes, the only way to straighten out the jumble she feels inside, is trying to make order of everything on the outside.

"Jesenia, what is it? Looks like a dark cloud passed over your face. Did I say something wrong?"

"No, I'm okay." I squeeze his hand and look out over the water. The sun is in its full expression and shining through the bright red and yellow leaves of the changing trees. "You said everything right."

"Tell me or this is never going to work. We've got to be upfront with one another. We've got too much riding on this— we owe it to ourselves. This is our second chance. Let's do the best we can."

"You're right, Ty. I'm sorry. There's something I should tell you about myself and my history. It's what I meant when I said I come with instructions. I'm definitely far from perfect, I, I—"

"Don't." Is all he says. He seals my lips with a swift kiss and stops my defeated words from leaking out. "There's nothing about you that I don't want or won't cherish. We all come with faults and I'll love yours as hard as I plan to love the rest of you. I know it sounds strange, but to me, it's a done deal. I've never felt so sure about anything in my life. I'm in it for real."

"But if you knew certain things, you might not be so generous with your heart. It's heavy stuff, Ty. It would be wrong not to warn you."

"If it's part of you. It's part of us."

He pulls my head onto his chest and I think I may be crying. His valiant acceptance of my flaws is more forgiving in one moment that my husband was in a lifetime. I think I may have just hit the pot of gold in the lover department. Ty is even more stunning inside than he is on the outside.

"Besides, I promised the most important man in my life, that I'd go light on the heavy stuff this weekend and just try to enjoy a fun, crazy, wild time. This crazy fun includes you and the brave, young Angie, so I'd be honored if you'd agree to join us. I understand where you're coming from. Believe me, I do and I'd be happy to talk about what's wrong with you any other time. But I can tell you right now, one hundred percent, that I already accept it, no matter how bad it is."

I gaze into the face of the most generous soul I've ever met in my life. He spoke to me that night in the diner and I recognized in him this incredible human spirit that couldn't be forgotten. And now he's in front of me once more, and we're embarking on making memories together, on sharing our lives. It all seems like too much. My heart is bursting and overrunning with emotion. I grab his face. I kiss him long and hard, like I can never get enough of him. My heart sings and then it soars. And in my mind, unspoken words are already humming, *I think I might be falling in love with you.*

⚓⚓⚓⚓

Angie and I are getting hot stone massages. It's great to spend time together and it gives Ty the opportunity to spend some alone time with his son. The masseuse places smooth, round stones down both sides of my spine. There's the flash of a hot burn before it morphs into muscle melting heat under a delicate pressure from the rock. I close my eyes and breathe deep. The relaxation is luxurious and carries me far away. But unlike the sorts of fantasies I've indulged in the past, things with Ty are my reality, so I only have to imagine as far away as last night.

"You are so glowy!. We should do spa retreats more often, you look amazing!"

"Ty makes me *feel* amazing, I don't mean to take away from the facial, but the light is on the inside, Angie, and if I'm glowing, it's from happiness."

"That's how Andrew makes me feel, like I'm lit from within."

"I know he does. That's why I went to battle against your father for your right to happiness."

The masseuse takes one of the larger stones from Angie's back and begins to gently roll it into her shoulder muscles and down the span of her back.

"Thank you." Angie mouths to me and it almost brings tears to my eyes.

That riff between her father and I felt like the last straw in a long series of disappointments. We disagreed about everything—we could never find common ground.

"I never could tell if it was just because Dad didn't trust me or because he really believed I was too young."

"A combination of both things, I think. Your father also harbored an unspoken belief that he could have a hand in choosing who you ended up with. You falling in love with Andrew extinguished his designs on marrying you off like a merger."

"He likes Andrew now that you're getting divorced."

"That's a good thing. I knew he would eventually come to his senses. Plus, you're his little girl so, technically, no one was ever going to be good enough."

I can't move after the massage is over. My face is still smushed through the hole in the massage table, denting my cheeks.

"I want to take a nap here."

"You can or we could go out to the hot tub."

Angie and I make our way out to the detox baths. They are wood, panel-surrounded hot tubs with various amounts of salts and herbs in them. Angie picks the one called, "energize," we drop our robes and climb in, wearing our bathing suits.

"Anyway, Mom, I feel like if it weren't for you, I wouldn't have Andrew. I'm so grateful for that."

"Well, now we're even, because if not for your diligence, I wouldn't have reunited with Ty. So, I'm grateful to you, too, Honey, for knocking some sense into me."

"Speaking of Titan, where are those two this morning?"

"On zip lines down the side of the mountain. I'd rather not have to watch, those things scare me to death."

"Tell me about it. You don't want to lose him before you even get him back again."

Just then a hawk flies above us in the pale blue, fall sky. He squawks and then glides with a grace that is mesmerizing. He surveys the treetops, circling and riding the air weightlessly, without moving a muscle.

"Losing him once was enough. That's part of the reason why I fought tooth and nail for your happiness with Andrew. I realize you're young and I know, first hand, that it can be problematic. There's a chance it still could be and you might even resent me later for being so lenient."

"Never!" Angie says and puts her palms together in the steaming, dark water. She lifts her hands to her face and rubs the water on her cheeks and her forehead.

"There's no way to be sure. But when I saw you with Andrew—I knew I would risk whatever it took to see you together. I agree that twenty-one is extremely young to get married, but after a loveless union with you father, I wanted a life full of love and true happiness for you."

Leaning back into the soothing water, I submerge almost up to my neck. It smells of balsam fir and arnica, maybe some lemongrass.

"Dad said no to Andrew's face when he came over to ask him."

"This feeling of regret, of loss, my missed connection with Titan—I've felt it my whole life. Regret wasn't something I was willing to watch you experience, if I could help it. I believe we know when it's true love and it's up to us to hold on tight. I made a mistake the night I met, Ty, Angie. One I've regretted my whole life."

"But now you've got a second chance and Ty feels the same way." Angie trails her fingertips through the water, making figure eights. Her face is flushed and her baby hairs are plastered to her head.

It's not something I'm used to—finding happiness in another person. But now that it's happening, I'm terrified of losing it, of it being taken away. I need ten more lifetimes to love Ty, to make up for what we've lost and to do it the right way.

CHAPTER 22

Titan

It's just past noon when Luke and I finish the zip line tour of the mountainside. I'm not sure I've ever seen a smile so large plastered on his face before. He really loved it. There was something exhilarating about it. Whizzing through the air suspended by a harness and wire. The excitement built as we harnessed up and climbed to the "launching pad." Then it was into the air, soaring like an eagle, with a tree-top view. It was adrenaline-pumping. The view of the foliage and lake were incredible. At one point, we were one hundred feet over the lake as we cruised the last section.

"That was insane!" Luke exclaims, removing his helmet and handing it to one of the staff.

"It was. The girls should have come. I think the view would have outweighed the scared-of-heights factor."

"Ha, I don't know, Angie seemed game but Jess was a little jumpy just talking about it," he says and laughs. I remove my helmet and hand it off.

"So what are we doing now?"

"We're meeting them at the restaurant for lunch, I think."

"Right," I confirm.

"You know," Luke starts, as we head up the path back towards our cabin, "you've been really smiley today."

"Is that weird?"

"Naw. It's good. I saw you and Jess this morning down by the dock." Luke slides his eyes at me then back to the path. He has a lopsided grin on his face.

"And?" I ask.

"You looked good together. Comfortable or whatever. I liked it." He kicks a rock out of the way and looks at me.

"It was comfortable. I liked it, too, Buddy. Jess is special—not just because of who she is to me, but as a person, she's one of those really solid, good people."

"And pretty. She's really pretty." Sometimes I forget that he's only fifteen and is ruled mostly by what's between his legs, when it comes to the opposite sex.

"Yeah, yeah, that, too. But that's not the important quality. It's a bonus. The personality is the important part."

"Do you think she will come visit our house? Or maybe we could visit her and Angie? You know, after this weekend is over," he asks.

"Is that something you're comfortable with?"

"Yeah, Dad, I'd like it, I think," he says and picks a chunk of bark off a tree.

"Well, unless I really screw something up in the next twenty four hours, it's likely we'll see them again." I bump Luke's shoulder as we head into our cabin to freshen up. I can't believe he asked about Jess visiting. That's big. Even in the brief relationship with Tara, I kept her away from the house as much as possible—away from Luke as much as possible. I didn't think he was ready to have another woman in our house. I didn't want him to ever feel like I was replacing Rory. My chest swells at his fondness already for Jess and Angie. It's one less thing I need to worry about. If he's good. I'm good.

I all but collapse into one of the bedroom chairs, winded from our little hike back here. I'm exhausted. I tossed and turned last night. My dreams were torturous. I dreamed of all the dirty, bad things I want to do to Jess. Of the sounds she'd make and the way her back would arch when I touched her. I couldn't relieve myself with Luke in the bed next to mine, so I suffered through the dreams and waking with a rock hard erection on and off all night long. This morning when she kissed me, when her hand slid down and grazed my erection, I almost threw her down on the forest floor and tore her clothes off. Good thing I didn't, since, apparently, Luke could see us down there. My desire for her is out of hand. The physical attraction is like a magnet drawing me in. Her voice, a siren's call that eliminates responsible thought.

I want to touch her, feel her, kiss her, hold her for hours, days even. We need to alleviate some of this tension between us or we'll both burst into balls of fire or implode. I bend forward and pull my shirt off. Standing, I swipe the activities list off the nightstand and look it over to see if there is anything that could entertain Angie and Luke for four or five hours tonight.

"There's a board game night with snacks at seven," Luke says with a grin. "I hear Monopoly takes a while to play through."

I drop the list to the floor and stare at him.

"Come on Dad, you're not an activities guy, why else would you be looking at the list?"

I don't know where this kid gets his balls from but they are etched in brass apparently. "Busted, I guess," I mumble.

"It's okay. Angie and I planned this so that you two could spend time together. The goal was for us to entertain ourselves anyway."

I dig through my bag for my Oxford shirt—the one nice thing I brought per Luke's request. "I think maybe this isn't a topic we should discuss any further."

"I'm almost sixteen, Dad. You should hear the guys on the team talk."

"I'd rather not," I shoot back at him. I can only imagine what those little punks talk about and what they're doing on a regular basis with girls. A shudder runs through me.

"Just saying, we will be playing monopoly for a few hours tonight. So, the cabin will be empty."

I button up the last of the buttons and straighten out the cuffs. "Can we just go eat now? Please?" I ask. Luke chuckles at me and nods his head.

"Is it weird for the kid to embarrass the parent?"

"It's rotten. Truly rotten." I clamp a hand on Luke's shoulder and usher us out of the cabin and towards the vixen in my dreams.

Jesenia

I put on a pale peach dress and a grey cashmere wrap to keep me warm. Sweeping my hair into a loose French twist, I secure it to my head with a tortoise shell clip. I put teardrop pearls in my ears and slip my feet into a pair of low heels. I dab gloss on my lips and a single coat of mascara to bring out the blue in my eyes.

"Holy Shit, Mom, you look gorgeous!" Angie says, jumping up from the bed. "Let me get a picture of you like that. No, wait till Ty comes, I'll get a shot of the two of you together. Are you doing the lodge for dinner?"

"I think so, Honey. Would you like to come with us or do you have something else planned?"

"Oh, plans with Luke already. More hot chocolate, board games and then S'mores out back by the fire pit."

A knock at the door makes my pulse jump like the little fish in the lake. I've been to a million fancy dinners in my life and I've never felt nerves like this. But it's anticipation and not necessarily bad. I'm excited to see Ty, to listen to him talk, watch him eat, and kiss him again.

Angie bounces to the door and rips it wide open. Ty is wearing a button-up shirt and has ditched the work boots for the time being. Even dressed up, he still screams rugged man, a nice shirt can't hide his physique which is lean and hard from years of physical labor. It makes my stomach flop and heat travel through me. I'm used to the pale fish bellies of politicians who work from a chair. The most exercise they get is rising up and coming down from the podium, that, or stroking their own egos provides a bit of a work out.

"You look edible."

I blush. Like a kid, like a schoolgirl, like a woman who knows nothing about sex. I don't know how I can seduce him with zero experience in the seduction department. He puts his arms out and I gravitate to him.

"You look like a peach, that I want to get a bite of," he whispers in my ear, as he wraps his arms around me.

"Smile!" says Angie as she snaps a few photos on her iPhone.

Ty is so affectionate and expressive with his touch. His hands are all over me as we ride in the elevator and coast through the main lobby. On the nape of my neck, around my waist, my shoulders and my back, he marks every part of me with his touch and it makes me feel so cherished.

There's another beautiful fireplace roaring in the dining room, a rustic, antler adorned wooden A-frame that fits, at the most, twenty white napkin-adorned tables. He pulls my chair out and as soon as he sits down, reaches for my hand under the table. Mine are cold, his are warm, and his large hands envelope mine like a blanket.

"Your eyes, they do strange things to me. They've haunted my dreams for so long and now, here you are in the flesh. It makes me speechless sometimes. I wonder how I got so lucky."

I massage his big hand and run my fingers over the calluses. My fingers slip into the cuff of his shirt and caress the pulse point of his wrist.

"I'm at loss for words with you, too. You're even better than a dream. You're a better man than I could have even imagined."

I order wine and Ty orders our food. We're trying both the house specialties, fresh-caught salmon and venison stew. Ty spreads butter on a piece of sourdough and hands it to me. His simple, considerate gestures mean the world to me.

"How was your father-son time with Luke today?"

"A blast. That kid is committed to having fun in the best possible way. He adores Angie and he even said you and I look good together. Mentioned you and Angie making the trip up to see us, if that's something you'd be interested in. We've got plenty of room in the house and actually, the garage out back, I've redone into a little guesthouse," Ty says. He eats with an appetite, doesn't shy away from vegetables and God knows why, but it's turning me on. The bigger his bite on the fork is, the more I'm squirming in my seat. My hand gravitates to his thigh under the table. I trace my fingers up as high as they'll go, maybe an inch from his zipper, then spontaneously lean in to touch my lips to his, even though he hasn't finished chewing.

"Is that a *yes*?" Ty asks, laughing. He leans back in his chair and brings the cloth napkin to his lips. After a day in the woods, he's got some scruff beginning to peek through. It makes him look younger, sexier, and even a tiny bit dangerous. I know my eyes have gone glassy from how much I want him.

"Yes. We'd love to. And you're welcome in the City, any time you want to. The townhouse is big, plenty of room for you both. Don't even consider a hotel, if you're coming in for work. You stay with me." I'm nodding my head as I say it and even to myself, I sound overly possessive.

"I would love to stay with you. What do think about dessert?"

"I think I can't stand another minute sitting next to you with all of my clothes on."

We both stand up at the same time.

"My thoughts exactly, the only thing that sounds appetizing to me, is you. And maybe peaches."

We manage to walk out of the lodge at a normal pace, Ty's arm around my waist, me leaning into his scent, my hands straining for his chest, his neck, any part I can reach. Once we near the trail, he steps in front of me, holds my hand and guides me into the thickly wooded area. The path is narrow and delicately lit with tiny lights along the side every four to five feet. The trees are dense and the rich, the fecund smell of soil and woodchips, rich undergrowth overcomes me. Ty speeds up his pace and I struggle not to stumble or lose my footing in the near dark. The moon is out and brilliant but almost obscured by the tall trees.

"Ty, wait, I'm caught!" I exclaim as craggy branches reach out and snag my sweater wrap. Turning, I unwind myself out of it and lay the wrap over my forearm. Ty pulls us forward again and I only make it a couple of feet before my heels catch a root and I collide into Ty's back. I'm giggling and winded and hopping on one foot.

"My shoe is back there somewhere in the dark."

Ty offers me his arm and I hop as we backtrack looking for it. Ty gets down on his knees in the dirt and leaves that seem to have a layer of slippery mud under them.

"These woods are conspiring against us. The want you all to themselves!"

"Just leave it! We don't have much time. You can find it in the morning and run it down to my room." In a moment of lunacy, I reach down and tug off my other heel. I toss it up into the air and we can hear it land but we don't see where it goes.

Ty grabs my hand again and we run toward the cabin. My bare feet are slipping in the cold mud and I can't stop laughing. As soon as the cabin comes into view, Ty reaches down and scoops me up in his arms, as if I were a short two by four. I squeal and he kisses me as he walks with me in his arms. He sets me down on the little porch of the cabin and fishes in his pocket for the key. Ty looks down at my feet illuminated by the light over the door.

"Jess, your muddy little feet against your pale skin make for one of the sexiest sights I've ever seen in my life."

"Really?" I ask, still winded, and laughing from our sprint. He answers by grabbing the back of my neck with force and kissing me hard and fast. His hand slides down my back and cups the curve of my ass, he squeezes gently at first, then steals bigger handfuls as he deepens his kiss. He lifts me again and gently kicks open the door; he flicks on the light and marches me straight to the bathroom.

It's brightly lit in the small bathroom but it's extravagant and modern, made to look rustic but no expense is spared in the design. Ty sits me on the edge of the tub and turns on the water.

"Let me wash your feet."

He looks deeply into my eyes and I want him to wash all of me, I want him to undress me and take me and do whatever he wants with my body. I want to surrender to him and offer up all that I have. The water steams as it streams out of the faucet, Ty lowers my feet in and gooseflesh rises up all over my arms and my upper thighs. He lightly pulls down the zipper on the back of my dress and I shudder in anticipation, as it falls away from my shoulders. Ty traces my freckles along my collarbone and chest. He brushes his lips softly along my shoulder blade and I close my eyes and tilt my head back at the delicate sensation. Ty gathers soap and a washcloth and a water glass from the sink, he lifts one foot into his lap and begins to lather it into a thick foam. Once it's thoroughly covered he begins to massage my feet. The man knows how to massage and I can't help but let out a tiny moan. He dips the washcloth in the steaming water and wraps my whole foot in it.

"Your feet will be bruised."

"I don't care, it was worth it."

"You were like Cinderella out there on the path."

"Only my shoes will get carried away by wolves and I'll have to go the rest of the weekend in flip flops."

"I could give a damn what you wear on your feet. But I would die, if you disappeared on me after midnight."

"Ty, I would never leave," I whisper and lean in to kiss his cheek.

"Give me your other dog," he says smiling. I laugh.

"You call feet, dogs?"

"What do you call them, piggies? I guess *dogs* doesn't work for these tender little things. He lathers up the other foot and I angle myself so that I can lean back against the wall.

"This is the most decadent foreplay I've ever had; it feels like a sacrament."

"Oh, no, Jess, we haven't even begun that part yet.

Anticipation gives me shivers and I close my eyes again at the rich pressure he's kneading into my arch. This time, he applies gentle pressure to my ankle, up my calf and ever so softly, his fingers slide up over my knee and down my thigh.

"I'd like to get you out of this dress."

I cross my arms, reach down to where it's gathered above my knees, I lift my butt momentarily and pull the dress over my head. I toss it onto the floor and lean back in my spot again.

"Should I hang it up?"

"No, you should take me to bed."

Ty uses the drinking glass to pour water down my legs. The sensation is pure velvet slipping over the soft skin. He pulls a fluffy white towel down from the rack and pats them dry, without ever looking at them. Instead, his eyes roam all over my body, my breasts, my stomach and down lower.

"I don't want to say this too much, but you are stunning. Even more beautiful than the first night I met you, time has done nothing more than polish the diamond that you are."

"I think the same of you. You're even more attractive now; it almost makes me afraid to touch you."

"If you like it, it's all yours."

With that, he wraps both arms around my back, lifts me abruptly until I'm straddling his waist. I hook my ankles behind him and sink into the deep kiss that he's offering. He carries me into the bedroom and lets me fall gently to the bed. I hear the zip of his pants and my heart starts pumping. He strips down to his boxers in mere seconds and is suddenly before me in all of his glory. Ty is fit, beautifully shaped and proportioned like an athlete.

I quiver at my need for his body and my simultaneous modesty. I'm insecure when it comes to prowess in the bedroom. I've only ever had one lover and he was not a generous or enthusiastic one. We had sex out of what felt like obligation. John made me feel frigid and undesirable, like a failure in bed when it came to love making.

"I'm kind of nervous, Titan."

He lowers himself onto the bed beside me and hugs me in close, caressing my hair.

"We don't have to do anything besides cuddle, if you don't want to."

That's not what I want at all. I want him to take me. I can think of nothing but him thrusting deep inside me. Arching into his kiss, I wriggle in closer to him and make my body flush with his. I'm nervous because I'm inexperienced. John and I hadn't had sex in ages, I've only ever had one partner and it never felt like lovemaking. Ty has probably had some vixens in bed, girls that are younger and daring, willing to do crazy positions and aren't scared of anything.

"I'm nervous because I feel like an amateur. I don't know what you're used to or what you like and I haven't experienced many things."

"I'll let you know if you ever do something I don't like, but I can tell you right now, that I'm doubtful that will happen." Ty takes my hand and lowers it to his boxers, he lays my palm right on top of his, huge, rock-solid erection.

His cock feels so incredible, that I roll my body on top of his, I sit up to straddle him with my panty covered groin even with his penis. His hands come around my back and he unclips my bra. I toss it to the floor and begin to move slowly on top of him. He cups my breasts and then thumbs my light pink nipples into tortured points of reception. Ty's hands fall to my hips and begins to control my movements, sliding his cock back and forth suggestively against the apex of my soaking wet panties.

"I want to taste you, Jesenia. Will you let me?"

I take a deep breath and nod. He pulls me down onto his chest and rewards me with a deep kiss, simultaneously slipping his thumbs into the elastic and sliding my panties off. I sit up and pull them down over my ankles and my very clean feet. I toss them onto the floor and turn my attention back to Ty who has also stripped down to nothing.

His chest is strong, his stomach flat, he's got shoulders like a linebacker and a cock like nothing I've ever seen before. My mind is blank, devoid of words or even thoughts. I take in his body like a child looking at an amusement park. So many place to explore, so many new things to try, I don't know where to start. Ty grabs my hand again and puts it directly on his hardness. I squeeze and loosely grip my fingers around the thick girth, moving them up and down slowly, I simulate what I'd like to do with another part of my body. Ty's hand covers mine and he moves it faster and squeezes harder.

He grabs me and kisses me ruthlessly, his stubble gnashing into my soft chin and cheeks and his tongue probing deep into our kiss. It's a kiss of desperation because our bodies can't catch up to how far our hearts have fallen. I whimper out loud. He pulls me into his chest and flips me under him so that now he's on top. I stare up at the ceiling of the cabin, the knobby logs so neatly fit together and the reddish mortar in between that keeps the cold rain and wind out. He spreads my legs using his knees, then with an arm on either side of me, he leans down and sucks my erect nipple into his mouth. I arch my back in response and grind my hips into his erection.

Ty kisses my belly and dips his tongue into the button, his fingers toy with my nipples making me wetter and wetter between my legs. He's slowly moving south and I'm delirious with anticipation. His face hovers just at the top of my thigh. He caresses me once through my folds and I jerk in response. His fingers slide right into me and I'm so sensitive, I cry out in pleasure. Then he lowers his mouth to my sex and his tongue melts into my flesh. His fingers slide in and out of me gently, as he teases my clit into torturously pleasurable agony. I'm breathing fast and rotating my hips, even though I'm consciously trying not to.

He inserts another finger, making the penetration tighter. It feels like he's hooking his fingers and a foreign sensation arises in the base of my spine. My body is aching, my muscles contracting and pressure keeps building deep inside.

"Oh, God, please stop. I'm going to come already." I say reaching down to his head.

"Perfect," he says and then, "I love how wet you are for me."

My muscles bear down and my back arches in a bow. Ty reaches up and pinches my nipples hard and the orgasm crashes over me like a crescendo. I scream. I grab his head. I grind shamelessly into his mouth. He gently fucks me with his tongue until I ride the orgasm out.

I've never been so verbal, so enraptured or turned on. Ty's face in between my legs is the sexiest thing I've ever done. He's still lazily thrusting his tongue gently in and out of my overly-sensitized flesh, while tremors and aftershocks of the orgasm run up and down my spine, tickling my back.

When Ty finally withdraws and sits up on the bed, his erection is so engorged it's pressed into his belly. I stare, openly, fascinated with his virility. He wipes his glistening mouth with the back of his hand.

"Do you like what you see?" It comes out hoarse and sinfully sexy, suddenly I'm mortified about my skills in the blowjob department.

I nod my head and bite my lip and gaze into his smoldering eyes.

"You, like this—on my bed, messy hair, glazed eyes, swollen lips, and yes, I mean both sets, red marks on your skin from where I touched you—this is a vision I'm never going to let leave my head."

"I've never come like that, Ty. Ever. Not in my life before you."

"There will be more, as many as I can coax out of you. I want you coming and saying my name because it's all you can think of when your body feels that way."

"Let me take care of you," I say, nodding to his swollen cock that is leading pre-cum at the tip.

"Let's save it for round two, the kids could be here any second."

"I'll be fast, I promise. We can go into the bathroom."

"I can take care of myself in the shower—no problem. Anyway I'm used to it," he says, tossing me my bra and panties.

"No, please, let me try. I really want to."

"If you insist," he says smiling. He starts stroking his big hand up and down his erection. I salivate at the size and at such a potent hardness. He's engorged and I don't think I've ever seen anything so gorgeous.

He steps off of the bed and walks up to me by the pillows. He's stroking himself gently the whole time and looking at me with intensity. Instead of letting me take charge, Tyson reaches for the back of my neck and pulls me up close to him. He gently grabs a fistful of my hair and guides my mouth to the head that is now drenched in precum. I lick it off and the taste of him melts on my tongue, a heady intoxication invades all of my senses. With a light pressure he pushes me down on his cock and as I slide down, my lips encounter every bulging vein, texture and color of him. He's big, but I'm confident I can handle it. I love his assertion, how he yanks and pushes to help me find the right rhythm.

"Jesus. That's fucking good." I peek up at his face and his head has fallen back in enjoyment. His muscles are tense and his spread leg stance is strong. He thrusts his hips forward carefully when I reach the peak of how far I can go. I reach out to tug and squeeze his balls. He runs his fingers through my hair and pinches my nipples.

"Jess, Baby, I'm close," he says.

I bob my head faster and add suction and pressure. I love how he strokes his hips more freely as he gets close. He's lost his restraint and with it, the pretense of treating me like I'm delicate. His breath comes faster and he thrusts hard into my mouth. I angle my head so that he has better access to my throat.

I've never wanted to give a good blow job before, the thought of it nauseated me and I'd avoid it all costs. But with Ty, I know that I would do anything to bring him pleasure. To see him let go is the greatest gift I can imagine.

"I'm coming!" Ty says and he withdraws from my mouth. His strong hands stroke his length rhythmically like he's milking his cock. I open my mouth to catch his semen, but Ty just takes my hand and adds it to the pressure he's already applying.

"I would swallow for you, Ty," I say tentatively. It sounds forward, considering how truly little we know of each other.

"I know, Baby. Next time," he says.

I move into the center of the giant cushy bed. I pat the spot beside me and Ty drops in, exhausted. He reaches his bear arms around me and pulls me to his chest. Less than two minutes later, his breaths even out and he's sound asleep on his back.

CHAPTER 23

Titan

I can still taste her. She's gone back to her room and I feel cold and let down but what else could I do? Her creamy skin laid bare to me was better than any fantasy I could have ever envisioned. All that silken hair spread over the pillow was enticing. Those freckles across her shoulders, her collarbone. I groan and turn the shower on. Cold. She's made me feel intoxicated to the point of never wanting to be sober again. The feel of her lips on me; sucking, pumping, licking was euphoric.

Her moans were the most religious thing I've experienced. The way her back bowed as she came, set my core on fire. I want to feel myself inside her. I need to be with her—more than we were. I crave it. She awakened something inside me that has been long dormant. I dread leaving tomorrow. Not seeing her face in the morning, the afternoon and at night. I step into the shower and try not to yelp at the cold water. The icy deluge does little to quell the need I still feel but it's better than nothing.

After stepping out, I towel dry my head then wrap it around

my waist. I wipe my palm over the mirror to clear the fog. My reflection shows a healthy looking man. A man with a deep contentment—an obvious contentment glow. A man with a future. It doesn't show the ache in my right side. It doesn't show the constant metallic taste in my mouth. It doesn't show my viral load or scarring or stigmas. I punch the mirror and watch as the glass splinters and falls into the sink. Blood trickles from my knuckles but it doesn't hurt. Or maybe I'm just too upset to feel the pain. I run the water and stick my hand under the flow. Blood tinges the sink pink before washing away. I look in the vanity for Band-Aids but can't find any, so I wrap my hand in toilet paper. It won't clot for a while. I'll need more toilet paper. I make sure the blood is all cleaned up. I pull on my boxers and toss my towel over the shower rod.

I flop into my bed and yank the covers up over me, fluff my pillow and roll to my side. The moon is barely a half moon but it seems to light up the entire world. Like Jess is lighting up mine. I don't want it to be over. I don't want to wait any longer. I don't want real life and truths and fears to infiltrate what we've just barely started. I shove the covers off me and fumble around in the dark for my pajama pants and a thermal shirt. Next, I slip on my sneakers and blow through the cabin door and down the path to the dock. I don't sit. I can't. I walk right out to the end and stop. It's fucking cold out here. I need to just come out and talk to her. It is completely selfish of me to not tell her.

Without thinking, I strip my shirt off and let it drop to the dock, followed by my pajama bottoms. I toe off my sneakers. The water is calling to me. It's calm and I need calm. It's clear and I need clarity. It's still and I need stillness. I dive in and all my breath leaves me. The frigid water steals all the feeling from my body. Numb.

My head breaks through the surface and I gasp. It's so cold.

"Dad!" Luke screams from the shore. He's running—sprinting, actually. I swim to the dock edge and pull myself up.

"I'm okay," I wheeze.

"What the fuck! Are you insane? What are you doing?" His comments ramble out without thought. I've scared him.

"I'm sorry, Luke. I'm sorry. I'm alright."

He picks up my shirt and pants and pulls on my arm. His frown is epic and the look of concern kills me. "Come on, Dad. Let's just get in the cabin where it's warm."

I nod, stand and let him keep hold of my arm as we walk back up to our cabin. I let him rekindle the fire while I towel dry. I get my pajamas back on and sit in an oversized chair by the fire. We're silent. There aren't the right words to express what we're each thinking—experiencing. Luke sits between my legs and puts his head on my knee, like he did when he was a little boy. I palm his head with my uninjured hand. And we both fall asleep that way.

⚓⚓⚓⚓

I wake with a cramp in my neck. Sleeping in a chair seemed like a decent idea in the moment, but now, not so much. Luke is curled up on the rug at my feet. I let out a sigh and stretch. My cut knuckles have finally clotted but they're sore. I push up and step over Luke. I push the heels of my hands over my eyes and rub the sleep away. It's overcast outside. It's okay though, the grey clouds suit my mood. I fill the coffee maker with water and get the brewing started. There's a quiet knock at the door. I tiptoe to it and crack it open.

"Jess," I whisper. She motions for me to come out onto the porch, so I do.

"I felt bad leaving when you were sleeping." She looks like she barely slept.

I reach out and pull her into my chest. "Don't be. Sorry I fell asleep. I was tired." Her arms squeeze my waist fiercely.

"I don't want to go home, Ty." Her voice changes pitch and I know that she's close to crying.

"I don't either, unless you're coming with me," I admit.

She sniffles once. "If we leave here, the magic will be gone."

"Real life can be just as good if we try to make it," I murmur into the crown of her head. She pulls back and looks up at me. Her eyes are full of torture, fear. I hate that.

"Ty," she starts. I bring my hand up and place my fingers over her mouth to silence her.

"Come home with me. Stay one more night. You can't drive all the way back on a spare tire. We'll get it replaced. You can drive home Monday." She smiles and wraps her fingers around my hand.

"What happened?!" she gasps, getting a good look at my knuckles. I pull my hand from hers and look to the lake, willing it to give me a good answer for her. It doesn't. I turn my attention back to Jess.

"Say you'll come home with me today, stay the night and we can talk all about it." I lean down until our faces are a mere inch from each other's. "Please." I kiss her lips gently, then more forcefully before pulling away and resting my forehead on hers. We need just a little more time.

"Okay," she says. I exhale a breath of relief. We just got a little more time and tonight, I'm going to show her just how much I need her. I'm going to give her everything she wants.

All of me.

Jesenia

I leave a distraught Titan to shower and wake up Luke. I told Angie I'd meet her in the dining hall and I find her at a table by the big windows, with a huge carafe of coffee and a basket of pastries.

"Hi, Sweetie, are you only having carbs?" I pull out a chair and sit facing the stunning view, a sight I feel unready to say goodbye to.

"I ordered a Swiss cheese omelet, it should be here in a

minute. Did you want me to get another menu or do you know what you want already."

"I'll just have the same. Can you pass me the coffee?"

"How'd things go with Mr. Black Coffee? You seem a little off?"

I can't help but think of his bloody, swollen hand in contrast to how beautifully things flowed last night, how natural it felt to be in his arms. How we ran down the path, how he cleaned my feet and eventually, how we gave one another a little taste of ecstasy.

"Things couldn't be better, that's why I feel so awful." I pour the steaming coffee into the mug bearing the insignia of the lodge. I add a little milk and drop in two cubes of sugar with the tongs.

"Why, because you didn't tell him about your glitches? I'm thinking we should do a show on rustic touches for the season, like hanging dry herbs and fall themed wreaths and centerpieces, maybe one of our, *switch out five things*, to get a rustic feeling for the season?"

"Yes. That's a great idea. Maybe we should snap some pictures before we leave. Dried corn braids would be nice, as well as pumpkin and gourd arrangements."

"I wouldn't worry about the stuff with Ty, Mom. It will work itself out. He seems pretty crazy about you and like an accepting kind of guy, so I think you might be stressing over nothing."

"I hope you're right. I already feel like a liar. Almost as if I'm trying to make him fall for me before I tell him the truth, which, of course, isn't fair."

"Whatever, Mom. No one does. Everybody sells themselves first—that's how it works. You don't get a boyfriend by going up to some guy and saying, '*Hello, I suck. I've got a ton of issues and I'm really high-maintenance. You might want to think twice before you get involved with me.*'"

"But with a man as genuine as Ty, I feel like I should be

upfront."

The waiter comes and sets down a perfect, fluffy omelet in front of Angie and we order another. Angie dumps first ketchup and then hot sauce all over hers.

"What do you think push-up bras are for or fake lashes or heels? What about all make-up or tight clothes or fancy underwear? Or lip injections or Botox or implants—the list goes on and on. It's all false advertising, trying to get someone hooked. No one states their flaws on the first date. It's counter-productive. Everyone hooks first and then dishes later. Ty, the man, probably even has his own secrets to bring to the table."

I bite into a muffin and look at the lake out the window. It's placid and dark, the overhanging clouds somehow draining this place of its magic. Or maybe it's my mood, my shame that's encroaching on our perfect getaway and reunion.

"He won't want to be with me after I tell him I'm crazy."

"It's not "crazy," Mom, you're being dramatic and oversimplifying things. Dad made you feel like shit about your condition because he was afraid it would cause a political scandal and he just didn't understand it!"

Angie bangs her coffee mug down onto the saucer. Coffee sloshes over the side and onto the tablecloth.

"I'm sorry, Ange, I'm scared is all. I really care about Ty and I want this to work."

"Do you want me to tell you what it's like loving someone who's bipolar? Because I know, Mom, I'm an expert because I've spent my whole life doing it!"

"Angie, I'm sorry," I say and lay my hand on her arm.

"Don't be. Let me enlighten you. My mom often had a lot of energy that other people didn't have, which meant sometimes she didn't sleep at night and did "crazy, reckless" things like bake more banana bread then we could eat, so we had to give some to the teachers at school or share with the neighbors. Other times she'd knit or sew or clean or organize, so you'd go to sleep with a messy room and you'd wake up with it spotless. Maybe she made the Halloween costume you'd been talking about in May or maybe she finished all the Christmas cards before the school year even started."

"Stop, Angelina. Please."

She's heated and she's speaking too loud and people are starting to take notice.

"No, I'll stop when I'm finished. Those were the good parts. The bad parts were when she was down and she'd be asleep on the couch when you got home from school or could barely open her eyes from crying so much. But even in those bad times, when she had to fight for normalcy, she always packed my lunch, she always wrote me a little love note on my napkin. Even when she was so depressed she walked around the house like a zombie, she still managed to put lavender bubbles in my bath or make me homemade macaroni. She got better as the years went on and knew how to focus her energy. She found out what made her happy and used that to manage her mood swings. She wasn't perfect, but she was there and she doted on me and she fought for me a whole hell of a lot harder than Dad ever did. She did her best and she loved me."

I'm crying into my mug of coffee. I've been selfish dealing with my disease and always trying to cope. I don't know if I've ever once asked Angelina how she was doing or how she, herself, was coping. I spent years trying to push it under the rug and hiding instead of trying to understand it and help my daughter manage her own feelings about it.

"Angelina, I feel selfish, we should always be open about this."

"Dad would slam down the subject as soon as it came up. And that's not the point, Mom. What I'm saying is that your mood swings don't make it any harder to love you. Yes, it can be challenging and yes, it can hurt, but by no means does it make you unworthy of real love."

I reach out and take her hand and we squeeze hard and smile.

I wipe my tears with my napkin and cut into my omelet.

"Anyway, at this point, you could tell Ty you had an extra boob and he'd be like, '*Cool, sign me up.*'"

"I do have one," I say taking a deep sip of orange juice and grinning at my daughter.

"No, you don't, Mom. Shut up."

"What if we drive to his place first and get the tire taken care of? If it gets too late, we can stay and drive back into the City on Monday morning."

"Another night? Andrew will kill me."

"Think it over, Sweetie. It might be safer not to drive at night and plus, it might be fun."

CHAPTER 24

Titan

I feel better after my shower. Less down, more up. I'm prepared for the drive to feel long and ominous because I'm prepared to tell Jess what's going on later at the house. It's both a weight lifted and disheartening. What if she runs? What if she assumes I was a dirty drug user at some point? Luke's about ready to head up to the lodge so we can eat before we have to check out. He eyes me as we exit the cabin.

"You cool?" he asks.

"Nothing to worry about, Bud, just had a moment."

"I know, but that moment ended with you jumping into a frigid lake. And what the hell happened to the bathroom mirror?"

I groan and quicken my pace up the path. "I broke it. Before the swim. But, Buddy, I'm alright. It's not your job to worry about me."

Luke trots to catch up with me. "We've only got us, Dad, we worry about each other." I smile at him and nod. He's right.

Since Rory's death, we've always had each other's backs. He's just being a concerned kid. If I stop to put myself in his shoes, I would have been scared shitless at what he witnessed his parent doing. I yank him into a sideways hug.

"Will they be there eating?" he asks.

"Probably, why?"

"Just wanted a little more time before we all left, I guess. Angie's cool."

"It really makes me happy to hear that you like them," I say. Luke pushes open the large doors to the lobby and we go in. Fires are blazing in every fireplace, which makes the place feel less overcast and gloomy, which is good. Luke spots Angie and Jess at a table by a large bay of windows and waves. Angie grins and motions us over.

I pull my chair out and sit next to Jess. She reaches out and rubs my bicep. "Coffee?" she asks.

"Yes, please. Can't have too much." I put my hand atop hers. I'll never get used to how soft she is.

"Luke! Gross!" Angie squeals. I look over and he's got what looks like an entire pastry shoved in his mouth. He's moaning—in a good way and chewing with his mouth open. Little puffs of crumbs fly from his mouth when he groans. Luckily, I'm used to it and I'm the one sitting across from him.

"Theserresogud," he says around his food. I face palm and bite my bottom lip to keep from laughing. The boy will never learn. Angie giggles and it sets me off. I burst out laughing at the buffoon my son is. Jess looks between all of us with wide eyes.

"I've told him a thousand times," I laugh out.

"He looks like a wildebeest," Angie says clutching at her stomach. Jess finally breaks down. A loud, hearty laugh pours out of her and it's like nothing I've heard before. It's full and boisterous and musical. Luke wipes some crumbs from his lips and chin and lifts up the pastry basket.

"Anyone want one?" he asks. This is the way family

breakfasts are supposed to be.

We finish breakfast with fun banter and all return to our respective rooms to pack up our stuff. The girls got specific instructions not to carry their own luggage out. Which I'm happy to find—they obeyed. I take Jess's two bags and Luke grabs Angie's. Jess stops at the front desk to check out while I load her bags into her car. Luke and Angie are leaning against the truck, laughing about something. Jess sneaks up beside me.

"It's strange to see them together. And getting along, to boot."

I wrap an arm around her shoulders. "It is. No one could've predicted this would all go off without a hitch."

"So . . ." Jess starts.

"I need to check out still. Maybe we should let Angie drive her and Luke in the truck and you and I can take the Volvo. It's safer."

"Oh, I don't know," Jess says. She looks to Angie. "I can ask her if that's alright, though."

"Deal. Let me go take care of my bill and I'll be right back." I lean down and kiss her gently before heading inside. I'm going to have to pay for the mirror. I'd rather not tell Jess that happened. After an additional two-hundred dollar charge to my debit card, I'm free and clear of the Lodge.

"Everyone ready?" I call out to the three of them. They're standing together, close, talking and smiling. I feel like they're up to something.

"Yes," Jess answers and starts walking toward me. Her hair is pulled back loosely, a few strands frame her face. Her smile is wide and white and aimed at me. She's got a sweater on and the sleeves pulled down over her hands. She looks adorable and beautiful.

"Angie okay driving the truck?"

"She said yes," Jess says and lifts up gracefully to her tiptoes. I meet her halfway and kiss her. Walking hand in hand around to the passenger side of the Volvo, I open her door for her and usher her in. In three hours, Jess will be inside *my* house. It's a fact that has me beaming and cringing simultaneously.

Jesenia

"How far is it to your place from here?"

"About three hours, give or take."

"Well, the ride should be beautiful. This time of year makes the scenery out of this world."

"You're telling me," Ty says, looking over and checking me out. I blush at his joke and reach out and put my hand on his knee.

"My dad always used to say that if a couple could get along in the car on a road trip, it was a true test of love and would define whether or not they could make it together in life," Ty says.

Ty is a great driver, even in a car he doesn't know well. He's confident, yet graceful and the way he hugs the curves of these winding roads, is turning me on.

"Your dad was a sage man, because I'd say that holds true. Are your parents still living? Do you get to see them often?"

"My Dad passed in '89, my Mom is still going strong. She's in an assisted living facility for Alzheimer's, but she manages to stay fairly active, she volunteers at church. She's in Stamford; Luke and I go down there for a visit near Christmas. She used to come up, but her dementia has gotten worse over the last couple of years."

"And your wife's family?"

"From New York, White Plains. Her parents are gone though, so my mom is the only grandparent Luke has left. Rory's sister, Emily, is still close; we see her at Christmastime, too, and she calls to see how Luke's doing. What about your folks?" He asks.

"I still have both of them, thankfully. Snowbirds now, in St. Augustine, Florida. I used to take Angie every spring when she was young but sometime around high school, she lost interest, already had too much going on. They're into cruising and they've also got an RV. Pretty average family, pretty normal childhood."

"Where did you grow up?"

"Oh, in Washington DC, both my parents are lobbyists. They were always deeply entrenched in politics. I met John when I came to college here in New York. My parents were thrilled that he studied political science and had his eye on the governorship."

"And John was who you were running away from the night we met?"

"Yes. I didn't tell you that night, but I'd just found out I was pregnant."

"I see. With Angie? It all makes more sense now as to why you left so abruptly."

I reach out, take his hand and give it a squeeze. I can do this, I tell myself. This might be my only opportunity before we part ways. If I care about him, even half as much as it feels like I do, I owe him honesty and transparency. It's the least I can do.

"I was young, in my early twenties and incredibly scared. I knew I wasn't in love with John, but I didn't want to give up the baby. As soon as I found out I was pregnant, I went off my meds."

I said it. It wasn't so hard. Ty looks at me curiously and affectionately squeezes my arm.

"I wanted to tell you before we took this any further. I'm manic depressive. I have bipolar disorder."

Ty nods and he looks at me with compassion. I wipe a few stray tears from my eyes. I don't feel sad, I feel unburdened— lighter. Even if my mental health scares him away, I feel relieved saying it out loud—giving it energy and space, instead of all the hiding and covering up I've been doing for years.

"I'm glad you told me. That couldn't have been easy for you."

"I am, in my own opinion, pretty high functioning. I take my medication regularly and see a psychiatrist. I have my moments, but for the most part, it's regulated. I've gotten adept at hiding it because John always felt like it wouldn't be good for business."

"When were you diagnosed?"

"End of high school. My parents never knew what to make of it. One thing I'll always be grateful to John for, is that he protected me throughout my pregnancy—made sure I stayed on track and saw to it that I was well cared for. It may only have been in the interest of his child, but it saved me, too, and I wouldn't have made it through the pregnancy without him."

"That must have been difficult for you. And you must have been scared."

"I couldn't have gone with you, no matter how much I wanted to."

"I'm honored to get to know all of the parts that make up who you are. I hope I can help you when you're having a rough time and I hope you'll be open with me about what your needs are. I don't know much about the disorder, but I'm willing to learn and I hope, if you're struggling, you let me help you ease the burden."

My hands are on my mouth to keep me from sobbing out loud. I peer at him with eyes clouded in grief and wonderment. He made me feel so at ease and accepted within the span of a few heartfelt sentences. I smile at him through the blur of my tears.

"Don't cry. I want us to happen, no matter the obstacles. I've got my fair share of baggage, too. I hope we can be there for each other as we unload some of these life scars. If we carry the burden together, it will make it lighter for both of us."

"You might not feel that way, once you see me in a bad spot."

"You know, let me tell you a story. Rory, my late wife, was an even-keeled person, but she had some of the worst PMS I've seen in my life. She'd cry and yell, sometimes throw stuff and break things. Snap at everything Luke did and a few times, at her worst, she even tried to break up with me. But when it happened, I always took it for what it was. Her hormones were raging and they made her do things, that later, she'd eventually come to feel ashamed of. So during those days or that week every month, I'd try to soothe things over, intervene where I could.

Once, when we were all sitting down to dinner, Rory pulled a giant casserole out of the over and when she saw that it had burned, with hot pads on and everything, she marched out the front door and smashed that sucker in the driveway. Poor Luke, he was stunned. Rory came back in, crying, and all I could do was hold her and give her hug. I made us all peanut butter sandwiches and we ate watching a movie.

Later that night, Rory was mortified that maybe the neighbors had seen her, that they'd call child services or at the least, deem her crazy. We cleaned up the mess after dark that same night. At one point, it struck us as funny and all three of us were laughing so hard. Luke kept saying, "Welcome to the Jenning's Drive-Thru, can I take your order?"

So those moments weren't her best, but they didn't define who she was. Rory was great the other three weeks out of the month. I was her husband, so it was my job to see the difference.

I know PMS doesn't compare to mental illness but it illustrates my point well. I know who you are today from our conversations and letters, the time we've spent together in the past seventy-two hours. I won't hold you to a breakdown you have or some behavior that might be questionable. I see who you are right now, and to me, that's all that matters."

"I want you to stop the car so I can give you a hug." I'm overwhelmed with the need to hug him, to pull him close to my heart. He turned what I was terrified of revealing, into an affirmation.

Ty pulls over to the side of the road without even thinking

about it twice. He stops in the emergency lane and pops out of the driver's side. He reaches my side just as I'm climbing out. The air is cool and the wind is whipping but the sun still seems strong. He pulls me into his arms and I throw mine around his neck, snuggling into his chest.

"Where have you been my whole life?"

"Right here, waiting for you to turn up again."

CHAPTER 25

Titan

As a person who enjoys culinary adventures, yet mostly still eats like an eighteen year old, I find cooking to be intriguing and sometimes tricky. Typically, I don't venture outside of culturally-familiar cuisine, mostly due to my fear of eating other species' reproductive bits. That's not to say I don't enjoy good Indian food, or Thai food, from time to time. As I mull through the fridge and sniff test everything I'm eyeing, I come up with an idea for dinner. We got home just in time to cook something, after we dropped Jess's car at Rusty's, so he could put a new tire on it.

"Everyone okay with pasta and bacon?" I ask.

I get a resounding yes from all three people, so I start pulling out what I will need. I can't botch this. I want it to be robust with flavor and to look nice, too. I don't need to impress Jess, but I'd like to. I put a large pot of water on to boil before browning the pancetta and bacon in olive oil. While that's underway, I beat some eggs and put a ladleful of boiling water into them. I can't believe Jess is bipolar. I would have never guessed. She doesn't seem off kilter at all. When the pasta's done, I mix all the ingredients together with some heavy cream, salt, pepper and garlic. She shared her baggage and I'm feeling guilty for not having the guts to share mine yet. I should have told her in the car but I didn't want to draw the attention away from her. The kitchen smells amazing and my mouth is watering. I'm impressed with myself. I resolve to tell her after dinner, when the kids take off for a little bit. It has to happen.

"Luke!" I shout over my shoulder. "Set the table, will ya?" There is a grunt and footsteps shuffling in my direction, so I assume he heard me.

Jess walks in and sidles up behind me. "How can I help?" She slips her arms through mine and kisses my shoulder blade.

I turn slightly and kiss her forehead. "No, no, you're a guest. Your job is to sit and relax."

"Titan." Jess narrows those sky blue eyes at me.

"Okay, your job is to entertain Angie," I say with a smile. She shakes her head at me but marches back toward the living room. I don't want her to do anything. I think, for once, it's her turn to sit back and let someone take care of things.

"Anything else?" Luke asks. I pour the carbonara into a serving dish and nod.

"Drink orders for the ladies." Luke yells to them, asking what they want. Not exactly what I had in mind but I'm glad he's treating them like he would any other family or friends.

Our dinner is surprisingly comfortable. Angie makes fun of the pictures along the dining room wall from when Luke was younger. Jess and I make a toast. Everyone oh's and ah's over the carbonara. We talk about how awesome the resort was, and get more detailed reports from the kids about what they did. All in all, it feels like a family dinner that's happened every night for the last twenty years. It's strange. A good strange, but strange nonetheless. I expected more awkwardness. I expected some hiccup or hang up between the kids not liking either me, or Jess or each other. I expected a lot of things once I knew the four of us were going to spend time together but I didn't expect that everything would be perfectly smooth and affable. It almost makes telling Jess that much harder. I'm about to throw a wrench in things.

⚓⚓⚓⚓

Luke took Angie to hang out in town with his friends and show her around. He was really excited because his friends would think she's hot. Angie was a good sport though and even touched up her make-up before leaving with him.

"Let's go into the living room," I tell Jess. She smiles and grabs our glasses of water before heading in. I watch as she sinks into the couch. She's perfect and it's going to be hard to shatter the angel sitting before me. I'm bad at this stuff and I'm trying to think of how to tell her when she pats the sofa cushion next to her.

"I have Hepatitis C," I blurt. I plop down on the old sofa, stretching my legs out and crossing them on the coffee table. Sinking back, I close my eyes, and rest my head against the cushion, hoping for some relief. I let the weight of my words sink in. Jess remains silent. "I had it for years before I was diagnosed. Last year, I started a new trial treatment. In the beginning, the results were hopeful. My liver function got close to normal and my viral load dropped. Last month my viral load skyrocketed, bringing me closer to cirrhosis. My blood tests still show high viral counts and liver inflammation. My platelet count is low, and my blood isn't clotting normally, because of the liver damage. I have a biopsy this week to see how my liver is looking these days." I open my eyes and find Jess staring at me. Eyes brimming with unshed tears. I decide to plow onward because I need to get this all out.

"I don't know how much you know about it, but it's usually spread when blood from a person infected with it, enters the body of someone who is not infected. Think unsterile tattoo parlors, needle sharing or transfusions gone bad." I take Jess's hands in mine. "People can live with Hep C for a lifetime now. The treatments have come a long way."

"Is it, can it be sexually transmitted?" she asks and runs her fingers through her hair.

"It *could*, but it's not likely. Better to use protection and be safe. One of the other patients in the trial study with me, just knocked up his wife and she did not contract it—and neither will the baby. But, if there is any blood contact, it's just not worth it to me, Jess, to mess around like that with your health."

"Is this why you didn't . . ."

I cut her off. "Yes. I didn't have condoms with me. I thought it was a weekend away with Luke. It nearly killed me not being inside you that night. There is absolutely no evidence that hepatitis can be transmitted through oral sex. I would never put you at risk. Never without your consent."

"So oral sex is safe?"

"One hundred percent," I tell her with assurance.

"That's good," she says, with a glint of mischievousness crossing her face.

"God, even after I woke up and you were gone, I was hard again. Torture, I tell you." I give her a grin. "If you feel at all uncomfortable, I can set you up a phone call with my doctor to answer any questions."

"No, Ty. I trust you. If you say it's safe—you know better than anyone."

Her eyebrows furrow and I have an urge to smooth them out. To soothe her somehow but I know she needs to process everything I've just shared. "But you don't seem sick? Are you suffering? I don't really know anything about Hep C. Please tell me you're not dying."

I stroke her thigh gently. "There's plenty to learn and you will—but no, I'm not dying right now. We just need to be careful and I need to stay vigilant with my health and this trial I'm doing."

Jess pushes her fingers through her hair. I'm beginning to think that's a nervous habit. "How did you get it?"

"I don't know. Could have been from the tattoo parlor, could have been a blood transfusion after the car accident all those years ago, who knows? I wasted a lot of time trying to answer that question and getting angry about it, but eventually, I had to let it go because I will never know."

"Did you use drugs? Did you get it from sharing needles?"

"Definitely not. I was never an addict. Tried some stuff in my early twenties but I never injected."

"Ty, I'm so sorry." I slide my feet to the floor and turn so I can pull Jess into my arms. She sinks into my embrace and I know everything will be okay. She didn't run screaming. She didn't scrunch her nose in disgust. She didn't say it was too much to handle.

"Don't be. It's not your fault. It's not my fault. It just is."

She nuzzles into my chest. I inhale her scent and kiss the crown of her head. "We have approximately two hours before the kids return and I've been dying to feel you. All our skeletons are out now, Jess, let's go upstairs."

Jesenia

He grabs my hand and I follow him up the refinished wood stairs. I'm in a daze from what he's told me, but strangely, I'm not scared. On the contrary, I feel a need to confirm to Ty that I'm not afraid of his body, that even if he's sick, his body is sacred to me and I want to show him how much I want it. But I am terrified for him and what this could mean. Will a trial cure him for good? Is he destined for an early death or degeneration because of the virus—or is it dormant enough that it's just a technicality and cannot affect his life?

He opens the door to his bedroom and it smells just like him. Old Spice, drug store soap, maybe cinnamon and cardamom.

His bed is made and the décor is minimal, dark slate colored drapes, dark slate colored everything. He's got an en suite bathroom and a nightstand on each side of the bed. There are condoms in those drawers. I haven't seen a condom in years.

"Jess, if you're hesitant or uncomfortable, please let me know. I don't want any pressure or to rush things."

"I'm sure. I've been sure since the night I met you. I missed my chance back then; I'm not letting another night go by without you.

"Thanks for trusting me," he says, looking deep into my eyes. Ty has a way of making me feel like my life is just beginning, forty years in and he gives me the sense that my whole future lays ahead of me. "I would never put you at risk. If it were even dangerous. No matter how badly I want you, I don't take it lightly. I wouldn't chance it."

"I'm ready. I want this for us."

Last week, I wasn't sure if I wanted to actually meet him. I thought it would taint the magic I could feel through his texts and emails—the decades old memories of our one chance encounter. But now, after only three days, Ty is more than I imagined. He makes me want a future for myself instead of just living vicariously through my daughter.

"Can I tell you, without sounding juvenile, that you are the most beautiful woman I've even seen in my life?"

"You can tell me, but I probably won't believe you. Let's talk about you and that body of yours. You've gotten better with age, in every way possible."

He pulls me close to his wide and warm chest, circles his arms around my back and kisses my head. He runs his fingers through my hair and pulls a small section apart with his middle and pointer finger. "It's like spun gold, not a white hair in sight."

"I think both Angie and I were meant to be redheads, but our DNA didn't get the whole message."

"I like it like this. Blonde like a sunflower. Like you're wearing a permanent halo."

His fingers press up from the nape of my neck into the base of my skull, massaging with a pressure that makes me weak in the knees and my body melt into his. He scratches my scalp with all five fingers and I relax more than I knew I could. I make a sound of pleasure that come out like a purr. Burying my face in his neck, I kiss him there and slide my hands up under the back of his sweater.

"I give good head . . . massages." Ty says, his lips bearing a sly smile.

"You are so good at both," I gush and his tongue pushes into my mouth. Ty kisses like a man much younger than his years, he thrusts deep and uses his tongue and soft suction to draw me into a state of frenzied arousal. It's strange to me, that with a kiss, he can simulate sex; even more foreign still, the way he can get me wet with just his mouth on my mouth, his lips tasting my lips. He walks me backward until the back of my knees hit the bed. I fall back into the soft down comforter and I push myself up until my head reaches the pillows. I'm rewarded with his sweet and spicy scent all around me. I flip on my stomach, hide my face and inhale deeply. Ty's hands come under my stomach and unfasten my jeans.

"Are you hiding from me or showing me your butt?"

"Both," I giggle. My skin sensitizes with gooseflesh as he removes my clothes.

"Turn over, Jess. I want to see your face."

I flip onto my back and help him lift my tunic over my head. I like the way he looks at me. No, I love it. I feel resplendent, beautiful, young and hopeful under his gaze. I don't know how he does it but I hope that my eyes on him bring him a fraction of what his do to me.

Ty strips down to his boxers and planks over me, holding his whole body just inches from mine. His biceps bulge, his cock is hard, he looks so virile and strong. I can't image that there's a virus that's silently attacking his body. His beautiful body that

I've come to adore in the little time we've shared. I feel desperate, frustrated, overwrought with emotion and longing. Linking my arms behind his neck, I pull him to me and wrap my legs around his back. His full weight bearing down on me is enough to crush the breath out of my chest.

"I'm scared for you," I whisper into his ear. Then I attack him with the kind of persuasive kiss he kisses me with. I suck his tongue into my mouth and press my hips into his until I'm lost in his body, his scent, his husky manliness.

"Do you want me to answer that, Jesenia?" he asks me when we surface for air.

"I want you to be okay. I can't stand the thought of you suffering." His eyes look sad, he nods his head and travels his kisses down my neck and over my collarbone. He pulls back the light blush-colored bra I have on and my nipple puckers in response to the cold air and anticipation of his mouth.

"God, this lingerie that's so close to your skin color, makes me lose my mind. All I can think about is being inside you." And truly, that's all I want, too. My insides are like gasoline and each time Ty touches and caresses me, is a match. I'm blazing like a bonfire at my core.

When he pulls one erect nipple into his mouth, I gasp and grind and arch my back, offering the nipple up more. Ty uses his teeth to lightly scrape it and then extends his tongue fully and laps at it, flattening my breast out. The sensation is so potent, I feel like I might come in my underwear.

"Oh, God!" I breathe and he pulls the other bra strap off of my shoulder. He squeezes my breast, licks and then thumbs the nipple. I tilt my pelvis, arch my back and tip my head back all at once. Again, I'm pushing my breast into his hungry mouth and rotating my hips, shamelessly pressing my crotch onto his hard bulge. With Ty, I'm overcome with something I haven't felt in years. Lust, making my teeth itch, the back of my throat scream and my body behave like it doesn't even belong to me.

He tortures my nipple and I brush my nails down the expanse

of his back. His brown skin, his rough hands, his solid muscles are driving me into a heady intoxication. He's not all that gentle with me either and instead of invoking fear, it makes me feel more daring. I tug at his boxers and pull them over his round butt. My hands, with a mind of their own, greedily massage and grab the flesh I've been dying to touch. He reaches down a hand and hurriedly yanks them off. Then, he's at my entrance, and all it would take is one thrust. I'm wet enough to receive him and more than eager enough. But he presses on my hips with both of his hands and sits up until he's straddling my hips. His erection is enormous, his cock pulsing with anticipation. I lick my lips and grind again into nothing.

"Condom. Sorry, it's non-negotiable. I'll protect you from me, even when you beg me not to. And believe me, you'll beg; I'll make you. A lot. But even if you cry, I will never gamble with your safety."

He leans into the night stand and the gorgeous erection presses up high onto my pale belly. Its heat and hardness make my head swim and I reach down to touch it. He sits back up, suddenly pulling it away. He tosses the gold square onto my stomach and it feels cold and foreign in contrast to his cock.

"Here, you put it on me," Ty winks and smiles. I smile back and decide that condoms aren't that bad after all.

CHAP TER 26

Titan

The sight of Jess's small, creamy hands rolling a condom on me is enough to bring me to my knees, if I weren't already on them. She takes her time. Her tongue darts out and wets her lip. I lean down to her mouth as her hands leave my shaft. Taking her bottom lip between my teeth, I bite gently and pull. The moan that escapes her, drives me wild. Her eyes are barely open, as I let go of her lip and nibble my way down her body. I want her teased to the point of begging. I want to taste every inch of her before I let myself sink inside of her. I want so many things but I'm not sure I have the willpower to wait any longer. We've waited twenty years for the culmination of this desire.

"Please, Ty."

"Please what?" I tease. I lick the underside of her breast and goosebumps break out along her skin.

"I want you." Her voice is husky and wild sounding. Like she's a different person. Lost in desire. It's the best sound I've heard.

"You have me," I answer before taking her nipple into my mouth. She raises her head and wiggles beneath me.

"Inside me," she says. She's resorted to begging. Which is good because I'm not sure how much longer I could have teased her anyway. I rest back on my knees and wrap my hands around her ankles. She watches as I lift each leg and place them on my shoulders. With one hand, I spread her wide as the other guides me in. She's tight and warm and hugs the entire length of me. I push in and withdraw slowly a few times. Her perfect toes curl. I put my hands at either side of her head and thrust. Jess, folded somewhat in half, gasps.

"Is that good?" She nods her head quickly. "Hold the backs of your knees, baby."

I kiss her lips and thrust again, deeper this time. Her lips stop moving against mine and her breath stops. "Breathe, Jess." Her hands leave her legs and she reaches around and claws at my backside. I speed up my rhythm.

"Do not stop, Titan," she pants.

"Never." I slam into her again and keep a steady pace this time. She squeaks, and moans and the headboard thumps the wall behind us. The sway of her breasts has me hypnotized. When I find the wherewithal to look away from them, I find her eyes burning into mine. Devotion. Need. Here we are, together, finally.

I hold her gaze and pick up my pace more. I will never last like this. She turns my insides outward. My brain doesn't exist. We are carnal, primal, skin and need, meeting in a hurricane of longing. A woman whom I have fantasized about endlessly, beneath me in the flesh, taking every inch of me. My balls tighten, her muscles contract and she goes rigid beneath me. Her legs drop from my shoulders and wrap around my waist. Hands come to my shoulders and clutch with a strength I couldn't have imagined she had. She moans sweetly, powerfully. Her eyes have gone glassy and lost in the sea of feeling and memory that we're both drifting in. Crushing her petite body to me, I pump into her desperately and stop deep inside as my orgasm hits me. Jess's back is arched. Her muscles squeeze my cock, milking it spastically as her orgasm tapers off. I slowly grind in circles until she relaxes. I don't want to stop taking her, even after I come. She shivers and gives me a lazy smile as we both gently fall back down to earth.

I brush some hair from her face. "Are you cold?"

"No." She shakes her head. "Aftershocks."

I laugh and let some of my weight rest on her. She glows in the dim light with a beautiful radiance. I pump slowly in and out and revel in her petite shudders. I pull out and roll to the side, but bring her with me. I pull at the condom and toss it into the trash next to the nightstand. Jess rests her head on my chest, her fingers trace lazy patterns over my abs.

"That was, perhaps, better than my fantasy," I admit.

"I can't make words," Jess says. I chuckle and kiss her temple.

"Then don't. Let's just enjoy this moment a while longer." I pull the blankets up over us. Jess throws a leg over mine. Nothing has ever felt this right before. No single moment in my life could have prepared me for being with Jess. Everything just clicked into place. I stroke her hair and whisper nothing and everything into her temple. I love the feel of her skin against my lips. Her breathing falls into a slow, steady pace and I know she's fallen asleep. There is nothing better than knowing I'm going to wake up in the morning with Jess in my arms. The world feels like it holds endless possibilities for me as I drift off.

⚓⚓⚓⚓

Flutters across my chest and abs raise me from a deep sleep. I squint one eye open. Jess is kissing, no, barely grazing her lips all over me. Blond hair trails behind her lips, tickling. I lift a hand and run it through her golden hair.

"Morning," she whispers on a smile. I grab her under her arms and drag her up onto my chest. Jess giggles and leans in to kiss me. I let my fingertips run against her flesh up and down along her back lightly, as she shows me exactly how good of a morning it is.

"We should put some clothes on."

I frown and pull her body to mine flush. "Clothes are overrated."

"Ty, the kids will be up soon. It's six already."

I glance at the clock. I can't remember the last time I slept in so late and groan. "Damn."

"You need to get Luke off to school."

"And we need to get your car picked up. Can I, at least, convince you to shower with me?" I ask with a grin. Her eyes light up with mischief and a smile takes over her face.

"I think that can be arranged," she says. Again, I feel immortal. That smile makes me feel eight feet tall. She pops up, taking the blanket with her. Her naked body is perfection. I watch the way her muscles contract and release as she stands and walks to the bathroom. "Coming?" she asks. I nod. My body starts to burn and fantasies about Jess using her mouth and voice on me in creative ways, plays out in my mind like a movie reel.

Jesenia

Here we are saying goodbye already and I feel like a jilted teenager in love. I want every minute with him, even the boring tedious ones, like watching him sleep or seeing him go about his busy day at work. I want endless hours curled up in bed, with the phone glued to my face while I twirl the cord around my fingers and listen to him breathe, while my parents threaten to take the phone away, if I don't go to bed.

I don't know if I've ever had this feeling of infatuation, giddy and restless all at once, the sound of his voice and his smile doing ridiculous things to me, sparking reactions that ring all the way to the tips of my toes.

"I've got everything in the car, Mom. Looks like we're ready to go." Angie says, her hair bobbing in its high ponytail. She's being indulgent with me, I can tell she really wants to get going. She's got her own Prince Charming at home and no matter how close we are, no one is that enthusiastic about their own mother's love life.

"Okay, we'll be right out, just give us a minute."

"You don't have to ask twice, guys. I don't want to watch you make out."

Ty smacks my butt as soon as she walks out of the kitchen.

"I've got a mind to drag you back upstairs and take you all over again."

I'm breathing hard already and trying to memorize his scent—the feel of his hands desiring me, and the profound physical awakening he's given me in the last few days.

"Me, too, I want you a hundred more times. Until it hurts, until we can't anymore. I need a thousand more weekends wrapped up in your arms."

"Jesus, Jess. You're making my dick hard. We'll figure out another visit as soon as possible. I want more of you, too. I've already got planned all of the dirty things I want to do to you."

"It's going to be a long ride home, I'm glad Angie is driving. I want to mention something really quickly and I should have brought it up earlier."

"What is it, babe?" he asks, concern dimming the brightness that was all over his face.

"We have to be low profile with this, until the divorce is finalized. It's not like there will be much press up here, but John is a public figure and you know how that goes. His lawyers asked me specifically—especially while they deconstruct the pre-nup." I feel like a jerk saying it. Like it somehow qualifies our love as not being important, not good enough for the shitty tabloids that would write it up.

"Okay, I know the guys at work will ask, can I say anything

to them?" he looks disappointed. I've hurt his feelings, which was the last thing I wanted to do.

"Probably not, Titan. Just to err on the safe side. I'm sorry, it's ridiculous, I know. But bad press can hurt John's campaign, so they'll go to great length to stop it. They aren't beyond threats or intimidations, so it's best to keep it quiet."

"I was looking forward to telling everyone. But I can wait, if we have to."

"Just this one thing and then we'll shout it together from the rooftops, as soon as it's finalized. You can come on the show and I'll publically strip you of your title, *most eligible bachelor*, in front of everyone."

"I like the sound of that," Ty says. He wraps his arms around me and hugs me to his chest.

"I can't wait already, until I see you again."

He kisses my tears away and touches his lips first to my cheek and then my lips. Reluctantly, with a sinking feeling in my chest, I let go of his hand and walk back toward the life I was so eager to run away from.

CHAPTER 27

Titan

I adjust myself and stretch out a bit. "I'll be okay. It's an outpatient procedure."

"I'm worried for you," she says and it melts my heart.

"I don't really know what I am doing but I didn't anticipate you to affect me this much Jess, being apart is torture," I say into the receiver.

"That sounds like an 'I miss you.'" Her voice is soft and melodic.

"It is. It's a giant I miss you. Two days feel like an eternity. I want to come see you this weekend."

"Really? You'd make the drive? It's Halloween weekend though, what about Luke?" She sounds surprised which makes my heart ache. She should know, believe how much I want to see her.

"Of course, I would. Luke has a football game Friday night, but I could leave after that. He doesn't trick or treat. There's a

Halloween party Saturday night at his friend, Dillon's house, anyways, he can stay there for the weekend. I'd be pretty late getting to you but it's worth it."

Luke yells from the living room. I check the time. Nine p.m. "Jess, I have to run, but think about it. I'd love to see you—the sooner, the better and this weekend is the soonest I can arrange.

"It's okay. Go be with Luke. Let me just make sure my schedule is clear and I will let you know tomorrow when we talk," she says. I smile into the phone.

"Sounds good, babe. I'll text you goodnight."

"Alright. Looking forward to it."

"Bye, Jess."

I hop off the bed and trot downstairs to watch a show with Luke. He's got something queued up already and a glass of water on each side table.

"You ready for tomorrow?"

"Yes. Luke, I'll be home by six. It's just a couple hours in the recovery room. Rusty's driving me. You can relax, Bud, a biopsy isn't too invasive."

"I know," he says.

⚓⚓⚓⚓

The room is chilly as I lay here on my back waiting for the general anesthetic to kick in. Dr. Hemphill told me not to worry about a thing, but I can't help be nervous. They're making small incisions in my abdomen and removing small pieces of tissue. It sounds like a bigger deal than it is.

"Titan, how're you feeling?" Dr. Hemphill asks.

"Like elephants. Sitting. Eyelids."

"That's good. Just relax." Is the last thing I remember hearing.

After a few hours, waking up and getting my legs under me again, I'm feeling alright. I assumed I'd be in pain, but I'm not really. Just sore where the stitches are.

"I've scheduled a follow-up visit for a week from today to explain the results, once they've come in." Dr. Hemphill says.

"Sounds good. What time?"

"Nine a.m., it's all I had open."

"That works. So, am I clear to go home, Doc?" Dr. Hemphill smiles at me.

"Yup. Do you have your ride all lined up?"

"Rusty should be in the waiting room."

"Good. I'll let him know you'll be out in a few minutes. Your clothes are right there," he points to the chair in the corner of the room.

"Thanks, Doc. See you next week."

I gingerly get out of the bed. I'll be moving a little slower than normal, apparently. I get my clothes on and pull my phone from my back pocket to text Jess that all is well, while heading to the waiting room to find Rusty.

Rusty is all jittery from free cups of coffee and when he sees me, he has a thousand questions for me. I try to answer them all but I'm feeling quiet and slightly withdrawn, which I think is irritating him. Every pothole the truck hits sends a wave of agony through my midsection.

"Rusty, you've got to go slower," I complain.

"Sorry. I really should have skipped that third cup of coffee." His fingers drum a beat to the radio.

"Edie made a casserole and sent it home with Luke after practice today. He should have it all warmed up by now. She didn't want you going hungry."

"That was sweet. Tell her thank you for me," I say.

"You can tell her yourself when she comes to check up on you tomorrow morning," he laughs. I whip my head to look at him. "What? I couldn't tell her no. She wouldn't hear it. She's going to get Luke off to school and make sure you're alright."

I groan. "I don't need a babysitter, Rusty. I'll probably be asleep when she gets there."

"Hey, everyone needs a babysitter once in a while and considering you don't ever get drunk, this is probably the only time we'll be required to pinch hit for you. It's not a big deal," he says and taps his fingers on the steering wheel to the beat of the song playing again.

"Fine. But tell her I don't want her cleaning up or anything. She's only allowed to make sure I'm still breathing."

Rusty lets out a loud chuckle and nods his head. "You got it, Ty."

My phone dings. *Happy you're out and doing well. xo.* Jess's response puts a smile on my face.

"Who's that from?" Rusty asks. I shove my phone back into my pocket.

"Luke," I say.

"Luke's got you smiling like that?" he asks. Damn.

"Drop it, Rusty."

"Aww, you got a secret relationship going on?" he laughs. I stay silent, despite his teasing all the way to the house.

Jesenia

Blue, red and yellow corn wreaths are lying in a row along the craft table, surrounded by pinecones, both natural and painted. We've got some wall hangings, a few southwestern-looking throw rugs and blankets. Pillows with embroidered mallards and Canada geese flying in V's, old wooden boxes turned into kindling holders, glass bowls filled with colored leaves and gourds. But really, the pièce de résistance is one half a barn door turned into a den table. I stayed up all night varnishing and attaching the legs.

"That thing is sick, Mom. I'm totally going to bring it home with me tonight instead of letting it go to auction. Andrew will probably hate it, but whatever, I love it."

"Well, they'll be expecting to be able to bid after the show. I have the other half of the door in storage. I'll make you an even better one!"

"Your hair is standing up on end and you look like a crazy person. Thank God this show isn't on camera, because you'd have viewers running at your Halloween costume."

"Thanks, Darling, for your kind words. I couldn't sleep, I got so excited about this project and the show. I thought one would look great in Ty and Luke's TV room, too, don't you think?"

"Maybe you're manic," Angie says, taking a small Mason Pearson brush from her purse and running it through my hair.

"I'd tell you if I were. Ange, for the first time in a long time, I'm happy.

"Because you've got a hot boyfriend. So what's our first "switch out five?" I'm going to write them all down, so you don't make it up as you go along."

"They love when I do that!"

"No, they love when I get mad at you and we start arguing over table settings or where a picture should go. It takes up the whole podcast, if we get started. Seeing as you're so happy today, I'm just taking precautions."

"Don't worry about me, honey. You're over-reacting. What's going on with you, Angie? Is something the matter?"

She drags the brush through her own hair and big, fat tears fall down her cheeks. I reach out and grab her hand and hold it in two of mine. I can't even imagine what's gotten her so upset.

"You told Ty, didn't you?"

"I did. When we drove back, I told him in the car. He accepted it, Angelina, he took it so well. He's not your father."

"I'm just afraid he'll dump you, if you get bad. And it hurts already, just thinking about it and what you'd go through—what it would do to your happiness."

"He's a good man, Angie and he accepts me as I am. It's not your job to worry about me. Even if Ty did decide that he was better off without me. I'm an adult. I can handle it."

"Seeing you so happy is breaking my heart. I want you to always feel like this and I'm already scared that it will end."

I pull my daughter into a hug and she cries into my shoulder. I'm only now realizing how much John putting me down affected her. She expects Ty to dislike my disease so much that he would lose interest in me entirely—that my mental health trumps every other good part of me. That's because he taught her that it did. John was so scared of my disease that he made her fear it as well—and even worse, made her question whether any man could ever love me or want to be with me.

"Angie, Ty has issues of his own. We make a good pair. We were just meant to be together, it's that simple. I trust him, he trusts me. We're at a point in our lives where there are things more important than measuring our faults. We both want the whole package. He's not going to leave me."

"Dad said to expect you to be delusional about it. He said the guy would probably swindle you and make you feel like it wasn't a big deal. That I should keep an eye out, so you didn't get hurt. He said you're too sick to be responsible about a relationship."

My blood is boiling and my ears ringing and I feel like smashing something. I grip the handle of my coffee mug, then think better of it and run my fingers over some blue corn that's intertwined in a braid.

"Did you believe him, Angie? What he said. Is that why you're crying because you agree with him?"

"No, Mom. I saw the way Ty looks at you. I know he feels like he's been waiting his whole life for you. I guess I'm just scared, that's all. And Dad was seriously asking so many questions—just digging and digging and it made me uneasy."

"What do you mean, questions?" I ask. I pop a blue kernel out with my nail and it rolls into my moccasin.

"Like, he heard some stuff from some people, so he was asking about Ty. He wanted to know if we met him upstate and what his financial situation is like—if he has a criminal record—stuff like that."

I swallow deeply and fight the urge to scream. I want to run from the room crying and go call Ty and complain. But I know divorces get messy, ugly and vindictive. I'm lucky John agreed to do a non-contested, considering he's so powerful, both financially and otherwise. I take a deep breath and grab Angie's hand again. I get the feeling she's been playing it cool, but underneath, she's hurting over the split and is too proud to admit it.

"I've made a mistake, Angelina and I want to apologize. I use you as a confidante because we are so close and sometimes I forget you're my daughter. But that's not fair to you and I know how much you love your father. From now on, your job is to manage your crappy manager here at the podcast, oversee the financials on our accessory line and love Andrew and get ready for your wedding. No more supporting me or turning against your father. Divorce can get tricky and I don't want you caught in the middle."

"So stay the hell out of it, in other words. Don't tell Dad shit and stay out of your relationship with Ty?"

"You are too bold, Angelina. You need to invest in a filter."

"That would be boring. And divorce aside, this table is the shit and even though you look tired as hell, I can see all the happiness dancing around in your eyes."

CHAPTER 28

Titan

I shouldn't be at work today. Edie scolded me when she saw me up and about this morning. I'm supposed to rest for five to seven days but I just can't. I have things to get done before I leave for the weekend. And there is no way in hell I'm not making the drive, just because I have a few stitches in me. I'm working out TCH's next build schedule when the door to my office flies open. It startles me and I jump, which in turn makes me groan in pain. A medium build man in a nice looking trench coat steps inside and looks around with his lip curled up. Like this place is the foulest place he's ever encountered.

"Can I help you?" I ask standing.

"Titan Jennings. Where is he?" The man demands, rather than asks. His personality puts me on edge.

"You've got him. What can I do for you, Mister?" I let my greeting hang in the air between us. He's stopped his approach and is sizing me up.

"Van Buren. John Van Buren," he states. A chill runs through me. *This* is Jess's husband? He couldn't be more wrong for her, if he tried.

"I see."

"Do you now?" he snaps. "Have a seat, Mr. Jennings, we have a lot to discuss."

Anger boils in my gut. "I don't think we do. I think you should leave."

John charges forward and I widen my stance. "Listen to me, you little prick, you do not get to make the rules here. I call the shots. It's my *fucked up* wife you're fucking and my image you're ruining."

"Jess is not fucked up," I say as calmly as possible.

John laughs long and hard. "You have no idea. You haven't lived with her for over twenty years. She's a train wreck mentally and should probably be institutionalized, but you know, that doesn't look good and the sympathy vote only carries you so far."

My hands clench into fists at my sides. "Why, exactly, are you here?" I grit out.

"To make you understand. This situation is extremely delicate. I can't have reports of my wife traipsing around with some, mixed scum from upstate. Do you know who I am?" He looks incredulously at me.

"Quite frankly, John, I don't give a shit who you are. Jess is out. Done with you. It seems to me, if you don't want the press to catch wind of all this, you should be hasty with the divorce proceedings."

"Listen, '*Titan*,' I haven't had the desire to fuck my wife for a long time, the divorce doesn't bother me, her image and how it reflects on me—does. If you can't shape up, I will take measures to keep you in line."

I take three steps backward to my desk, slide open the drawer and pick up my revolver. I slide the safety back. "I think you misunderstand the situation, '*John.*' You have no say here. This is my life. My world. My town. Get the fuck out," I say. "And so help me God, if you cause Jess one more tear of anguish, I will put a bullet in you."

John puts his hands up, like I'm actually going to do something to him and backs out of my office. My hand shakes. The gun shakes. I've never had to actually use the gun. I took a couple shooting and firearm safety lessons when I got my permit for it but that's it. The gun was just a failsafe, really.

I don't sit until I hear John's car kick up gravel on his way out. Adrenaline leaving my system rapidly, makes me feel weak in the knees, so I lean on the corner of my desk. I'm worked up and pissed. I give myself thirty minutes to calm down and resume work. I still need to appear at Luke's game before I head out, too, and confirm with Rusty and Edie that they're all set to have him for the weekend. None of that is going to happen, with me freaking out. I never thought I'd meet him or see him. I never anticipated the violent reaction I'd have to his sorry words. How did Jess ever survive that marriage and why would she put up with that kind of man? My heart breaks for her. For the last twenty years, I've experienced a wonderful marriage to an incredible woman. And Jess silently suffered alone.

I finish up my work and lock up the office. When I arrive at the football game, Rusty and Edie have saved me a seat. I desperately want to tell Rusty what happened but I keep my mouth shut because Jess asked me to keep our relationship a secret. I don't know if I should tell Jess what happened or not but I have a little more than a three hour drive ahead of me to figure it out.

Jesenia

"Coming," I yell, as the doorbell chimes. My heart thuds with my footsteps, hoping it's Ty. I pull open the front door of our townhouse on the Upper East Side. It will be strange to have him in the residence I shared with my husband, but I have to start thinking of it as my house now. I'm starting over, it's a new life and this new life includes the gorgeous man standing on my doorstep.

"Hi. Did I wake you?"

"Come in, I slept a little around ten and then I woke up again. How was the drive?"

"Awful. I couldn't get here soon enough. I've been aching for your arms."

We embrace in a warm hug and Ty's hands go to my neck and head, massaging in the way only he knows how. It puts me in a trance and I whimper into his strong neck.

"I missed you so much. I barely survived the week without you."

"I know how you feel. This week took ten years to get through."

"Sorry, I'm being rude. Let me take your bag and your coat. Would you like tea or water?"

"Just a bed with you in it would be fine, at this point. What time is it anyhow?"

"A little after two, last time I checked." I take Ty's coat and hang it up in the hall closet. I flick on the light and put his bag at the bottom of the stairs. "Do you want a tour tonight or can that wait until tomorrow?"

"Tomorrow, I'm beat after the drive."

"You do look tired." In fact, something about Ty's expression worries me. His eyes seem more creased, his brow looks more furrowed. Not that it, in any way, robs him of his looks. He's as dashing as ever, but he looks somehow defeated. "Come on, follow me," I say, heading up the stairs. "I didn't prepare a guestroom for you, I figured we'd share."

"That's fine with me, Ty says, hoisting up his duffel bag. As long as it's not the marital bedroom you shared with the senator, I'll sleep anywhere with you."

"Oh, well, John and I haven't shared a bedroom in years. When he left, I had my bed moved into the master suite. I repainted and got rid of all of the furniture that was in there. I hung some tapestries that I'd always dreamed of having in the bedroom."

"Was there anything good about your former marriage?"

"Angie," I say, without any hesitation.

"And besides the lovely Angie?"

"Nothing I can think of. Maybe some vacations in the very beginning. He liked my cooking and would compliment me on that."

"That's all you got? Pretty sad, I'd say. But I actually met the guy this week and I don't have anything good to report."

I turn around on the stairs and come face to face with him.

"What do you mean?"

"He came to my office. Tried to pick a fight. I had to shoo him out with my 38 Special."

"Are you serious? You pulled a gun on John?" I feel a twisted smile creeping onto my face and quickly lift my hand to cover it.

"Oh, you like that, huh? When I've got to fight for you?" Ty says and digs his fingers into my hip. He pecks my lips once, twice and then goes in for a rougher, deeper kiss. "I'll fight them off, Jess, if I have to. Cause you belong to me now. Excuse my French, but I could give a fuck if he's the state senator."

Our kiss goes off like a firecracker, a sonic boom courses under my skin. Ty kisses me so enthusiastically, that I reach my hands out for the wall behind me. He gropes my breasts, thrusts a hand up under my shirt and flicks my nipple hard. I cry out, only to be silenced immediately by his tongue. I start losing my footing and stumble back onto the landing.

"I didn't peg you for a girl who would get turned on by jealousy," he says, rapidly unbuttoning his shirt.

"I didn't know I was, but somehow you make everything sexy." I'm already wet, so responsive I am to him. He tugs down my linen pants and makes as short work of my underwear.

"I hope the politicos have cameras and spies watching us, Jess. I'm going to show them all how hard I like to fuck you."

I moan into his ear and thrust my tongue inside, biting his ear lobe; I wrap my legs around his back just as he tears his own pants down.

"I hope they have the walls of this place bugged, so they can all hear how it's my name you scream when you come."

"Ty," I say, wrapping my fingers around his thick shaft and pulling him toward my entrance.

"Condom," Ty says, scraping his teeth down my neck. "Wallet," he says as he takes my hard nipple into his mouth. I reach out with a blind hand, patting the landing; when I feel his pants, I search for the back pocket, pull out the wallet and thrust it at him.

"Do you want to get in bed?" I ask panting. He responds without words, shoving both hands under me and lifting me up. "Careful, Titan. Don't hurt yourself, I can walk."

"Nonsense, you weigh less than Luke. Which way?" he asks as we stagger through the darkness.

"First room on the right. Light switch is on the wall, just inside the door." I'm biting his other ear lobe and running my hands all over his pecs and biceps, feeling the muscles strain from lifting me up. He tosses me onto the bed and steps out of his boxers. He's a dark shadow, a profile, highlighted by a bit of street light leaking in the through the window. His cock is rigid, pressed up against his belly. I watch him tear into the condom wrapper with his teeth and roll it down his stunning length.

"On your stomach, Jenny. I'm going to fuck you from behind. Let's see if we can get a real orgasm out of you this time.

"A real orgasm?" Each orgasm I've had with Ty has been better than the last. He's a tiger in bed and I shudder at what his appetite must have been like when he was in his prime. And *Jenny*. A nickname already. My stomach flips with intimacy and affection for this man.

I do as I'm told and crawl forward on my bed, resting my head on the pillow and raising my back up to him. His hand comes under my stomach, the other goes to my hip. He guides himself inside me and I swim in the feeling of fullness, at being so connected with his body. He pulls out slowly and then slams into me with a quick pump. I gasp and push back brazenly right into his cock.

"I like you like this," he says with satisfaction. His hand dips into my crack and starts exploring, coming around front to massage my clit. My legs are already shaking. Ty increases his speed and his cock is hitting me on the inside in such a way, that I'm moaning into the pillows. I can feel the orgasm building in intensity and I see red when I close my eyes instead of darkness. Yet, there's color swirling in a frenzy all throughout my body, building until the pressure threatens to unhinge me.

"Titan!" I scream into the pillow. The orgasm rips through me violently, stealing my senses, hurling me through unknown territory, where my body fights for equilibrium and to grasp anything it recognizes. "Titan!" I scream again thinking I'd hit the peak, but the orgasm doesn't let go, it builds until my mind and body threaten to break. I keen into the pillow and completely collapse as the tremors unwind like fiery coils, pulsing red-hot and springing right through whatever calm was left in my body.

I distantly hear the condom snap through the blur of disorientation. Ty touches my genitals and gathers up lubrication. He rubs his cock on my ass cheeks and strokes himself. I hear the slip and can feel the passes of his hand working his erection. He tenses, almost stops. Then he groans loudly and threads of hot semen hit my ass and my back. He falls forward onto me and slides to the side, pulling me into his arms. We're sweaty and tangled, breathing hard, and messy with the evidence of our frantic coupling marking our bodies.

"I knew I could make you come harder," Ty nuzzles into my ear and tousled hair. He pulls me onto his strong chest and I lie in a stunned and utterly fulfilled state, listening to his heartbeat thunder in my ears. I think he hit my G-spot. I think maybe I'm in ecstasy. Is this what I've been missing out on over the last twenty years?

CHAPTER 29

Titan

I roll over and sling an arm over Jess. She's warm and still asleep. My stitches ache. I overexerted myself last night and it's obvious I will be paying for that today. I kiss the back of Jess's neck before sneaking out of the bed and heading to the bathroom. Jess doesn't know it yet but I have a whole day planned out for us, starting with breakfast. I clumsily bang around her kitchen looking for coffee and filters, so we can enjoy a cup before we head out.

"Time to wake up," I whisper into her ear. I set a mug of coffee, sweet and light, on her nightstand, hoping the smell will draw her out of slumber.

She sniffs the air. "Is that coffee?" she asks with her eyes still closed.

"It is."

"You're a good man, Ty." A groggy smile spreads across her face. She rubs her eyes before slowly opening them. She looks good first thing in the morning. Softer, more pure somehow. I lean down and kiss her forehead.

She wraps her fingers around her mug and lifts it to her lips. "Oh, no!"

"What? Too hot?" I ask.

"I forgot, I'm so sorry." Her eyes are glued to my incision.

"It's okay. There was no way we were going to take it easy last night. I knew that."

"But you must be so sore."

"I'm fine. I promise. Now enjoy that coffee because we have a full day ahead of us, starting with breakfast."

"What are you talking about?"

I shrug and sip my coffee. "I may have planned a few things for us to do."

"Really? Ty, you didn't have to. You're my guest this time."

"Jess, relax, I wanted to and it will be fun."

She relaxes and grins at me. "So where's breakfast?"

"Norma's at the Le Parker Meridien Hotel," I say.

"Ty! That place is expensive."

"And romantic, I hear." I wink at her and finish my mug of coffee. "I'm hopping in the shower."

It's nine thirty by the time our food arrives and I can hear my stomach grumbling, which means Jess must be hungry, too. "Sheer decadence," Jess groans. The shareable fruit-stuffed waffles and French toast à la foie gras are delectable and filling. I'm glad I took up the Vanderbilts on the suggestion. "Can't be beat," I agree.

"This is so nice, Ty. I haven't gone out to breakfast at a nice place in a long time."

"It's just breakfast, Jess." I reach across the table and take her hand in mine. "How are you really? I know John coming to visit me set you off."

She sighs and looks at her plate. "I'm so embarrassed that he did that. It makes me crazy to think that he'd behave that way, when he doesn't even care about me."

"Let it go. It's not worth harping on and it didn't scare me off."

She nods. "What else have you got planned for today?"

I scrape the last bite off the plate and motion for the check.

We enter Central Park at 59th Street and Fifth Avenue and head north past Wollman Rink before catching a ride on the antique carousel. Jess laughs when I tell her we are, in fact, riding the carousel. I ride next to her. She throws her head back and laughs, citing a man my size looks ridiculous on a toy horse. I can't disagree. I'm sure I look utterly absurd.

We talk about everything. Luke, raising a teen alone, Angie, her wedding, the ups and downs of running your own business and more. It's easy and comfortable. There's no awkward pauses, no uncomfortable silence. It's as if we've been together all our lives. We take our time and wander through the Literary Walk, a path lined with statues of Shakespeare and Sir Walter Scott, before I lead her to the Boathouse Restaurant. We're seated in the lakeside dining room, and have a spectacular view of the gondolas on the lake and the surrounding gardens. I hope that Jess is enjoying herself. She has a faraway expression and she keeps blinking back what looks like tears.

"Want to order something to share? I'm not super hungry yet," I ask. She looks from the window to me and a tear falls. "Jess, what's wrong?"

"Nothing at all. I'm being silly. I'm happy. These are happy tears. In all my time in Manhattan, no one's ever spent a day with me being a tourist; just, exploring and holding hands and talking. It's as if I'm seeing everything for the first time."

I move my chair to her side and wrap an arm around her shoulders. "I don't want tears, babe, I want smiles."

She smiles at me as I wipe her teary cheeks dry. "Titan, you are an incredible man."

"Maybe you bring out the best in me," I say.

She wrinkles her brow. "Doubtful."

"Let's agree to disagree. Our day isn't over yet and I have more in store for us. It's nice having so much alone time to be together and enjoy what the City has to offer."

"I will agree with you on that. And on sharing something, what did you have in mind?"

⚓ ⚓ ⚓ ⚓

We pick up a paddleboat at Loeb Boathouse near 74th Street. Jess looks at me incredulously, as I hold her hand to help her in. "It's too cold for this!" she squawks.

"Simmer down, woman. It's the perfect time of year for this!" I sit in my seat and kiss her until she's grinning. "Now come on . . . pedal."

We take a fifteen-minute ride on the New York Water Taxi to Brooklyn from Battery Park, and motor around the tip of Manhattan to Fulton Ferry Landing and go to the River Café. Jess orders lobster for us both, claiming it would be a complete waste to order anything else, so I let her. We share handmade chocolates under the Brooklyn Bridge for dessert.

Jess swings our arms as we walk back to her place. "This was the best day ever."

"I'm glad you think so."

She tugs my hand, so I look down to her. "I mean it, Ty, everything about today was amazing. You're amazing." I walk her backwards until her back is up against a tree on the sidewalk. "I'd do this for you every damn day, Jess. All your days should feel like this." Her breath is ragged and little puffs of fog billow out from her lips. I drop my head and nudge under her nose, she raises her head slightly and I let my lips graze hers. "I love the way your eyes light up when you're really happy," I whisper against her lips. I press my lips against hers and let my tongue tease her a bit. "I love the way it sounds when you laugh." I kiss her cheek and gently bite her earlobe. "I love that when you hold my hand, I feel like the most important man on the planet," I whisper in the shell of her ear before kissing a path from her neck back to her mouth. "And I love these lips." She mewls when I kiss her again. Her hands paw at my back, drawing me impossibly closer to her. We're making a spectacle of ourselves and it doesn't bother me in the least. Someone hollers 'get a room' and I finally pull away and laugh. Jess is flushed, her hair mussed and she's wearing the sexiest grin.

"Let's get you home," I tell her.

Jesenia

Sex all weekend. Every night, in the morning, even in the middle of the sunny afternoon. Moony, love-struck eyes, swoony whispered words, stolen kisses and indulgent food. Although I know it can't last forever and I'm wary of how fast it began, nothing has ever felt as sweet as falling asleep in his arms, or as easy as waking up to his kisses. And I'm sleeping. Actually sleeping, six hours, then seven, even eight. Not waking up, not compulsively crafting or organizing bins. I feel lazy, love drunk, and at ease with myself.

It feels good to give Angie some space, let her live her own life and not worry about taking care of me or making sure I feel included. I've got my own life and I'm living it with Ty—all thanks to a chance encounter outside a diner that fateful night. I'm having the kind of honeymoon I always imagined. John and I never enjoyed one another like this. We didn't communicate, verbally, sexually, in any form other than negotiating the terms of our relationship, who was up two points and who was down. Tallying up the score for which one of us was better, who was sacrificing more. We didn't hold hands and stare into one another's eyes. I never got to experience the feeling of my blood warming and sending tingles all the way down to my toes, with just a quick look or a smile. Of worshiping his physical body and getting to know his skin. With Ty, I want more and I'm getting it, we communicate freely and openly, like we've been doing it forever. I no longer feel the shame I had about my body, about my mental health, about even my hobbies. Ty accepts all of me and even asks for more. I'd do anything for this man, anything at all.

"This is it. Tomorrow we part ways and we've got to deal with the separation again."

"Move in with me. We'll send a driver down to get Luke and his things."

I'm standing between his legs, pulling a brush through my wet hair. He's sitting on the bed, his palms splayed, elbows locked, holding up his weight. "What? Why are you looking at me like that?"

"Because you're beautiful. Because I can imagine throwing it all to the wind and doing exactly what you just said."

I'm going to miss the adoring look in his eyes. I'll miss showering together, scrubbing off our mingled sweat and the evidence of his lust from my butt and the backs of my thighs. I love how Ty comes on me, almost as if because he can't come inside me, he still wants it to touch my body, make contact with my skin. He pulls the condom off just before climax and I offer up a part of my body for the hot ribbons of his ejaculation to land. Maybe it would be awful with someone else, unpleasant or dirty, but with Titan, I want all of it, as much as I can possibly get.

He pulls me back onto the bed and I land on top of him. His cock is hard again and we've just barely finished making love.

"Again? You're insatiable!"

"Only for you, I am."

"What will I do when you're gone?"

"I guess the same you were doing all these years we were apart," he says. Ty's hands go to my neck and I flatten out on top of him like a pancake. His touch, especially there, melts me. I love his hands—they are magic. I love his cock; it's magic, too.

My hands instinctively move to his boxers and slip in the flap. I run my palm up and down his erection and he presses into my hand with his hips. He's hard. I grab his shaft.

"I was sleepwalking all those years. Now I'm awake and you're leaving."

"I don't want to go, either. It hurts to leave you. Let's plan our next visit and if it's not too soon—no pressure, but we could start to discuss a long term solution for us."

I slide down his chest, pull at the waistband of his boxers and wrap my lips around the head of his cock. It's both long and thick, almost intimidating, but Ty assured me early on that he likes whatever I do. I'm not insecure or shy around Titan; on the contrary—I feel sexually confident and competent, for the first time ever.

"What about next weekend? You could come up Friday after the show, either that or Saturday morning?"

I nod my head "yes," looking up at him without removing my mouth.

A half an hour later, we're a pile of spent limbs and body parts lying tangled in the sheets, our earlier attempts at dressing are now wrinkled at the base of the bed.

"Okay, should we try again?" Ty says. He laughs at the ceiling. I keep telling myself to go easy on him because of the stitches, but I'm like a wildfire spreading out of control, I have no resistance around Ty, no restraint. My body, in response to him, has gained a will of its own.

"I guess we can't live in this bed," I say curling into the form of his body. I lightly kiss the outside of his bicep, his shoulder, my palm rests on the flat of his belly that still holds the impression of abs, of a well-earned six pack. He's in amazing shape for his age—that's part of why it's so hard for me to accept that he's sick. I hate the disease that is tainting his blood, this beautiful man, with so much to give and so much love. If the results of the biopsy are serious, I'm afraid I'll die. My heart races into a panic just at the thought of him suffering or getting worse.

He is so pure and good; it's not fair. It's not fair and it hurts. I snuggle in closer, ignoring intentions of rising. I lay my ear to his heart and listen to it fire. Ty is barrel chested in the best sense of the word; he's a huge man and I adore it, there's so much of him for me to love. I hypnotize myself with the drumbeat in his chest, praying to all gods, all heavenly bodies, to preserve this one piece of human flesh. Tears roll down my cheeks and pool in the concave of his sternum.

"Are you crying again, Jess?" he whispers, his voice hoarse with contentment.

I don't think I ever loved myself as an adult. I think I figured it was unnecessary and frivolous and then there was John, who was only capable of accentuating my very worst parts. On Ty's chest, my fears and insecurities slowly slip away and take flight. I don't focus on my faults and in turn, the very best parts of me shine brilliantly bright. I forgive myself and love myself fully in his arms.

"It's okay if you cry. All of those tears slip into my heart, and it helps fill me up. I want the sad parts of you, just as much as I want the good stuff."

I sob into his chest and my whole chest cavity shakes. He squeezes me harder and it steals my breath away.

"I wish we'd spent our whole lives together. I'm mourning all the moments we lost. My husband drove me to extreme insecurity and self-doubt and I can't help but think how much better I would have fared in your arms."

"You did great, despite the circumstances. I'm sorry you were unhappy. But I wouldn't trade my memories of my wife or the birth of our son. Maybe we needed the time apart to grow and become who we are. I would take away the suffering, if I could. I'm sorry he was cruel, but you did an amazing job with Angelina, Jess. You started a huge, successful business; you left him as soon as you had the strength to stand on your own. I see a strong woman here. One who changes the light whenever she walks into a room. One who thousands of fans tune into every week to see how her mind comes up with new creative ideas. It seems pretty damn good to anyone looking in from the outside."

I pull away from him and stare into his beautiful, warm eyes. He looks content and I resolve to feel this way, too. To let go of anxiety surrounding the future as well as regrets about the past. I vow to myself to live in the present and enjoy every single moment, every meal, every hug, every breath.

I grab my robe off of the floor and slip it over my shoulders. Ty stands and pulls on his boxers and pants for the second time this morning. I walk over to the window and pull open the drapes and roll up the blind, bathing the room in sunlight. I peer down onto the street and see paparazzi. Three of them, with their cameras. One news truck—no bystanders. John must have gone public with the news of the divorce. It looks bad that Ty's here with me. There's no way he can leave without it becoming a scandal.

"Where'd you park the truck?"

"In that garage on 72nd. Why, what's up?"

The tabloids would love it—not only the backstory, if they could get their hands on it, but *all* of the rest. The fact that our divorce was just announced and I'm already sleeping around, that Ty's so handsome, and most of all—that he's black.

"Do you have your sunglasses?" I ask. I am loathe to hide him. I want to scream to the tabloids and the news how wonderful he's been to me—what a fabulous man he is. That he's a better man than John could ever dream of being. I want to protect Ty, to shelter him, to hide him from scorn. I don't want the reporters to dig and come up with parts of his past that they could and would sensationalize, drag his name through the mud. What a heyday they would have, drunk driving, vehicular manslaughter, Hepatitis C positive. They'd make him look criminal and would crucify him publicly. All in the name of selling copies—I'm well aware of how they work. So after years of hiding my own less than savory details from them, I now have to hide Ty—the man I'm likely in love with.

"In the truck," Ty says buttoning his shirt. He comes to stand by my side and slides an arm around my waist. He kisses my head. "Is it that sunny out—Fuck."

"There's a back exit that goes out to the yard. You can walk through the courtyards until you end up on 5th and slip into the park."

"Like I did something wrong or like I'm the help, who you fucked."

I turn around in his arms and look up to his face. I'm surprised at his outburst, but I understand his rage.

"It's the only way. Not to protect John. I've not a single consideration for him. To protect you. To protect Luke and your past."

"And if they catch me? If there are more of them waiting around the corner? What do I say?"

"That you're a contractor giving appraisals. That your luggage is your tool bag. That I'm not home, you were dealing with the overseeing realtor on the estate. That you've never met Jesenia Van Buren. Ever. And no, you don't have any comments on the divorce that's just hit the papers."

I can see the anger flashing proudly in his dark eyes. I can see the primal Ty, who can fight, and pull guns on men, regardless of what their social or political power is.

"For you," he says, his voice tense and vibrating with fury. He grabs the back of my head and kisses me possessively, dipping his tongue in deep, widely sweeping my mouth. He bites my bottom lip, growls and squeezes my hip through my robe. I step backward away from the window and Ty almost falls into me.

"I know what you're doing. Those vultures have telephoto lenses," I say, smiling into our kiss.

"You're mine, Jesenia Van Buren, I'm not the help, I'm your lover and I can't wait to tell the whole world how we met and what we mean to each other."

CHAPTER 30

Titan

I miss her already. It's corny. Sappy even. I've never felt so lovesick over a person before. That saying, I left my heart . . . that's how I feel, like I've physically left my heart behind with her and it hurts almost. We need a better plan than winging it for visits and calling each other daily.

⚓⚓⚓⚓

"You have your camera ready?"

"Huh?" I mumble.

"Dad, Homecoming. Tonight," Luke says, staring at me like I have four heads.

"Right! Homecoming. Okay, camera." I run around the house looking for the camera. I can't remember the last time we actually used it. I almost always use my phone for pictures now. The truck! I used it for the Vanderbilt house.

I trot back into the house. "Got it." I set it on the dining room table.

"Okay, so don't be late. Bree hates being late. She said she'd be here at seven and that she wants to be at the dance by seven forty-five."

Luke is a nervous wreck and it's the most adorable thing I've witnessed in a long time from him. "Luke, Bud, it's all going to be fine. I will be home by six, we can eat, you can get dressed and when she arrives, I will take loads of pictures and then drop you at the school, okay?"

He lets out a long breath. "Yeah. Solid plan." I laugh at him as he throws his backpack over his shoulder and heads out to the bus.

"Breathe, Buddy!" I shout after him. He turns beet red and glares at me over his shoulder.

I head to the truck for a half day of work and my follow up appointment with Dr. Hemphill.

⚓⚓⚓⚓

"Hi, Ty, good to see you." Dr. Hemphill ushers me into his office. "We got the results of your biopsy yesterday. Why don't you sit, so we can go over it?" I shake Dr. Hemphill's hand and sit like I'm asked.

"Always a pleasure, Doc."

He smiles at me, but it's a sorrow-filled smile. My stomach drops to the floor. I've never seen that smile before and it raises red flags. My heart speeds up. "There's no easy way to say this, Titan. You have hepatocellular carcinoma. Liver cancer." No. The fine hairs on my arms prickle and stand at attention. No. "The cancer occupies a third of your liver, and though its advance may be slowed, this particular sort of cancer is terminal." His words are garbled. The lump in my throat threatens to choke me. I need to get out of here. "The prognosis isn't great, Ty, we're looking at eight months to a year." I'm numb. I'm in denial. This can't be right. I've only just told Jess. She's accepted my Hepatitis C. We can make it all work. We can. We have to. "Titan, did you hear me?" The words and voice sound far away. I can't see Dr. Hemphill at all. Where am I? Things are rushing past me. People. Memories. Places. Luke, Jess, Angie, Luke.

"I have to get out of here," I say more to myself than anyone else. I push up from the chair. Wobble.

"Titan! Sit. Down." Dr. Hemphill orders. I collapse back into the chair. My body folds. My head hits my knees. A deluge of tears hit me. "Do you want me to call someone for you?" The pain I feel is everywhere, right down to the cuticle. I feel like an exposed nerve in a broken tooth. I'm stripped down to something I don't recognize.

"Titan, are you okay?" Dr. Hemphill asks again.

"I don't know. What's the likelihood of a transplant?"

"Slim to none, Ty. Being Hepatitis C positive doesn't make you a priority for a good liver, since your blood will infect it. Maybe another infected donor, but you can imagine how limited that database looks."

"So what are my options?"

"Live out your life with or without treatment for the cancer."

"I can treat it?" I look up to him, eyes hopeful.

"We can, but it will only slow it down, not cure it. It might give you a couple extra months but the thing you need to take into consideration is your quality of life, Ty. Chemo is rough on people." I know all too well what chemo and radiation does to a person. Rory suffered horribly during her treatments. I stand and pull my coat on.

"Titan, let's talk a little more," Dr. Hemphill says.

"I'm all done talking for now," I answer. I walk from the doctor's office through the small town main street. The leaves have all dropped, leaving barren sticks behind. They look gnarly and morbid—like I feel. I hang a left at the coffee shop and park my rear on a bench in the park. I don't know what to do. I imagine Rory perched on her cloud above, weeping at the unfairness of the situation. I try to envision Luke five years from now, thriving without me. Of missing his graduation. Of Jess, alone. Of my company disbanded. My friends watching their children grow.

I don't want the looks of pity or the tears that will come with telling them all. I don't want to be treated differently or handled with care. I don't want the long talks or the heartbreak. I want to live in the richest, deepest, most productive way I can and that won't happen, if anyone knows.

It's a selfish thought, because of course, I have to tell everyone. I need to arrange care for Luke, a plan of action for the business, give Jess an out from what we've just barely started. She deserves a life filled with happiness and joy and love and I've got that to give her, but only for another eight months. Twenty years from now, I want to look across the dinner table with a handful of grandchildren under our feet and know Jess still makes me feel immortal but that's impossible. Eight months is nothing. Ephemera. I drop my hands to my knees and stare up at the cloudy sky.

"Fuck you!" I scream. I wipe the tears from my cheeks and stand. I need to go back to the office and get my truck. I still have to pick up some groceries and beat Luke home to make dinner. I have to take pictures of him and Bree. I have to drop them at Homecoming, entertain myself until ten and then pick them up. Drop Bree at home and get Luke and me home. And I have to do it all without giving anything away.

Not tonight.

Jesenia

"Ty?"

"I'm here, what's wrong?"

"Nothing. I can't sleep without you. I'm miserable. My thoughts are racing and I don't even own a dildo." I sound like a crazy lady, even to myself. He's not going to like this. He has a normal life, a son, he has to work in the morning.

"What time is it? Hold on." I hear him groan, probably sit up, adjust the phone.

"It's late. Early. I don't know. I shouldn't have called. It's just that I slept so well with you beside me and now I can't sleep at all. I got worked up, I—"

"Wait, Jess, slow down. I can't understand when you talk so fast. Let me catch up. One thing at a time." Ty's voice is somehow soothing, with the perfect mix of authority and concern coming through the phone.

"I can't sleep."

"Okay. Let's start with that. You mean tonight, you haven't gone to sleep yet?"

Tell him the truth or try to gloss over it? Risk how he feels about me by showing him the real parts?

"Jess, are you there?" I love the sound of his voice, traveling across invisible lines, entering my mind and providing calm and order among the chaos.

"I haven't slept since you left. Not a wink."

"You haven't slept in three days?" I can picture him sitting straight up.

"A while, I know."

"Does that mean you're manic? Are you having an episode?"

"Probably, but I don't like that word. The borders are so blurry and undefined and it's not a great way to describe it anyway. It's not a solid state of being—it's more like a cloud. A cloud that hovers and won't let me sleep."

"Jess, I'm here for you. What's the best thing for me to do? Should I drive up to the City? Are you safe?"

My eyes are expressing tears but I'm smiling into the phone. Crazy, I may be, but that is the nicest anyone has ever been to me about my disease.

"Oh, love. I'm safe. I'm not operating heavy machinery and

I know better than to drive on days like these. At some point, I'll crash. I just wanted to hear your voice."

"Alright, well in that case, I'll keep talking. You sound out of breath, were you running?"

"No, I got worked up. I was thinking about you and our bed and how you make me feel. The things you do with your hands and your mouth."

"Turned on? Horny? That's what you mean by worked up?"

"Yes. I don't own a dildo. I never have."

"I can help you with that. You have Facetime, right?" I can hear the smile in his voice and the distinct note of pleasure. I was wet before and now I feel like I'm so turned on, I could climax just from hearing him speak.

"I'm too shy!" I'm startled by his suggestion, it's not what I expected.

"Let's get you tired out, Jess. I'll exhaust you, so you can get some sleep. I'm Facetime-ing you right now. You'd better pick up!"

My phone rings and Ty's face appears immediately. I'm almost expecting something obscene from the get go, but it's just his sweet face, so I'm the one with a dirty mind. But I know what's coming and I feel simultaneously out of my league and too old, yet more excited than ever. More excited than when Angie and I first did the show, maybe even more excited than when Ty appeared out of nowhere, when we were stuck with a flat tire.

"Ty, can you hear me okay?" I ask.

He releases a warm and booming laugh. It puts my heart at ease.

"It's not a walkie-talkie, you're coming in fine."

"I'm so excited! And nervous, but excited, too," I'm completely failing at expressing myself.

"You look so gorgeous. Is that a nightie you're wearing?"

He's sweet, but I know I look crazy. Not sleeping does make my eyes go all bright, but in a deranged sort of way. My hair is tousled—clean—but not styled once in the last three days. I'm alert. Like a rabbit. Too alert. Vigilant. I could take a pill to bring me down. But I hardly ever do. A few occasions in the past, a Valium or Xanax, for a state dinner or event—something to help me crash before we went on a trip, when I hadn't been sleeping for days on end.

I don't need anything now. I'm happy, albeit jittery, maybe a little too sped up. I'm rational and lucid. I've got nothing to hide and nothing to prove to anyone. I'm already on the downside of this upswing, it won't last much longer.

"Are we having phone sex?" I ask Ty, feeling shy and adventurous all at once.

"We're doing whatever we want—whatever makes us feel good."

"I'm, uh . . . I'm aroused. I can't say the other word. I searched three closets for a toy—I thought I remembered having one in college."

"We'll get you some new ones, until we can be together all the time. I don't want you suffering with being *aroused* and nothing to fix it."

"Fine, horny. But, I don't like the way it sounds."

"It sounds good to me!"

He's laughing still. He sounds so sexy, all amused and yet sleepy. I want to crawl in bed with him and snuggle into his body. I do sit on my own bed, even though I've been hating the empty, Titan-less bed, ever since he left.

"One stipulation, when you use it, or anything, even your hand; you have to be thinking of me."

My heartbeat catches a little because it sounds so domineering. I like Ty possessive. I like him telling me how he wants things.

"Of course, what else?"

"Are you wearing panties?"

"I am." I can't help but smile. I feel like a naughty kid.

"Slide them off slowly; over your thighs, down your calves, ankles and toes. Hold them up to the phone, so I can see. I want to see if they're wet, if you're wet for me."

You can do this, I tell myself. *You trust him with your secrets and your faults. Let go of your inhibitions. Ty would never belittle you.*

I pull my panties off just like he said. I hold them up to the phone so he can inspect them. Sure enough, they are slick with my arousal.

"Take your top off and slip under the sheets naked," Ty says, carefully. His voice is assertive, self-assured and almost domineering. I like it. I like him like this. I do as he says and slip in naked between the cold sheets. The sensation is exhilarating. My flesh is a plane of reception, hyper vigilant, awaiting Ty's hands, or in his absence, perhaps just his commands.

"Jesenia, my cock is so hard. I'm stroking it now. Let me show you how hard I am, just thinking about you waiting for me, your pussy wet and ready."

I hold my breath when he speaks. My thoughts seem to slow and come into a steady focus. I'm looking at Ty's penis, his strong hand moving up and down it. There's not a lot of light and the image comes across grainy and with a shade of green that's not there in real life, but the effect is mesmerizing, it somehow heightens the mood. I reach out to the bedside lamp and twist the switch between my fingers. I feel delicate and feminine, yet I long to be crushed by him.

My fingers find their way to my nipples and I squeeze them into points. I focus the phone on them but I have no idea if he's even looking or just stroking himself.

"Show me your lips, I want to watch your fingers run through them. Are your nails painted?"

"Red," I say.

"Perfect. Do it."

The image of bright, red nails and soft pink flesh makes me dizzy. Bending up my knees, I toss off the covers. One hand slips to my sensitive flesh and I balance the phone on my knee, aiming the camera to try to give him full view of my wet center.

"Christ, Jesenia. You are perfect. Use two fingers inside. I want to see them slip in and out."

I cry out in pleasure from him talking dirty. I want to tear him apart. Bite him. Punch him. Fuck him and kiss him hard. I want to let him take me brutally. I want him to worship me and hurt me, to love me, to humiliate and bruise me. My thoughts are out of control, but crazy has never felt so good.

"That's right, baby. Fuck yourself good."

I whine and cry out, doing what he says. I drop the phone. I arch my hips in the air as my fingers slip deeper inside me. I can't stop. It's too much, as if the mania and my arousal have joined forces and taken me hostage.

"Jess, can you hear me?"

"I'm going to come. I'm coming!"

"I'm with you. Where do you want me to come? What part of your body?"

"In my mouth. Please? I don't care if you're sick. If your blood is contaminated, then I want to be contaminated with it. Come on my tongue. I want to taste you in my mouth. Slide all the way to the back and come down my throat."

I'm a madwoman. I've never talked dirty in my life. Maybe I'm unhinged, my sanity gone, finally slipped off down the rabbit hole.

"Stick out your tongue but don't stop fucking yourself. I want to unload on your face. On your lips and your tongue. So much that it drips down your chin and your neck—onto your tits."

His voice and words hit the spot, perhaps even better than my fingers. I scream into the dimly lit bedroom, so loud the neighbors will likely think I've been murdered. I bite on my own knuckle to keep from spewing forth curses. I come harder every time with Ty—one of these days I'm bound to hurt myself.

"Jess, are you there? Everything okay?"

"Yes," I whisper. So good."

"I'm gonna grab a towel and pee. I'll call you right back on your house phone."

My head crashes back to the pillow without the weight of all my demons. They were frightened away by my Titan-fueled orgasm—they're now quieter than they've been in three days.

A few minutes later the phone rings.

"Titan."

"You feel any better or should we try again?"

"I'm sleepy. My eyelids feel heavy. Brain is finally quiet."

"Good. I'm going to talk about boring stuff. Construction and accounting, until you fall asleep on the phone."

"You mean the world to me. I already can't imagine a life without you."

"Shhh, baby, I'm here. Now try to sleep before I'm ready for round two."

⚓⚓⚓⚓

"Hey, Jess, I'm glad I caught you."

"Hi, what's up?"

"I don't suppose you checked your email yet this morning?"

"I didn't. Something going on?'

"Well, unbeknownst to me, Luke took it upon himself to invite you and Angie and her fiancé to Thanksgiving up here. That kid of mine, I swear he's not normal. At fifteen you're supposed to be separating from your parents and he's playing matchmaker and setting up dinner parties."

"He loves you, is all, and he's had a slightly different experience from other kids his age. He appreciates family, is all I'm trying to say. It's a good thing. Consider yourself lucky. I'd love to come. I might have to do some juggling with my schedule—run a prerecorded show that Friday, if possible."

"I would love to spend the holidays together." I notice how he says *holidays* and it makes my chest flutter. We're moving forward fast, but we haven't yet lost our footing.

"I don't know about Angie and Andrew, I'll call them and see."

"Seems Luke already did and they RSVP'd."

"Even Andrew?" I ask. It comes out more surprised sounding than I'd intended. I guess we're a blended family now and Andrew will inevitably have to meet Titan. It's unfortunate that he's so close with John. I'm sure it will make Ty uncomfortable and we'll all be wary that he'll report back once he's gone.

"What's wrong with Andrew? Will we not get along?"

"No, I think you would. It's just that he's more or less sided with John. I think I'm on his shit list for stealing Angie that weekend. But it will have to happen sooner or later, so we might as well do it and make the best of the circumstances."

"Anyway, read the email Luke sent, it's a trip. The whole thing rhymes. I swear, he's obsessed with the Van Buren ladies or something. I never taught him poetry—maybe Rory."

"Maybe he just loves his family and he misses his mom. He probably wants to make the holidays memorable, you know, in case he ever has to deal with a loss like that again." We're both silent for a minute. I hear Titan breathe into the phone. The tension is thick and I know I have to ask him. I feel like he would have told me already if he'd gotten good news. "Did they give you the results for the biopsy, Ty, you still haven't told me?"

"Uh, yeah. Inconclusive. Said they need to run some more tests. Getting information out of those guys is like pulling teeth, you know how it goes."

"Tell me as soon as you hear anything, Titan. I'm your partner now and I want to be the first to know."

"Of course, baby. I'll let you know."

I want to say I love you. I want to reach my arms through the distance and pull his head to my chest, to caress his temple. I want to make love to him all night, until we can't anymore. Until our bodies hurt from touching and fall asleep in rebellion. I want to erase the distance between us and the obstacles we face. I want forever with Titan and deep inside, I'm in anguish, terrified that we're already too late for it.

CHAPTER 31

Titan

A million thoughts sweep through my brain in mere seconds, trying to decipher what I'm feeling. My palms are sweaty. My heart is racing. My breaths are shallow and quick. I can't do this alone. I lied to her. I lied to Jess and it has my stomach in knots. I couldn't tell her over the phone. And I didn't want to worry her in the meantime by telling her we'd talk about it in person. In person means a holiday and I refuse to ruin a holiday, especially since I have so few left to celebrate.

They should be here any moment. Dan and his wife are setting the table. Rusty is with the boys in the living room and Edie is with me in the kitchen, prepping food.

"Are you excited or nervous to have them meet us all?" she asks.

I stop cutting potatoes and sigh. "Both," I admit.

"Don't be, Titan. I promise to kick Rusty under the table if he gets unruly and he's the only one you really need to worry about anyway." We both laugh and go back to prepping. She's right. I shouldn't be worried. The family we celebrate Thanksgiving with are friends but friends I've chosen to consider family. They are good, kind people who have supported me and lifted me up in the worst of times. Of course, Jess will like them. I'm more nervous that I have to see her today, knowing that I lied to her. In a way, I've lied to everyone here by not telling them about the biopsy results. Omission is still a lie, right?

I drop the potatoes into the boiling water and wipe my hands on a dish towel. Luke comes bounding into the kitchen. "They just pulled in!" I smile because his excitement is infectious. Edie pats my shoulder and pulls a piece of potato peel off my shirt before telling me now I can answer the door.

Luke swings the door wide and tackle hugs Angie, rambling a thousand, 'I'm so happy you came,' at her. Jess laughs and Andrew gives a half grin. I'm glad that he gets to see how much Luke and Angie get along. It may help him deal with the situation better if he sees how happy his bride-to-be is here.

"You made it." I open my arms and Jess steps into them. She's warm from the car ride. I kiss the top of her head and usher them all in, hugging Angie and shaking Andrew's hand as they enter.

"It smells amazing in here," Angie says.

"We've been at it all morning, so it should." Jess tucks herself under my arm as we enter the living room. A cacophony of hellos and 'nice to meet you!' greet her. "Jess, that is Dillon, Rusty's son, Rusty, Dan and Anna, their daughter Bridget and . . ." I turn us toward Edie, "Rusty's wife, Edie," I finish. Jess says hello to everyone, as do Angie and Andrew. "Alright, what can I get you to drink? Wine, soda, beer or water?"

Edie and I get everyone's drink orders and hand them out, before heading back to the kitchen. Angie pops in and asks if she can help with anything, so I let her mash the potatoes for me.

"How's everything going, Ty?" she asks.

"Really well. I'm glad you could join us today."

"Me, too. This is really cozy and fun. It's much better than our normal Thanksgivings which are cold and formal."

I slide my eyes to her and give her a grin. "We're definitely not formal here." Angie smiles and goes back to mashing.

By the time the turkey is ready, it's after one. Dan, Rusty and the boys are dying to eat so they can catch the game. Our table is packed and there is barely enough room for our plates with all the food out. Jess's hand on my thigh makes my shoulders feel heavy with guilt. I need to tell her. I know that now trumps later every time. I've lived it before, only I wasn't the one dying. Tell the truth now and deal with the fallout. That's what I should have done. We'd get through it, maybe, and have a short future to live out together. The only thing that's real is the present and I'm plundering it. Robbing Jess's future. I squeeze her hand and push the thoughts from my mind so I can focus on this moment.

Jess at my dinner table, sharing a holiday meal with my family, my friends. Plates scrape plates. Jokes are shared. Laughs had. I'm moved by it all. I stand and raise my water glass. The din dies down until it's quiet.

"I need to tell," my voice cracks. I compose myself and try again. "I need to tell you all that I am so grateful for this day. To see you all sitting around this table, making memories." Everyone raises their glasses and clinks circle the table. "Cheers."

By the time we've finished eating, most everyone is in the living room, reclined somehow, watching the football game. It's quiet outside of the game announcers. Luke's pumpkin pie is demolished on the coffee table which makes me smile because he worked hard to make it, so he must be proud that everyone ate it. Bree stopped over and is snuggled between Luke's legs. Everyone seems content. I'm content, yet not. My secret looms over me like a dark shadow; tainting the happiest of moments. I don't know how long I can keep it. I also don't know how I can make the words leave my mouth and destroy lives with its truth.

Jesenia

We're wrapped up in each other's arms. After a glorious meal, happy family and pumpkin pie, which Luke made and was so adorably proud of. Ty drew a warm bath and we soaked indulgently together. The kids were down in front of the fireplace when we left them, Angie and Andrew drinking cognac and Luke and his girlfriend having hot cocoa.

I never knew that life could feel like this, where every moment manages to be somehow better than the next. I'm in pure bliss and my love for this man has permeated every single cell. Every syllable I speak, every breath I take is different and better because of Ty in my life. I no longer hate myself, I no longer feel like I'm just waiting—waiting for life to pass me by or for something bad to happen. Instead, I'm living and in doing so, my universe is expanding. There are so many things I want to do, to see, to conquer with Ty by my side. I want to build our business together, I want to build our dream house. I want to travel and see the world with him. God, I want everything. There's even a part of me that wishes I could give him more children.

He pulls me on top of him and I'm naked under my towel, my skin still flushed with the heat of the bath. He brushes my wet hair back from my face and lays it over my shoulder.

"Ty?"

"MmmmHmmm?"

"I didn't know life could feel like this," I whisper it, almost scared to jinx the beauty, the fragile balance of perfection. Tears run down my face, but they're not tears of sadness.

"I wish we could take the moments and stretch them out forever."

"I want to move in together as soon as the divorce is final. Like have the house sold, my stuff in storage, all ready to go."

Ty is quiet and I take it as hesitation. I'm moving too fast for him or he's not ready to move in with a basket case. It's my disease, I know, that is making this hard. I'm not a contract without conditions, I'm not a hole in one, nor am I cut and dry.

"I don't get manic that often, and after so many years, I'm fluent at handling at. I do have trouble sleeping and I may do a few things that you find crazy."

"I realize all that. It doesn't change how I feel. What's it like when it happens? How do the episodes make you feel, how do they affect you?"

He always surprises me, always makes me stop and think. Ty is unpredictable, he's always more thoughtful than I expect. The way he treats me and how he thinks about the disorder, is so different from how John was, that it takes me a minute to acclimate, to realize he's truly interested in an answer.

"Mania makes me lighter, it makes me quick and strong. I can see things with clarity that were murky before. I have the confidence to make attempts at more unattainable things and the drive to keep trying again and again, ad infinitum. But sometimes it goes too fast or it gets a little askew—that's like heat turning into a burn. Or like looking through a camera lens until the focus is just perfect and then tightening it up more until it's so sharp it starts to hurt."

"Do you like it? Do you ever have sex when you feel like that?"

God, just Ty's curiosity and interest are enough to make me get wet.

"Masturbating with you was the first time I tried it. Except for maybe in the early stages of my marriage. But I was so self-conscious and so ashamed, I did everything I could to suppress it."

"I think we should use it. Explore it and see what happens. Do you feel emotions more intensely? What about physical sensations?"

"Yes. But you should know, it's the same when I'm low. The

depression is severe and my self-esteem non-existent. I don't have the lethargy as bad as some others do, but I get very detached, disinterested in life itself and everything around me."

"I haven't seen you like that yet, but I'm ready for it when it comes. I think we should try sex almost therapeutically with both the highs and the lows. If you're more sensitive, both physically and emotionally, it could be potentially mind-blowing and I think it's something we should try together—that is, if you're up for it."

My heart soars with everything that he says. The emotion is overflowing like hot lava falling into the ocean, there are so many reactions happening inside me at once, that my mind and heart have gone haywire on overload. I kiss him with a fervor and zeal that feel like starvation. His cock reacts against my thigh and my hand immediately grabs it. I want sex like an addict needs another hit. I don't think I can live another minute without this man inside me.

"I didn't think it was possible to fall any more deeply in love with you."

It comes out fluidly with a life of its own; surreptitiously, without my heart asking permission from my mind or my mouth. I freeze and go stiff like a terrified animal. It's my truth, I'm madly in love with Ty, but the problem is, that up until now, neither one of us has yet said it.

CHAPTER 32

Titan

I'm stunned momentarily. Not because I don't feel the same way but because she said the words out loud. Desperation to tell her overwhelms me but this isn't the ideal time. Not after saying those words. She's stiff in my arms. Clearly unsure if she should have let those three little words slip.

I lift her chin until she's looking at me. "I love you, Jess." The words aren't hard to say. I feel no hesitation putting them out there. I want this; I want her. I wrap my arms around her, not caring that our towels fall away. We're flush against each other and my need for her is evident. "I've probably always loved you. It's ridiculous, I know, but there you've been, holding a corner of my heart since the night we met." I scoop an arm down, under her knees and pick her up. It's not far to the bed but I don't want to put her down. I'd hold her forever, if I had the time. Guilt claws at me but I push it away. I revel in the feeling of her swept up in my arms. Of the way she weighs so little and the feeling of her arms clinging to my neck.

"Ty," she whispers. I silence her with a kiss. We don't need words right now. Setting her on the bed gently, I watch as she lies bare for me. She squirms, whether in need or lack of self-esteem, I don't care. I want to look at her. I love her body. I trail a finger from her collarbone downward. Goosebumps break out along the path I've traced. I push her ankles apart, kneel between her legs and lift her hips with my hands. Her entire body shudders when I bring her pussy to my mouth and lick her center. Her knees are hooked over my shoulders. I use one hand to spread her lips wide and I dive in. Licking, gently biting and sucking. I want her to explode. I want her to come undone. I want her. It's simple as that, really. She tastes clean and smells soapy from our bath. I push her bottom up with my palm, bringing her center more firmly to my mouth. Pushing my tongue inside her yields me a groan that I haven't heard before.

Her hands clutch the comforter. It twists in her fingers. I replace my tongue with two fingers and use my mouth to focus on more sensitive areas. When her hips start bucking, I don't slow; instead, I speed up all my movements. She mumbles something about it being too much but I know her body and I know she's wrong, so I continue on with fever. I swing the arm under her rear up and hook it at her pelvis to keep her from thrusting so hard. Flattening my tongue, I run it up the length of her, then nibble on her clit. Jess cries out as she comes. With both hands, I pull her core more firmly to my mouth and slowly bring her down from ecstasy. Tiny earthquakes ripple through her body. Muscles tightening, then going slack. Like little shivers. It drives me wild, knowing I can make her body react that way.

I set her hips down to the bed and open the nightstand drawer for a condom.

"I want you on top, babe," I say handing her the condom. She blinks in rapid succession as I lie on my back, hands tucked under my head, erection standing at attention. She kneels on the bed beside me. Her hair is tousled and wet still. Her face has a glow to it and her eyes are cloudy with desire. She rolls the condom on slowly, no doubt toying with me, but I like it. The feel of her and the deliberation with which she makes her movements, is sensual. She lifts one leg and straddles me, hovering just above my cock. I want to push my hips up and take her, but I don't. I want her to be in control. I want her to own her sexuality; to believe in it.

She sinks down on me slowly. It's torture. Her hand's come to my pecs to steady herself as she lifts up again. I crane my neck upward so I can kiss her. Her kiss is hungry and feverish. She rotates her hips around leisurely and clenches. A moan slips from the back of my throat. "You like that?" she asks. I nod and she does it again. Pulling a hand out from behind my head, I place my palm flat between her breasts and push slightly. The angle is just right. She lets out a breathy cry and starts moving her hips faster, grinding down on me. Her breasts bounce. Her back is arched and she feels so incredible. The sensations coursing through me overwhelm and I come. Her hips grind faster until she squeaks out a sound I've never heard before and collapses onto my chest.

"Oh, God, I'm sorry, did you finish?" she rasps. I chuckle and rub her back in slow circles.

"Yup." It's the only word I can form. We lie in a tangled mass of limbs, silently, and it's perfect.

Jesenia

I'm a grown woman hiding in a closet. What's even worse, is that it's not my own closet, it's Ty's, and he'd think I was insane were he to find me in here. But I've been crying and he's sleeping. No, I've been sobbing. I don't want to. I'm trying to keep it under control, but I've lost it. I couldn't sleep anyway; I was tossing and turning when I heard his phone vibrate with a message. Then the screen lit up, casting a greenish hue all over the room. I ruminated. I thought it could be Luke. Maybe he snuck out and he got hurt. Maybe he needed a ride or a rescue from a sticky situation. I was worried. I could have woken him up. What if it were just his cellular service reminding him how much he had left on his data plan. Maybe it was a family emergency, a distant relative died and they were notifying next of kin. I ran over every single possible scenario in my head.

When the phone buzzed again, I decided to look. Look first and then wake him up only if it were important, information that absolutely could not wait until morning. When I snuck out from under the covers as carefully as possible and tiptoed around his big bed, I did have the inkling that I might be invading his privacy. I'd be lying if I said the thought didn't occur to me. If not, how could I explain doing everything so quietly.

But it wasn't Luke or his family, at least I hope she's not family. It appeared to be something far worse, a problem in which I had no experience dealing.

> HEY, SEXY, I'M OFF ALL THIS WEEK. READY FOR ROUND TWO? I COULD DRIVE UP AND YOU COULD GIVE ME ANOTHER TOUR, LOL!
>
> I GET WET JUST THINKING ABOUT YOU AND THAT PACKAGE UR CARRYING.

Then a winking, yellow smiley face. I'd never seen a smiley face look so threatening. I dropped the phone and clutched my heart like a bad daytime soap opera. I fell to my knees and picked it up again, thinking maybe it was a joke from one of his male friends. But her name was Emily, it was written at the top. I did the worst thing then, I became a snoop. I scrolled through their texts. They know each other well, she's the reporter who wrote the article on him for that magazine. It seems they hooked up. My heart hiccups, then drops like a stone to the ocean floor, hard, fast and straight; a heartbroken deadweight.

I hide like a thief in the dark. Into the closet, right back where I hid my mania so many times from John. I retreat between rows of shoes so that my back is flush with the cold wall and I'm partially hidden by coats. I use his phone to Google images of her. She's beautiful. Of course. She's probably twenty years younger and much better in bed. She's probably funny and smart, ambitious but at the same time, genuine. I hate her. I want to tear out her gorgeous hair and claw at her face. Then I hate myself for feeling that way and I pull my knees to my chest. Face in hands, hands against knees, I cry into oblivion. I don't know what Ty sees in me. He can obviously have anyone he wants. He's obviously had better than me.

I don't know for how many hours I sit there and cower, torturing myself with images of his hands on her, him whispering in her ear. Ty bringing her to orgasm, or even worse, him coming for her. Ty ejaculating on her body like he does on mine, his moan of satisfaction, the weight of him, spent, resting on her. I torture myself so much, that I fear becoming physically sick. I can't puke on Ty's clothes or in his shoes, I've got to get into the bathroom.

My head knocks the shelf above me and boxes tumble down on all sides. It was loud. I squeal and jump back to my hiding spot.

"Jess?" I hear his sleepy voice murmur.

Quiet! Say nothing. He'll fall right back asleep, like a baby.

"Baby? Are you in here?"

I hear him get of bed. He goes to the bathroom. He pees. I'm mortified. He can't catch me hiding in the closet. But I'd die before I'd come out willingly, face swollen from bawling, delirious with jealousy.

He comes out, stands in the middle of the room. Walks toward the bedroom door but probably sees that it's closed.

"Jess, are you in the closet?"

I must have told him my former hiding spot. I'm so embarrassed I could die on the spot. I'm filled up with gallons of humiliation, sprinkled generously with self-doubt.

"No." I say, like I'm four years old. This is it, Jesenia. Say goodbye to your dream future because you just lost yourself a boyfriend. And a best friend. As usual, you fucked up and flushed it all down the toilet. Mental illness wins and you lose the whole game.

He pulls the door open and some light from the bathroom leaks in. I scurry back further, trying to escape my predicament.

Ty always surprised me. John used to feel around with one arm. He'd grab at me, catch any part and drag me out aggressively, always with anger, always with rage. Almost as if he took my shortcomings as an insult to his own character. He'd yank me out and scream at me to act like an adult, scream that I should be ashamed of myself. It wasn't enough that I already was, that I am. Hiding was about me feeling safe, but he never understood that. John never tried to understand, he tried to rid me of it and it never worked.

Ty kneels down and tentatively grabs one of my ankles. His hand whispers its way up my leg and squeezes my knee reassuringly when it gets there. He pulls the door closed behind him with his foot. It's pitch black inside and I can hear only my heart pounding and his breathing. He ducks under the clothing and pulls himself up beside me. Ty can barely fit in the closet, such a strappingly huge man, he is. But soon he's sitting right next to me, feet pulled in, knees bent. He reaches his arm around my back and presses my head into his chest.

His heart is beating hard, too, and I know I have to tell him what I'm upset about, why it is that I'm hiding. If I were more resilient, I could deal with this more eloquently. But instead, I'm a mess.

"It's tight in here," he whispers. "Quiet and dark."

I nod my head and sniffle into his T-shirt. I lift up his phone without looking at it and press it on. I hold it in front of where I think his face is but I can't hold in the sobs.

"Ah. Emily," he says. There is no fear in his voice or any sound of culpability. He doesn't sound angry that I've read it and audaciously invaded his privacy.

"Are you sleeping with her, too?" I ask. I can't keep it together. My heart is breaking when I speak and I'm so terrified of his answer.

"I did once. Before you replied to my letter."

I cry. I cry because he slept with her. I cry because she knows his body, too, and I feel jealous of her. He rubs my head. He massages my neck like only Ty knows how.

He presses a button on his phone and the screen lights up again. He texts with one thumb, never removing his other large, comforting hand from my neck.

> Emily, Happy Holidays! The article looked great! I'm in a very committed relationship now and I'm happy.

"Will you send this for me, Jess?" He passes the phone to me. My hands are shaking and I wipe away the tears, realizing how silly I am. How pitifully insecure I am about myself, and my lover.

"Are you sure?" I ask him, my voice in vibrato with emotion.

"Your heart is part of me, it's the most precious possession that I own. You entrusted it to me and I will guard it and honor it with my life. I won't cheat on you, ever. I shudder at the thought of you thinking I'd want anyone else. We are way beyond dating. This isn't about the sex or hooking up. Twenty years ago, you walked out of a blizzard and into my arms. You were a vision to behold in that green dress. In a little under *an hour,* you'd captured my whole heart.

"Don't, Ty. It's me, I was being unreasonable."

"Shh, just listen to the story."

"Do you know how many times I replayed that moment in my head? Where I was in the bathroom, second guessing my own feelings and you, full of your own doubts, slipped away into the night. You disappeared right before my eyes, like magic. I beat myself up for not running with it, for not telling you the effect you had on me in that moment. I left it up to fate, when I should have been a man and grabbed it with everything I had in me. But back then, I guess, I just didn't have enough."

"You were hurting. I should never have run away and left you alone."

"But that's the way it worked out and we can't change the past. I know your ex-husband didn't do enough to let you know how special you are. I know he didn't make you feel desirable. I'm not him, Jess."

"I know you're not him, I'm sorry."

"You've held my heart as collateral for the last twenty years. I only want you. I couldn't care less about a one night stand before I found you. It's over. It never even got started. Please don't be jealous about something in the past, that I have no control of."

"Okay," I whisper and straddle his lap.

"Okay? Just like that? I mean, I was kind of flattered."

"Shut up," I say and kiss him tenderly on his smart mouth.

"Can we get out of the closet then?" he asks through the kiss.

"I love that you came in here with me. I love everything about you."

"This?" Ty says, pressing his erection to my center.

"Especially that," I say and tip back my head as he nibbles my neck.

"On a serious note, fate has a strong arm and we're blind to its intentions but whatever we have left, whatever it grants us, I plan on using every moment of it and loving you the best that I can."

CHAPTER 33

Titan

My heart is still racing. Emily's text really upset Jess and although I think I've rectified the situation, I know it was a big blow to her confidence.

"Are you real?" she asks. I chuckle and nod my head.

"Can we please get out of the closet now, babe? I'm all bunched up." Jess laughs lightly and helps me out of the closet, since she can maneuver the tight space easily.

Once we're in bed, I pull Jess close. She's warm. My arm is heavy across her waist. Taking my hand, she put it on her breast, as I look at the clock by the bed. It's going to be a rough morning.

"I love you, Titan," her whisper dances slowly across my lips and I grin.

"I love you too, babe." I squeeze her to me and close my eyes.

⚓⚓⚓⚓

At eight, I'm awakened by the smell of bacon and coffee. Jess isn't in bed, so I snag a tee shirt from the floor and head downstairs. Angie, Andrew and Luke are sitting at the dining room table eating a full breakfast. Jess is in the kitchen, at the stove cooking. A pang of grief hits me square in the chest. Seeing her here, in my kitchen, doing normal everyday family things, makes me so happy that I could burst but knowing that this future is short lived, sends my stomach plummeting to the floor. I can't go on like this. I can't lie to Luke, my friends and I especially can't lie to Jess. I have to tell her before she leaves. It will be the best of a shitty situation. She will have Angie and Andrew with her for support.

"Morning, honey," Jess coos when she sees me. *Honey.* I like it. I mosey over to her and kiss her forehead. "Morning."

"There's coffee ready and your breakfast will be up in just a minute," she tells me.

I fix myself a mug of coffee and sit with the kids at the table. "Morning, guys."

Luke grunts through his food and Angie and Andrew say hello. "Did you two sleep alright?" I ask.

"Yes, perfectly. It's so nice here. Quiet and peaceful," Angie says.

"I'm glad you like it. You know you're welcome anytime."

"Ty, do you think we could come to Luke's football game tonight?" Andrew asks.

"You a big football fan, Andrew?"

"I played in high school." I smile at him. Luke beams at me.

"Of course. You are all welcome to join me. It'll be cold, so bundle up," I tell them.

Jess saunters in with two plates. She sets one in front of me and sits down with the other one. "Bon appetite," she says smiling.

⚓⚓⚓⚓

Luke's team won the game, in overtime. It was an incredible game, both teams equally matched. Angie and Andrew are sharing a hot chocolate. They look hilarious wrapped up in scarves and baggy knit hats from the closet chest at home. Jess's cheeks are tinged red, as well as the tip of her nose. I pull her to my chest to warm her up. We're waiting at the locker room exit for Luke.

"Hey, Dad," he says as he makes his way through the crowd.

I let go of Jess to talk to him. "Bud, I need you to skip the dinner tonight and come home with us."

"But I'm supposed to meet Bree." Luke's face is nothing but disappointment.

"It's important," I state. Something flashes in his eyes but I don't have time to dissect it before it vanishes.

"Okay, Dad." I take his duffel bag from him and use my free hand to catch Jess's in mine, as we all head back to the parking lot.

I stop at the convenience store and grab two bottles of wine on the way home. Jess gives me a funny look, but everyone drank the wine that I had yesterday at dinner and I have a feeling she will need a drink tonight. Maybe Angie, too. I'm starting to feel bad for Andrew because he's going to be in the middle of an awkward conversation in just a short while.

We all pile out of our vehicles and into the house. Scarves are unwound. Gloves and mittens shed. Hats tossed on the bench. Coats are hung. It's all perfectly normal. Chit chat and laughter ring out. I feel cold and shaky. A pit forms in my gut. A lump in my throat. I clear it. "Hey," I say. Everyone stops and looks at me.

"Could we all sit in the living room for a minute?" Everyone nods and heads in. Except Luke. He narrows his eyes at me. He knows something's up. I blink a couple times to try and keep my composure. His eyes well up. Luke and I don't need words after what we've been through together. He shakes his head no and lunges at me. Fists pound on my chest. I let him give it all he's got. Angie squeals and rushes to the entry way, followed by Jess and Andrew. I grab Luke's fists and hold them together at my chest with one hand. "It's okay, Buddy," I say to him. My other arm wraps around his back.

"What the hell, Luke!" Angie shouts.

Luke and I sink to the floor together. My breathing goes from rapid to lazy, as we sit piled together. Luke sobs in my chest, clutching my shirt. I hold him tightly to me. I look up to Jess and Angie. I clear my throat again.

"The biopsy . . ." I stammer. There are no words good enough for this situation. "I'm dying," I say. Tears leak from the corners of my eyes as I squeeze Luke to me. "I have liver cancer."

Angie gasps and Andrew tucks her into his side. Jess drops to her knees on the hardwood floors, stunned. Luke pushes away from me.

"How could—?" he shouts. "How could you not tell me?" He scrambles backwards before I can utter a word. Angie reaches out to him but he shrugs her off. He storms out the front door. I leap to my feet to go after him but Andrew's large palm hits my shoulder.

"I think he needs time. Let him go," he says. I turn and wipe the tears from my cheeks and face Jess. I scoop her up under her arms and cradle her to my chest while carrying her to the couch.

"I'm sorry, Jess. I'm so sorry." I repeat my words over and over.

Jesenia

I'm tipsy. No, I'm drunk. Probably more than I have been in a really long time. Angie handed me a glass of wine and I think I drank it in one gulp. She told me her and Andrew were driving back to the City, gave me a hug and then she hugged Ty and cried. She kissed his cheek and it brought tears to his eyes. I stood by in silence and watched and felt number and number by the second. My eyes glassed over and a brain fog completely overtook me. I didn't want to process what I'd just witnessed.

Andrew went into the kitchen and brought me the whole bottle. He set it gingerly next to my wine on Ty's coffee table. He spoke in a low voice to Ty and I already knew Andrew was good, but tonight I saw just how good he truly could be.

"We're going to drive around and look for Luke, we'll bring him to Bree's house for the night. I'll speak to her parents. Angie grabbed his sleeping bag from his room. If Jess needs a ride or you two need anything at all, call Angie's cell and we'll turn around. We can be back here in a matter of hours, at any time. I'm sure you've got your resources figured out, but please, let us know if we can be of any help."

Ty nodded his head, hugged Andrew and slapped him hard on the back. So much emotion between virtual strangers. I fill up the wine glass. Drink it. Refill it.

We are silent when everyone is gone. I can hear the pendulum swing on the grandfather clock in the dining room.

"How long have you known?" I clear my throat when I ask. It comes out almost accusatory and that's not how I mean it. "What are our options?" It sounds clinical, detached, but that's how I feel. I don't feel like myself. This exchange is surreal. I fill up the wine glass again.

"I didn't want it to be the answer. I didn't want to tell the truth. Not to you, especially not to Luke. I wished it away for a while. The guilt was killing me though. Figured I was going to die of a guilty conscious before my liver started to fail me."

"What about the trial?"

"Didn't work. Maybe I got a placebo, who knows."

"What about chemo, is that an option?"

"Palliative only, at this point, Jess."

"What about a transplant? Are you on a list?"

"Hep C patients aren't a priority because it's the blood that's infected and carries the virus. My body would contaminate a healthy liver—just a matter of time."

"What about alternative treatments? We could do research, go to Germany or Mexico, they're always testing new things that haven't been approved here yet. We've got nothing to lose if it's advanced!" I can feel my face making expressions for the first time tonight, like I'm coming back to life at a little glimmer of hope in the distance.

"I don't want to shoot you down, kid, but we tried that path with Rory and it really cut into what we had together as a family. I'd rather spend the little time that we have enjoying each other, not fighting this disease until we're both exhausted and I die anyway. I want to say goodbye. To my son. To you, Jess."

Ty's head falls into his hands and he cries. He's so big and strong. Everything about him seems healthy and robust. I can't believe that he's sick. I can't believe that he's going to leave me.

He looks at me and his expression is so pained, like he's been slaughtered already and cannot fight the battle in front of him. Defeated before it begins. My heart is breaking. I love Ty. We finally found one another and had only gotten a tiny taste of our forever. But fate is so cruel, she's doing it again. I squeeze his hand and we hold hands, staring into one another's eyes. We are cold and clammy, flushed and awkward. What do we say? Where do we go, when there's nothing but a chasm in front of us?

"I can't, in good faith, ask you to stay. I understand completely if you want to go and leave this behind you. It's not what we had planned for being together as a couple. I may not have long at all. Six to eight months is what we're looking at. I love you, Jess, but I won't ask you to stand here and watch me suffer. I know, first hand, how awful that is, and I don't want you to go through it, if you can save yourself from it."

I climb down the couch and tumble into his arms. I drank the whole bottle and what I really want to do is cry, but I can't cry anymore.

"I love you, Ty. It wouldn't be suffering. It would be an

honor for me to stand by your side anytime and anywhere. I never thought I'd see you again. And now here we are. I loved you for twenty years. I can love you for six months. If that's all we have, I won't give it back. I'll take whatever we're given. I'll love you for six days, if that's all we get. I'll love you for six minutes. I'm proud of our love and I would never willingly give it up."

"Jesenia, you cut right through me."

He wraps his big arms around me and kisses my hair. His heart beats hard under mine and my body rises and falls with the rhythm of his breath. He's so alive. Titan. My anchor. My lover.

CHAPTER 34

Titan

I'm starting to lose my mind over Luke. He hasn't called to check in and Angie hasn't called to say they found him. It took a while, but I managed to stop crying. Jess is asleep on the couch. She will no doubt feel like dirt tomorrow morning from the bottle of wine she consumed. I pick her up and carry her to the bedroom where I remove her clothes and tuck her in. I text Rusty to see if Luke showed up over there. Heading back downstairs, I slip on sneakers and grab my keys. Rusty responds that he hasn't seen Luke, he asked Dillon and he hadn't heard from him either. He wants to know what's up, but I ignore his text and leave without responding to him. I snag an extra coat from the closet.

I hop in the truck and start it up. Backing out of the driveway, I turn left and head to the one place not many would think to check or drive by. It takes ten minutes to drive there and in the light cast by the headlights, I can see a small, curled-up form atop the small hill. I park the truck, grab the jacket and head up to him.

He's curled up on his mother's grave. He shivers. I put his coat around him.

"Luke," my voice cracks. He looks up and tears start pouring down his face.

"It's not true, right, Dad?" he asks and my heart shatters. I sit down next to him as he pulls on his coat and leans back against Rory's headstone.

"It is, Buddy. I wish it weren't, but it is and it's bad."

"How much time?" he asks leaning into me.

"Maybe eight months." A sob rips through my boy and I want to make everything better for him, but I can't. I can't change that he will lose both his parents before he graduates high school. I can't change that he will lose both his parents to cancer. I can't change a God damned thing and it eats at me. I squeeze him into my side hard. "Bud, I'm not doing chemo. I want quality of life over quantity. You won't have to watch me go through that. We will live in the house until I need to be in the hospital and once I'm admitted, I'm sure I'll go quickly. It won't be like mom." I kiss the top of his head. "But I need you here with me. I need you to be my son. I want more football games. I want more movie nights and pizza binges. I want you to bring Bree over to hang out so I have time with you and get to know her." I stop because I can't talk anymore. I can't speak over the lump in my throat.

"What about after, Dad?"

"You'll live with Aunt Celia," I say. Rory and I decided a long time ago that if anything happened to us, her sister would take Luke.

"No. I don't want to go there. I don't want to move," he yells at me.

"Luke, we have plenty of time to talk about this. We don't have to have all the answers tonight." He slumps down further into the grass.

"This isn't fair, Dad," he says and wipes tears from his face.

"It sure as hell isn't," I agree. "It's cold out here. Let's go home."

"I miss her," he says and puts a hand on her headstone.

I wrap my arm around him. "I miss her, too, kid, every damn day. She would be so proud of the man you've turned out to be, Luke. You've got to know that. Your mother loved nothing more than you, not even me."

We walk to the truck together in silence. Luke climbs in and I toss him the keys to start it up so he can get warm. Before I get in, I look up to the millions of stars shining in the night sky and say a silent prayer to Rory to help us out with this transition because I sure as shit can't do this alone.

"Do me a favor and text Angie so she knows you're safe, they were out looking for you."

"They were?" he asks.

"Yeah."

"That's really nice. I'm sorry, Dad. I shouldn't—." I interrupt him.

"It's okay, Bud. It's understandable. You did nothing wrong," I say.

Jesenia

I've researched every single thing I can find on Ty's situation. I've spoken to doctors, I even went to a conference. I don't tell him, though. I pretend to respect his wishes, but it's just not in my nature to accept it. I have to fight it. And if that means doing it on my own, I'm okay with that. I will look at every possible angle and try to fight this disease for him, while pretending I'm accepting it. But how do you accept the death of the man you just figured out you're in love with? I can't swap the visions of a dream house with picking out caskets, the hope of a wedding dress with a simple, conservative black dress. So I'll fight silently in my corner and if I figure out a cure or a solution, I'll rescue my lover.

I have done some drastic things to change my life. Angie is taking over the business and I'm now retired. I see Ty every weekend. But this week, I close on the townhouse in Manhattan and I make my way to Fairfield to be close to him. He's getting weaker by the day and Luke needs someone to look after him, he's still a child who needs a parent.

I don't know what I'll do once Ty's gone. I don't know if I'll survive the moment when I have to say goodbye to him. When I was small, my grandmother used to sit me on her knee, "Jesenia," she'd say, "what we put into this world, we're allowed to take out of it. If you do good things, then good things will happen. Remember that always." Then she'd pinch my cheeks and braid my hair. I remember when she died, everything felt so morbid. It was breast cancer and my parents never explained it to me. I thought she took all the good things with her when she left because she always did good things for me. I cried for weeks and then I got angry. She's the only person close to me that I've ever lost. I have no experience with death, but Ty does and Luke does. They know how to plan and Ty is doing an amazing job. He's got Luke's whole life mapped out and every night he writes a journal entry to his son. I don't know how he does it, how he stays so strong. But I'll walk alongside Titan and hold onto his hand. I'll do it, until he can't hold on anymore.

"Ma'am, that's the last of what's going to storage. We've got the van going to Fairfield packed up as well."

"I'll write you the check for the moving today. In Fairfield, I don't want either of the men who live in the house to do any of the lifting."

"I hear you."

"But know that they'll try to, so the movers on that end have to be informed. I know it's not heavy, but I don't want them helping."

"Understood, Ma'am. I'll relay the message."

My heels echo on the hardwood floor, the house stands empty, there's nothing to absorb the sound. I have a lot of memories here but not that many of them are happy. Flashes of Angie running around in stocking feet as a kid, helping with homework, giving her baths, measuring her growth on the wall in the kitchen. Most of the others are with Titan. When I first saw his face on the television screen and learned that he was looking for me. Showing up at my door in jeans that night when he first came to visit me, barely leaving the bed or the shower. Falling into bed exhausted after all of the thoughtful New York things he made me do with him. How he devoured me with kisses and how it felt to wake up in his arms. I shut it down because I refuse to think about it like it's over. I still have new memories to make with Titan.

Grabbing my purse and small rolling suitcase, I open the front door. I take one last look back in the hallway and slip my sunglasses back on.

"Mrs. Van Buren! Will you give us a statement? Is it true you left the senator for your true love? Has he really been diagnosed with cancer? How does it feel to be part of this year's most romantic viral story? Is he seeking treatment? Is it true you're moving in with him?" The questions come at me like a firestorm. I'm not prepared for this. I should have realized the moving vans would attract some attention.

I yank my purse over my shoulder and tug my suitcase, bumping down the stairs. I parked the Volvo at least four blocks away. I wish we had a garage.

"Mrs. Van Buren, can we get a statement on camera? Has the senator contested the divorce? Is it true you cheated on him?"

"No! I never cheated on him. I mean—oh, none of your business!" I didn't mean to speak out loud. But I never cheated on John. I wasn't with Ty until John and I were separated. I walk briskly away, yanking the stupid suitcase behind me. The flashbulb mob follows close behind. I'll never shake them, even if I start running. I turn to face them and consider giving them a statement. I promised John I wouldn't talk to them but I don't see any easy way out of this.

"Did you leave the podcast? Did you give the business to your daughter? Are you under a gag-order, Mrs. Van Buren?"

"No! I'm just—I'd like some privacy, please."

"Jesenia!" I'd recognize that authoritative voice anywhere. I thought the town car with the tinted windows that was slinking along beside us had come with the reporters. Turns out, it's the senator. He lowers the window and glowers at me with his ice cold blue eyes.

"Jess, get in the car!" he barks before rolling the window up.

I don't have a choice. I'm about to get trampled by reporters. It starts to rain. I run to the car. A secret service agent steps out from each side and come to my aid, one takes my suitcase, the other has an umbrella and shields me from both the rain and the onslaught of the paparazzi.

The interior of the car smells like money. John is dressed impeccably, as usual. He gives me a condescending smile and gestures to the mob, raising one eyebrow at me.

"Thank you," I say quickly.

"You're welcome. What was your plan back there? Just curious."

"Outrun them."

"Listen, I don't want to take up any of your time. Where are you headed, we'll drop you off."

"Uh, Stanton St. between Norfolk and Essex, on the Lower East Side, right off of Houston."

"What are you doing there?"

"None of your business."

"Look, I'll make this quick and painless. My campaign manager doesn't want you moving in with him until the divorce is final. We're almost there with the paperwork, it's just a matter of getting a rush job with the court date."

"I'm moving in with him tonight, John. We don't have much time left."

"Right, I heard about the cancer. So the only other option is for you to go public with the story. The media might have more sympathy, if they knew he was dying. I look like the martyr but still retain my image. I'm dating an actress. I'm sure you've heard of her."

"That is entirely up to Titan. I won't make him do anything he doesn't want to. I spoke with my lawyer, John, and told him to work around the divorce proceedings—this is more important to me. If you want everything—take it. I've got enough for retirement with the accessories line. I'll be fine."

I'm counting the seconds until we make the turn onto Houston.

"Don't lose your head over some boyfriend, and screw your whole future. You're a sick woman. What happens when he dies? You can't really expect Angie to pick up the pieces. You've sold the house now. Essentially, you're homeless. I'm just supposed to stand by and watch you make terrible decisions until you destroy what little is left of your life?"

"That's it right there," I yell, leaning toward the driver.

"On the right side, Mrs. Van Buren?"

It's Clyde, we've known each other for years. He helped me pick Angelina up from school and from her piano and dance lessons.

"Yes, Clyde, with the fluorescent sign. Right there, number 127."

"You're looking lovely these days, Mrs. Van Buren, if I may say so, better than ever."

"Oh, thanks so much, Clyde. What a pleasure to see you again!" I lean all the way and crane my neck through the divide so I can kiss his cheek.

"Getting ink, today? I've got one right here. Best present I ever gave myself," Clyde says patting his bicep.

I grab my purse and the secret service man on my side opens the door for me. John looks up from his phone, his eyes still steely.

"*Hardcore Tattoos?* You've got to be kidding me?"

"I've got to go, I have an appointment. I'm moving in later tonight, John. You can speak to my lawyers."

"What if I flinch or jump when the needle goes in?"

"I'll be holding your arm down, you don't have to worry about it."

Royal is a burly man with a long beard and a leather jacket covered in patches. He's got tattoos on every inch of him, including his knuckles. Inky images crawl out of his shirt and all the way up his neck, stopping flush with his jawbone. He apparently likes scary things, demons and devils from the deep, skulls, daggers and flames. His face holds no ink but some impressive piercings I can't take my eyes off of. The skin is stretched and the holes are so huge.

I close my eyes when I hear the loud buzz of the needle. My muscles feel tense and ready to spring forth like a racehorse. It hits and the pain is milder than I'd imagined. It's a sweet burn that stings but I don't even have to squirm like I'd imagined I would.

"If you breathe, the pain is minimal. Holding your breath like that will get you nowhere, except passed out on the floor." He slams his steel-toed boot down. I jump a little in my seat, but his plastic gloved hand is in the air, not filling in the anchor on the inside of my wrist. "It's possible that it's going to swell and bruise on you, Miss Buren."

"Van Buren. But call me Jess, please."

"No way? Jesenia Van Buren? What a trip!"

"You've heard of my husband, I guess?"

"Well, shit. That and you're all over the news. The Craigslist romance of the century. The handsome black guy. Sorry to hear about the cancer. If that ain't cruel irony, then I don't know what is."

"Thank you. Yes, a lot of coverage on our story, although I'm not sure it warrants it. We're just two regular people in love."

"Yeah, but wait until I tell Wendy, she's gonna flip. You think I could get a picture with you for my wife? I mean, I've been paying attention to the news because I have to, she doesn't stop talking about it. Wendy is maybe the biggest fan of your show in the universe. All of the guys make fun of me when they come over. We're a bunch of bikers but we got a sign over the bathroom door that says W.C. Water Closet. They never let me live it down. Jesenia Van Buren. What a riot!"

"Indoor Stencils and Homemade Signs, episode 82."

"She is going to love it. Seriously. For my wife, meeting you is better than Elvis."

It's starting to burn more as he fills in the shape he's made with the black contour lines. I squirm just a little and clamp down on my teeth.

"Is this for him, the guy? What his name, Tyson, right? Is the ink for your man?"

"Titan," I say. I nod at Royal and a surge of heat flushes through my heart. *My man.* The one I want to be anchored to for life.

CHAP TER 35

Titan

"Whoa! Slow down," I say, scared I won't get to live out my remaining months. Luke's in driver's ed class and we're practicing his skills every day. I *will* see him get his license. Maybe. If he slows the hell down. I'm white knuckling the handle by the window currently.

I've tried to keep my emotions in check lately. I managed to tell Rusty, Dan and family what's going on, without tearing up, which I thought was a big deal. I've been to my lawyer to make some alterations to my will and estate. I contacted the Hepatitis C Virus World Community Advisory Board about becoming a donor. Organ donations to the non-infected have been done, but now, as a general guideline, they transplant from positive donor to positive patient to avoid complications. They say as long as the cancer doesn't metastasize, I can donate what organs are cancer free.

Luke and I have resumed our sessions with the family counselor to help us get through this and Jess is moving in with me. I wouldn't admit this to anyone, but I have a mental bucket list going. See Luke get his driver's license, live with Jess, spend a weekend on the boat, take Jess to Hope's, go camping one last time with the boys, to make this Christmas epic. Small things that all involve time spent with loved ones. I'm livid I'm being taken away from Luke and Jess and frustrated that the wellbeing of both of them is out of my hands when I pass. But another part of me is calm. Another part of me just wants to spend this time with the people I care about.

I've temporarily handed over the reins of Titan Custom Home Builders to Rusty and Dan as long as they keep the business running a percentage of company profits will go into to an account for Luke. It won't be enough to live on but it will lessen the stress of supporting himself after the life insurance runs out.

Luke pulls up next to a parked car. "Okay, so I cut the wheel first, right?" he asks.

I laugh because we've tried parallel parking at least ten times today and not once has he been able to nail it. "Yes. You know the drill." I look out my window as he inches backward. This won't be the time he nails it either. He's already too wide. I keep my mouth shut though and let him do this on his own.

Luke slams his hands on the steering wheel. "Why do I have to know this? I mean no one ever has to parallel park here."

"Because in the event that you leave this town, you will have to know," I tell him. "I think it's time to call it quits for today, Bud."

"Can I drive us home?" he asks. I nod and grip the handle again as he pulls back onto the road.

"Stop at the store so we can pick up some things for Jess," I tell him.

Jesenia

"I'm here!" I call out after the exhausting drive. My wrist is wrapped in saran wrap and sealed with masking tape. If John could see me now, he'd be appalled, the thought makes me grin.

I put a bag of groceries down on the counter with my keys. I picked up bars for Luke after practice and some new protein powders for Ty, I'm going to make him start drinking smoothies to keep his strength up. But as far advanced as the doctor says he is, Ty seems remarkably resilient—either that or he just tries very hard to hide it from me.

"Hey, kiddo," I say, walking into the living room and kissing Luke on the head. He's absorbed in his homework and wearing headphones, listening to music.

"Where's your dad?"

"Upstairs, doing the journal thing. He's writing about sex and I told him he could talk to me about it, I'm sixteen. But he says he's got to write it all down, he's driving me nuts."

"Luke, I get the feeling this isn't about the diagnosis. He'd avoid this topic, even if he weren't sick. Ask Angie anything you want to. She's really open about sex. I'd help you out if I could, but I don't want to step on your dad's feet. Let him write it, it will be something you'll treasure later on."

"Are you here for good now?" Luke asks me. He's got dark circles around his eyes. But he still seems so hopeful. The pain he'll have to endure, yet again, just kills me.

"I closed on the house, so now you guys are stuck with me."

Luke smiles and suddenly yells, "Jess is here!"

"I guess I'll go help him out with his research."

"Gross! God, you guys are hopeless."

When I walk into the bedroom, Ty is stretched out on the bed, he's still clad in his work clothes, pen tip in his mouth, reading glasses perched on his head.

"Luke said you were writing about the birds and the bees."

"Come over here," Ty says. I cross the room and he tugs me onto the bed. I curl into his side and breathe in his scent.

"Where are we at?"

"I'm working on the technical stuff like verbalizing and consent. It's in the news so much at all of the colleges. There are rules that you've got be aware of—stuff that didn't even exist when we were growing up."

"Don't look so concerned. It's great that you're doing this. But you raised a very sweet and conscientious young man. I don't see him as capable of ever disrespecting anyone."

"I know. I just feel desperate to cover it all before it's too late."

"I'll be here for Luke. So will Angie. We both know how women should be treated. Besides, Ty, you've modeled behavior for him his whole life."

"He's driving."

"Yeah?"

"Terribly, but still—the permit's a done deal."

"I know you need to do all of these things so that you can find some peace and closure. I do understand. But I can't help but feel that it's bringing us closer to the end."

"We are moving closer to the end. We're not going toward the beginning. You never know how much time you'll have left in life, with anyone."

"I know you're right, but I don't have to like it." Ty kisses me and tucks my body into his. I reach up and take the glasses off his head and toss them onto the bedside table. Ty catches my arm on its way back. He jerks it to him and sits up fast. I smile at him through tears and yank my white cowl neck sweater up over my head.

I offer him the inside of my wrist and he takes it in his hands. Carefully he pulls back the masking tape and lifts the saran wrap. I almost turn away at the sight of what must be blood mixed with ink and maybe some pus, swimming nauseatingly over what truly is, underneath, a beautiful anchor. Ty looks at it adoringly and then looks at me in wonder.

"Did you go to a safe place, sterile and all?" he asks. I nod my head, I know how concerned he is about clean needles. "Did it hurt?"

"Not a much as I expected," I say. My fingers find their way to his anchor tattoo, I run them over the ink that covers his wrist; I can feel the blood pumping in his veins underneath my fingertips. Blood that's his life force but that's also killing him.

"Oh, that reminds me," Ty says, grabbing his notebook. He scribbles down the word, tattoos, under the paragraph he'd been writing. He then tapes mine back up. "Tomorrow we wash it."

"Why don't you go spend some time with Luke. I'll make his lunch for tomorrow and clean up the dinner dishes."

"What about you?"

"I live here now. I'm not going anywhere."

"Okay, but first I need to taste this dangerous, tattooed lady."

He rolls me under him. Titan may be sick, but his libido is healthy.

CHAPTER 36

Titan

We are hauling in our Christmas tree. Luke and I really razzed Jess over the length of time she took to pick one out but she said it had to be perfect. It's been a few weeks since she's moved in and for the most part, everything is wonderful. She has cute habits that I didn't know about before. Like the way she stands when she brushes her teeth, one arm behind her back, like she's a captain. Or the way she has to have music on in the kitchen. She swings her hips whenever she's cooking. While watching TV, she twirls one clump of hair repeatedly. All these things are endearing and intimate.

"Let me help, Titan," Jess says trying to nudge me out of the way. I shake my head no and continue carrying the tree inside. She positions the stand under it before we set the trunk in and then we hold it straight while she screws the knobs tight.

"Can I go over to Bree's now?" Luke asks as soon as the tree is standing upright on its own.

"Sure, Buddy, be home by ten, though." He hugs me, then

Jess, and trots out the door. I thought maybe having Jess live here would make Luke uncomfortable but so far, he seems fine with it.

Snow falls quietly outside. The first snow of the year. It's beautiful and makes me wonder how many winters I complained about it, rather than stood in awe of it. It falls softly just barely covering the grass and road. It's clean and unblemished and has this static smell about it. I leave the view from the window and head to the garage to pull the ornament box with the tree lights from the top shelf.

"Let me carry that," Jess says. I carry it to the kitchen and slam the box down on the island. I'm sick of being treated like an invalid. I'm sick of the special treatment. It's not how I want to spend my days.

"Dammit, Jess, you've got to stop!" My voice booms.

She steps back. Her shoulders slump and she looks at her feet. I feel like a jerk for yelling at her. I walk to her and put my arms around her. "You're not here to watch me die. You're here to watch me live. To live with me. You've got to stop treating me with kid gloves. I'm not an invalid, okay?" She looks up, tears fill her eyes. I've never yelled at her before and I feel like a schmuck. "I'm sorry I yelled." I lean down and kiss her.

"I guess all couples have a spat once in a while," she says.

"You know what that means right?"

She tilts her head and narrows her eyes at me. "What?"

"Make-up sex?" I try. Jess bursts out laughing and I follow suit.

She twists out of my hold and grabs the Christmas box. "Come on, stud, let's get these lights up."

I smack her rear as she goes and she jolts. "A guy can try, can't he?"

⚓⚓⚓⚓

The lights are up. They cast a dewy glow throughout the room. I love this moment, when the tree is up and lit but no ornaments hang yet. If I squint, the whole room turns into a prism of light. Jess is curled into me on the couch, sipping a glass of wine.

"When do you decorate?" she asks.

"Christmas Eve usually. There's no real reason except we just always have. We play Christmas music and hang all the ornaments. When Luke was little and went down for his nap, we'd put out all the extended family gifts and before bed that night, he was allowed to open one gift."

"What else do you do for traditions?"

"Well, a couple nights before Christmas, I used to rig up bells to a string outside his window. And when Rory would put him to bed, every so often I would pull the string. The bells would jingle outside his window and Luke would shoot straight up—even if he were almost asleep—asking, Did you hear that? Did you hear that?!" I laugh because the memory is so close to my heart. "We really went to town on the holidays around here."

"You're wicked!" Jess says and playfully slaps my chest.

"It was great when he still believed. And we kept him believing longer than most. It was only around twelve when he finally caught on to me."

"That's great. Luke had a great childhood."

I nod. "He did."

"What about you? How have you celebrated? What are your traditions?" I ask.

"Growing up, my parents always did the anti-Christmas. We went to Miami or Palm Springs. Palm trees and a pink or white tinseled tree in some condo rental or swanky hotel. My parents would drink cocktails and plop me in front of *A White Christmas* or *Miracle on 34th Street* on television. Those were the times of year when I'd wish for a sibling more than anything else. My mother didn't cook, couldn't really be bothered to decorate. That may be part of why I became so obsessed with those things."

"So all your crafting is completely self-taught? That's

impressive. You and Angie have a reputation that's up there with the best in the business."

"Well, I read books, watched Julia and later Martha, religiously. The Joy of Cooking was my bedside book instead of fiction and I was the first one in line when they opened the Home Depot in Manhattan. It was, for me, a convenient escape mechanism. John never wanted me to work because he thought me mentally fragile, so I had a ton of time and a daughter who shared an intense passion for creating."

"Having a love for something is one thing, but turning it into a successful business is another skill entirely. You're pretty amazing, Jesenia Van Buren."

"Ever since she was small, Angie and I went berserk during the holidays. We pillaged other cultures' traditions and made decorations the likes of which our neighborhood had never seen before. A couple of times, the town house was featured in magazines. We did three trees every year in the City and a huge one at the house upstate. An outdoor light display on both houses that took weeks to create. We did a British Christmas once and came up with a Charles Dickens theme. We had a goose, made fig pudding and even roasted chestnuts. John thought we were crazy. Another year, we did a Swedish one and Angie dressed as Lucia with real candles on her head. It's my favorite time of year, Ty. I can't wait to spend it with you and Luke. If you won't kill me, I might do some decorations around the house *before* Christmas Eve."

"You can decorate the house anyway you'd like, we only save the tree decorating for Christmas Eve," I tell her. She smiles and nuzzles into my side a little more.

Jesenia

It's almost Christmas. Ty is still with us. He's fighting hard, but little things are changing. We don't talk about them, mention them out loud, but both of us notice and commiserate in silence with guarded, furtive looks. He gets winded easily and is always tired. All of the jeans he looks so good in, don't quite fit his hips the same way anymore. I bought him a belt. I cried when I bought it, tried even harder not to cry when I gave it to him. He used to gobble up my meals with enthusiasm, complimenting every bite and asking for seconds. Now he eats less than I do and I can tell he feels sheepish when I ask him if he's full already. His coloring looks different, just enough for those close to him to notice. I notice. I notice every little change and I resent all of them.

If it were up to me, we would go out with guns blazing—try every new method, swallow every trial antidote. But it's not up to me and I have to respect his wishes. Ty wants to enjoy what's left, so that's what we do, we enjoy it. We love one another the very best we know how and we wait for the final bell to ring, for God to reclaim his soul.

And it's remarkable how much fun we manage to have, how much sex and love and intimacy we can cram into every evening. How much we uncover about one another by telling stories of our pasts, remembering our adventures from childhood. We talk about the future sometimes, too. We see it as a bright place, where I continue to love Luke and support him as much as I can. Where I spend more time with Angie and Andrew and at Ty's insistence, I pick back up with my crafting and maybe rejoin the podcast. It doesn't seem terrible when Ty describes it, but it's a future I don't want, one I'd sacrifice anything to not have to face. A future without Ty seems to me a very frightening, broken and cloudy place.

"What time do Angie and Andrew arrive?"

"They'll be here before dark for sure. Angie's got it in her head that she wants to go caroling."

"I might have to pull out the cancer card on that one," Ty says smiling. He takes a sip of his coffee and shakes his head sheepishly.

"Oh, I don't know if you can get out of it. She talked to Luke and he found a group from school that's going. He said he's up for it."

"Alright, alright. Don't want to be Scrooge. Did you make that list of last minute groceries? I can swing by after work."

"You don't have to go in if you're not feeling up for it. Rusty and Dan have everything under control, I know they can manage—you said so yourself."

"It helps me to feel useful. I can't just sit around and wait." He runs his hands through his closely cropped hair. There's more grey at the sides now. Streaks so perfectly placed they make him look like he should model for a menswear catalogue, distinguished, elegant, but still rugged in his Carhartt work pants. I walk over to him, twisting my hands in my apron. I've got two loaves of homemade bread rising under tea towels on the counter. I don't know what to say and I know my expression is pained. I don't want him to stress. I don't want him to overexert himself. I just want to preserve him. I know he hates it when I act like he's fragile.

"Did you do this?" he asks, a smile reanimating his face.

I nod in silence. He's pointing to the mistletoe I hung up on the arch in the kitchen that leads to a small mudroom, a door, the back yard and the driveway. It's the entry we all always use, as if the front door never existed.

"Are you going to kiss me under here or what?"

I rush into his arms and he kisses me long, deep and hard. I throw my hands around his neck and he lifts me off the ground.

"I promise to stop working when I can't anymore. I'll stay home and let you take care of me. But for now, just let me make sure everything is in order. Luke deserves that."

"I know," I say nodding. I think the hardest part of our relationship is that Ty accepts dying. He accepts the disease, he doesn't believe he's been robbed. He thinks all of this is atonement for the damned car accident in his past. Sometimes I want to remind him that he was under legal limit—that he wasn't drunk driving, that he doesn't have to carry with him the blame he holds onto. But Ty has lost people he loved and his mind is already made up about it.

"Where's my list?" he asks, smacking me playfully on the rear. I hand him the paper. "Call me at work if you think of anything else you need. Edie left a message that she's doing potatoes, both kinds and call her if you want her to bring another pie—I don't know, it's on the machine, you can listen to it."

⚓⚓⚓

Angie and Andrew bustle through the door, covered in snow. It's practically a whiteout, so there's no doubt we'll get a beautiful Christmas. Ty is in the kitchen dealing with the meat. We're doing both ham and turkey for tomorrow to satisfy everyone's needs. Luke is used to a ham and Angie grew up with turkey. This is how blended families manage—twice the food and twice the work preparing it.

Hugs are genuine and the kids are happy to be together. Andrew decides to help Ty, while I go hang out with Angie and Luke in the living room. Luke has a box of ornaments out and he's filling the tree. Angie is untangling lights, she looks up at me when I walk into the room. Hey eyes are wide and she gestures with her head toward the kitchen.

"How is he?" she mouths, barely making any sound.

"Okay. He's tired. His good counts are low and the bad counts are high. But I'm lucky if he even updates me, let alone shows me the tests results."

"Jess, let's not get into it. It'll ruin his Christmas," Luke says. His eyes are pleading with me.

"He doesn't want to be treated any differently, that's the main thing." I tell her and Luke nods his head solemnly.

"Ty, you lazy brute, get your ass in here and help me with these tangled lights!" Angie screams in the direction of the kitchen. "Like that?" she asks Luke, smiling.

"Oh, my God, I love you, Angie. You just made my Christmas and my whole life," Luke says, grinning.

Ty pokes his head around, peeking in at us.

"Somebody need me?" he asks.

"Yeah, next time, could you maybe splurge more than the dollar store? You've got the shittiest lights I've ever seen and your family is weird and apparently sucks at Christmas because this should have been done like a minimum of three weeks ago!"

Ty is smiling like he couldn't be more amused. Andrew walks in and looks disapprovingly at his wife to be.

"So you want me to hang them?" Ty asks.

"Yeah, I want you to hang them. What do I look like, your building superintendent? Get to work! These ones go around the fireplace." Angie tosses the lights at Titan's feet while Andrew looks on in shock.

"Like that, Luke?" Angie whispers as she saunters over to the couch. Luke's got his hand to his mouth, barely containing his laughter.

⚓⚓⚓⚓

Christmas dinner is a feast, the likes of which I've never seen before, Rusty and Dan and their kids, and our little family of five, but we've got enough food to feed the block, if not the whole town. We gathered at noon and we were seated at the table by four.

"The table looks like it should be in a magazine, you've really outdone yourself," Edie says, admiring the décor.

"Probably was," Luke garbles with his mouth full, "That's what the Van Buren ladies are famous for."

Angie and I planned it all out on Pinterest, like the decorating nerds we are. I wanted it to be perfect, a memory that Luke would always have, his last Christmas with his father. A blue spruce centerpiece, intertwined with birch bark and red berries, silver and gold glittering pillar candles. Candy cane bark fudge truffles at each place setting Angie made and hand packaged at home. We combined some of Rory's decorations that Luke knows from childhood. Not just the table, the whole house looks magical. I almost choke on my food, thinking that this time next year, Ty most likely won't be here with us.

We eat until we can no longer hold anything in. The boys want to play football and boast and brag that they aren't deterred by the snow. Anna and Edie offer to help with dishes and we begin to clear the huge table, dropping down the extra wings as we go. I didn't know if we could make it, so many people squished around an ancient oak table that belonged to Ty's grandmother. But we managed it just fine and the tight squeeze only added to the ambiance.

"How are you holding up?" Edie asks me. She warmly rubs my back through the sweater I'm wearing.

"Okay. It's hard to live your life like every moment matters. Exhausting actually, then you beat yourself up when something doesn't go as planned or doesn't live up to how you'd imagined it."

"You're doing an amazing job," Anna pipes in.

"And Ty is stubborn, he's always been. That's just him. He wants to be a man for you, protect you, even though the symptoms are starting to show. Just let him take care of you, it's what he wants more than anything else."

We load the dishwasher and put away the leftovers. The noise coming from the backyard sounds more like a snowball fight with tackling than a light game of touch football. A snowball hits the window with a loud thump and we start.

"Is Angie playing, too?" Anna asks.

"No, believe it or not, she and Andrew went caroling, they found a group going from a nearby church."

"That's such a fun idea!" Edie says, pulling on her boots. Anna throws on a puffy white coat and pulls a red hat with a huge pompom on her head. "Are you coming out, Jess? We might take a stroll around the neighborhood, just to make some room for pie. I volunteer to whip the cream as soon as we get in."

"I'll be out in a minute, I just want to warm the pies a bit. Thanks for all the help. It would have taken me twice as long without you."

I'm drying a ceramic gravy boat with a towel when I hear a yelp and commotion that sounds like someone got hurt. I wipe my hands on my apron and rush to the back door. Ty is charging away from the group looking distraught. He's holding one hand in the other. I rush out the door in my socks and don't even notice until I hit the landing.

"What happened?" I ask.

"I'm fine," Ty growls at me. Then he looks over his shoulder and yells, "I'm fine!" at all of his friends, but sounding far from it.

I step out of his way as he charges past me into the house. He goes to the sink and frantically starts washing his wrist. It's cut, maybe on ice but from where I am standing, it doesn't look too bad. At least not an emergency room trip to the hospital on Christmas Day. I rush over to him, grabbing a towel from the drawer.

"Stay away, there's blood."

"Oh, for crying out loud, Titan, it's not that contagious!" I ignore his requests and stand right next to him, reaching my hands into the sink.

"I said I'm fine, now stay back!" Titan booms in his loudest voice. I drop the towel and step away, my hands coming to cross over my chest. Tears stream down my face; I've never seen him so angry.

"I'm sorry, Jess. Jesus! I'm sorry," Ty says. He throws the towel into the sink and begins walking toward me. He grabs me around the waist and presses his face into my neck. "I'm weak. I can feel it, it's starting. I'm going downhill and there's nothing I can do to stop it. I feel so fucking helpless and I hate it."

His anger is monstrous, like he might snap in an instant. I rub his head and neck, bring my hands to press against his chest. He's no longer worried about the blood or even the injury.

Then, suddenly, he's all over me, like a reckless fire spreading out of control, his hands splayed across my back, his mouth devouring my neck, biting, sucking and licking. His anger and desperation morph into passion. He touches my breasts through my sweater and I can't help but glance at the door. Then his hands are on my ass and he's shoving his tongue into my mouth.

"I want to forget, help me forget, baby," he says, between kisses. We're mixing blood and tears, and it's just like how fear and hope are both converging in on us. He pushes me back until I'm up against the wall. One hand goes between my legs and the other holds my chin steady while he forces his heavy, unraveled kisses into my mouth.

"Let's go upstairs," I say. Warmth is already running its way through me, a fire trail of lust and sorrow, of defeat, of true love and ruin. I'm turned on by his desperation, by his raw, savage pain that's both physical and existential. It's tragic, yet somehow it's so beautiful. I don't recognize this woman who leaves her own dinner guests for sex, she's a stranger to me, but whoever she is, I kind of respect her. The senator would be mortified if he knew of the vixen and lover his ex-wife has turned into.

We rush up the stairs, our bodies crashing into walls and railings, yet softening against one another. He's pawing at my clothes and getting them partway off of my body. We're leaving behind a trail of garments as we make our way to the bed.

"Ty," I breathe into his kisses.

"Make love to me."

Then we're naked and rolling in the bed. He's hard in all the places I'm soft and his body looks anything but sick. Ty is virile, he's passionate, he's as alive as any man can get. I slide down beside him and lick up his thick length. Taking him in my mouth, I savor the feeling of his flesh against my tongue, I savor his taste. He grabs his shaft at the base and guides himself into my mouth.

"I'm not going to last like this," he says. I'm not sure if he's speaking about ejaculation or his emotional state.

Ty grabs a condom from the drawer and I help him roll it on. His cock is rock hard, the veins pulsing, balls cinching in anticipation. If this is sick Titan, I can't imagine what he would have been like in his prime. He shoves me back onto the bed, straddles me and hovers just over my hips.

His cock is thick and engorged, all of the muscles in his body flexed, his chest is heaving and his nostrils flared, his fingers balled in fists. He leans down and kisses me brutally, once again holding my chin in place.

"Don't scream too loud when you come, I think I just heard them come in." He says it with a smile, like a mischievous boy with his hand in the cookie jar.

He uses one hand to steady himself and with the other, he spreads my own lubricant up and down my folds. I grind into his fingers, desperate for him to enter me. He does, in one slow thrust that nearly undoes me; I move my hips to meet him stroke for stroke. Arching my back as the pressure builds, it all starts to become too much. Ty's fingers crawl up to my throat, his thumb hesitating against my jugular. His fingers caress my jaw and then he quickly ducks his fingers into my mouth. I desperately try to suck as he pulls them in and out. My own fingers answer the pulsing throb in my clit. I arch into his body and whimper as the orgasm fast approaches. I'm undone, he's undone, our bodies frantically syncing with the rapid beating of hearts, the wild thoughts in our heads. Our union feels crucial, dangerous even, as we furiously reject that any one of these times could be our last.

"As long as I can do this, I won't feel like I'm failing. I love making you come. I can't, I won't ever get enough of it."

His words are too much and I tumble into climax. I want to hold Ty to my heart, to bind him, to memorize him; I never want to let go of him. My muscles contract and spasm until the orgasm shatters through me. I cry out anyway, despite guests, despite Christmas; I've got no control over it. Ty tears the condom off and ejaculates in hot ribbons of come onto the swell of my belly, the valley of my hip. We are both breathing hard, our faces stained with tears. There's blood on the white sheets. The weight between us is so heavy, so loaded, neither of us have strength enough to bear it. He falls on top of me and we're sweaty and spent; so emotionally drained.

"Merry Christmas," Ty whispers into my ear.

"You are the very best present a girl could ever hope for," I whisper back into his ear.

CHAPTER 37

Titan

I watch from the side of the house as Luke carefully makes his way up the driveway. As soon as he's close enough, I launch my snowball at him. It pelts him right in the chin. He grunts and cries out while looking around. "You're going down, old man!" I watch as he squats and scoops snow into his hands. When he stands, I step out from the side of the house and launch another snowball at him. I miss but only because he ducks.

Another one soars through the air and hits me square in the chest. Luke does a little victory dance, which is stupid because he's distracted and I'm able to pelt him twice before he can retaliate.

We're laughing, hard. White puffs of air cloud the space around each of us. The front door opens and Jess pokes her head out. "What's going on out here?" she asks. Luke looks at me, his eyes alight with mischief. I grin back and we both turn to the door and throw snowballs at it. Jess screams and ducks. I turn to Luke and double over laughing. Snowballs start exploding on the ground around us. Luke and I look up and Jess is armed and ready to retaliate.

"Oh, shit!" Luke cries out. I should scold him for his language but I'm equally stunned at Jess's reaction. Luke and I split up, each diving behind snow plow mounds along the driveway. Jess creeps along the side of the house. She's so slight, I can't see her behind the snow pile. I'm concentrating on listening for snow crunching under her feet when I hear Luke squeal. I pop up from my spot, slightly out of breath from exertion and see Jess on top of Luke, white washing him. She tackled him. I can't stop the laugh that bellows out of me. Her head whips in my direction. "You're next!" she shouts, with a smile on her face.

⚓⚓⚓⚓

"You're sure you're okay with this?" I ask Luke.

Luke raises an eyebrow at me. "Yeah Dad."

"And Bree's parents are okay with you going over there until midnight?"

"Yes, Dad," Luke says and rolls his eyes.

"And Bree will give you a ride to Rusty's right after, yeah?" I ask.

"Oh, my God, Dad, everything is all set. For the love of all that is holy, will you focus on what you're about to go do instead of me?" he says throwing his hands up in the air.

"I can't. I'm too nervous," I admit. Luke grins at me and slaps my shoulder.

"It's going to be fine and you know it."

I take a deep breath and blow it out slowly. He's right, but I'm still a ball of raw nerves. Jess comes around the corner, her hand at her ponytail, she pulls at it, letting her hair down and all mine stands up. She's so damn sexy.

"Is it time to go?" she asks.

"Yeah, we should get going."

"Am I allowed to know where we're going yet?"

I grin at her. "Nope."

The drive to the City isn't so bad. I'm guessing most people headed in much earlier for the night's festivities. Jess and I talk and laugh and sing along to songs on the radio. I pull over when we're a ten minute walk from our destination. The parking situation is atrocious but I manage to find something. I pull out a tie from the center console and dangle it in front of her.

"Titan, you can't be serious," Jess says incredulously.

"Oh, yes, I can." I pull her closer and blindfold her.

"But it's slippery out there!" she protests.

"I'd never let you fall, babe." I hop out and round the truck to her side. Helping her down, I make sure she can't see and that she's bundled up before we start walking. The streets are alive with people celebrating the impending New Year. No doubt trying to get as close to Time's Square as possible, but not us.

It's eleven when we arrive at our destination. Which is perfect. It gives us time to talk and have coffee. "Ready?" I ask. My hands shake as I raise them. I untie the blindfold. Jess blinks a few times, letting her eyes adjust, then, she gasps. Her hand flies to her mouth and her eyes well up.

"Oh, my God, Titan."

"I hope this is okay," I say. She leans into me and squeezes me tightly.

"It's perfect." I kiss the top of her head before we walk into Hope's Diner on New Year's Eve, like we did so many years ago.

The coffee is hot and the conversation easy. Memories of the last time we were here bombard me. Nothing has changed. The seats are more worn and the countertop more faded but besides that, it's all the same. "If I get up and go to the restroom, you'll be here when I get back, right?" I give her a stern look.

Jess laughs. "Absolutely."

My nerves are getting the best of me by the time eleven fifty rolls around. I stop Jess from talking with a finger over her lips.

"There's something I need to do," I tell her.

She cocks her head left and looks at me curiously. "Okay."

The Hope's Diner matchbook is in my shirt pocket, burning a hole. I'm almost certain she can see it. "Twenty years ago you saved my life. You couldn't have known then, but you did and part of me fell in love with you right then for that alone. These last three months have been better than any fantasy I could have concocted. I know, Jess, that the situation before us isn't ideal. I know it's tragic and will leave you hurting. I know that and it kills me, but I still want this."

"I want this, too," she says.

I reach into my pocket and slide the twenty year old matchbook across the counter to her. "Marry me, Jess. It doesn't have to be legal. We can have a ceremony without the paperwork, but before I die, I want you to be my wife."

I hold my breath as she lifts the flap of the matchbook. I pulled out all the matches and put an engagement ring inside, protected by her anchor drawing. Tears leak out from her eyes. The rest of the crowd in the diner looks on silently. Wide eyed and mouths agape. She runs a finger over the faded anchor she drew so many years ago before lifting the ring from its spot. Jess hands the ring to me and my stomach drops, but she holds her left hand out waiting. I slide the ring on her finger. "Yes, Titan, always yes for you," she says. I stand and scoop her up into my arms. Patrons cheer and clap as I hold her to my chest. The cooks come out of the kitchen to start the countdown. Jess looks up to me, mouths two . . . one . . . and pushes up on her tiptoes. Our kiss is like a bomb exploding. Static electricity zapping every nerve ending in my body. "I love you so much," she mumbles against my lips.

A waitress shouts out that a slice of pie is on the house for everyone. Jess pulls away, eyes sparkling, and smiles. "Celebratory pie?"

Jesenia

"Mom, I'm going to attach it right under the spot where the braids crisscross," Angie says, her voice distorted from holding bobby pins in her mouth. We have the exact same hairstyle except for the veil. Loose princess curls and two braids that come around the sides to hold the curls back. We did one another's make-up and giggled the whole time. We were calling it "trial for Angie's wedding," until halfway through, she decided it would be better to hire a professional. But Angie did a wonderful job on me, my cheeks are flushed pink and my eyes done a little smoky.

"Here, put the garter on now, before you forget." Angie hands me a blush pink garter that matches my bra and underwear. My wedding dress is cotton with a high empire waist, but the neck is scooped low and almost off the shoulder. It has bell sleeves with scalloped lace edges. It's very seventies inspired. I wanted something simple and beautiful, elegant, yet casual. Angie told me I looked like a "sexy peasant," when I first showed her. My wedding to John was so formal and over the top. I want my wedding with Ty to be about love and the union, not the extravagance or anything material. I'd marry him barefoot in the back yard, but Ty wanted to come up to the Lodge. I protested, he's not doing well with long trips or being away from home for too long.

"I'll take extra pain meds," he pressured.

"Yeah, and then you'll be out of it!" I countered.

But I do want to do the things that make him happy. Ty is ceremonious about things—he wants to make this special. I want to fulfill all of his wishes and make these good memories. So here we are at the Lodge and it's been so stressful. Andrew has been working like a dog to stave off the press and keep away any photographers. It's crucial because my divorce isn't yet final, but Ty has started to fade and we might not have much time left. So we're gathered here, our little family, a few close friends. It's an illegal wedding, so we don't have a real minister, we've got Ty's friend Rusty to officiate.

Angie's dress is burgundy and backless, her flowers will match Luke's corsage and mine will match Ty's. Our children are walking us down the aisle and giving us away to each other. Who knew that a wedding, which is supposed to be a moment of hope, could feel like the last leg of a journey, a final closing door at the end of our story?

I couldn't have imagined twenty years ago in Hope's Diner that I would come to love this man with every ounce of my being. That he would be the greatest light in my life and the only man who ever took the time or the care to look close enough and carefully enough to really see me.

He joked on the way here, "Luke, you might have to wheel me down the aisle. Carry me piggyback and then drop me in Jess's arms."

It was maybe too close to the truth and we all felt the urgency. Hurry up and marry him so that I can become a widow. I'm not ready to say goodbye, I'm not ready to face a world without him. But Ty is strong and convincing about the methods. I'll keep putting one foot in front of the other and preparing for his exit. He's not scared. He's not regretful, he is accepting and humble. He loves us so fully and completely, that we'll be covered for life. Ty couldn't possibly love us more than he already has. That's the type of man he is—going to great lengths to prepare *us* for *his* death.

"Mom, the eye makeup is waterproof," Angie says handing me a gorgeous bouquet of calla lilies, tied up with a burgundy bow.

"Am I crying already?" I ask slipping my finger along the rim of my eye.

"Not yet, but I'm your daughter, so I can tell what you're thinking. This wedding is for today, Mom. Remember, no future, no past. Just like Ty said, we do it in the moment and we'll get through it. Together. It's going to be okay."

"Is Andrew going to make it to the ceremony?"

"Doesn't matter. It's time. Let's go give you away to your man." But Angie is crying and I feel my lip start to quiver. She grabs my arm and links hers through mine and we head to the great hall where Ty waltzed with me by the fireplace.

When we enter, Ty is already standing by the big picture windows, Luke at his side. They are so handsome in tuxes, I lift my hand to my face to force back the cry. The music starts and Angie and I make our way toward them, among the wooden folding chairs with ivory silk bows tied to them. It's the smallest and most perfect wedding I've ever seen, our family, a handful of good friends and the world's most handsome man. His eyes are kind and understanding just as they always have been. He nods sweetly at me, as if he knows this is bittersweet, so precious and so painful.

He takes both of my hands in his and Angie takes her place by Luke. Rusty has decided to do the formal church vows and Ty was all for it. I lose myself in Ty's compassion, in his unconditional love and dedication.

"We are gathered here today . . ."

Our vows are exchanged, my heart hurts with the words, *in sickness and in health, until death do us part*, it's almost too much to bear, but Ty gives me strength when he looks at me.

"I've loved you since the moment I met you. You've brought me such peace, such comfort and pleasure. I want you to be my wife, until I'm no longer here. I want to honor our love and our story and the power of us being together."

He slips a gold band onto my finger. On the inside, is engraved an anchor and the words, *"Ty and Jess, Forever."*

"Remember our love, Jess, if and when you struggle. My heart will always be with you, even when I'm not here, I've got your back forever," his face breaks into a smile with those words, despite the tears pouring down his face.

I look up at Angie and Luke, who are gripping hands and

smiling with red, swollen eyes and running noses and tears falling all over the place.

"I love you, Titan Jennings," I say and lean in to kiss him. Our small group of attendees starts clapping and shouting and it puts a desperately needed smile on everyone's face.

"I pronounce you, man and wife: Mr. and Mrs. Titan Jennings," Rusty says and Ty gives him a hearty high-five. Then Ty goes in for a dramatic kiss, sweeps his arm behind me and dips me.

"This dress is the sexiest thing I've ever seen you in, but I still can't wait to tear it off you tonight in the cabin."

I smile at his words but know the truth isn't so glamorous, it's hard for us now, we take it slow and deliberate. But I wouldn't have it any other way. Ty's love is a universe in and of itself. He loves me so completely, that I revel in every moment of basking in his affection. Be it slow or hard, difficult or easy, our love is a communion, it's an honor to be with him.

"Oh my God, you two are married, can you believe it?" Angie yells, lightening the mood dramatically. "Pictures with the photographer start in ten, I need a drink—anybody with me?"

"Can I have a beer, Dad?" Luke asks, looking up at Ty, hopefully.

"No!" Ty says with a frown.

"One, and not another sip and don't move an inch away from Angie," I say quickly and Luke flashes me a huge smile.

"He's sixteen," Ty says to me, shaking his head.

"Oh, live a little, you old man!" I say, tickling him hard in the ribs. "Anyway, I'm his step-mom now, so I do have some say."

Ty grabs me and swings me around to face him. His eyes look tired, I can tell the pain is resurfacing, he needs to rest and maybe sleep.

"Mrs. Jennings, there's something I have to tell you." I wrap my arms around his neck and look up at him adoringly.

"I know that today wasn't ideal. I know you deserve *forever* and it's not something that I can possibly give you. But I want you to know, that today, you made me not only the happiest, but the proudest man on earth. I hope you know, that if I could, I would give you the stars. But instead, all I can give you is everything I have in my heart."

"I don't want the stars, Titan, and I don't need eternity. This moment, in your arms is more than enough for me."

CHAPTER 38

Titan

March

The front door flies open and Luke storms through it. He comes to a stop by the couch. I've been impatiently waiting here for hours. Too exhausted to go with him today.

"Well? How'd it go?" I ask. He looks upset, which is making me upset. He practiced so hard for his test.

He stays silent a beat longer before a huge grin takes over his face. "I passed!"

"I knew it," I tell him. He leans down to me and hugs my neck. "Now let me see that license, boy." He pulls it from his pocket excitedly and hands it to me. In his picture he's got the biggest, goofiest grin. It's perfect really. The perfect first license picture. "I am so proud of you, Luke."

He swipes the license from my fingers and tucks it back in his pocket. Jess walks into the living room and sits with me. "Thanks for taking him today," I tell her. She kisses my cheek.

"Of course."

"Can I take the truck to Bree's?" Luke asks. I laugh.

"Right now?"

"Uh, yeah."

I nod and pull the keys from my back pocket. "Be careful, okay?" I tell him.

"I will. I promise."

"Wait!" I call out. Luke stops and turns on his heel. "Let's take a picture with your license."

He smirks and pulls it out again, along with his phone. He plops down on the couch next to me. Holding his license with one hand and his phone with the other, we lean in, head to head. He snaps a picture and jumps back up. And just like that, he's gone again.

I shake my head in disbelief that he's truly old enough to have a license. "Wow. My boy. A licensed driver. Scary!" Jess chuckles at me.

"I remember when Angie got hers. I felt the same way," she says. Her hand rests on my thigh. "How are you feeling?"

"Tired mostly and nauseous. It's frustrating because I'm hungry but every time I eat, it comes back up." I sigh and rest my head on the back of the couch.

"How about I make some pot brownies and we watch a movie?" Jess says. I think I misheard her.

"What?" I ask incredulously.

Jess looks me directly in the eyes. She's serious. "Andrew gave me some. It's supposed to help with the nausea." I'm flabbergasted. I can't imagine Jess and pot on the same planet. I can't stop the laugh that bubbles up from my gut. Jess high? I can't see it. I can't remember the last time I got high either. It seems ridiculous to even consider. "Don't you laugh, Titan," she wags a finger at me. "Even the doctor said it could help you feel better. Settle your stomach and all that." Her hand waves through the air as she talks.

"It seems so silly, though. A grown man eating pot brownies." Jess laughs, too.

"It really does, but I'll have one with you. We can watch a comedy. You keep stressing quality of life over quantity, Ty, so let's have some fun."

I can't beat her train of thought. "Alright. Let's do it. I'll pick out a dvd, while you bake."

⚓⚓⚓⚓

Three hours later we're laid out on the couch both quiet and staring at . . . nothing. Eating pot is a very different high than I recall from smoking pot. My body feels like a cloud. My head is happy and mostly free of thoughts. I feel like I am floating.

"My lips are numb," she says, "but not in a bad way."

I think about my words long moments before I can get them out. "I feel, light."

"Light?" she asks, then giggles.

"Yes, like I weigh very little."

"Very little," she repeats. I chuckle at her imitation of my voice. There's a knock at the front door and I jolt upright.

"Oh, shit, who is here? You get it, Jess!" My heart pumps furiously in my chest. Jess laughs at me and gets up. I hear the door swing open.

"Rusty, Dan! Hi," she greets from the entry way. "We're high, care to join us?" Her hands clap together. Oh, no, why would she say that? I hear jackets discarded and mumbles. Rusty and Dan's heavy footsteps get louder and louder until they are standing in front of me. Rusty's face has a devilish smile. "Partaking in edibles these days, Ty?" I stay silent. I don't know what to say. I feel like this is out of character for me to be doing but I can't really pinpoint why.

"I have some stuff to get done," Jess says. "Pot brownies are on the counter. I'll leave you to it!" Jess sounds perky. Too perky. Maybe it's the brownie. Why is she leaving? I can't seem to really form a rational thought at the moment. Dan disappears.

"Sit," I say.

Rusty sits, still grinning like a fool. Dan appears with two napkins. "Rusty, you ready for some fun?" Rusty nods and takes a napkin wrapped brownie from Dan. They both pop them in their mouths in one bite. I can feel my mouth hang open and my eyes widen.

"Seriously?" I say.

"I think we're all in need of a little fun and relaxation. I can't even remember the last time I got high," Dan says. He stretches out in his spot.

"Me either," Rusty adds. "Let's enjoy it while we can."

"You guys are awesome," I say. Rusty starts laughing and Dan grins at me. "Give it an hour, guys, and you will be feeling as stupid as I am right now."

⚓⚓⚓⚓

Jess appears two hours later with a pizza in hand. "Look. My wife," I say with a grin. Dan and Rusty start laughing. I join in. The sound of their laughter is infectious. We can't seem to stop it from happening. Jess flashes a huge smile at me. The theme song for the show we have on feels like it's been on for an eternity. Time is prolonged somehow in this state. We've talked about how we have all changed over the last fifteen years, about the kids being so grown and how we've managed to stay friends throughout a lot of ups and downs. No one talked about me dying, which was exactly what I needed. My nose smells the pizza in Jess's hands. I realize I am starving and my sentiment is obviously shared by Rusty and Dan. They stare at the pizza box like it's the last female on the planet. Jess sets the box on the coffee table and we tear into the pie. I look up to Jess. "Hey, pieces are missing," I say.

Jess shrugs. "I had the munchies, so I hate some in the car."

"I love you," I blurt out.

Jess cocks her head to the side and smiles. "I know."

Jesenia

April

"I don't want to leave him, I don't care about the stupid divorce. If he dies while I'm gone, I would never forgive myself." I'm having coffee with Edie in the kitchen and am absolutely dreading having to drive all the way to Manhattan again tomorrow.

"You can't control it and there is no such thing as a perfect death. You could be sitting vigil by his bed for two days, get up to pee once and when you come back, he's gone. What are you going to do then, never forgive yourself for having a bladder?"

"I guess you're right, it just seems so unfair that I have to go deal with John and our shitty divorce instead of being with him in these important moments."

"You've been here the whole time, Jess, every single minute. You've got to start letting go a bit. Do you think he's getting close? What have the doctors said?"

"Not much, they don't want to commit to a timeline. They told us to call hospice and they don't do that, unless it's a matter of weeks we're talking about."

"Did they come?"

"Who, the angels of death? I mean that in the best way; they were so helpful. That's what Luke and I called them after we had our first meeting. They're pretty amazing, death is their business and they put all of your worries to rest and make it sound easy. Ty was up and walking around—that was three days ago. He hasn't been able to get out of bed except to make it to the bathroom. The pain is minimal so that's the most important part, but the painkillers mess with his cognition, he's not one hundred percent Ty anymore."

"If you want to move him into a place, you know we'd all support you. It's too much for you try to lift him and you're not a nurse, for crying out loud."

Edie takes a bite of the coffee cake and I get up to refill our mugs with fresh coffee.

"He wants to die at home and I want to honor that. If it gets to be too much for Luke, then we'll move him for the last part."

"You're a strong woman, even though you come in such a small, innocent-looking package."

"I've got to go check on him and give him his afternoon meds. Take the rest of that cake home to the boys."

"I would get so fat if I could bake like this," Edie says as I put Reynolds wrap around the cake. She's become such a good friend, checking in on us every day. She's offered to stay with Ty all day tomorrow, while I suffer in a courtroom hundreds of miles away, trying to finalize John Van Buren out of my life.

"He's not eating at all. At least not in the last three days. When the paid meds wear off the abdominal pain is terrible and when the painkillers are working, they kill his appetite. You can try the Ensure shakes or the Boost, they're all in the pantry. But if he doesn't want to eat, don't force it. He always said he didn't want us to prolong it." I want to cry, but I force myself not to waiver. "He's wet the bed a couple of times, Edie. There are pads underneath him if—"I can't finish the sentence. I remember Ty's huge body and strong arms picking me up as if I were a child, how he'd touch me in bed; he was so masculine, so muscular, so sexy and virile. His light is fading and I'm not ready for it to switch off and leave me in the dark.

"Listen, it's not a big deal at all. We all come into this world in diapers and we leave that way, too. It's fitting, he was always such a big baby, what a rotten, loveable jerk." Edie is crying now, too, and she hugs me hard and sniffles into my shoulder. "What an asshole for leaving us. You two were, *are*, so perfect, Jess. A vision, the both of you. Your love is palpable, inspiring. I'm gonna get the hell out of here before I really start blubbering."

"So, tomorrow at four. I'll leave all the written instructions, you can text me. Luke needs to be up by six thirty and out of the house by seven. I'll just leave him cash for his lunch."

"I got it. Don't worry at all. Go divorce the piece of crap, it would make Ty so happy to see you leave him in the dirt."

I walk up the stairs with my ears perked, listening for any sound. I hold my breath every time I walk into this room. I'm terrified to find him without any life left in his body, frightened there will be pain, more tears or blood. I wonder how soon it will be before his death feels like a release, or how sick he can get before letting him go feels like a relief.

But he's sleeping peacefully, his chest rising and falling. His color is off, his skin has taken on a sallow cast, but his face looks placid, there's almost a hint of a smile gracing his lips.

I walk around the other side of the bed and kick off my slippers, pull the comforter back and slip in between the sheets next to him. I snuggle into his body that's still warm and provides me with extraordinary comfort. I nuzzle his neck and rub my cheeks against his stubble. He stirs and pulls me close to him and I throw one leg up over his legs.

"Jess," he murmurs and kisses my forehead.

"I'm here, baby. Can you eat something? Do you want to try to use the bathroom?"

"Just want you here," he says. He feels so thin in my arms. I'm afraid we're counting days at this point, if he won't take in any sustenance.

"I have to go out of town tomorrow, to the City, for divorce court."

"Good," he says and a smile plays on his face. He opens his eyes and looks at me lucidly for the first time in days. "Come back after you're done. I don't want his name attached to you. He doesn't deserve it; he hurt you."

We whisper and hold each other as the sun goes down and darkness overtakes the bedroom. I don't bother to eat or pee or even undress myself. All I want in this world is here in my arms. The minutes are ticking. Soon, even this will be too much and we'll be forced to say goodbye.

⚓⚓⚓

"Mrs. Van Buren, is it true you wed your lover in a secret ceremony in the Adirondacks?" "Are you contesting the pre-nup? How much are you getting in alimony?" "Mrs. Van Buren, won't you give us a statement? Can we get a word with your lawyer?" "Is it true Titan Jennings is a former intravenous drug user and contracted hepatitis from shared needles?"

My lawyer shields me with his briefcase, practically lopping me in the face. I've worn sunglasses and my hair different from usual, but it didn't matter, they were already circling like sharks, when we arrived at the courthouse.

"No questions, please. Mrs. Van Buren would like to keep the proceedings private!" my lawyer shouts as we make our way up the steps. They can't come into the courthouse without a press pass, but they'll gather and swarm until we leave and then they'll attack us. My attorney's shoes click and clack more than my heels on the hard marble floor. I've donned cream-colored slacks and a navy blue blazer, oversized sunglasses and platform heels to bolster my confidence.

"Jesenia, take the ring off. It doesn't look good. If we're lucky, they won't even bring it up because it was a symbolic wedding and not, in any form, a legal ceremony," my attorney says, he's so matter-of-fact.

"I won't take it off. It means too much to me. He's dying."

"I'm aware of the issue, but—"

"No, I mean *he's dying*, like right now and I'm here doing this," I don't want to cry or go in there with smeared make-up all over my face. I don't want to break down before we even set foot in the courtroom.

"Do you have a necklace on?" he says quietly out of the side of his mouth.

"No, I—"

He casts a quick glance around and then digs his fingers into his tight collar. He produces a thin gold chain with a crucifix on it. He undoes the clasp quite expertly and zips the crucifix off and slips it into his pocket.

"Ring?" he says speaking in a low voice.

I twist it off and hand it to him. He slips it onto the chain and in the blink of an eye fastens the chain around my neck.

"Slip it into your shirt. I lost my first wife to breast cancer. Okay? It's close to your heart." My eyes well up with tears at this short, and impatient man's gesture. He's loved and lost, too, my crazy-expensive, divorce lawyer.

Court is dry and much quicker than I expected. I'm not trying to get any money or property out of John, so we agree to all of the equitable distribution. It's, in essence, an uncontested, run of the mill divorce. Just so happens that John is the state senator and I'm, in my own right, a somewhat public persona. But less than an hour later and they're already filing the agreement.

In the hallway after we exit, my lawyer is running over final instructions, John approaches us, says, "excuse me," and puts his hand out for me to shake it.

I look up at him and offer him mine, feeling a bit surprised and uneasy.

"Angelina just called me. Take one of my cars and a driver. You'll get back upstate faster and it's not safe for you to be driving under stress."

"John, I'm fine really—"

"I'm not referring to your mental health. I'm referring to Titan Jenning's health and I thought you'd want to get back to him."

I'm speechless and stunned; it's been so very long since he's been kind. So many unfeeling years made me numb. I stand with my mouth agape, searching his eyes, waiting for the catch. But there is none, John is genuine. He suggests we leave together so I can utilize his bodyguards and the few secret service agents lingering in the hall.

"I'll leave you at the steps. It's necessary for me to make a statement to the press. I'm calling this 'a divorce filled with admiration and mutual respect.' I mean that, I wrote it. It's not a political tactic, it's the truth. I hope you make it back in time. I'm sorry that this is what you have to go through."

He shakes my hand again and I'm still shocked into silence. We move as a large group toward the exit and as we near the door, the flashbulbs start popping and the questions flying, a full-blown media circus stands before us. We're finally divorced, but the only thing on my mind is getting back, as fast as I can, to be by Ty's side.

⚓⚓⚓⚓

The door to the bedroom is ajar and I hold my breath. I push it open and Edie is asleep in a chair by the bed. I rush across the carpet and reach my hand out to touch Ty's face. He's warm, he's breathing, I exhale a huge sigh of relief.

Twenty minutes later, I turn off the light and crawl into bed next to him. He pulls me close immediately and kisses my head.

"I'm no longer a Van Buren," I whisper to him.

"Jennings," Ty mumbles sleepily.

"How do you feel?" I ask him. He's quiet, like he doesn't want to answer. *Miserable*, I think. Probably suffering in pain. I wrap my arms around him protectively and snuggle into his body as much as possible.

"Perfect, now that you're here with me."

CHAPTER 39

Titan

May

I feel like I have the flu. Fever. Chills. Stomach pain. I haven't had the strength to get out of bed for the last two days. I itch everywhere. I've been shaking so badly that I knocked my water glass off the nightstand by mistake yesterday and where my hand hit the glass is bruised. Jess says that it is time to go to the hospital but I don't want to. Not yet.

I need a little more time. I want a little more time. Luke says, if I lose one more pound, he will carry me to St. Mary's himself. I need to relieve myself. Badly. I push the covers off me and swing my legs slowly to the floor. I take my time getting to my feet. Holding on to the edge of the bed, I take two steps. They are slow and lethargic. On the third step my right left leg doesn't cooperate. I fall to the floor. My head hits the hardwood and I'm too tired to get up.

Footsteps rush the stairs. My head hurts. Warmth trickles down the side of my neck. The bedroom door blows open.

"Dad!" I'm just so tired. I close my eyes. "Jess, hurry!" Luke sounds frantic. *Don't be frantic*, I think. *It will be okay.* I just need to sleep for a moment.

⚓⚓⚓⚓

I'm warm. I stretch in my spot. I feel better. Well rested. There are strange noises coming from the bedroom though. Carefully, I pry open my eyes. The room is bright and harsh. Machines surround me. Tubes vine around my arms. Why am I here?

"Titan," Jess gasps. I smile at her. "You're at St. Mary's, love." Tears roll down her cheeks. Her eyes are bloodshot. She's been crying for a while. I don't want her tears. I don't want to be the one causing them.

"When?" I ask.

She scrunches up her face and shakes her head violently. "They aren't sure. A few days, maybe." Days? There are things I need to do still. Words I want to say. Letters I want to write. Kisses I want to share. Days is not long enough. I'm not prepared for mere days.

"Where's Luke?" I ask beginning to feel panicked.

"Grabbing some food. He'll be right back." I lift my hand, hook Jess's neck and pull her face to mine.

"I love you, baby. So much. Please don't cry. Your tears gut me." I bring my lips to hers. She tastes salty with tears. My stomach clenches in agony. I can't stand to see her cry like this. I need to make things right.

"I'm not ready yet, Ty," she whimpers.

"Neither am I. I'm still here, aren't I?" She nods her head and presses her forehead to mine.

"What do you need me to do?" she asks.

"Get Angie here, for one. And two, don't leave my side."

Luke called Angie hours ago while I was out. Andrew was driving her and they should arrive any time now, so Jess says. I feel like I've missed precious hours with them all.

Luke comes back with a haul from the cafeteria and a vending machine. I can't help but chuckle at his stash. "What?" he says, "I didn't want to have to leave again for a while."

"Come here, Bud," I tell him. He empties his arms and comes to the bedside. "Get in." For a moment he looks confused. I pat the bed next to me. He swallows hard but climbs in. I wrap an arm around him. "You're the best son a man could have, Luke. I'm so proud of who you've become and I know you will only get better the older you get. I love you." Luke sniffles and buries his face in the crook of my arm. I hold him there, as if he were still a little boy for a long while. "Hey," I whisper to him. "I need you to do a favor."

He looks up and leans in close. I whisper what I need and how to make it happen.

Luke nods. "Now?"

"Yeah, Bud, we've got time, if you do it now."

"Okay, Dad." He climbs off the bed and jogs out the door to run an errand for me.

Dr. Hemphill arrives to administer morphine so that I'm comfortable. I appreciate it, but it also makes me less lucid. Jess is snuggled into my side, whispering I love you and peppering kisses wherever she can reach, when Angie shows up. She throws herself on top of me and squeezes me fiercely.

"Hi, to you, too," I say smiling. She bursts out crying and I feel terrible. Jess gets up and wraps her daughter in a tight hug, letting her sob. Andrew shakes my hand and asks how I'm feeling right now. It might be the most appropriate thing anyone's said to me all day.

"Right now? I'm happy. Everyone is here and it makes me happy," I tell him. Andrew smiles at me and nods his head.

"Where is Luke?" Angie asks, suddenly realizing that he's absent.

"I sent him on an errand. He should be back soon," I explain.

The nurse comes in once more before Luke arrives. He's out of breath and red in the face. Angie and Andrew are sitting on the small loveseat. Jess is in the bed with me and the TV is on but I've been in and out of sleep.

"I got it, Dad," he says. He hands the paper to me and smiles.

I nudge Jess. She lifts her head and I hand her the marriage certificate. "Angie," I say, "think you can find a notary?"

"I'm one," Andrew says, lifting a brow.

Tears well in Jess's eyes. "Be my wife, legally."

Her bottom lip quivers but she nods and signs her name to the form, then hands me the pen. I sign my name. Angie and Luke sign as witnesses and Andrew signs as notary before heading to his car to get his stamp.

"Jess, you've got to file this," I say sternly.

"I will."

"No—now," I say. "I want you to go and do it now." She shakes her head no. And I understand, she doesn't want to leave but it has to be done before anything happens. "I can barely keep my eyes open anyway. Just go get it done." It takes all my effort to get the words out. I'm exhausted and the morphine makes me want to sleep for endless hours.

She wipes her tears with the sleeve of her shirt. "Fine. But I want you to know, it's under protest." I smile and lay my head back on the pillow as she gets up. She kisses me possessively. "Do not die, Titan Jennings. Not until I'm back." She turns on her heel and scoops up her purse before heading to the door.

"I love you, Mrs. Jennings."

"I love you, too," she calls over her shoulder.

"Luke, sit over here," I say. He sits in the chair next to my bed. I reach for his hand. His hand is warm and holds on to mine tightly. "I love you, Bud."

"I love you, too, Dad." Things are in order for the most part. Everyone's here. As soon as Jess files that license, we're legally wed. I am more at ease, so I close my eyes to rest for a bit.

☫☫☫☫

I can't be sure how much time has passed, but another nurse has come in to check my vitals and Jess is back in the bed next to me. I can smell her hair and feel her body pressed into mine. I want to open my eyes but it seems an impossible task. I say 'I love you' but I can't be sure the words were out loud. Did they hear me? My hand is squeezed. Luke. I'd know his firm grip anywhere. I want so badly to say something.

Instead, I drift back off.

Jesenia

When he finally passes, it's uneventful, like quiet becoming silence. He's been unresponsive now for more than twenty-four hours. In the early morning hours, just before the sun rises, Luke and I sit on either side of him and hold each of his hands. He would squeeze back when you squeezed just yesterday, but now he's too far away from us. I lean forward onto the bed, holding his one hand with both of mine, occasionally bringing it to my face. I can still hear his heart beating, we can still see every rise of his chest. I keep fighting off sleep, trying so hard to stay present. His skin is mottled, his hand growing colder against my skin. Then peacefully, the air stills as the sun hits its apex and the room becomes bathed in bright daylight. Even the external hospital noise seems to grow silent. Ty's heartbeat slows, his breathing stops, and he slips softly away from us.

☫☫☫☫

Ty's funeral is the most profoundly painful and excruciating experience. And not for me, I am devastated but I can live with this loss, the pain is for Luke, who has now lost both parents. After Rory's death, Ty and Luke became closer than any best friends. They were inseparable and loved so hard that, for Luke, losing Ty has meant utter desolation. To see him, head down— defeated, dressed in black, being a pallbearer and burying another dead parent, was probably one of the worst experiences of my life. I've been by his side ever since, cooking his meals, reminding him to do his homework, to shower, taking him to his therapy sessions and even gently waking him up in the morning. Luke's pain is incomprehensibly big. I cry, too, but never in front of him. I don't want him to have to deal with the weight of my own sadness.

But I mourn. Day in and day out. I wear his shirts. I wear his jackets. I smell his clothing when what I really long to smell is his skin. I stare at pictures of him for hours. At night, when I'm alone in our bed, I whisper to Ty as if he were right here beside me. I ended up in a ball on the floor in the laundry room when I washed his last heap of laundry. I was horrified when I was folding his clothes and realized that there was no one to wear them, no one to fill the giant hole that he left in my world.

Today is the day they are reading Ty's will. Luke and I will go together and Dan and Rusty will be there, because as Titan explained to me, he left his whole business to the two men, with a clause that Ty's share of the profits from the continued, active business were directly deposited into a trust for his son. It was, of course, up to Rusty and Dan if they'd choose to continue and for now they have.

I hold my arm around Luke's shoulders as we walk through the dark wood and heavily carpeted law offices. Rusty and Dan greet us in the waiting room. They offer hearty hugs to Luke with emotional thumps on his back. Luke holds it together and I, too, manage to contain myself.

The executor who drones on about the legality of Ty's assets is bald and shiny with tiny, wire-rimmed glasses. He doesn't tell us anything we aren't expecting, until he gets to a lumberyard Ty owns the lion's shares of. All of us look at one another with surprise. The shares are left to Luke and are really quite substantial.

"The house was owned outright, notwithstanding the yearly property taxes. Mr. Jennings leaves his home to his wife, Mrs.

Jesenia Jennings," he says, without looking up from his paperwork. My eyes widen in surprise. Ty left me his house? I look at Luke and he smiles for what seems like the first time in weeks.

"Really?" I mouth, a smile also creeping onto my face.

"Yeah," Luke whispers.

I tilt my head in wonder. What else has this beautiful man of mine got up his sleeve from the afterlife?

When all of the legalities are finalized, the executor has us all sign some papers. Then he hands me an envelope. I take it from him with shaking fingers. Tears are already flowing and I nod my head. I know my husband, I don't have to ask what it is. I think about him every minute and it feels as if he's still with me, but I'm unprepared to hear his voice, to read the words that he wrote for me.

"If none of the other beneficiaries mind, I'd rather not read this now. Is that okay, guys?"

Dan and Rusty nod and Luke gives me a quick hug.

"The letter is for you alone, Mrs. Jennings, for you to read at your discretion. I was only legally bound to make sure it was in your possession. You're under no obligation to read it now or ever, if you don't want to."

As Luke and I make our way back to the car, I'm not sure who's holding up who, anymore.

> To my wife,
>
> Jess, I can't imagine what you're feeling right now, but know this, you are forever in my heart. You brought me hope when I had none. Joy when it was in short supply and unconditional love. You were the seafloor to my anchor. I will never stop loving you. Death cannot stop my love because we are anchored together in this life and the next.
>
> Without you, I'm not sure I would have been able to

get through these last months. I wouldn't have been okay with my diagnosis. You've given me a peace that I can't put into words a second time around.

So long as my heart beats, you'll be able to feel its presence in the world. And if it stops, your love will live in my spirit, in my soul, Jess. We are eternal and I will always be nearby. When a light flickers, or a rush of wind comes seemingly out of nowhere, know that it is me, with you. Please don't mourn the loss of me because you haven't, nor will you ever truly lose me. I'm forever a part of you.

Luke and I were able to talk and he made it clear that he wants to stay in Fairfield to finish high school. I'd like that for him. To be near Rusty, Edie, Dillon and Dan and family and Bree. To be with you. I've left the house to you. I want you to stay. There is no mortgage, so it's yours free and clear. I need you to be happy. To make a life for yourself (and Luke). I can't imagine anyone outside of me or Rory, loving and caring for him the way you will, so I hope you will accept this last wish of mine.

Do not be afraid to love again, Jess. You have so much to offer. Your heart knows no bounds and your kindness expands each day. Please know that I want you to follow your heart in the future, without guilt, without sadness and without doubt.

If I could have given you all the stars in the galaxy, I would have. Please be happy. Please be grateful for what we were able to share together and please, love again.

Forever yours,

Titan

EPILOGUE

I shut down the cash register and flick off the lights.

"Hurry, Mom! I swear if you don't finish up, we'll miss all the good seats!"

Angie is shooing me out of the store. I made a sign for the door that says, "Luke's Graduating Today! Normal business hours will resume tomorrow." I tape it over the OPEN sign and lock the heavy front door.

It's been one year since Luke and I cut the ribbon on "Jenning's Home and Hardware." It's been a full-time job for us both and a therapeutic experience to build something from the ground up, while we struggle through our loss. We found the old feed barn that's almost eight thousand square feet, about two miles from the house. The location was perfect, just off the highway on an old county road. Dan and Rusty did the construction, while Luke and I worked with a consultant to figure out the business plan. We sell everything from lumber to bulk sequins for crafting. There's even a small cafe in the front where we sell cakes and pastries, espresso drinks and to-go coffees. I'm the overseeing manager with two employees and Luke, who helps out most days after school. He does the day shift on Saturdays and has saved enough money to buy himself a used car. I'll be devastated when he leaves, but Dillon, Rusty's son, will take his place, since he's not going away to school.

I slide into the backseat of Angie and Andrew's car, Charlotte is in her car seat and grins at me with two adorable bottom teeth.

"Oh, my, baby girl! When did those happen?"

"Over a long sleepless week with lots of fevers and diarrhea," Andrew says, twisting to look out of the back window. He backs up down the driveway and pulls out onto the street. "How are you holding up, Jesenia? Ready to see Luke graduate?"

I caress Charlotte's tiny pink cheeks and she giggles and coos. Angie did not have an easy pregnancy and I wonder if my granddaughter will be her first and last attempt at procreating.

"I'm doing fine, Andrew, thanks. A little manic here and there, but nothing that couldn't be put to good use. After two nights of banging around in the house, Luke sent me to do overnight store inventory. Seems that's his new strategy and it's working out for the both of us. I've been a little anxious about today because I know how much Ty wanted to be here, but I know he's watching and I'm happy we can make it special for Luke."

"You sound great, Mom. To tell the truth, we were a little worried." She glances at her phone and then smacks Andrew on the arm. "Step on it, slowpoke, you're going to make us late for the ceremony!"

We arrive in plenty of time and somehow sit in front of a rowdy group of college kids, who from the sound of it, seem like they've already started celebrating. The atmosphere is festive and the air is crackling with energy. They ask all of the families to withhold their applause until the end. Angie can barely sit still in her seat.

She's as close to Luke as any stepsister can be. She talks to him, maybe, more on the phone than she even talks to me. I think our experience with Ty changed her a lot, too; she decided on a smaller wedding without the pressure or fanfare. Wanted just close family instead of a guest list that rivaled the Statehouse.

She even asked Luke to be in her bridal party and to stand up for her. There he was, sticking out like an adorable sore thumb among all of her sorority sisters clad in taffeta.

Rory's sister arrives with her family, they shuffle down the aisle to the seats that we've saved them. Rusty and Edie are a few rows ahead, waiting to see Dillon walk. We've got a huge party planned at the house. I did the unthinkable, I hired caterers. But with all the work at the store, I've been really exhausted. It was great to let someone else take over and to dole out the orders.

It's been almost two years since he left us. I still sleep in his bed. I still sleep in his T-shirts. Sometimes, when I'm struggling, I remember the things he used to say. He had a sensible wisdom to him that helps me along, to this day. I remember how when I tried to explain my disease, he always listened, always tried to understand and would often break it down to me. Once, I told him that it wasn't straight ups and downs, that I could be insanely depressed inside of a manic episode. He nodded his head and said, "I call those great, shitty days, Jess. Where everything sucks but for some reason, you feel great, or everything is going great, but for some reason, you feel like shit." I burst out loud with my laugh and threw my arms around his neck.

"Everybody has those same feelings, Jesenia, you just feel them a little deeper than the rest of us." I loved him for those profoundly simple explanations. He made me feel normal and so greatly loved. The man who climbed into a tiny closet beside me, to show me that he wasn't afraid of who I really was. I spent so many years hiding and it was only through Ty's unconditional love, that I grew to eventually love myself.

I can feel him all around me as we listen to the names and watch the graduates make their way across the stage. They are projected onto the big screen, so we get an up-close view of all the tears and reactions.

"Lucas James Jennings," the announcer says.

"Here, hold the baby!" Angie yells, practically throwing her into Andrew's arms. "Go, Luke! Go, Luke Jennings, woot, that's our boy!" she screams, while standing.

"Angie, they said to withhold the applause," I say uselessly.

"Just let her go," Andrew says shaking his head and smiling. I giggle, too, and offer to hold baby Charlie.

She finally sits down after they hand him the diploma, his face momentarily lights up the big screen, Ty's kind eyes in spades, Luke definitely has them. I feel my heart swell with pride. I make a silent vow to my Titan to always watch out for his boy.

"Oh, my God, who is that? He's totally hot," says one of the enthusiastic girls behind us.

"Oh, Luke?" Angie says twisting in her chair to glare at them. "He's my little brother—hands off! Why don't you go pick up some frat boys, huh?"

Andrew looks alarmed but I'm barely containing a smile. The girls get really quiet. "Go, Luke, you did it!" Angie yells again and then they call the next person.

We wait by the exit for the seniors to come and throw their hats up outside, it's a Fairfield High tradition and a great photo opportunity. Angie and I tackle Luke with hugs as soon as he comes out. He's grinning ear to ear and has Bree at his side. I snap a few photos of the two of them together, then with Charlotte, then Angie and Andrew and then Luke and Dillon and even more with Rory's family.

A man standing nearby wearing sunglasses and a suit jacket smiles and approaches us.

"Here, go ahead, let me get one of you and your son together," he offers amiably.

Luke and I look at each other for a moment. He smiles and I smile back at him, then I step forward to get in the picture with him.

When we're finished with the photos, Andrew hands me the bouquet in school colors I made earlier at the house. I pass it to

Luke and he crushes me along with the flowers into a huge hug. The boy learned to bear hug from his dad.

"Thanks for being here, Jess. It really means a lot to me."

"Wouldn't miss it for the world! I'm so damn proud of you, Honey. Know, Luke, that your dad is smiling down from above."

⚓⚓⚓⚓

"No, Angie, really. It's no problem, I'll get it. It will take me two seconds and besides, you've got to feed Charlotte, look at her little face."

"Why didn't you have the caterers bring the coffee?"

"I just forgot."

Guests are already streaming into the house. We invited a lot of people, it feels like a really big deal. Bree and her parents arrive, with Luke in tow.

"Skip it then, we don't need it!" Angie shrugs.

"Skip coffee? I don't think so. Ty would have wanted coffee for sure."

I hand Andrew the bowl to have everyone put their keys in.

"Just have them drop them in, even if they're not drinking and especially check all the kids on the way out, because, well you know, they're good kids but it's graduation."

"All over it, Jess, go get the coffee and get back here for the slideshow!"

"I'm running!"

The drive to the store takes me under five minutes. I'll just run in and get two pounds of ground coffee beans and the large, industrial thermoses to keep it hot throughout the party.

I park in the gravel driveway and yank the keys out of my purse, flick on the huge buzzing barn lights and lift the wooden hinged bar over to enter the café corner. Into a big, thick brown paper bag with handles, I load the coffee and two empty thermoses. There are still two full ones on the bar from this morning. I need to drain out the coffee before it leaves a bitter flavor to the container. I lift one into the sink and press down the release.

"Hello?" Someone calls behind me. I practically jump out of my skin and immediately realize that I left the front door open.

"Sorry, we're closed!" I say to the nice looking man.

He makes a disappointed face and holds up a travel coffee mug.

"I always pass by on Saturdays and Luke makes me a great one."

He's stepping closer as he speaks. Part of me feels like I should be afraid but there's something about him that sets me at ease.

"I can fill you up if you don't mind that it's from this morning. It's still hot," I gesture to the steam rising up from the one I'm pouring off.

"Great, thanks. I appreciate it. I really love this store. I used to admire the barn and wish somebody would do something with it."

"It's been a labor of love, to say the least. Almost two years in the making, but I wouldn't trade her for anything," I say, as I fill up his coffee.

"Mike Blackard," he says, reaching out his hand to shake.

"Jesenia Jennings," I say. When my skin touches his, I feel a breeze blow near my neck. My skin rises in goose flesh and one of the giant fluorescent barn lights flickers above me.

"They do that sometimes for a few minutes after you turn them on." He nods at me and keeps looking into my eyes.

"Sorry, how much did you say that was? Should I carry that bag to your car? It looks kind of heavy."

"On the house. If you're friends with Luke and a loyal customer, we give out free refills. Besides, it was going down the drain anyway," I hand him the bag over the counter and he smiles at me. His eyes are soft and friendly. I notice a med alert bracelet on his wrist.

"Peanut allergy?"

"No, I wish, he says smiling. Hepatitis C positive, I'm afraid. It's not necessary to wear the bracelet but I do, just in case. Safer for first responders and things like that."

"I'm well acquainted with the disease."

"Yeah? I'm responding to treatment, my enzymes are great."

"That's wonderful. Good for you."

My mind keeps telling me I should be on guard; I'm all alone, the store is closed, the safe is full of cash and the security cameras are turned off. But the stranger has such a nice feeling about him. We walk to the car and chat about Luke, the store and the warm, balmy weather we're experiencing.

"Well, I'll come back to see you again, if you don't mind. Luke is great, but I somehow I think I like your coffee better." He winks when he says it and it is a little flirty, but I don't take offense. I feel flattered, truly.

"I'll make sure to have a fresh pot next time you come." I think I might be flirting back and suddenly I'm blushing. I hop in the car, put it in reverse and roll down the window.

He leans down a bit and raises his thermos.

"Funny thing is, I never drank it. Then two years ago, I almost died in an accident. I survived a full heart and lung transplant from a single donor. When I woke up out of surgery, I felt like I wanted it. Strangest thing in the world. The whole surgery was such a huge transformation, I figured a black coffee addiction afterwards was the least of my worries. Thanks for this, Jesenia! And I promise this won't be the last you'll be seeing of me!"

I pull out of the parking lot and wave goodbye in wonder to the man with the black coffee. The sun is setting as I make my way back to the house, in brilliant golds and deep pinks, putting on a spectacular show. It's funny how much I can feel Ty all around me, like he's not really gone but instead he's close and watching out for me. I can look at something beautiful, like the sunset in front of me and I feel like he's here, like he's sharing it with me. I smile when I feel his presence and a sense of utter peacefulness washes over me.

So long as my heart beats, you'll be able to feel its presence in the world. And if it stops, your love will live in my spirit and in my soul. We are eternal and I will always be near. You haven't, nor will you ever, truly lose me. Jess, I am forever a part of you.

THE END

ACKNOWLEDGEMENTS

Thank you to my family, my beta readers for all of the amazing feedback, Sunny, Katy, Yaya, and Supreet. Thank you to K. Larsen for sharing her writing space with me and for the kick in the butt it took to get me producing again. Thank you to all of the bloggers for spreading the word and giving this book a chance—you guys are our lifeline and we couldn't do this job without you. Thank you to all of the readers, you are the reason I keep coming back to the keyboard. I couldn't do this job without your amazing support. I am grateful for each and every one of you!

m a r a   w h i t e

I'm going to keep this short and sweet.

To start, a huge thank you to Mara White. Not only did you pull me from my writing funk, you made it fun again and easy and I will forever be grateful for that.

To my family and friends for always being there and being supportive of me.

A giant thank you to all the bloggers who take a chance time after time on my work.

To my Beta's; you are amazing. You are necessary. And, you are loved. Thank you for the time you spent helping this book be its best. Pat yourselves on the back for that loves.

To you, the reader. Thank you for picking up this book and giving it a chance. Thank you for leaving a review and sharing with your friends (if you enjoyed it-or not). Thank you for kind words and being an amazing community.

k. larsen

ABOUT THE AUTHORS

k. larsen

K. Larsen is an avid reader, coffee drinker, and chocolate eater who loves writing romantic suspense and thrillers. If *you* love suspense and romance on top of a good plot, you've hit the mother-load. She may mess with your head a bit in the process but that's to be expected. She has a weird addiction to goat cheese and chocolate martinis, not together though. She adores her dog. He is the most awesome snuggledoo in the history of dogs.

Seriously.

She detests dirty dishes. She loves sarcasm and funny people and should probably be running right now . . . because of the goat cheese . . . and stuff. Sign up for a chance to win a $5 Gift card every time she sends a newsletter out.

Stalk her—legally

Newsletter: www.klarsenauthor.com/5-gift-card/

Amazon: www.amazon.com/K.-Larsen/e/B00AN1BSIE

Facebook: www.facebook.com/K.LarsenAuthor

Twitter: @Klarsen_author

Want more of K. Larsen's work?
30 Days ~ FREE
Committed

Bloodlines Series—All can be read as stand-alone books.
Tug of War ~ FREE
Objective
Resistance
Target 84

Stand Alones
Jezebel
Lying in Wait
Dating Delaney
Saving Caroline

ABOUT THE AUTHORS

m a r a w h i t e

Mara White is a contemporary romance and erotica writer who laces forbidden love stories with hard issues, such as race, gender and inequality. She holds an Ivy League degree but has also worked in more strip clubs than even she can remember. She is not a former Mexican telenovela star, contrary to what the tabloids might say, but she is a former ballerina and will always remain one in her heart. She lives in NYC with her husband and two children and yes, when she's not writing you can find her on the playground.

Links:

Email: authormarawhite@gmail.com

Twitter: @authormarawhite

Facebook: www.facebook.com/heightsbound

Website: www.marawhite.com/

Printed in Great Britain
by Amazon